DELIA'S HEART

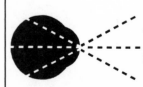

This Large Print Book carries the
Seal of Approval of N.A.V.H.

DELIA'S HEART

V.C. ANDREWS

THORNDIKE PRESS
A part of Gale, Cengage Learning

Detroit • New York • San Francisco • New Haven, Conn • Waterville, Maine • London

GALE
CENGAGE Learning·

Thorndike Press® Large Print Core.

The text of this Large Print edition is unabridged.

Other aspects of the book may vary from the original edition.

Set in 16 pt. Plantin.

Printed on permanent paper.

LIBRARY OF CONGRESS CATALOGING-IN-PUBLICATION DATA

Andrews, V. C. (Virginia C.)
   Delia's heart / by V. C. Andrews.
     p. cm. — (Thorndike Press large print core)
     ISBN-13: 978-1-4104-1203-4 (alk. paper)
     ISBN-10: 1-4104-1203-2 (alk. paper)
     1. Girls — Fiction. 2. Mexicans — United States — Fiction.
   3. Aunts — Fiction. 4. Palm Springs (Calif.) — Fiction. 5. Large
   type books. I. Title.
   PS3551.N454D46 2009b
   813'.54—dc22
                                2008046820

Published in 2008 in arrangement with Pocket Books, a division of Simon & Schuster, Inc.

Printed in the United States of America
1 2 3 4 5 6 7 12 11 10 09 08

DELIA'S HEART

PROLOGUE

Looking down from my bedroom window, I see Señor Casto bawling out one of my aunt's gardeners for doing what he considers sloppy work. Señor Casto is as upset and as animated as he would be if he actually owned the estate and not just served as my aunt's estate manager. She is lucky to have such a dedicated employee, but I think his dedication and loyalty are still more to my aunt's dead husband, Señor Dallas, than to her. He talks warmly about him quite often, although usually not in my aunt's presence.

Casto is waving his arms and thrusting his hands in every direction. It brings a smile to my face because it looks like his hands are trying to fly off his wrists but keep being caught in midair and brought back.

The gardener, a short, thin man whose pale corn-yellow sombrero is at least two sizes too big, stares without expression and holds the rake like a biblical prophet might hold his staff. The shadow masks his face. He waits patiently, occasionally nodding. He doesn't try to defend himself. I am sure he is thinking, *Soon it will end; soon it will be time for lunch.* With the other gardeners, he will sit in the shade of my aunt's palm trees and unwrap his taco. They will drink their Corona beers and maybe have some beans and salsa.

Sometimes I watch them talking softly and laughing, and when I do, I'm jealous of their conversation. I know they speak only in Spanish, and they are surely talking about Mexico, their relatives, and the world that they, like me, have left behind. Despite the poverty and the other hardships of daily life back in rural Mexico, there was the contentment that came from being where you were born and raised, being comfortable with the land, the mountains, the breezes, even the dust, because it all was who and what you were.

The weather and landscapes here in Palm Springs are not terribly different from the weather and landscapes in my village back in Mexico, but it is not mine. I don't mean in the sense of owning the property. The land truly claims us more than we claim the land. And it does that for all of us, no matter where we are born. No, I mean that I am still a stranger here.

I wonder, will I ever truly be a *norteamericana?* Will my education, my aunt's wealth, my cousins, and the friends I have made here over the past two years and will continue to make here change me enough? Probably more important is the question, will they ever accept me as one of them, or will they simply treat me as a foreigner, an immigrant, forever? Will they finally see me for myself and not just "another one of them"? What must I give up to win their full acceptance?

Can't I hold on to what I loved and still love about my people, my homeland, my food, my music, and my heritage and yet still be part of this wonderful place? Except for the Native Americans, wasn't that what everyone else who came here had and kept? Italians, Germans, French, and others hold on to their sayings, their foods, and their ancestral memories. Why isn't it the same for us?

Nearly a year and a half ago, I stood by the door of the bus in Mexico City and said good-bye to Ignacio Davila, the young man I loved and thought I had lost forever to the desert when he and I fled back to Mexico. He was fleeing because he and his friends had taken revenge on my cousin Sophia's boyfriend, Bradley Whitfield, who had forced himself on me. During the violent confrontation, Bradley was thrown through a window, and the broken glass cut an artery. He was with another girl he was seducing, Jana Lawler, but she did not call for medical help quickly enough, so he died. Ignacio's friends were found, quickly sentenced in a plea agreement, and sent to prison, but through a friend, Ignacio's father hired a coyote to lead us through the desert back to the safety of Mexico.

A little more than halfway across, bandits attacked us when we stopped to sleep in a cave. Ignacio fought them so I could escape. I thought he had been killed but later discovered he had faked his own death in the desert. Only I, his family, and a few of their very close friends knew he was alive and well, working out a new identity for himself. That day we parted in Mexico City, we pledged to each other that we would wait for each other, no matter how long it took for him to return.

Through our secret correspondence, I knew that Ignacio was doing well and waiting for enough time to pass so that he could return and not be discovered. He had to earn enough money so as not to be dependent on his father and put his father in any more danger. Both his family and I realized that he couldn't come back here, however. It would be too dangerous. Bradley Whitfield's father was an important businessman, wealthy, with connections to government officials and politicians. When the news was spread that Ignacio had died crossing the desert, Mr. Whitfield had retreated from driving Ignacio's family out by destroying his gardener business. The Davilas even had a memorial service that I attended. In a real sense, I imagine they felt their son was dead and gone. Anyway, I suppose Mr. Whitfield believed he had gotten his revenge or what he thought was justice and was satisfied.

Although Ignacio was just as angry as his friends were about my being raped and Bradley going unpunished for it, he swore to me that when they had gotten to the house that Bradley and his father were restoring and found him with Jana, he did not lay a hand on him. It was mostly his amigo Vicente who was so violent. Although Ignacio was technically only an accomplice to what was finally ruled manslaughter, he was afraid that he would not get an even-handed, just punishment. He regretted fleeing; he didn't want to be thought a coward, and he didn't want to leave his family with all the trouble, but his father was worried that Ignacio wouldn't survive in the prison system and that Bradley's father was so angry he would secretly arrange for some harsher punishment after all.

I had fled with Ignacio so I could return to my little village, hoping to be with *mi abuela* Anabela again, even though I knew it would break my grandmother's heart to see me leave what she believed was a wonderful opportunity for me in the United States. Here, living with my wealthy aunt Isabela, I would enjoy a far better education and have the chance to make something greater of my life. Of course, she knew that *mi tía* Isabela hated our family and had renounced her heritage and her language. She thought it was all because Tía Isabela's father had forbidden her marriage to Señor Dallas, a much older American man, but I knew from her own lips that her rage came from my mother marrying the one man *mi tía* Isabela had loved, the man she thought loved her. Grandmother Anabela was hoping my aunt had regretted disowning her family and would give me opportunities as a way to repent and relieve her of her guilt.

In my senior English class at the private school I now attended, my teacher, Mr. Buckner, quoted from a play by an English author, William Congreve, to describe how angry someone whose love had been rejected could be. Mr. Buckner was a tall man, with a shock of light brown hair that never obeyed the brush and comb. He was a frustrated actor and enjoyed dramatizing his lessons. He had a deep, resonant voice and took a posture like an actor on a stage to look up at the ceiling and bellow, "Heaven has no rage like love to hatred turned. Nor hell a fury like a woman scorned."

Everyone in the classroom, even my cousin Sophia, roared with laughter — everyone but me, that is, because all I could think of was *mi tía* Isabela's blazing eyes when she described her disappointment and rage at losing my father. She accused my mother of being sly and deceptive and stealing my father from her. Of course, listening to her spout such hatred and anger at my mother and my family, I wondered why she wanted me to come live with her after my parents' tragic truck accident on their way to work. It wasn't long before I realized, as my cousin Edward so aptly put it one day, I had become a surrogate. My aunt couldn't punish my mother, because she was dead, so she transferred her hunger for vengeance to me and wanted to make my life as miserable as she could. She did just that, so I had little hesitation when it came to my decision to flee back to Mexico with Ignacio.

Grandmother Anabela used to tell me, *"Un corazón del odio no pueda incluso amarse por completo."* A heart full of hate cannot even love itself.

I saw how true that was for my aunt. She flitted from one younger man to another in a determined effort to look pleased with herself and get her friends envious. She flaunted her wealth and was at times ruthless at seizing property, claiming she was protecting her dead husband's fortune for her children, but her children were cold to her and she to them. She had little respect for Sophia, and Sophia was constantly in trouble, doing rebellious things just to annoy her half the time.

Edward was different. I sensed that he wanted to love his mother and, at times, I saw how much she wanted his love, but he, too, did not respect or approve of her actions and lifestyle. He was especially angry at her for the way she had treated me when I first arrived after my parents' deaths. She immediately turned me into another one of her Mexican servants and practically put me into the hands of a known pedophile, John Baker, who was to serve as my language tutor. She forced me to live with him in what he called a "Helen Keller world," in which I was completely dependent upon him for everything, supposedly to enhance and speed up my development of English. But after he tried to abuse me that first night, I fled, and Edward came to my rescue.

For a while, thanks to Edward, my aunt was forced to treat me as her niece and not her house servant. However, she was always conniving, searching for ways to isolate me. She got me to spy on Edward and his close friend Jesse Butler, claiming she was worried that they were falling into a homosexual relationship, when all the while she knew that was just what it was. What she was really trying to do was drive a wedge between Edward and me.

She nearly succeeded. Edward was very angry at me for doing that spying, but when he learned that his mother had put me up to it, he was at my side again, even after his terrible car accident.

Edward had tried to come to my rescue a second time when he heard what Bradley Whitfield had done to me. In anger, he had chased after him before Ignacio and his friends did. He was going so fast he lost control of his car and got into a terrible crash that resulted in his loss of sight in one eye. For a while, it seemed as if old Señora Porres, a woman back in my Mexican village who believed in the *ojo malvado,* the evil

15

eye, might have been right to predict that it could follow someone anywhere. I thought it was stuck to my back, and all I could do was bring trouble to anyone who wanted to help me.

But in the end, it was Edward who wrote to me in Mexico and sent me the money to return. He and my aunt had learned of my grandmother's death while I was crossing the desert with Ignacio, before I had reached my Mexican village. I was so depressed and lost when I arrived there that if it weren't for Ignacio appearing like a ghost one night, I probably would have married a man in the village, Señor Rubio, and condemned myself to the life of a drudge with a man who was ugly and weak. He owned a *menudo* shop with his mother, who ruled him as she did when he was a small boy. She would have ruled me as well.

With the promise of a future for me once again and the hope that Ignacio would join me in America, however, I returned, willing and strengthened to deal with whatever my cousin Sophia threw at me or whatever my aunt would do to me. Ignacio's love for me and my love for him gave me the courage.

I can't say, though, that my legs weren't trembling the day I deplaned in Palm Springs and met Edward and Jesse at the airport.

They were both very happy to see me return and rushed to my side.

"We'll be your knights in shining armor," Edward promised.

"No one will bother you with us around," Jesse bravely assured me.

It disturbed me that I was accepting their generosity and love and yet would be unable to trust them with the deep secret of Ignacio's existence. Keeping secrets from the people you loved and who loved you was a recipe for a broken heart. I was afraid, however, and out of my affection for them, I also did not want to weigh them down with the burden of such a secret.

There was so much more here in America than there was back in my little Mexican village, so much more opportunity and comfort, but there was so much more deception here as well. Back in my simple village, everyone seemed to wear his heart on his sleeve. Here, most people I met wore masks and were reluctant to take them off and show you their real faces. For me, even with my vastly improved English, I was still like a young girl wearing a blindfold and told to maneuver through a minefield.

However, much had improved for me since my return. As Edward explained in his letter to me when I was back in Mexico, his reaching his eighteenth birthday triggered some financial power and independence through the trust arrangements his father had created before his death. Edward explained that my aunt wanted his cooperation on a variety of investments and properties they jointly owned, and to get that, she relented and granted me many new privileges and benefits. I was, as Edward had predicted, now attending the private school my cousin Sophia attended. Sophia and I were still taken there every morning by my aunt's chauffeur, Señor Garman, and when he wasn't available, Casto would drive us. I didn't know it yet, but Edward was planning to give me a new car someday soon. He was trying to get his mother to do the same for Sophia, because he recognized she would make my life a living hell if I had a car and she did not.

Edward and Jesse had both been accepted to the University of Southern California in Los Angeles, but they were home so often people wondered if they were really enrolled in a college. My aunt continually complained about it to him.

"Why are we paying all this money for you to attend college if you're not there?" she demanded to know.

"I'm there for what I'm supposed to be," he replied.

"College is more than attending classes. It's a whole world," she said.

He didn't reply.

In my heart of hearts, I knew that Edward was worrying about me all the time, how I was being treated and what new injury or pain my aunt and his sister were planning for me.

I tried to assure him that I was fine whenever he called, but he was still concerned, despite how unafraid I sounded. I did have far more self-confidence now, and I think my aunt realized it. I would never say she accepted and loved me. It was more like a truce between us, or even a quiet respect and awareness that I was no longer as gullible and as innocent as the poor Mexican girl who had just lost her parents. The events of the past few years had hardened me in places I had hoped would always be soft. I didn't want to be so untrusting and cynical, but sometimes, more often than not, those two ingredients were important when building a protective shield around yourself. Here, as everywhere, it was necessary to do so, especially for a young woman my age, whose immediate family was gone and whose future depended not so much on the kindness of others as it did on her own wit and skill.

In one of her softer moments, when she

permitted herself to be my aunt, Tía Isabela admitted to admiring me for having the spine to return and face all the challenges that awaited me, challenges that had grown even greater because of the previous events.

But her compliments were double-edged swords in this house, because she often used them and me to whip Sophia into behaving. As a result, Sophia only resented me more.

"Instead of always doing something behind my back or something sly and deceitful, Sophia, why don't you take a lesson from Delia and draw on some of that Latin pride that's supposedly in our blood," she told her once at dinner when she discovered Sophia had been spreading nasty lies about a girl in the school who disliked her, the daughter of another wealthy family. The girl's mother had complained bitterly to Tía Isabela. "Believe me," she told Sophia, "people will respect you more for it. Look how Delia is winning respect."

Sophia's eyes were aching with pain and anger when she looked at me. Then she folded her arms, sat back, and glared at her mother.

"I thought you weren't proud of your Mexican background, Mother. You never wanted to admit to ever living there, because you were so ashamed of it, and you hate speaking

Spanish so much you won't even say *sí*."

"Never mind me. Think of yourself."

"Oh, I am, Mother. Don't worry, I am," Sophia said, and smiled coldly at me. "Just like our Latin American princess," she added.

Frustrated, Tía Isabela shook her head and returned to eating in silence.

Most of the time, silence ruled in this *hacienda,* because the thoughts that flew about would be like darts if they were ever voiced. They would sting like angry hornets and send pain deep into our hearts. It was better that their wings were clipped, the words never voiced.

There was little music in the air here as well. Oh, Sophia clapped on her earphones, especially when she went into a tantrum, but there was no music like there was back in Mexico, the music of daily life, the music of families. Here there was only the heavy thumping of hearts, the slow drumbeat to accompany the funeral of love, a funeral I refused to attend.

Instead, I sat by my window at night and looked out at the same stars that Ignacio was surely looking at as well at the same moment, somewhere in Mexico. I could feel the promise and the hope and vowed to myself that nothing would put out the twinkling in the darkness or silence the song we both heard — nothing, that is, that I could imagine.

But then, there was so much I didn't know.

And so many dark places I couldn't envision.

1
DARK PLACE

"I'll make a deal with you," Sophia told me one evening just after the start of our senior year. She had called me into her room when I came up to go to mine and start my homework.

"And what is this deal?"

"I'll do our English homework if you'll do our math. You're better than I am in math, because you don't have to speak English to do numbers."

"I'm better than you are in English, too," I said.

Tía Isabela had tried pressuring her into working harder last year by saying, "A girl who barely spoke English a year ago is now achieving with grades so much higher than yours it's embarrassing, Sophia."

"The teachers feel sorry for her and give her higher grades out of pity, that's all," was Sophia's response.

"Every teacher? I doubt that."

"Well, they do! She puts on a look so pathetic sometimes that it is . . . pathetic."

Aunt Isabela shook her head at Sophia and walked away, which was what she usually did. She would rather retreat than spend the time and effort to cause Sophia to change or improve.

"I'm trying to be more of a cousin to you, Delia," Sophia continued, with a sickeningly sweet smile as a way of urging me to do her math homework. "You can at least meet me halfway."

"Okay, I will. I will help you with your math homework whenever you ask."

"Help me? I'm not asking you to be my teacher!" she flared back at me. Then she quickly calmed down and again slipped that phony smile over her face, a smile I had grown so accustomed to that it no longer had any effect.

Why she never saw the futility of these antics, not only with me but with others, especially her teachers and her supposedly close friends, I didn't know. She was so obviously being phony. I was tempted to tell her time and time again that she wasn't fooling anyone with her false faces. Just be yourself, believe in yourself. And then again, I was beginning to wonder if she even had a self. Maybe she was just a mixture of this deception and that lie, a bundle of phoniness that when unraveled left nothing.

"Look, if you do my math, I'll help you make more friends. Everyone needs more friends, Delia."

Now I was tempted to laugh aloud at her. On my desk in my room was an invitation to Danielle Johnson's birthday party, an invitation she had yet to receive. I had learned never to mention any invitation before she received it, because if she wasn't invited to the same party, she went into a sulk and then a tantrum. It only made life more miserable for everyone in the *hacienda,* especially the servants she badgered and abused, such as Inez Morales, the assistant maid to my aunt's head housekeeper, Señora Rosario. Poor Inez desperately needed the money, since her husband had deserted her and her twin boys, so she had to endure whatever abuse Sophia unloaded on her. Sophia was like that, quick to pounce and take advantage of someone who was practically defenseless. I remembered how defenseless I was my first days here and how she had abused me.

Never again, I vowed.

"I am pleased with how many friends I already have, Sophia. When your mother and your brother told me I would attend the private school, I was worried that so many

25

of the other students would be snobby, but I'm happy to say it's not so," I told her with a deliberately exaggerated happy smile.

Of course, there were snobby girls and many who were not friendly to me, but give her back the dishonesty she doles out to me and to others, I thought. Or, as my Señora Paz would always tell my grandmother whenever someone would say something insulting, *"Páguela en su propia moneda."* Pay her in her own currency.

I could see the frustration boiling inside Sophia, the crimson color coming to her cheeks, the tiny flames dancing in her eyes. I knew my grandmother Anabela would not like to see me so vengeful, but sometimes I couldn't help it. Was I becoming too much like my cousin?

More than once I had heard my father in conversation with other men say, *"Cuando usted se convierte como su enemigo, su enemigo ha ganado."* When you become like your enemy, your enemy has won.

Was that happening to me? Was my living in this house with my aunt and my cousin turning me into a woman with a character just like theirs? Was I doing it to survive or because I had come to enjoy it?

"Don't be fooled, Delia. You speak English okay, but you're not sophisticated enough yet to be an American. They're lying to your face and talking about you behind your back. You don't hear what I hear in the girls' room. They still think you're some wetback Mexican who just happened to fall into a good thing."

"If that is so after all this time, then there is not much you can do to change them, Sophia, but thank you for thinking and worrying about me," I told her, smiled, and went to my room.

Even before I crossed the hallway, I could hear her heaving things about in anger. It brought a smile to my face, until I looked into the mirror above my vanity table and thought I saw *mi abuela* Anabela shaking her head.

"I'm sorry, Grandmother," I whispered. "But I've turned the other cheek so many times, I feel like I'm spinning."

I dropped myself onto my bed and stared up at the ceiling. Yes, I was back in this beautiful room with this plush, expensive furniture, and I had a closet almost as big as the room Abuela Anabela and I had shared as a bedroom back in Mexico, but it still felt more like a prison at times.

I'm the Lady of Shalott in the Tennyson poem we were studying, I thought when I rose and went to my window to look out on the estate. Just like her, I'm trapped in a tower, hoping somehow to be with my true love but cursed if I dared look at him. If I acknowledged Ignacio, I would have the same fate.

All of the clothes, the cars, the riches of this *hacienda,* and the privileges I now enjoyed did little to relieve me of my aching heart. Sometimes I thought I was torturing myself by continuing to hope. On many an occasion, I heard Señora Paz bitterly say, *"Quien vive de esperanzas muere de hambre."* Who lives on hope dies of hunger. In her old age, she could only look back at missed opportunities and be cynical, but I was determined not to be that way.

I glanced at my desk. Under my books was the letter I had started, the secret letter I would have to get to Ignacio's family so it could somehow travel through the clandestine maze and find itself in his hands. During these past two years, we had the opportunity to speak to each other on a telephone only a half-dozen times. He was afraid to call his home and certainly could never call here, even though, thanks to Edward, I had a phone in my room with my own number. Ignacio and, especially, his father were afraid that somehow someone would overhear or trace a conversation. It was better to be extra careful. Everyone except someone like my cousin Sophia knew that an ounce of prevention was worth a pound of cure.

But when it was possible, I went to a pay phone in a strip mall and answered the phone for a secret, prearranged telephone rendezvous. Once, one of the girls at school, Caitlin Koontz, saw me do it and asked about it. I told her I had just heard it ringing and picked it up. I said I quickly learned it was an elderly lady who had made a dialing mistake.

"Why did you speak so long?" Caitlin asked.

"I was just trying to calm her down and help her call the right number."

"Was she desperate for some kind of help?"

"No, just confused."

She smirked and shook her head. "Boring," she sang, and sauntered off.

I was afraid she would tell some other girls, but she either forgot or didn't think it was important enough. Nevertheless, just that little confrontation filled me with such fear and anxiety that my body trembled all day. I knew Ignacio's father didn't want him to have any contact with me other than the letters, and he wasn't happy about that, either. Reluctantly, because of promises he had made to Ignacio, he would get a message to me that a letter from Ignacio had arrived. I would have to wait until I could find a way to get out to the Davilas' house to read it. Right after I had, his father would burn it, and his mother would turn away and cry.

Ignacio's father was a very proud, strong man, and he wouldn't permit tears to be shed in front of him. I thought he forbid it because it would only make him more aware of his own pain and sorrow. Despite his attempt to be stoic and firm, I saw the glitter of deep sadness in his own eyes, too, whenever Ignacio's name was spoken.

Going to the Davilas' house was difficult, not only because of the distance and the arrangements I had to make to get there but because my aunt disapproved. The first time she learned I had visited the Davilas, she summoned me to her office. Señora Rosario informed me that I was to appear immediately. It was as if she was bringing me a court subpoena. Edward was already away at college, but that didn't matter. I hadn't told either him or Jesse about my visits with the Davila family. I did not know how my aunt had found out. It gave me pause to think she might be having me watched, even followed, perhaps for other reasons. After all, I had been shoved down her throat, so to speak, and *mi tía* Isabela was never one to be told what to do. That I knew from what my family back in Mexico had told me of her.

She made me stand in front of her in her office for a good thirty seconds while she shuffled papers.

"First," she began, lifting her eyes toward me and focusing sharply, like a sniper taking sight of his target, "I would have thought you would want to widen your relationships and take advantage of the opportunity to know young people from substantial families."

"Substantial?"

"Rich, well-off, people with status, authority, people who could do you some good," she rattled off. "Don't pretend not to understand me, Delia Yebarra. I know you better than anyone else knows you, even Edward, and I know you're not stupid, so don't pretend."

"I'm not pretending anything. I just wanted to be sure I understood," I said softly.

She glared at me a moment and then took a deep breath before continuing.

Forgive me, Grandmother, I thought, but I do enjoy frustrating her.

"Second, this boy you knew from this family was a felon and would have gone to prison. He was selfish and foolish to take you along on a very dangerous desert crossing, and yet now I learn you still remain friendly with his family. Why?"

"They have suffered."

"So has Rod Whitfield. And so has your cousin!" she added, widening her eyes.

I knew that Tía Isabela would blame me for Edward's loss of his eye forever, even if Edward did not. On more than one occasion, she had suggested that I should have kept what Bradley had done to me to myself, swallowed it back and forgotten about it, just like that, like snapping your fingers, and *poof,* it never happened. She could do that with unhappy events, disappointments. She had steel skin and an iron heart. She told me that if I had kept what Bradley had done to me locked away, Edward would have both eyes, and the Mexican boys would not be in prison.

"And one wouldn't be dead and food for buzzards," she added, believing, as did everyone else, that Ignacio was dead. Maybe she was right. I did feel some responsibility for it all, even though I was a classic victim.

"Continuing any relationship with these Mexicans, especially now, can come to no good. I forbid it!" she told me.

I just stared at her.

"Did you hear me?"

I turned away and looked out the window

at the clouds, which seemed to be reaching for each other. It was as if the sky were in sympathy with me, with my longing to reach out to Ignacio and feel his hand in mine.

"Do you understand me?" she demanded.

I did not respond. I went to that wall of silence so familiar in this house, that wall that fell so often between everyone in it. In this *hacienda,* it was safer to be deaf and dumb and even blind.

"I'm warning you. I won't stand for it," she threatened. "Don't you ever even think about bringing any of those people here!"

I smiled.

"What are you laughing at?"

"Would you even know if one of them came, Tía Isabela? In your eyes now, all Mexicans look the same."

For a moment, she looked as if her face would burst.

"You insolent . . . get out of here. You'll make your own disasters, I know. You won't need me to help," she said, nodding. Suddenly, she waved her right forefinger at me, her entire demeanor changing. *"El pez que busca anzuelo busca su duelo,"* she recited. I was certain it had been recited at her so many times when she was younger that it was embedded in her brain. A fish that looks for the hook is halfway cooked, a lesson her father had tried desperately to teach her.

Her returning to her Mexican roots, even for a split second in anger, brought a gleeful smile to my face. Perhaps she hated me most because I reminded her of who she had been and who she still was. The moment the Spanish words came from her lips, she slammed them shut and turned away, angry at me but shocked at herself as well.

"Thank you for worrying about me," I said and left.

She never spoke of the Davilas again, but I had no doubt that she would be infuriated if she knew I continued to defy her and visited them many times after her lecture. She did complain to Edward.

"If you feel comfortable with the Davilas and feel you should visit them, that's fine," he said. "But it's better my mother does not know. I have made her swallow as much as I can, but always be careful. She'll always be looking for something she can use against you, Delia. Try not to give her any other opportunities. She'll pounce on you."

I almost told him the truth about it all then, but fear of his deserting me, too, kept me from speaking about Ignacio. In the end, it would be okay, I told myself, even though I had no idea when such a conclusion would ever come.

Lifting away my schoolbooks, I slipped out the nearly completed new letter to Ignacio. I wrote to him only in Spanish, just in case Sophia came into my room and inspected my things, looking for something she could use to make me look bad in front of Tía Isabela or the other girls at school. It was like living in the same house with a pair of scorpions.

While I wrote to describe my days, my school experiences, and my longing for us to be together again, my eyes drifted to Danielle Johnson's party invitation. I was always reluctant to go to any of these parties, but in the end, I usually did, just to keep anyone from suspecting anything. Why I was invited before Sophia was invited did puzzle me. I was beginning to believe that whoever invited me was afraid that if Sophia wasn't invited, I would be unable to attend. If Sophia knew that her social standing was so dependent on me, she would be inconsolable, and I didn't need another reason for her to despise me.

So, usually, I did not reply until she was invited, or if I were asked in school, I would say something about Sophia, and that would trigger an invitation. She did hang out with a different clique of girls at the school, and more often than not her friends were not invited to the same parties, but Sophia, not to be outdone by me, certainly, always attended and almost always had bad things to say about the girls, the party itself, or even the food. Unless it was something she did or chose to do first, it was never any good.

Usually, I did not mention social activities when I wrote to Ignacio. I didn't want him to think I was with other boys and having a good time while he suffered because he was away from his family and those he loved. I spent most of my letter describing my schoolwork, my life in the *hacienda,* and the things Edward and Jesse did for me. I knew he would like to know I was being so protected.

Edward and Jesse really were like two mother hens, I thought. They called me at least twice a week and returned to Palm Springs almost every other weekend to take me to the movies or to dinner or just to hang out with me in the house. I always told Edward when I was invited somewhere, and he would give me advice about the girl's family, if he knew them, or advice in general about how to behave with what he called "the poor little misunderstood rich kids."

As if he could sense when I was thinking about him, he called.

"What's new on the battlefield?" was always his first question, and I always laughed.

"Your mother has been very busy with business and business dinners this week," I said. "I've seen her only twice."

"Lucky you. Jesse and I won't be there this weekend. We have some research papers and will sleep in the library, but we're thinking of coming down the following weekend," he said.

"Oh."

"You don't sound happy about it. Have you fallen in love or something?"

"No, but I have another party invitation for that Saturday night, Danielle Johnson."

"Johnson? Yes, that should be a nice party," he said immediately. "They have a beautiful property in Palm Desert. Her father built himself his own golf course on the property. He owns a railroad in Canada, you know, among other things. Well, you're at the top of the food chain now, Delia."

"Food chain?" I laughed. "What are they eating?"

"Each other. It's called social cannibalism. Did you tell my mother?"

"Not yet."

"What about Sophia?"

"Not yet," I said.

He was quiet a moment. I could almost see the realization settle in his face.

"She wasn't invited?"

"I'm sure she'll get her invitation tomorrow. Mine came today. It's happened before," I reminded him.

"I see. So, you haven't mentioned it yet. You're getting pretty smart, Delia. We'll be down anyway. We can spend Friday night with you and some of Saturday, and we'll love to hear the blow-by-blow about the party on Sunday morning before we head back to Los Angeles."

"I love you both," I said, "but you don't have to worry so much."

"Hearing you say that makes me worry more," he replied. *"Tenga cuidado."*

"Be careful yourself, Mr. Big Shot college man," I said, and he laughed. I heard Jesse ask him what was so funny. When he told him, Jesse laughed, too, and then got on the phone.

"I met an exchange student from Costa Rica today," he said, "and she was very impressed with some of my Spanish. Thanks to you."

"I met an exchange student from Texas, and she was impressed with my English, thanks to you," I replied.

I never heard either of them laugh so hard.

"We miss you," they chanted together, and then we said good-bye.

Despite my telling them I didn't need their protection so much, I loved to hear from them and to see them. They were truly sunshine for me on any dark, rainy day in this house. It was comforting knowing they were always there.

As usual, the moment I hung up, Sophia burst into my room without knocking first. If she heard my phone ringing, she perked up like a sleeping snake. I wish I could lock my door, but then I thought that would only make her more suspicious and more intruding. Somehow, it was all right for her to lock her door when she wanted it locked, but it was not all right for me.

"Did you get an invitation to Danielle Johnson's party?" she demanded immediately. "Well, did you?" she asked, her hands on her hips. "I was just on the phone with Alisha, and she told me about it. She wasn't invited, and neither were Delores or Trudy," she added, mentioning her three best friends, the girls who had been with us that fateful night when Bradley was killed. "I told them that if we weren't invited, you certainly wouldn't be."

I didn't answer immediately. I had always thought that lying to Sophia wasn't as terrible as lying to anyone else. Lies were so much a part of who and what she was that it was as if they were her own language. She was comfortable with them, and she would rather be lied to and remain happy than to be told the truth and be angry or hurt. She took baths in deception. It was second nature to her.

But I was suddenly filled with a raging desire to hurt her in some way. Her arrogance and her meanness were just spilling over.

"As a matter of fact," I said, "I was." I picked up the invitation and showed it to her.

I could see that despite what she had said and probably told Alisha, she was anticipating this.

She stepped forward to rip it from my fingers and read it.

"A night in Paris? How ridiculous. Just because her mother came from France, she thinks she can parade about with her *oui, oui* and *pardon moi*'s."

She ripped the invitation in half and tossed it into the little trash can by my desk.

"Well, you won't go," she said.

"Why won't I go?"

"You're my cousin. You live in my house. If you're invited and I'm not, you just tell them no thanks."

"Maybe you will be invited," I suggested.

She looked at me suspiciously for a moment. "If I get an invitation now, I'll know it was not really sincere."

"Since when did you care about that?"

"About what?"

"Being sincere," I said.

Her expression dissolved. "Very funny. I want to be with you tomorrow when you tell her where to go with her Paris party. I'll tell you exactly how to say it," she said, turned, and marched toward my bedroom door.

"I can't. It's too late," I said.

She spun around. "What?"

"I already called her this evening and told her I would be there. You know I've been taking French." I smiled. "When she answered her phone, I said, *'Merci, Danielle. Je serai heureux de m'occuper de votre partie.'*"

Her mouth opened and closed.

"I have a wonderful dress to wear," I continued, rising from my chair. "You remember it, I'm sure. It's perfect for an evening in Paris."

I opened my closet and started to pull the dress off the rack, but when I turned around, she was already gone.

Even Abuela Anabela would be unable to hide a small smile, I thought.

But then she would chastise me and tell me to ask God for forgiveness.

Later, I thought, I would pray for forgiveness. I was enjoying the moment too much right now, and I knew that pleasure was not going to last very long.

Sure enough, in the morning at breakfast, something we rarely shared with Tía Isabela on weekdays, Sophia complained to her mother about my being invited to the Johnson party and her not being invited. Tía Isabela was genuinely surprised to hear it. I could see a look of amazement and then a faint smile of amusement when she glanced at me.

Either to help Sophia feel better about it or maybe to make me feel less happy, she said, "I'm sure Angelica Johnson asked her daughter to invite Delia as a favor to me."

"Well, what does that say about me, Mother? She didn't invite me. Is that a favor for you?" Sophia asked, wagging her head so hard I thought she would give herself a headache.

"I'm sure it's probably because of the girls you hang out with. I have told you many times, Sophia, that I don't approve of the friends you've made. You make your own bed. Apparently, Delia's making some nice friends."

"Huh?" Sophia said. She thought a moment and then threw her spoon down and folded her arms. "You mean you're going to let her go to the Johnson party even though I've been snubbed?"

"You've been invited to things I haven't been invited to," I said softly.

Rarely did I interject myself between them when they argued, but I also rarely heard Tía Isabela defend me, for whatever reason she had.

"She has a point, Sophia."

"A point?"

"Do you want me to ask Danielle's mother about it? I'm sure I can get her to invite you."

"Absolutely not! Do you think I'm desperate to be invited to parties, desperate for friends?"

"So why are you making such a ruckus about it?" Tía Isabela asked.

I kept my eyes down, but I could almost feel the heat and frustration coming from Sophia.

"Forget about it," she finally said. "If you don't care, I don't care."

"Good," Tía Isabela said.

I looked up at her. She was too pleased, I thought. She wasn't only trying to teach Sophia some lesson. She was hoping for something else. It was so hard to live in a house with two spiders weaving their webs in dark corners, hoping I would fall into one of them.

The silence started to weave its own co-coons around each of us, but Sophia, never one just to accept and retreat, made a new demand.

"When are you going to decide about my having my own car? I have to wait for her after school if I want to come home in our limousine or ride in that stinking car with Casto. It's embarrassing! You don't like me riding with Alisha, who happens to have her own car even though her parents don't have a quarter of our money."

"When I think you're responsible enough to have a car," Tía Isabela said, "I'll get you one. And I told you, I don't want you riding around with Alisha."

"If my father was alive, I'd have it by now. I'd have had it on my sixteenth birthday! He would want it. He left me a fat trust fund, didn't he?"

"And when you're old enough to have control of some of those funds, you can waste them any way you like, Sophia, but once you do," Tía Isabela added, her eyes quickly glowing into hot coals, "you won't get any money from me." She sat back. "And I doubt you would get any from Edward."

"No," Sophia said wagging her head. "I wouldn't get anything from Edward. He'd give it all to her," she said, nodding at me. "The two of them don't fool me, even if they fool you," she fired back at her mother.

"Fool me? Fool me about what? What are you saying, you idiot?"

"Nothing," Sophia replied, picking up her cereal spoon again and smiling. "Only . . . you'd better start wondering why Edward and Jesse spend so much time alone with her."

Tía Isabela looked at me.

The implied accusation now brought a crimson tint into my face.

"Sometimes the innocent look guilty because they are so embarrassed by the innuendos and they are so outraged they are too vigorous in their denials and fit Shakespeare's great line in *Hamlet,* 'The lady doth protest too much, me thinks,'" Mr. Buckner had said just yesterday during our reading of *Hamlet.* "The line between the innocent and the guilty gets blurred."

I looked at Sophia when he told us that. She was doodling in her notebook and not paying attention, as usual. I wondered, if she had paid attention, would it make any difference?

"That's not funny, Sophia," Tía Isabela said. "What happens in this house reflects on me. Just remember that."

"What happens in this house reflects on all of us, Mother. I live here, too. You, yourself, have told me that you think Edward dotes on her far too much. Well, maybe they do more than dote, and right under your nose."

"That's enough," Tía Isabela snapped. "I have a full day today, and I don't need to be aggravated before I even begin. You had better watch your own behavior, Sophia, and not worry about your brother."

"Suit yourself, Mother," Sophia said, keeping that infuriating smile. "If you want to bury your head in the sand, you have no problem. We live in the desert."

Tía Isabela slammed her spoon down, rose, her breakfast half eaten, her coffee nearly untouched, and marched out in a fury.

I looked at Sophia. She was so content with herself for getting to her mother that I had to wonder if they ever loved each other. Did she ever cling to her when she was little? I couldn't remember a time since I was here when she and her mother kissed or hugged.

"Satisfied?" she asked me, as if I had been the one to cause the trouble.

I didn't reply.

Two days later, without my saying a word to anyone who might have said something to Danielle, Sophia received an invitation to her party. She came into my room that night wearing a very deep, satisfied smile.

"Well, look what came in the mail to me," she said, showing me the invitation.

I started to deny having anything to do with it, but she stopped me.

"I know it wasn't you. It's my mother's doing," she said. "She was worried about her status in society, I'm sure."

And then she tore the invitation in half and threw it into the wastebasket, just as she had done to mine. She spit on it as well.

"I wouldn't be caught dead there," she said. She turned and marched away, slamming my bedroom door behind her.

The following Saturday, however, she was out shopping for a new dress that would outdo mine, no matter what the price.

She wouldn't be caught dead going to the party? I guessed she'd hired a hearse to bring her to it, I thought, and laughed to myself. It felt like I had won a small victory and any victory, no matter how small, was an achievement in this house.

But I should have remembered what she and her girlfriends were so fond of saying all the time.

"He who laughs last laughs best."

2
CHRISTIAN TAYLOR

"Bonjour, Delia. Comment allez-vous?" Christian Taylor asked me as we were entering French class.

This was the one class that Sophia and I did not share at the private school.

Considering her opinion of Mexicans, I found it ironic, even amusing, that Sophia had chosen Spanish class over French class, something most of the students at the school actually had done. There were only eight students in our French class, but because this was a private school, the class could still be conducted.

Of course, the students who chose Spanish, thinking it was far easier, claimed they chose it because it was more practical to learn Spanish in our community, with so many Latinos working and owning businesses here. There weren't only people from Mexico. There were people from Nicaragua, Venezuela, and Costa Rica, as well as some other Central American countries.

"Je suis très bien, et vous?" I replied.

"Bien," he said, and then looked worried that I would continue speaking only in French. I could see it clearly in his face, a face I would be the last to deny was quite handsome, with his luminous blue eyes highlighting his classic Romanesque nose, high cheekbones, and strong-looking firm lips. He had rich light brown hair gently swept behind his ears and halfway down his neck. Six feet tall, with a lean swimmer's physique, he was the school's track star and thought to be a shoo-in for a sports scholarship at some prestigious college. Most of the girls in our class and the class below swooned over him, and the problem I saw was that he knew it far too well. He had an arrogant strut, and when he walked through the hallways, he wore a self-satisfied smile that, in truth, put me off despite his drop-dead gorgeous looks. I thought that conceited smile was just another mask.

Ironically, avoiding him seemed to be just the right thing to do to win his attention. Either it bothered him very much that I wasn't doting on him as were most of the other girls, or he was genuinely intrigued and interested in me for being so indifferent to him. Whatever the case, I was not going to become another one of his conquests, nor would I forget Ignacio to be with him. In fact, just thinking about Christian made me feel guilty.

He tried to ask in French if I were going to Danielle's party but gave up after *"Etes vous"* and added, "going to Danielle Johnson's birthday bash?"

"Mais oui," I said, and then hurried to my seat.

Monsieur Denning, our teacher, had entered. He was very serious about the class, annoyed if we wasted a second of our time. We were at the point where he wanted us all to try to say anything in class in French and would make a student look up the words and attempt the correct pronunciation, no matter how long that took.

I glanced at Christian, who was sitting two rows over, and saw him smiling at me warmly. I also saw how some of the other girls in the class were looking at me with shadows of envy darkening their faces, but I did not smile back at him.

Just before I had celebrated my *quinceañera,* my fifteenth birthday, in Mexico, a birthday that was very significant for us, a time when we were moving from being a girl to a woman, my mother passed on some of her advice about men.

"You must be careful about the messages you telegraph to them, Delia."

"Messages?"

"In your eyes, in your smile. The secrets in your heart can be revealed very quickly. Be careful," she said, and then told me a saying her mother had. *"Mujer que no tiene tacha chapalea el agua no se moja."* It meant, a woman who's innocent can splash around in the water and not get wet.

"Be careful where you splash," she added with a twinkle in her eyes.

So, although I felt a smile trying to come out to answer Christian Taylor's smile, I recalled my mother's advice and looked away quickly. I concentrated on my French to avoid thinking about him, and not once during the remainder of the class did I look his way.

However, now I really was caught in a paradox. Seemingly, no matter what I did, Christian saw it as encouraging. It continued. The more I ignored him, the more he pursued. Perhaps it had become a matter of pride for him. After all, what other girl in this school would turn down his attention?

Tía Isabela wasn't wrong about the friends I had made and the friends Sophia already had. At lunchtime, we sat far apart from each other in the cafeteria. Otherwise, it

51

would truly be like trying to mix oil and water. I had quickly learned that in one way or another over the years, Sophia had alienated, insulted, or somehow embarrassed most of the girls I found as friends. They were all somewhat suspicious of me in the beginning, because Sophia was my cousin, and I lived in her *hacienda,* but eventually it was easy for them to see how different we were. Also, the fact that Sophia was so obvious about her dislike and jealousy of me pleased them.

Sophia did little to help me adjust when I first entered the private school. I didn't know it at the time, but that turned out to be a blessing. When Edward and Jesse arranged for me to return from Mexico, he and my aunt, with Sophia sitting in and sulking, discussed why I should now attend the private school. They were worried about my continuous exposure to other Mexican teenagers at the public school who knew about Ignacio and his friends and my involvement with them. Edward thought some would blame me, and in the end, it would only bring more trouble to the family. My aunt, to my surprise, agreed quickly and was willing to spend the thousands of dollars for my private-school tuition. Of course, Sophia was not happy about it.

The private school had a far better language tutor than Mr. Baker could ever have been, and with my previous experience in the public school's ESL class, I made very quick progress. There were a few other Mexican students, one being the daughter of a family who owned a chain of Mexican restaurants. I didn't immediately make friends with her. I could sense she was being snobby. She spoke fluent Spanish but usually avoided it. I thought she had begun to see me as some sort of competition. Her name was Estefani, but she insisted on being called just Fani. She was tall, nearly five-eleven, with a runway model's figure. Her father was from a wealthy Mexican family in Houston, Texas, and her family was very close to the family of the most influential Indian families in the desert.

The Indians here owned a great deal of land and made money on the land leases. They also ran casinos and were very wealthy. All of the politicians courted their favor, so Fani was at grand events and parties and often had her picture in the local paper and magazines. The friendliest thing she said to me that first year was, "Maybe I can get you a job as a waitress at our Palm Desert restaurant. We're always looking for authentic Mexicans."

"What's an authentic Mexican?" I asked. She just smiled. I knew what she meant was someone not as fluent in English and dirt poor.

I avoided her, which pleased Sophia, because Fani's friendship was something most of the girls craved, even Sophia. With Fani, Sophia could admit to her mother being Mexican without feeling inferior.

"We're alike," she would tell Fani. "We come from aristocratic Mexican family lines."

Sophia concocted some fantastic tale about her mother's family being descendants of wealthy Mexican businessmen and politicians. I was the only poor relative they had.

If the girls she told these things to could see where my aunt really had lived, the house she had lived in, they would probably laugh in Sophia's face, but because no one knew the truth about Tía Isabela, Sophia could make up anything she liked. As long as I didn't contradict her, of course.

That first year, she was quick to lay down that rule. She did it as we walked into the building, seizing my wrist and tugging me back.

"Don't you dare tell these girls how poor my mother's family was. Whatever I say, you just nod, and if you're not sure, you don't say anything, understand? I'm warning you," she threatened. "I don't like you being here, and I don't want you to embarrass me."

I pulled my wrist out of her grip, but said nothing.

Those early days were very difficult for me, and on more than one occasion, I considered quitting, but gradually, I made more friends and became more and more comfortable, especially with my teachers. Before the first year ended, I was on the honor roll and cited at a school function as the transfer student who had made the most improvement of anyone with language disadvantages. They meant in the history of the school, too. My aunt accepted the congratulations as if it had all been her idea. Sophia was burning up with so much jealousy one of my friends, Parker Morgan, suggested we spray her with one of the school's fire extinguishers.

On this particular day, Parker, Katelynn Nickles, Colleen McDermott, and I had just begun eating our lunch and talking excitedly about Danielle Johnson's party, when Christian approached with his tray of food and asked if he could sit with us. Since he had not shown interest in any of the other three, they all looked at me as if it was to be my decision. Whether I liked it or not, I had to be the one to say yes or no.

"Yes, of course," I said. "Only you will be bored. We were just talking about dresses and shoes."

"Oh, I'm very interested in dresses and shoes," he said, slipping into the seat beside me. "I'm something of an expert on them. Just ask me anything."

He smiled at me and started to eat.

"Oh? What do you think of kimono-sleeve dresses?" I asked, looking at the other girls.

He pretended to give it serious thought, which only titillated the other three.

"Well . . . if I were a girl," he said, "I'd worry about the elbows. Most girls don't know it," he continued, leaning in as if he were going to impart a great secret, "but boys get turned on by elbows."

Everyone laughed. I couldn't help being amused, either. He turned those devastatingly beautiful eyes on me. I felt like someone trying to climb out of a grease pit. The more effort I made to ignore and avoid him, the more I went in the opposite direction.

"Anything you wear is going to look good on you, Delia. Don't worry about it."

I saw how my girlfriends' eyes widened with surprise and jealousy. They exchanged quick glances. I blushed and ate my sandwich. Across the cafeteria, Sophia stared with a look of absolute amazement on her face. She whispered something to Alisha, and then all of them turned our way.

Edward hadn't been wrong about why I should attend the private school instead of public school when I had returned from running away. Although the students here knew what had happened to Bradley and what had happened to Edward, of course, they didn't know much about my involvement and certainly nothing about my flight through the desert with Ignacio. One of the conditions my aunt had set down for my attending the private school was that I was never, ever to talk about the events with anyone at the school.

Of course, Sophia was warned as well, but her friends knew it all, and keeping them silent about it was not as easy. Up until now, Sophia had managed to keep them in tow, but I was always worried that one day, someone like Fani or Fani herself would step up beside me in the hallway and say, "So, I just heard you were raped, and that was what started all the trouble."

It wasn't any different here from anywhere else. The victim never stopped being a victim and never lost the stain on her image. That was another irony I didn't understand. Boys would easily go out with girls who were loose with their own bodies but would hesitate about going out with a girl who was raped. I had seen that in Mexico and knew the same was true here.

Wasn't it enough that I carried the dark memory forever? Why did they have to add to the tragedy?

When the bell rang to go back to our classes, Christian walked with me.

"Any chance you might want to go to a movie with me this weekend?" he asked before we entered our social studies class.

He wasn't the first boy to ask me out on a date. Most of the time, I said something that discouraged them. I did go to a movie with a boy who was a senior last year, Stevie Towers. It turned out to do me good, because he came away from the date believing I was too proper and religious to be any fun and spread the word. Few boys bothered to ask me out after that, which pleased Sophia. She did not know why it pleased me, but she thought she was annoying me whenever she flaunted her dates. She even went on a date with Stevie Towers herself and then spent the whole next day telling me how much fun they had. When he didn't ask her out again, I asked her why, and she told me she had decided he was too immature.

"But I thought you said it was fun to be with him," I reminded her.

"Only as a distraction," she quipped. "I would never go steady. I can't imagine anything as boring as being with the same boy every weekend."

"How do you expect to get married, then?" I asked her.

"I don't," she said. "Well, maybe when I'm tired of playing the field and just want someone to take care of me, someone who worships me."

"You're right," I said. "It might be a long time before you get married."

She didn't understand what I meant, that no one would ever worship her. She just nodded as if I had agreed with her philosophy of love.

Although I should have anticipated it, Christian's invitation threw me. I couldn't think of a good excuse not to go out. Edward and Jesse weren't coming, and there was no other event taking place to compete with a date.

"What movie?" I asked, to delay my response, hoping I could think of something.

"Whatever you like," he said. "I'm not just going to a movie. I'm going to a movie with you," he added.

The late bell was going to ring any moment. Other students walked by, every girl and even some of the boys looking at us with interest.

"Can I tell you tomorrow?" I asked.

"How about tonight? I'll call you," he pursued.

"Okay." I started into the classroom, and he grabbed my arm.

Laughing, he asked for my telephone number. I smiled and gave it to him.

Across the room, I could see Sophia glaring at us, her face twisted and as sour-looking as an overly ripe lemon. I slipped into my seat just as the bell rang. Christian sat two seats behind me in the row to my left. It took all of my self-control to keep from turning around, but I could feel his eyes on me. My heart was being challenged. It would be dishonest for me to say I was absolutely not interested in him. Every time his face, his smile, those eyes flashed in my mind, I drew up my memory of Ignacio's face to stop it, especially the way he'd looked as the bus pulled away from the station in Mexico City and he stood there waving. It would surely break his heart to know I had even looked at another boy with such romantic interest.

When the class ended, I anticipated Christian waiting for me again, but this time he just looked at me, smiled, and went on to his physical education class. I couldn't help but think that everything he did, every move, every look and word, was calculated. I tried to think of that as false so I could turn my heart against him, but it wasn't working.

Sophia came up beside me as I walked out.

"What's with you and Christian Taylor?" she asked — demanded was more like it. "Everyone's buzzing."

"Nothing," I said.

"Don't lie to me, Delia. You're not good at it, so don't try. And you shouldn't be keeping secrets from me. Well?"

"He asked me to go with him to the movies this weekend," I admitted. I was also curious about how she would react to the news.

"And what did you say?"

"I told him to call me. I would think about it."

She smirked. "He's poison on a stick," she said. "There isn't a girl here he hasn't tried to ruin or ruined."

I smiled.

"And don't give me that fable about the fox and the grapes he called sour because he couldn't reach them, either. It's not sour grapes. I've been with Christian, and it's no big deal," she added.

"Oh?"

"Now that I think of it," she continued, smiling herself, "in your case, it's not a big

61

problem. You should go out with him."

"And why is it not a problem, Sophia?"

She leaned in to whisper. "You've already been ruined, remember?" she said, and walked on ahead of me to join Alisha. She whispered something, and the two of them laughed extra loudly.

All sorts of curses slipped out of my tight lips as I watched them and then, maybe looking for the excuse I needed, I hurried down the hallway and reached Christian before he stepped into the boys' locker room. He turned, surprised.

"You don't have to call me," I said. "I cannot go to the movies with you."

"Why not?" he asked, his shoulders rising with indignation.

"I've decided not to date anyone yet. I have too much to learn. I'm not ready."

"Huh? You've been out on dates. I know for a fact that you once went on a date with Stevie Towers."

"And it was not successful. For either of us. Thank you for the invitation," I added.

"What are you going to be, a nun?"

"Maybe," I said.

He suddenly widened his eyes and raised his eyebrows. I could see he believed me.

"You're making a big mistake if you do," he said, and went into the locker room.

I looked in the direction Sophia and her friends had gone. The fire burning inside me died down, and now I chastised myself for my Latin temper. *"La cólera es el mejor amigo del diablo."* Anger is the devil's best friend, my grandmother would say.

I was sorry about being impulsive and doing exactly what would surely please Sophia. I considered calling Christian later and telling him I had changed my mind, but now I thought I would look foolish. It wasn't a good idea. He would ask why I had changed my mind, and I would have no answer.

Either Christian was too proud to tell other boys he had been turned down for a date, or there simply was no time for him to discuss it with anyone, but at the end of the school day, Sophia apparently still did not know what I had done. I enjoyed watching her brood about it in the car while Señor Garman drove us home.

When she got out, she turned to me, however, and asked what I intended to say to Christian when he called.

"I'm not sure yet," I told her. Why not let her turn and twist in the agony of her jealousy for a while longer?

She marched into the house ahead of me.

While I was up in my room changing my clothes and organizing my homework, she went down to see Tía Isabela and give her the latest gossip. Contrary to what she had anticipated, however, Tía Isabela wasn't disturbed or worried about it. She brought it up at our dinner table.

"Sophia tells me Christian Taylor has asked you out on a date for Friday," she said.

Although she hadn't set down any rules about it, I always told Tía Isabela about any activity I was doing and any place I was going, except, of course, my visits to the Davilas' home. Usually, she acted indifferent.

"Yes, he has asked me," I admitted.

"Really? Christian Taylor. His father is a cardiologist at the Eisenhower Heart Institute. Did you know that?"

"No."

"What do you know about him?" she asked.

"He's a good athlete," I said. "And a good student. He plays an instrument in the band, too. Trumpet."

"That's what you know about him?"

"He just asked me today, Tía Isabela. I didn't have time to learn a great deal."

Sophia and she both laughed at me.

"No time to learn a great deal? You've been at the school almost a year and a half, Delia."

I shrugged. How was I to explain my deliberate indifference to boys while Ignacio remained in my heart and mind?

"Maybe you aren't as sophisticated as I thought," she said. "I don't know why I ever thought it, now that I consider what has happened to you when it comes to men."

"That's for sure," Sophia said.

"I wouldn't pat myself on the back just yet, Sophia," Tía Isabela snapped at her. "Your relationships with boys have been nothing to brag about. Do I have to remind you about some of the situations you got yourself into, situations that could have been very embarrassing for me?"

"It's always you, isn't it, Mother?"

"If you had half a brain, you'd realize it's both of us, Sophia. You can't live in a bubble."

"I'm not the one living in a bubble, Mother. I'm not trying to be eighteen again."

"That's enough," Tía Isabela said sharply. She glared at Sophia who just calmly continued to eat. "Disregard any advice she gives you," she told me.

"She doesn't listen to my advice," Sophia complained. "She's a big expert when it comes to boys now. Haven't you heard?"

Tía Isabela thought for a moment. "Maybe she is," she said. "Christian Taylor's father was my husband's heart doctor. Finally, you're socializing with the right sort of people," she told me. "Don't do anything to embarrass me."

"I wouldn't do anything to embarrass you or myself."

"We'll see," she said.

I said nothing more. As usual, we finished our dinner in silence, the air so thick with tension around us it could be cut with a knife.

To my surprise, a little after nine o'clock, my phone rang. It was Christian.

"I'm just calling to see if you rethought your decision," he said. He made it sound like a business decision. "Girls can be impetuous. Maybe you were just in the wrong mood."

It would be like him to find a way to blame me, I thought.

"I do not mean to be disrespectful of your invitation," I said.

He laughed. "I'm not your teacher or your father, Delia. I'm not worried about respect."

"But you should worry about that," I countered quickly. "We must first respect each other. We must always respect each other's feelings."

He was quiet a moment, and then he said, "Maybe you are cut out to be a nun."

"It is not a bad thing to be."

"Hey, it's nun thing to me," he said, laughing. "Let me know if you have a change of heart," he added, and said good-bye.

I suspected that, as usual, Sophia had kept one ear out for the sound of my phone ringing. Almost the moment I hung up, she was in my room.

"So?" she asked. "Where's he taking you Friday night? If he told you he's taking you to a drive-in, that's bull. There's no drive-in. He just means he's taking you parking and pretending you're watching a movie. That's his big joke he pulls on innocent, stupid girls."

"Did he pull it on you?" I asked her quickly.

She started to say yes and then realized and nearly spit out her answer. "I'm not stupid. Well, what did he say?"

"He asked me if I had changed my mind."

"Changed your mind? What does that mean?"

"I had already told him no," I said.

She was obviously quite taken aback. For a moment, she couldn't think of anything clever or mean to say. "Why?"

"I listened to what you said," I told her. "How he flits about ruining girls. I want nothing to do with such a boy."

She stared for a moment, smiled, and then grew serious, actually looking to the doorway as if someone could overhear our conversation. "Don't you dare tell my mother I said those things and that was why you turned him down," she warned.

"Why not? You were only trying to protect me."

"My mother won't see it that way. She's a social climber, always. She would go out with the devil if it got her picture on the social pages or in the magazines. Just . . . don't blame me for your not going out with Christian, understand? If you make more trouble for me, I'll find a way to get even, Delia," she threatened.

I smiled. "Do not worry, Sophia. I make my own decisions for myself. By now, I think Tía Isabela understands that."

"Yeah, well . . . okay." She thought a moment and then smiled. "This is good. I'll tease the hell out of him. Tomorrow will be a fun day at school, and there aren't too many of those," she said as she walked to the door. "Now I'm glad I decided to go to Danielle's stupid party."

She opened the door but paused and then turned and looked at me. Her eyes narrowed with suspicion.

"Why did you really say no?" she asked.

"I have already told you."

"Did Edward have something to do with it?"

"How could he? I have not spoken with him today."

She nodded, still smiling coolly. "Nevertheless, I bet he did," she said. She looked very pleased with herself coming up with such an idea. I could almost see her brain twirling with possibilities, ideas, ways to deliver more pain and set more traps. "Nighty-night or, as we say, *buenas noches*."

The air in the room seemed to follow her out.

Living here was like walking through a field with areas of quicksand and having her lead the way, I thought.

3
THE DAVILAS

Christian was cold to me the following day at school. I was not surprised, but it did make me very nervous. He avoided looking my way or walking too closely to me. It did not take long for my friends and the other girls in the school to realize there was now a wall of ice between us where there had just been soft, warm sunshine. Their faces were full of questions. Unbeknownst to me was the stream of underlying ugly lies and innuendos Sophia and her girlfriends were generating through whispers all morning. By the time I went to lunch, I could see the seeds of rumors and suspicions planted in the faces of other students, and instinctively I feared it had something to do with my cousin Edward and his companion, Jesse.

Girls who wanted to win Christian's attention surrounded him, but contrary to what they had hoped, he didn't want their sympathy. I could easily see it in how he reacted to their remarks. How dare they think he needed sympathy? It wasn't he who had lost out here. It was Delia Yebarra. I could practically hear him saying that to any girl who tried to comfort him about being turned down for a date. That, at least, brought a smile to my face.

My girlfriends agreed with me when I gave them my reasons for not going out with Christian Taylor.

"I do not trust his intentions," I said. "He flits about from one girl to the next as if we were different pastries in a bakery."

They laughed at my analogy, and those who thought Christian would never ask them out anyway really lavished compliments on me for being so strong-minded.

"Delia's right," Colleen said. "Christian is too much in love with himself to love anyone else. I don't even think he loves his own dog."

The girls laughed, but our small group was isolated for the most part. However, to my surprise, Fani couldn't resist talking to me when lunch hour ended.

"You're the big topic of conversation today, Delia. Tell me, do you have a boyfriend back in the public school? You once did, didn't you?" she asked, fishing for some personal information. "Do you still see those Mexican boys?"

Like some queen bee, she did not like being the last one to learn what was happening in her hive.

"I have no one," I said, perhaps too quickly, but of all the girls in the school, I feared her the most, because she had some contact with the Mexican community.

"Your cousin is telling people you are so in love with her brother that you don't have interest in other boys. I know she's feeding that line to Christian."

"She knows that is not true."

"Yes, but I assure you, Christian Taylor likes that explanation. It makes him feel good. He's passing it out like free candy."

"But it's a lie."

She shrugged. "I don't care one way or the other. Your business is your own business, and I'm no fan of Christian Taylor."

And then, whether she wanted to be more friendly with me or just felt an obligation finally as a sister Latina, she said, *"Tenga cuidado, chica, usted magulló un ego grande aquí."*

I watched her walk away.

Katelynn had overheard her and stepped up beside me.

"What did Fani say? I hardly ever hear her speak Spanish."

"She said I should be careful. I bruised a big ego here," I told her.

"Really? Wow," she said, as if she had been told what the queen had advised me about something.

"I didn't need her to tell me that," I said sharply. Katelynn's eyes widened. "You wouldn't either, would you?"

"Yeah, but . . . Fani. This is getting to be a big story," she added, and rushed off to tell the others.

This was getting to be a big story? If only they valued their schoolwork as much as gossip, they'd all be honor students, I thought.

Later, I saw the look of satisfaction on Sophia's face. Whatever she had planned and hoped for was now happening, and she was very pleased with herself. She had turned her rumors and innuendos into facts that wouldn't go away. Christian looked even more arrogant now.

Tía Isabela was not happy when she heard about it all by Friday and immediately assumed it was somehow Sophia's fault. I discovered that apparently the parents of the wealthy talked about the social lives of their sons and daughters all the time.

"What did you do, Sophia? What did you tell Delia? Why isn't she going on a date with Christian Taylor? I'm sure you did

something, so don't give me that look of in-
nocence," Tía Isabela said to begin our dinner conversation that night.

"I didn't do anything. She decided herself. Or," she added, her lips dripping with
venom, "it was Edward's doing."

"Edward's doing?" Tía Isabela turned to
me. "Is that true? Did Edward advise you
not to go on a date with Christian Taylor?
Don't lie to me, either. I'll find out," she
warned.

"No, Tía Isabela. I have not yet spoken to
Edward about it. He called me early in the
week before Christian had asked me on a
date."

"I see. So, why did you decide not to go
out with him? I told you he comes from a
distinguished family. I didn't disapprove,
did I?"

"No. It's simply that I do not like him, Tía
Isabela. He is too much in love with himself. He should just go out with a mirror," I
added, and to my surprise, she burst out in
loud laughter.

"Well," she said, catching her breath and
looking at Sophia, "maybe when it comes
to romance and boys, you really should be
taking lessons from your cousin after all,
Sophia."

She couldn't have said anything more

hurtful to Sophia. Her face finally began to shatter, her lips trembling and tears flooding into her eyes. I prepared myself for her outburst, but to my surprise and to Tía Isabela's, she just stood up, took a deep breath and said, "Believe me, Mother, you will be sorry in the end, not me."

Before Tía Isabela could respond, she rushed out of the dining room and to the stairway.

"Well, I guess our little stone princess can be embarrassed after all," Tía Isabela said, and continued to eat.

Such indifference to each other's pain made me sick inside. I ate what I could and excused myself. When I reached my room, I thought I could hear Sophia sobbing. I hesitated at her door and then decided not to get between her mother and her. In my room, I sat and stared out the window. It was partly cloudy, with the moon looking as if it was trying to avoid being trapped by the clouds. It seemed to slip every which way to remain uncovered. It was how I felt. Trapped and searching for an escape.

Despite the comforts I enjoyed and the affection of both my cousin Edward and his very close companion, Jesse, I could dream only of escape, dream only of a life with Ignacio, no matter how simple that life was to be. Perhaps we both should have remained in Mexico after all, I thought. Yes, we would have so much less, but we would at least be together. On the other hand, he would be without his family, and I knew how painful that was for him. After all, I was without my parents and my grandmother. They were gone from everything but my thoughts and memories, which to us meant they had not yet passed through the third death.

According to what I had been taught, there were three types of death. The first occurred when your body stopped functioning and your soul departed. The second occurred when you were interred in the earth. And the third death occurred if and when you were no longer remembered by anyone.

I was so deep in thought about it all that when the phone rang, I nearly jumped out of the chair. As soon as I heard Edward's voice, I suspected Tía Isabela might have called him to interrogate him.

"What's new on the battlefield?"

"Your mother nearly succeeded in bringing your sister to tears," I began, and told him the whole story except for the real reason I had turned down Christian Taylor's invitation. It was apparently all new to him. "So, your mother did not call you?" I asked.

"Why should she call me?" I didn't want

to tell him about the rumors Sophia was spreading. When I didn't respond, he continued, "Yeah, Christian Taylor's a bit of a horse's ass. You made the right decision. Don't worry about Sophia. She has a thick hide. She'll get over it quickly and do something to bring someone else to tears."

"There is so much anger swirling about in this house, Edward. Will it ever change?"

"I don't know," he said quickly. "You sound pretty melancholy, Delia. I guess we should have come home this weekend."

"No, I'm fine. It's all right," I said.

"You have to hang in there, Delia. Things will change for you. It will get better. You have too much to offer. Just be patient," he said.

"I'll try, Edward. I don't hear Jesse."

"He's at the library. We're sharing the work this weekend. I'll call you again tomorrow," he said.

"It's all right. You need not call. Do your work, Edward."

He laughed but insisted he would call.

When I looked out the window again, I saw Casto standing in the driveway and gazing up at my room. I knew what that meant and hurried down the stairs and out to him. He lingered in the shadows, which confirmed my suspicion.

"There is something waiting for you at the Davilas'," he said. We both knew what it was.

"*Gracias, señor.*"

"I am going up that way late in the morning," he said. "I need to get some things in the big hardware store that is near there."

"*Gracias.* What time?"

"Ten."

"It's still perhaps better *mi tía* Isabela not know."

"*Sí,*" he said.

He had taken me there once before, and what I had done was walk toward the bus station and have him pick me up. We would do the same now.

"I am very grateful, *señor.*"

"*Es nada,*" he said, and left me in the darkness.

But now my heart was full of happiness, and the melancholy Edward had heard in my voice was quickly swept away. I hurried back inside to add more to my letter to Ignacio. Although his letters to me were usually quite short, I knew he cherished mine and wanted them to last weeks. I would bring it with me, and his father would get it to him wherever he was in Mexico.

I was on pins and needles all morning but tried not to seem so when Tía Isabela appeared at breakfast. Sophia was back to having her breakfast delivered to her by Inez. I was confident that would be hard on Inez, and sure enough, she returned with the tray to tell Señora Rosario that Sophia claimed her eggs and her coffee were too cold. An entirely new breakfast had to be prepared for her.

"I'm going into Los Angeles today," Tía Isabela told me, and then she did something she had never done. She asked me if I would like to go with her. "It's business, but I have time to do some shopping."

"*Gracias,* Tía Isabela," I said, "but I have much to do today for school."

She pulled her shoulders back so quickly I knew my rejection was like a slap to her. I realized I should have said yes and planned on going to the Davilas' home the next day, perhaps after they had returned from church. But it was too late. I had let my heart speak quicker than my head.

"Suit yourself," Tía Isabela said, finished her coffee, and left.

It seemed that every decision, no matter how small or large, would have a negative effect on our relationships here. It was probably far better to find ways to avoid each other so we could avoid even the possibility of conflict.

Thinking about that, I realized that if Tía Isabela didn't leave before I did, she would see that I had lied at the table. I had one eye on the clock and another on the door. Just at nine forty-five, she came down the stairs and went out to get into her limousine. I hurried after her, watching Señor Garman drive her down the driveway. As soon as the car was gone, I walked quickly down the driveway myself. It was still better that I be out of sight when Casto picked me up. The worst thing that could happen would be Sophia seeing him do it. She might even get him fired.

I felt very sneaky, but I felt confident that I had not been seen leaving the house. A little after ten o'clock, Casto pulled up to the curb, and I got into his car.

"*Gracias,*" I said again. He nodded.

There were three employees at *mi tía* Isabela's estate who had been there before her husband had died: Señora Rosario, Señor Garman, and Casto. It was natural for me to wonder what things had been like back then. Señor Garman was not as friendly to me as Señora Rosario and Casto, but both were still reluctant to say too much, even after all this time with me.

"It is good that you are careful, Delia," Casto said. "The Davilas are good people. I would not like to see any more trouble come to them."

"Nor would I."

"I'm not sure they could survive here if the truth about their son was revealed. Are you sure this is all still a good idea?"

Tears came to my eyes before I could respond. I took a deep breath.

"La esperanza no engorda pero mantiene," I said. He looked at me and nodded. It wasn't just my grandmother's saying. All of the people in my village lived by it. Hope doesn't fatten, but it nourishes. Our lives were so hard, hope was sometimes all we had, but somehow it was enough to get us through terrible droughts or sicknesses and accidents.

How desperate for hope poor Ignacio must be, I thought. To do anything that would wound and destroy that hope would be cruel and painful now, not only for him but for me. Our current living conditions were as different as could be, but we shared the same dream.

"My aunt and her children," I said, "were they always so unkind to each other?"

I thought he would not answer because he was quiet so long, but then he shook his head. "When Señor Dallas was alive, he doted on the two of them and Señora

Dallas. His love was like the glue that held them together. Sophia was always spoiled," he added, smiling, "but Señor Dallas could keep her in the corral.

"Señor Dallas was not happy that Señora Dallas was at war with her own family in Mexico. He tried many times to mend fences, but the flames of her anger never diminished. I think he was always worried about this."

"*Por qué, señor?* They were poor people back in Mexico. How could they do him any harm?"

"He wasn't worried about what they could do. He was worried about Señora Dallas. If she could hate her own family so long and so much, how could she love her new family? I once overheard him say such a thing," he revealed. "Sometimes they would shout at each other, and ears that weren't meant to be filled with these things were flooded with them.

"It is not right to speak unkindly about your employer," he continued, "but this is a mother who was jealous of the love her husband had for his own children. I do not think I say anything you do not know yourself."

I nodded, and we settled into our own quiet thoughts until we reached the street on which the Davilas lived. Just being here where Ignacio once lived helped me to feel better. I saw his younger brother, Santos, out in the front yard trimming some bushes. He had grown quickly since Ignacio's leaving and had the same broad shoulders. From the rear, he looked so much like Ignacio my heart actually skipped a beat. What if he turned around and it was Ignacio?

He did, and of course it wasn't. His brother looked more like their mother than Ignacio did. He had his mother's eyes and softer features. When he saw it was I who was going to get out of the car, he smirked with displeasure. Even though Santos looked more like his mother, his father had the greater influence on him.

"*Gracias,* Señor Casto," I said.

"I will be back in an hour's time," he told me, and drove off.

I walked slowly to the gate. Santos returned to his bush trimming as if I weren't even there.

"*Buenos días,* Santos," I said anyway. He nodded and grunted a response, but he did not look at me. I imagined he was afraid of being too friendly because it would upset his father.

Ignacio's mother greeted me at the door and smiled. It would be the only smile for me in that house for now, I thought. His father was sitting in the living room reading a newspaper. He glanced at me and continued reading. Ignacio's mother led me back to the kitchen and had me sit at the table. She poured me a glass of Jarritos lime soda without my asking. She knew it was my favorite Mexican soda.

She told me Ignacio's younger sisters were at the home of a friend.

"*Cómo estás,* Delia?"

"*Muy bien, gracias.*"

She handed me the letter, first holding it as if it were a precious jewel, stroking the envelope, her eyes mixed with joy and sadness.

"*Gracias,* Señora Davila," I said, and carefully opened it. She left me in the kitchen to read it in private.

Dear Delia,

I miss your face as much as I would miss the sun if it died in the sky.

I am afraid I have some hard news for you and for my family. I was robbed last night. All the money I have saved was taken. I am exhausted from raging and screaming. It was my own stupidity. Too often I counted it where other eyes could see. I trusted the men I work with on the soy farm, and now I am paying dearly for that trust.

Rather than feel sorry for me and try to help me find the thief, the other men just think me stupid. In this world, if you are a victim, you are the one at fault. I know that makes no sense to you, but it is so.

It makes me want to be a thief myself, but don't worry. I will not become one. I will just work harder and longer or find a cut-rate coyote to help me get back. But, as you know, it is not just a matter of getting across the border. I must also find work waiting for me and a place to live and hide. Without money and a false identity, I would be a desperate lizard, and I will not be so.

So I must ask you to be patient longer. I hope your love for me is strong enough to last.

As before, I must keep my exact where-abouts unknown not only to you but to my family. These letters are all that I can risk. It is better that they remain unable even to make a mistake. It would be an unfair burden to put on them and on you.

Kiss my mother for me.

Ignacio

I lowered my head to my arms and sobbed silently. Then I took a deep breath, drank some more of my cool soda, and rose. When I looked into the living room, I saw that Ignacio's father had left the house. His mother sat sadly, her head turned to the window.

"Here is my letter to him," I told her, and gave it to her. She looked at his letter in my hand. Her husband forbid her to read them, and even though he was not in the room, she would not disobey.

She took the letter from Ignacio and gently closed the envelope.

"He asked me to give you a kiss for him," I said, and leaned over to do so.

She smiled through her tears. "You will have something to eat with me," she said, "and tell me about school."

What she hoped was that I would reveal what was written. I wondered if I should give her the hard news and was reluctant to do so but then thought it was better she understood why it would take him longer to return. We retreated to the kitchen for my visit.

It was truly as painful for me to tell her the contents of Ignacio's letter as it was for her to hear them. However, Ignacio's mother reminded me a lot of *mi abuela* Anabela. She had the same power of acceptance for bad news. I say power because she was able to keep it on her shoulders and go on. She, as did Abuela Anabela, believed in the will of God.

"Perhaps this is his penance," she said, which was her only comment.

We both looked up when Ignacio's father stepped into the kitchen. He looked from Ignacio's mother to me and back to her.

Without comment, she handed him the letter. This time, he simply tore it into shreds and threw it in the garbage. My heart ached to see him do that. He knew, however, that if he didn't and I took it with me, I would probably sleep with Ignacio's letters, and there would be danger.

"I'm sorry, Señor Davila, but Ignacio does not send good news. He was robbed of all his money."

"Maybe God is telling him to stay where he is, then," was his response.

I couldn't blame him for his hardness. He had suffered great pain, and in having to pretend to mourn his son, he probably buried him in his heart, not believing there would be any happy ending to our story.

Ignacio's father left us to do some work, telling Ignacio's mother he would have lunch with some of his friends at a local eatery. I continued to visit with Ignacio's mother, trying to tell her only good and happy things about my schoolwork.

Afterward, she walked me out to wait for Señor Casto. He was there already, however, parked and waiting patiently on the side of the road. Ignacio's brother apparently had gone with his father.

"I'll see that your letter is delivered the usual way," Ignacio's mother told me. "I am sure he waits as anxiously for it as he did for the others."

"*Gracias, señora*. I will see you soon, I hope."

"Yes, soon," she said.

We hugged, and I hurried to Casto's car so she would not see the tears that I could not hold back.

Casto glanced at me and drove off without speaking. We rode a long time before either of us spoke.

"You do not have good news," he said, confirming what my face easily revealed.

"No, *señor*." I told him what had happened to Ignacio in Mexico.

"I am not surprised," he said. "Desperate people do desperate things, and there are too many desperate people back home."

"Yes," I said, smiling at how even after all these years, he referred to Mexico as his home.

I got out of his car a few streets back from *mi tía* Isabela's *hacienda* so no one would see that he had taken me anywhere. Again, these precautions were wise to take.

"I need a little walk anyway," I told him.

It was just fall now, early October, and contrary to what people who didn't live here thought, the desert did enjoy seasons. It could get surprisingly cold during December, January, and February. It always began to warm in March and was almost perfect in April. Sometimes April would have some summer desert days, where the temperatures might even reach 100 degrees. Today, it was in the mid-70s with a gentle breeze and a sky that looked like what the first sky for Adam and Eve must have looked like, a deep blue, cloudless.

It was hard to be sad here. Nature could be so comforting and fill you with optimism. It was easier to believe in tomorrow. Somehow, Ignacio would find a way, I thought. The obstacles would be overcome. We were too strong to be defeated. Gradually, my steps became stronger, my gait faster. By the time I turned into the *hacienda,* my heart was not as heavy, and then it skipped a beat when I set eyes on Edward's fancy Jaguar sedan.

Why was he here?

I hurried up the driveway. Both he and Jesse were sitting in the living room sipping some iced tea and obviously waiting for me.

"Why are you home?" I immediately demanded.

"Well, that's not a very nice hello," Edward said.

I would never get used to that eye patch, even though he joked and told me it made him exotic-looking. "Like some pirate or soldier of fortune," he said.

"We decided we were working too hard and would take the day off," Jesse explained. He wasn't quite as tall as Edward, but they had similarly slim builds.

I looked at them both skeptically.

Edward laughed. "She's not buying it, Jess."

"Okay, we were worried about you," Jesse confessed, "and decided we would come down to take you to dinner. We can't take you out next weekend. You're going to a high-society party."

"If you both flunk out of college, I will be the one blamed," I said.

"Good. I hate being blamed for anything," Edward replied. "So, where have you been?" he asked. "And where's my mother?"

"Your mother went to L.A. and is probably looking for you."

"That would be a real surprise," he said. He waited, because I had not said where I had been.

"I've been visiting friends," I told them, and he nodded, glancing quickly at Jesse.

He assumed correctly that I had been to the Davilas' home.

"Where would you like to go to dinner? You name it," Jesse said.

"I don't know. We rarely go to restaurants with your mother."

"I know," Edward interjected. "Let's take her to La Grenouille. She has to get more familiar with French cuisine, doesn't she?"

"Good idea," Jesse said.

"That is such an expensive restaurant," I said. I had never been there, but I had heard Fani talk about it and Danielle Johnson, too.

"We'll cut back on the dark chocolate," Edward joked.

Of course, I knew he could afford it.

"I'll go make the reservation," Jesse said, and rose to go to a phone.

"Where's the stone princess? She's not home," Edward asked me.

"I do not know."

"So . . . how are things with your friends, the Davilas?" he asked, with his soft smile.

"As they have been," I replied. I couldn't say much more, and I was terrified of accidentally revealing Ignacio's existence.

He asked me about schoolwork and told me about their classes rather than talk any more about the Davilas. He sensed I was reluctant to do so. Jesse returned to say we had the reservation, but we had to be there at six forty-five.

"They're having a big night. It was only because I used your name that we got in at all," he explained.

"We don't have to go there," I said

"It's done. I have an idea. Why don't you wear what you think you'll wear to the Johnson party? Let's all go French tonight. I have a beret, and I know my mother has a great French chapeau that would fit you, Delia."

"I cannot take her clothes without her permission," I said.

"You won't. I will," Edward said.

Just then, Sophia came in with Trudy and Alisha. They burst in laughing, until Sophia set eyes on the three of us and immediately changed her expression.

"Well, I wonder what brought you home today," Sophia said, a cold smile cut so deeply in her face it looked sliced with a bread knife. Her girlfriends wore similar smiles.

"We missed your sweet voice and face," Edward said.

"Ha-ha. Why are you here, Edward? Did she call for help or something?"

"I think she's doing just fine for herself," he said, nodding at me. "What crime are you three preparing to commit this time?"

"We're getting ready for a party, a real party," Sophia added.

"I bet."

"You're all invited," she said. "Even you, Delia."

"We need to skip it," Edward said. "None of us has the right inoculations."

"Funny, funny. C'mon," she told her girlfriends. "Three's company here, and we don't want to get in the way. We're not welcome, anyway."

They marched to the stairway.

"You know about the three witches in *Macbeth*?" Edward asked me.

I nodded and smiled at his comparison.

"Fair is always foul around here," he told Jesse.

"Let's just hope we all don't suffer Macbeth's fate," he replied.

It was a legitimate worry. There wasn't a cloud outside, but I could hear the thunder rolling in our direction.

4
RUMORS

Jesse and Edward left to visit Jesse's family. They told me what time to be ready, and I went up to shower and dress and do my hair. Now, probably filled more with curiosity than anything else, Sophia and her friends invaded my room. She saw the dress I had laid out to wear.

"That's fancy and expensive. My mother bought that for you at Dede's Boutique. Isn't that the dress you're planning to wear to Danielle's party?" she demanded as soon as I emerged from the shower.

I had shown her what I would wear after she bought her new dress, and for a few minutes we had talked to each other about fashions. I had thought we might just get along and actually enjoy the party.

"Yes, you know it is," I replied. I could see she was just performing for her two friends.

"Where are your two lover boys taking you?"

Her two friends had been inspecting all of my things, poking through my clothes, even looking in my drawers. They stopped when I appeared, but neither looked sorry.

"To dinner," I said. "I thought you had to get ready for your party."

"We don't have to doll up for our parties," Trudy said.

"We don't have phonies at our parties," Alisha added.

Both had still not been invited to Danielle's party.

"You mean, neither of you are going to the party?" I asked, sitting at my vanity table.

I would never claim not to be afraid of them. I just knew it was better never to show them my fear. They would trample me under their insults and crude remarks as quickly as a raging bull in the bull ring. Sometimes I did feel like a matador, deflecting their sharp horns and gracefully stepping out of their way.

"You're so funny," Sophia said. "Don't think my brother will always be around to protect you, Delia. And don't think we're going to keep all your little disgusting secrets locked up forever. Just watch your mouth."

I brushed my hair and didn't look at her.

"I asked you where they are taking you to dinner. I'd like an answer," she demanded.

When I didn't answer quickly enough, she came at me. "Well? My mother's going to want to know, too."

"They made a reservation at La Grenouille," I said.

"They did?" She turned to her friends. "You see what kind of money he spends on her?"

"What does she do for it, I wonder," Alisha said, smiling lustfully.

"She'll never tell," Sophia said, and they laughed.

I spun on them. "Get out of here with your dirty talk," I said.

"You're chasing me out of a room in my house?" Sophia asked. "You, who once cleaned my toilet?"

I rose, ignoring her, and went back into my bathroom. For a while, I just stood there behind the closed door, trying to calm my racing heart. I heard them laughing again, and then they finally left. After I caught my breath, I came out of the bathroom. For a moment, I just stood there, grateful they had left me alone.

And then I saw my dress.

It had been ripped apart where the zipper began at the waist. The tear was clear down to the hem. I held it in my arms like something or someone precious who had died.

The rage inside washed over me. I charged out of my room and to her bedroom, but the door was locked.

"Why did you tear my dress? Open this door!" I cried, pounding on it.

I heard their laughter, and then Sophia came to the door and opened it, her two friends at her side. They looked like hungry coyotes surrounding a puppy.

"How could you do this?" I screamed, holding up the dress.

"It was an accident," Sophia said. "Alisha tried it on, forgetting how thin you are, and the dress just tore. You're good at sewing. Sew it up."

"Aliméntese en su propia bondad y muere de hombre," I said, actually spitting the words at her.

For a moment, the three of them simply stared at me.

"What does that mean? What did you say?"

I turned away and headed back to my bedroom, ashamed at my own rage now.

"Delia, come back here and tell us exactly what that means, or else!"

I slammed my door closed.

"I'll find out what it means. You'll be sorry if it was a curse."

I sat in a chair, my torn dress in my lap,

and let the steam stop coming out of my ears. Finally, I felt my heartbeat slow down. I had no fear about her translating the curse that had come to mind. I had simply said, "May you feed only on your own goodness and starve," which was something I had overheard my grandmother mumble to herself when someone made her so angry she couldn't keep it bottled up. I had no doubt that if Sophia were left to feed on her goodness, she would starve.

Before they left the house, she came to my door and rapped it hard before telling me I would be sorry.

Sorry? I was sorry already, I thought, now feeling guilty that I had let her get to me, but they had destroyed my beautiful dress. Sewing it would not work. I tossed it to the side and closed my eyes. The confrontation and the angry outburst drained me, and without intending it, I fell asleep. I woke when I heard a knock on my bedroom door and then Edward's voice. The realization that I had slept nearly an hour shocked me. I leaped to my feet, scrubbed my cheeks quickly with my palms, and opened the door.

Both Edward and Jesse gaped at me, the shock clearly written on their faces. I imagined I looked like a crazy woman.

Edward wore a beret and had one of Tía

Isabela's fancy hats in his hand to give me.

"What's going on? Why aren't you ready?"

"Sophia and her friends," I began, and choked back the words.

"What?" Jesse asked.

Without explaining, I picked up my beautiful dress and showed it to them.

"That little mean . . ."

"When did they do that?" Edward asked.

"While I was in the bathroom, they came in, and they saw my dress on the bed. It was the one I was going to wear to the party next weekend."

"Before we leave tomorrow, we'll take you to buy a new dress, Delia," Edward said. "I'll have a few words with the stone princess, too."

"Don't waste your breath," Jesse told him.

"I'll waste hers," Edward vowed. "C'mon, Delia, throw something else on. Don't let her ruin our night. We'll wait downstairs. Here," he added, handing me the hat. "Wear this anyway. We'll still make it a French night, *d'accord?*"

"*Mais oui,*" I said, and took the hat. I chose another dress and quickly washed my face, put on some lipstick, and ran a brush through my hair.

As I came down the stairs, the two of them

began to sing the French national anthem. It was very hard to be sad or upset in their company. My heart was light and happy again. Arm in arm, they escorted me out, with Señora Rosario looking to see what was the reason for all the commotion.

When we arrived at the restaurant, I was surprised to see one of my girlfriends, Katelynn Nickles, there with her family. I could see she was even more surprised to see me, especially with Edward and Jesse. I waved to her, and she waved back, her parents looking our way.

But the bigger shock came an hour later, when Christian Taylor came in with Zoe Stewart, a girl in the tenth grade. He stopped dead in his tracks when he saw us. He smiled and went to his table. Up until that moment, I was really having a good time with Edward and Jesse. They had me laughing constantly with their imitations of some of their teachers and fellow students at college. Both Edward and Jesse recognized Christian, too.

"No moss grows on his rolling stones," Jesse said, and they laughed.

I didn't. I had not told either of them about the rumors and stories Sophia had been spreading about us at school. After what she had done to my dress tonight, I was afraid of adding salt to those wounds. In my mind, perhaps too naive and innocent, despite all I had been through, I couldn't imagine people readily believing such sordid tales about Edward, Jesse, and me. However, I got my first hint that things were not going to be smooth for me when Katelynn got up with her family to leave and not only didn't come over to say anything on the way out but avoided looking my way as well.

"Hey, you're not falling into another funk because of that idiot being here, too, are you, Delia?" Edward asked me.

"Funk? I do not know this word, Edward. Where is this funk?"

Jesse smiled. "It's not a place, exactly. It means depression, sadness."

"Oh, no. I don't care about him. I just don't want there to be more trouble at home," I told them.

"My sister will push and push if she's not slapped down," Edward said. "If anyone lived by the rule, give her an inch and she'll take a foot, it's Sophia."

"I cursed her tonight," I confessed.

"Cursed? How?"

"I told her that she should feed on her goodness and starve."

Jesse roared.

"That's neat. I have to remember that one," Edward said. "You see, Jess? As I told

101

you, I've got to reconnect with my Latino heritage. One of these days, we're all going to take a trip into Mexico."

I perked up at the idea.

"Really?"

"Sure. I especially want to see where my mother came from. You'll be our guide, Delia. Right, Jess?"

"Sounds like a real trip to me," he said.

"This would be wonderful," I said, my mind reeling with the possibilities. If there was enough time to tell him, Ignacio could actually meet me. The possibility of such a reunion filled me with new optimism.

"We'll give it some serious thought. Maybe we can do it during the spring break," Edward said. "It coincides with your spring school break."

"That would make me very, very happy," I said.

"We aim to please," Jesse said, and we were back to laughing and joking again.

Every once in a while, I looked at Christian and Zoe. I thought he was putting on an act for me by being so cozy with her. Sometimes they looked our way, whispered, and laughed. Edward saw where my attention was and assured me I had made the right decision in turning Christian down.

I was very nervous when we started for

home, afraid of what would now occur between Edward and Sophia. When we arrived, Tía Isabela appeared, obviously just returning from Los Angeles. Sophia wasn't home yet, which didn't surprise anyone.

"I thought you two weren't coming home until next weekend," she began almost as soon as we entered the house.

"Impulsive decision," Edward told her, "and as it turned out, a very good idea."

"Why?" she asked, looking from him to me and Jesse.

Edward told her what Sophia and her friends had done to my dress.

"You're kidding," she said. "That dress cost eight hundred dollars!"

"Well, if you're keeping accounts, deduct it from her inheritance," Edward suggested.

"Where did you get that hat?" she asked me. I quickly took it off.

"I gave it to her. It fit the night," Edward explained.

"Fit the night? Where did you three go?"

Edward told her.

"Weren't you a little extravagant, Edward?"

"It was educational," he said, smiling.

"Um. Where did your sister go tonight? All she told Mrs. Rosario was that she was going to a party. What party?" she asked me.

"I do not know of any party, Tía Isabela."

"Wherever Sophia goes, it's a party," Edward said.

"Well, I'm not waiting up for her. I made up my mind long ago that I would not permit that girl to destroy my health," Tía Isabela said. "We'll deal with her in the morning. I'm going to sleep."

I started to hand her hat back to her, and she looked at me as if I were insulting her.

"I don't lend out my clothes, Delia. My son gave you that hat. It's yours now," she said, and walked away.

"Great," Edward said. "You'll wear it to the party next weekend."

"She was not pleased you went into her closet," I said.

"Delia, you ever look into my mother's closet?"

I shook my head.

"There's more in it than in most clothing stores. She doesn't even know what she has anymore, believe me."

"She knew this was her hat," I said, and he laughed.

"She only said it because it looks better on you," he told me. Jesse agreed.

We went up to our bedrooms. I kissed them both good night and thanked them for a wonderful evening.

"You are truly my knights in shining armor," I told them, my arms around them both.

They wore identical smiles. It made me laugh, and for that I was grateful. I would not toss and turn within a kaleidoscope of emotions, as I had expected. Instead, warmed by their love and concern for me, I settled comfortably into my bed and didn't awaken until I heard Sophia's loud laughter very late at night. She stumbled down the hallway to her room. Edward stepped out of his to chastise her, but it was a waste of time. She was either too drunk or too high on something even to know he was there. I held my breath until she went into her own room and closed the door. Then I fell back asleep, just as I would had I been woken by a nightmare and then driven it from my mind.

But nightmares need not worry about their future in this house. There was no more fertile soil for their well-being and growth than the Dallas family. Rain the color of blood moistened it, and the pale yellow moon replaced the sun and gave the dark dreams the light they needed. They moved freely from Tía Isabela's sleep to Sophia's to Edward's and then to mine. Casto had told me that Señor Dallas's love had kept his family together. Now it was Tía Isabela's bitterness that bound them, chained them together like prisoners of their own troubled souls. What would free them was still something impossible to imagine.

Sophia did not get up for breakfast, nor did she call down for any late into the morning. Jesse, Edward, and I ate alone because Tía Isabela was taking her breakfast in her room this morning, perhaps to avoid any more conflict. True to their word, Edward and Jesse insisted I go with them to buy a new dress, something even more beautiful.

"And something definitely more expensive," Edward said.

We went directly to a boutique in the upscale shopping area of El Paseo in Palm Desert, which was comparable to Rodeo Drive in Beverly Hills or Worth Avenue in Palm Beach, according to both Jesse and Edward. Of course, I had been to neither of the other places.

The truth was, both Jesse and Edward knew more about women's designer clothing than I did. They rejected dress after dress as being too ordinary and finally settled on a beaded gown that sold for fifteen hundred dollars, nearly twice the cost of the dress Sophia and her friends had destroyed. It was red with silver-tone beaded shoulder straps and waist. It had an open back, a surplice

V neckline, and a gathered front with a full skirt.

"What about shoes?" Jesse asked, and the saleslady immediately brought out a pair to match the dress. Before we left the store, Edward had spent more than two thousand dollars. When I thought what this money would mean back in my little Mexican village, I was speechless.

"I want to be there when Sophia sees you in the dress," Edward said gleefully. "Don't show it to her until next Saturday."

He didn't have to tell me that. I was afraid of another sabotage job. In fact, as soon as we drove up, I hurried upstairs and hid everything deep in my closet. Sophia had still not risen and come out of her room. Tía Isabela was furious about it and forbade anyone to bring her anything.

"I do think it's the perfect time for us to leave, don't you, Jesse?" Edward said, smiling at his mother. "We have weak stomachs."

"You're just like your father was, Edward, when it comes to facing unpleasantness."

"Maybe that's because there's so much of it here, Mother," he snapped back at her. Then he smiled, said good-bye until next weekend, and started out.

"You mean you're coming back again next

weekend?" she shouted after him.

"We just can't seem to stay away, Mother, which shoots down your theory about facing unpleasantness."

Jesse said nothing. I followed them out to their car.

"Thank you for everything," I told them.

"Just keep your chin up, and don't let either of them get to you," Edward advised.

They both hugged me. It was on the tip of my tongue to tell them about all the nasty rumors now, but I held back. Why let them drive off worried more than they already were? I stood and watched Edward's car turn out of the driveway, and then I walked back into the house. It was deadly quiet, but I knew that was a deception. Soon, as soon as Sophia was up and about, there would be a great deal of static and noise.

However, Sophia had such a bad hangover from whatever she had done the night before that she didn't get out of bed all day. Tía Isabela finally went up to her room to see about her at dinnertime and returned furious. I was afraid to ask anything. She sat fuming. Ten minutes later, Sophia appeared, looking like she had just risen from a grave. Her hair was disheveled, her eyes bloodshot, and her complexion pale. Even her lips were a pale red. She kept her hand over her eyes and leaned over her food.

"I'm not hungry," she moaned.

"You should eat something, Sophia. And don't give me that story about someone putting something nasty in your lemonade. I'm not a fool."

"Well, someone did!" she cried, and immediately cringed from the pain of shouting.

"You know why you're a dummy, Sophia? This is not the first time or the second you've suffered after being so reckless, and if I had to gamble, I'd say you're going to do it again and again."

"I'm going to throw up," Sophia said, and she lifted her head slowly and glared at me. "I'll tell you why I'm in such pain, Mother. It's her fault."

"Her fault?" Tía Isabela smiled. "How, pray tell, is it her fault, Sophia?"

"She put a Mexican curse on me, and she wouldn't tell me what it was. It was probably this."

Tía Isabela held her smile, but the humor left a vacant mask. She looked at me.

"What curse is she talking about, Delia? Does this have something to do with the dress?"

"*Sí*," I said. "Yes."

"Why did you tear up that dress, Sophia?

That was a very expensive dress."

"It wasn't deliberate. Alisha tried it on, and it ripped."

"She is lying," I said softly.

"I am not. You weren't there. You were hiding in the bathroom."

"Enough," Tía Isabela said. "We don't believe in curses. That's primitive. It's ridiculous for you even to think such a thing. It's just an attempt to pass blame away from yourself."

"I can't believe how much you take her side now, Mother," Sophia whined. Then she paused and smiled. "Maybe you're more of a Mexican than you want people to believe. Maybe I should talk about it."

Tía Isabela's face nearly exploded from the rush of blood into her cheeks and forehead. Her eyes bulged with rage. Even Sophia saw she had crossed some line. She tried to swallow and then quickly looked down.

"I'm sick!" she screamed, and got up to run out before Tía Isabela could respond.

Minutes seemed to pass. I didn't move, didn't lift my eyes from the plate. Finally, she spoke.

"What was the curse?" she asked.

I shook my head.

"What did you say?"

"I was very angry, Tía Isabela. It

means nothing."

"I know it means nothing, but what was it?"

"I told her that she should feed on her goodness and starve."

Tía Isabela said nothing. I looked up at her. She was nodding.

"My father . . . he said the same thing to me," she said.

"I was very angry," I repeated.

"Someone put a curse on this family," she muttered, more to herself than to me. "It's been with us for years. Never mind," she added, returning to herself quickly. "I don't want to hear any more about any of this. Get through a week without any turmoil. I have a lot to do this week."

She rose and started out, then paused and turned back to me.

"You should have come with me to Los Angeles. Maybe none of this would have happened," she added, and left.

Maybe she was right, I thought. Perhaps she was changing. Perhaps she was tired of the bitterness in her heart and was hoping to rid herself of the past. Despite how cruel she had been to me and all of the unhappiness she had caused or participated in, I couldn't help having this desire to win her over, to bring her back to her family, to have her see me as her niece, her blood. Was I weak and stupid for wanting this, or was it what my mother would have wanted?

I spent the remainder of the day keeping to myself. Sophia did the same. I finished my homework, did some reading, took a walk around the grounds, and spoke in Spanish to the pool man who had come to clean it and treat the water. Then I changed to have dinner. To my surprise, neither Sophia nor Tía Isabela appeared. Tía Isabela went out to meet someone, and Sophia ordered her dinner brought to her room. I half suspected she would not rise in the morning to go to school, but she was there at breakfast, bouncing about with unexpectedly renewed energy. I thought nothing of it. After all, she had slept away most of the day.

However, her enthusiasm and flashy smiles came from a different source of rejuvenation. I should have realized she was spending more of her day on the telephone plotting with her other two witches, as Edward and Jesse would say. I was not fooled by her overly friendly behavior toward me at breakfast and in the limousine. Señor Garman had returned from delivering Tía Isabela in time to be the one to take us to school.

"I hope Mr. K isn't going to pull one of those Monday-morning history quizzes on us," she said. "I didn't have time to study. What do you think?"

"I think yes," I said, and recited some of the areas and answers to questions I expected him to ask. I didn't do it for her. I was reviewing it for myself as I described it.

"You really are better at school than I am," she admitted. "I don't understand why. I thought girls were thought to be too stupid to go far in school in Mexico."

"Who told you that?"

"My mother."

"It is not so."

"Whatever," she said. "I'm not worrying about it. If I don't go to college, I don't go."

"What will you do?"

"I won't work hard, I can tell you that. I'll do something simple in one of our businesses just to pass the time maybe. Maybe not. I have time to decide. Well, here we are. In Wonderland," she added, smiling at me. "Have a good day, Alice."

"Alice?"

"Alice in Wonderland, *stupido*. I thought you were supposed to be the well-read one, not me," she said, getting out of the car to hurry in.

Señor Garman, who had overheard us, turned to look at me as I got out slowly. His face was full of skepticism and warning.

"Count your fingers and toes every time you're near her," he told me, and drove off.

I looked at the entrance to the main building. Sophia was already inside with her friends. Something really wasn't right, I thought, but I headed for the entrance, too, walking slowly, like someone who was anticipating an ambush.

5
DOWN THE RABBIT HOLE

When I was little, no more than six, there was a very old lady in our village, Señora Baca. My mother told me she was one hundred and five years old and had outlived all her children. Her grandchildren looked after her now. Because of her age, she was venerated and revered. Everyone wanted her blessing, and no one would pass by her without stopping to ask her how she was and, more important, what the weather would be.

The belief was that her aged bones could predict the weather better than any weatherman on radio or television. She put her right hand under her left elbow, closed her eyes, and foretold rain, clouds and sunshine, warmth and cold. The story was that she was right far more than she was wrong.

But this fortune-teller's power to read the wind and the clouds could be applied to reading the future of people's lives as well. This was more subtle and happened very quickly. When she looked into your face, her face would instantly react with a smile or a look of pain. Woe to those who saw pain in her face. They waited every day for some disaster to occur, and when one did, it reinforced the legend of Señora Baca. It was said that she predicted the hour and minute of her own death and simply told her grandchildren it was time for her to pass on.

My grandmother, who remembered Señora Baca well, told me that being old, living longer, simply meant you were walking side by side with Death longer. He was always there, patiently waiting, sometimes annoyed, especially with Señora Baca, because he had to tag along so long and began to feel more like a servant than a master. Señora Baca especially teased and tormented him with her longevity.

I don't remember the incident all that well, but my mother told me that one day, Señora Baca put her hand on my head and predicted my life would be like a river, sometimes low, sometimes high, but never discouraged by any turn or twist. As water finds its way, I would find mine.

Of course, it was years before I understood what that meant, and even today, I wasn't completely sure about it, but its meaning clearly made my mother happy. She thanked

Señora Baca and from that day on told me never to pass her without greeting her. Although her face was thin and wrinkled like dried peaches, her eyes refused to age. I was nine when she died. It was a big funeral, because she belonged as much to the village as she did to her own family, and there was never a *Día de los Muertos,* a Day of the Dead, when everyone didn't celebrate her.

I thought of her this morning as I walked into the school, wishing that she was sitting just inside so I could greet her and ask her what the weather would be for me, where my river would flow now. I tried to conjure her and hold on to the image of her tiny body planted in that big chair which was really the seat taken out of a truck, with the umbrella opened over her and her jug of cucumber water and a glass beside her.

It was said that she was one hundred and eight when she died, and Death was so tired from waiting that he gladly carried her off on his shoulders and played the donkey.

These rich memories from my village gave me strength to overcome any fear. I was sure that anyone looking at me entering the school would be taken aback by the smile on my face and the firmness in my body and in my gait. Almost immediately, however, I felt the tension. Apparently, the phones had been ringing in the homes of other students all weekend. Sophia's disgusting accusations had gained firm footing in minds and conversations, not only among her friends but among mine, because of Katelynn and what she had seen at the restaurant.

Now it was known that I had clearly turned down a date with the school's heartthrob, Christian Taylor, to go out with my gay cousin, Edward, and his companion, Jesse. Something untoward and unhealthy was obviously going on. What else could it be? Why else would I avoid a date with Christian Taylor? Now the truth was known.

I saw the whispering going on behind my back, the hesitation in the greetings the other students gave me, and felt the chill in the air between myself and the girls who had befriended me. Perhaps to avoid sitting with me at lunchtime, my three closest friends had spread themselves out to sit with other students. For the first time since I had walked into the private school, I found myself alone at a table.

I saw that Christian had found allies now in Sophia and her two friends. They sat together, talking and laughing loudly for my benefit. I tried to look as indifferent as I could. However, I was twisting and turning into knots inside. I attempted to read, but my gaze kept floating off the page, and I found myself reading the same lines repeatedly.

And then, perhaps to show that she could do whatever she wanted or perhaps to be the first to know everything, Fani suddenly appeared at my table. She usually had only a yogurt and some fruit for lunch and took it out of her cloth bag after she sat. I stared at her and closed my book.

"I warned you about your cousin Edward and what could be made of it," she began.

"I'm not going to insult and be unfriendly to my cousin Edward because my cousin Sophia is jealous of me," I told her. "Edward and his friend Jesse worry about me. They are my best friends. If the others believe Sophia's lies, they do because it pleases them to believe nasty things about . . . about Mexicans," I said. I could feel the heat in my own eyes, and I could see that my outburst and determination startled her.

She dipped her spoon into her yogurt and ate quietly for a moment.

"Sophia doesn't deny being half Mexican when she speaks to me."

"That's because she wants you to like her, invite her to your parties, whatever. She'll tell you whatever she thinks will make you happy, but she treats the Mexican servants and workers like dirt."

Fani kept eating and then paused to look at me. "Well, you obviously don't care what she says about you."

"I refuse to let her bully me. My father always told me, *si usted actúa como una oveja, ellos actuarán como lobos.* If you act like a sheep, they will act like wolves. It's as true here as it was back in Mexico."

She finished eating and nodded. She didn't look at me when she spoke next. "My parents are having a dinner Friday night for one of the candidates running for United States senator, Ray Bovio. His son, Adan, will be coming, too. I will send a car for you at six-thirty," she said.

"You are inviting me?"

She pretended to look around the table. "Is there someone else here? Six-thirty," she repeated. She put her empty yogurt container in the bag and stood up when the bell rang. "It's formal, so dress appropriately," she added. She looked toward Sophia and her friends and then flashed me a smile before walking off.

I sat amazed.

I truly am a river, I thought, meandering through places I have never been.

Fani's joining me at my table stirred up even more chatter. By the end of the day, the news about my invitation to a dinner at her home had spread with electric speed, shocking Sophia. Apparently, Fani had deliberately told the girls she knew would do just that. Incredulous, Sophia had to approach me before the beginning of the last class to ask if it were really true.

"Fani invited you to dinner at her home?"

"Por supuesto."

"What?"

"Oh, sorry. I just thought since you've been taking Spanish, you would understand. That means of course," I said, and took my seat.

When the school day ended, she told me she wasn't going home with me.

"If Garman asks, tell him I've gone over to one of my friends' homes."

"Por supuesto," I said, and she smirked.

"I'm only taking Spanish to get the language requirement off my back. I don't intend to speak it, so I don't need to practice with you."

Before I could reply, she walked off. When I came out of the school at the end of the day alone, Señor Garman didn't really care where she was. He just asked me if he should wait for her and I told him no, she had gone to a friend's home. As soon as I got home and up to my room, I called Edward to tell him of my invitation to dinner, a dinner for a United States Senate candidate.

"That's terrific, Delia. I'm happy for you. We'll wait until Saturday to come down, then. I hate the traffic on Friday night, anyway. Take notes. We're going to want to hear all about it. Oh, does Sophia know?"

"Yes," I said.

"I'm sure she's having a nervous breakdown. Let me know the mental clinic she gets checked into," he said. I had to laugh. "Maybe I should drive back to help you get another dress."

"No, no, I have other dresses," I said, laughing again.

"Actually, I'm more interested in my mother's reaction to the news," Edward said.

So was I. In fact, my curiosity about it was so great I looked for an opportunity to tell her as soon as she was home. I went to her office and knocked on the door.

"What is it now?" she asked, looking up from her desk.

"I came to tell you I have two nights out this weekend."

"I know. My son and his Tonto are returning."

"No. I was asked to a dinner being given by Estefani Cordova's parents for a senatorial candidate named Bovio. It's Friday night."

She stared at me. "Who invited you?"

"Estefani. We call her Fani," I said.

"Well," she said, sitting back, clearly impressed. "I do think we've underestimated you, Delia. In this case, I'm happy to be wrong. I have taught you formal etiquette at the dinner table, so I imagine you will not embarrass me. However, I would like to see what you decide to wear."

"Very well," I said. *"Gracias."*

I left her quickly, smiling to myself. I could almost hear *mi abuela* Anabela warning me, "You're enjoying all this too much, Delia."

"Just a little longer, Grandmother," I whispered. "Just a little longer."

Although Sophia seemed to shrink and avoided me for the remainder of the week, even when we were home, I didn't for one second believe she was in any sort of retreat. For the moment, her efforts to hurt me with rumors and accusations were frustrated. Gradually, my friends returned to my side, if I could call them my friends. Real friends would have given me the benefit of the doubt, I thought, but I had learned how to wear a mask, too, so I smiled and accepted their friendship again.

Fani was friendly in school but didn't go far out of her way to be at my side. I thought she was standing on the sidelines, enjoying the way other girls behaved toward me, some still quite tentative, others, more curious than anything now, drawing closer. I caught Fani's small smile when girls I rarely spoke to began speaking to me, and especially when Sophia sat off to the side, glaring, fuming, muttering under her breath.

On Friday morning, Fani reminded me to be ready at six-thirty. Tía Isabela had offered to have Señor Garman take me, but when she heard the Cordovas were sending their car and driver, she thought that was far more impressive. Although she had a date herself, she made certain to take the time to stop into my room and check out my choice of clothes, my hair, and even my makeup. Her excuse for this unusual attention was, "I don't want the Cordovas thinking I don't take an interest in your appearance. After all, you do represent me when you go anywhere in this community."

She spoke as if I were some sort of an ambassador. It made me wonder how she went about explaining Sophia, with her rings in her nose and belly button, her sloppy appearance, torn jeans, and often ridiculous overdoing of makeup, especially her blackened eyes. I didn't say anything contrary, however, thanking her for her suggestions and her offer of a pair of her diamond-studded earrings and matching necklace and bracelet, all of which she insisted enhanced my appearance. She even took a brush to my hair to correct some loose strands.

Sophia kept her bedroom door shut, but she had to hear her mother attending to me. In my heart, I knew that this was not going to change anything. If it did anything, in fact, it only would make Sophia's resentment of me deeper, but I was not going to suffer anymore in the hope that she would somehow have a miraculous change of heart. She had snapped every olive branch I had held out to her, and I had no doubt she would continue to do so.

Tía Isabela was at the door waiting with me at six-thirty. The Cordovas had a newer-model Rolls-Royce. When she saw it coming up our drive, she patted me on the shoulder and said, "Enjoy yourself, but never forget who you are," which I knew meant "who I am."

I thanked her and hurried out to the car. The driver was waiting with the door open. When I looked back at the house, I was sure I saw Sophia peeking out a window. Was I more excited and happier because of the invitation or because of the pain it had brought to my cousin? At the moment, the answer didn't matter. I was truly curious about the Cordovas and Fani, especially after what Edward had told me about them. It was difficult to think of anyone wealthier than Tía Isabela or an estate and *hacienda* more beautiful, but I was about to see it. Ironically, it would make the simplicity and the poverty from which I had come seem like some dream.

I was really feeling like some Latina Cinderella, hoping that this golden chariot would not turn into a pumpkin and leave me questioning my own sanity.

It was a long ride to the Cordovas' estate, and when we turned toward the entrance, the shiny brass gate, at least twice the size of *mi tía* Isabela's gate, opened as I imagined the gates of heaven to open. The driveway was seemingly endless, winding up a hill and around. The *hacienda,* all lit up with lights like huge candles on the walls and a large courtyard, was truly the size of a palace.

Fani must have to get up in the morning twenty minutes earlier than Sophia and me just to get out of the house and down the endless driveway to the road.

I saw many more cars than I had anticipated parked in front, some with drivers who had gathered to pass the time. As soon as I stepped out of the limousine, I heard the music of the mariachis. When I walked through the arched front door, I entered a very large courtyard, with stone benches, a huge fountain, and a carpet of grass for a floor. I immediately saw that this was no small family gathering. There were at least forty people attending, all formally dressed, the men in tuxedos and the women in beautiful gowns bedecked with jewels. Tía Isabela was right on target when she had offered me her diamonds.

The waiters and waitresses walked about with trays of champagne and all sorts of hors d'oeuvres, and the mariachis circulated, playing and singing. I immediately recognized the father of a girl who had been in my ESL class at the public school I had attended. Her name was Amata, but we called her Mata. He saw me and nodded slightly, his eyes clearly revealing his surprise at seeing me. For a few moments, I stood gaping at everything, unsure what I was supposed to do. Then Fani left a group of women and headed in my direction.

"You look very nice," she said. "I knew you would."

"*Gracias*. This is so beautiful."

"Come, have a treat, a mimosa. You know what that is?"

I shook my head.

"It's champagne with orange juice. Don't worry. I won't let you get drunk. This is not one of your cousin's parties," she added, and I smiled.

"I'm glad of that."

She laughed, handed me a glass of mimosa, took my hand, and began to introduce me to people, simply calling me a girlfriend from school. I met presidents of banks, mayors and councilmen, very rich businessmen, builders and owners of chain stores, before she introduced me to her parents. Her father was a tall, slim, elegant man with a closely cropped goatee. It was from him that Fani inherited her dazzling ebony eyes, but it was clear that her mother, a strikingly beautiful woman with light brown hair and dainty features, had passed on the aristocratic demeanor and royal beauty that enabled Fani to stand out no matter where she was or how she was dressed.

Finally, I was introduced to Señor Bovio, the candidate, and his son, Adan, a young man about Edward's age. I had taken only three sips of my mimosa, but the moment Adan looked at me and I at him, I felt my head spin. His father looked senatorial, firm, wise, and wittily charming, but Adan was one of the most handsome young men I had ever seen. Unlike Christian Taylor, however, he didn't radiate any arrogance. Maybe because he was standing in his father's shadow, he was quiet, polite, and even a bit shy.

If a group of girls my age were told to conjure a rock star or a movie star, they would create a duplicate of Adan Bovio, I thought. He had very sexy dark green eyes, which glittered like rich jade in the light cast by one of the electric simulated torches nearby. The lines of his face weren't as male-model perfect as Christian Taylor's, but Adan's face, perhaps because of its small imperfections, was more manly, stronger. He was at least six foot one or two, with firm-looking shoulders under his tailored tuxedo jacket. I thought he had the sort of complexion that was just dark enough to look as if he had a permanent suntan.

I learned later that his mother had been an Italian movie star who was killed in a tragic car accident just outside Amalfi, Italy, only four years ago. She had been on location. Fani would tell me that the rag entertainment magazines made it seem like she had been having an affair with the director, who was seriously injured in the accident but not killed.

Adan was an only child, now working with his father in their oil and gas company, which had customers throughout the state.

"So, you are the famous Latina Cinderella," he said when Fani introduced us. He held on to my hand as he spoke to me.

I looked immediately at Fani. I had never told anyone that I often felt like Cinderella, but she obviously had come up with it, too.

"Yes, I do feel that way sometimes," I said, smiling. "Especially now."

He stared at me, holding my hand. "Fani has told me how you have moved like a comet through the school, mastering English, becoming an honor student."

Before I could reply, he leaned toward me and in a lower voice added, "Despite living with a cruel cousin."

"I have had some help," I said.

"I have been only to the fanciest places in Mexico, resorts in Acapulco, Ixtapa, Puerta Vallarta, but I have seen some of the poverty and hardship. I understand why Fani might think you a Cinderella. You must tell me about your life in Mexico. My father," he said, eyeing him, "is always telling me to appreciate my heritage, especially now, since we're trying to get the Latino vote," he said a little louder.

His father shifted his eyes toward us but then looked away quickly to continue his conversation with some prospective donors to his political campaign.

"C'mon," Fani said. "We've got about twenty minutes before we go to dinner. I'll show you the grounds."

"Am I invited?" Adan said.

"Of course," she said, winking at me. "We always need a bodyguard."

We walked through the grand lobby of the *hacienda*. It had a dome ceiling that reminded me of a grand church. We exited again through a side door and walked to where there were a half-dozen golf carts.

"You two sit in the rear," Fani said. "I'll drive."

Adan helped me in and sat beside me. Fani started us off down a path toward the golf course and then wound around a garden and small pond to the tennis courts and the pool, but the most amazing thing to me was to see a helicopter on a helicopter pad.

"My father bought that a year ago. He hates being caught in traffic."

"He flies it himself?" I asked.

"No. We have a pilot for that and for our plane."

"Plane? Where's the plane?" I asked, looking around.

Both Adan and she laughed.

"It has to be kept at the airport, silly. We have a lot of land but not enough for that, and besides, we couldn't have an airport because of some zoning laws or something."

I was speechless. Was there any end to

the wealth of these people? No wonder she moved like someone walking on a cloud. To have all this money and be beautiful as well — it made me wonder what wonderful things her ancestors had done for them to inherit such happiness. Or was it all a matter of luck?

"Adan's father has a plane, too," Fani told me.

"Yeah, but your father's plane is bigger than my father's," he said.

"You have a yacht. We don't have a yacht. My father isn't interested in a yacht," she said.

"You have your own golf course and your own tennis court."

"I don't play golf much, and you have a tennis court."

"Your pool is bigger than ours."

"Your father owns horses, we don't. My mother wouldn't want horses on the property."

"You want to trade houses right now?" he challenged.

Fani laughed.

I felt as if I were watching a ping-pong game being played with a ball made of gold. It wasn't that long ago that I was proud of the fact that we had two bedrooms in our small house and an old black-and-white television set that worked occasionally when the electricity worked.

"You'll have to come to my house and make comparisons," Adan told me. "Fani likes to pretend she's modest, but she considers us the poor relatives."

"Relatives?"

"My father is Fani's father's second cousin."

"Third, but who's counting?" Fani said.

"Oh, I didn't know you were related," I said.

"See," Adan cried, "she never told you. She's ashamed of us."

Fani laughed harder and then swung the golf cart around sharply. I fell against Adan, who held me in his arm for a moment.

"She is so reckless," he said.

I started to sit back again.

"It's all right," he said. "I don't mind."

I smiled but sat up and held on to the side of the cart until we pulled back into the cart parking area.

"Thank you for the tour," I said.

"Yeah, thank you," Adan told her. "It worked up my appetite."

We went back into the house and followed the guests to the enormous dining room. Only in books had I heard of a table that could actually seat forty people, but this hand-carved dark cherry-wood table was dressed with gold-plated settings and sparkling silverware with goblets for the wine and water. There were more than a dozen waiters and waitresses ready to serve and pour the wine.

Fani led us to our seats. Adan sat between us, which meant I was seated beside his father on my left. He immediately introduced himself to me again and began asking me questions about my life in Mexico.

"My family comes from Sonora. They owned a great deal of land just outside Hermosillo. Adan has been there a few times," he said, looking Adan's way.

"Yeah, right," Adan said, obviously not happy about the visits.

"Perhaps you can help him appreciate his heritage better than I can," his father said.

"Maybe she can, Dad. I think I would be more attentive to her than I have been to you," Adan quipped, and his father laughed.

"Watch him. He's as deadly as a scorpion when it comes to young women. He pretends to be harmless."

"Hey, no fair. If you warn her, I'm at a disadvantage," Adan said.

"I doubt that you're ever at a disadvantage," I said, perhaps too quickly, maybe because I had finished my mimosa and begun sipping the wine. I felt the flush in my face.

Adan's father laughed, and Adan smiled. I looked at Fani, but she was in her own conversation with a man to her right. Adan turned his attention completely to me. He told me more about himself, the work he did with his father, and some of the traveling he had done.

"If my father gets the nomination and wins the Senate seat, I'll have to work harder," he said, "so I'm torn between hoping he wins and hoping he doesn't."

"That's selfish," I said.

He shrugged. "He knows. We don't keep secrets. I suppose I'll be proud if he wins, not that I'm not proud of him now. He's always been a successful man."

"He's a good example for you to follow, then."

"I know. Now, tell me about yourself and especially this war between you and your cousin."

"It's not a war, exactly," I said, laughing.

"Oh, I know about women. It's a war," he assured me.

"It will take a long time to explain it," I said, hoping to change the topic.

"Fine. I'll pick you up tomorrow night, and we'll continue the story at dinner."

Fani was listening to us now, a soft smile on her face.

"Oh, I can't. We're going to a big party tomorrow night," I said.

"That's all right. Adan will go with us," Fani said. "Won't you, Adan?"

"If I'm invited," he said.

"Of course, you're invited," Fani told him.

How could she invite someone to someone else's party? Wouldn't he feel strange being invited that way?

"There," he told me instead. "See how easy it is when you're in Fani's hands? If anyone can guarantee that you won't be an overnight Cinderella, it will be Fani."

"She doesn't need my help, Adan. She's quite capable of taking care of herself, even with you."

He laughed and said, "Sure, go ahead and gang up on me. Two against one."

"*Nosotros solo tratamos de hacer una lucha justa*. Right, Delia?" Fani said.

"*Sí, absolutamente,*" I said.

"Hey, that's definitely not fair. You know I don't speak Spanish that well," Adan said.

"It's your own fault. Your father has tried to get you to learn."

"Well, what did she say?" he asked me.

"She said we are only trying to make it a

fair fight."

"Ha-ha. Haven't you two ever heard the saying, all's fair in love and war?"

"Oh, we've heard it, Adan. We know all about it," Fani said. "And we plan on practicing it as well."

"I'm in trouble," Adan said, and drank some more wine. "But I have the feeling I'm going to like it."

All three of us laughed so loudly we stopped some conversations and drew the amused looks of some of the guests. I didn't know whether it was the mimosa and the wine or what, but I felt as happy as I ever had since I had left my grandmother. Maybe, just maybe, I, too, could end up living in a palace and forever be Cinderella.

Was that too much to ask? Was I filling up with too much pride and conceit?

Was the *ojo malvado,* the evil eye, watching and waiting somewhere in this grand room?

Fortified with the courage I gathered from my new rich and powerful friends, I gazed about, just daring it to show itself.

I was not the poor, innocent little girl whose heart was shattered years ago when she was dragged away from the only family and world she had known.

I was Delia Yebarra, I thought, and I was a

raging river now. Señora Baca was right.
Yo no voy a ser derrotada.
I would not be defeated.

6
ADAN

Before dessert was served, Señor Bovio was introduced. He made a speech about his candidacy, why he was running, and how much he appreciated the support he was getting from the people present at this dinner and from the community. He pledged to give his candidacy a real and determined effort, and then introduced Adan, who stood up to applause.

"My son and I are partners in business and partners in life, in all either of us does," Señor Bovio said, looking at Adan so proudly it brought tears to my eyes. "He's going to watch my back as I go forward."

Everyone clapped harder. Adan and his father hugged, and then Fani's father stood and pledged his support, announcing that he was donating a quarter of a million dollars to Señor Bovio's campaign. I think my mouth fell open. I had no idea how wealthy these people were. He could buy my whole village and more with that donation, I thought.

I gazed around at these people, these men in their fine tuxedos and these women dripping with diamonds and gold. Look where I am, I thought. How did I get here? Where will I go from here?

The waiters and waitresses brought baked Alaska around for our dessert. Immediately afterward, guests approached Señor Bovio and either gave him envelopes with checks in them or pledges for money. The supporters and well-wishers surrounded Adan as well.

"C'mon," Fani said. "We don't have to stay here any longer." She led me out and then to her room on what she called the east end of the *hacienda*.

For a moment, I thought I had entered a castle in some fairy tale. Fani's bedroom was at least twice the size of Tía Isabela's. I couldn't even begin to imagine what her parents' bedroom was like. She laughed at the expression on my face.

"I have never seen such a room, even in pictures."

"It's not my fault," she said. "My father thinks I'm a princess. And don't say I act like one, either," she added before I could speak.

"I do not think even a princess has such a

room or such a grand bed."

"Probably not. My father had it custom-built. It's a good two feet wider and longer than the normal California king-size bed."

The four posters went all the way up to the ceiling. Carved in each were angels with their heads and eyes skyward, so that it looked as if they were ascending to heaven. The headboard was a work of art itself, depicting dawn, the sunlight waking the birds and opening flowers. Whoever had done it truly had to have been an artist. It looked as if everything was in motion.

"How do you sleep in such a beautiful setting? There is so much for your eyes to feast upon."

The bedroom had grand arched windows with light pink velvet curtains and gold sashes. There were two gold chandeliers with the most unusually shaped bulbs I had ever seen. They curved up at the ends and looked a little like the beaks of birds.

To the right was a sitting area with her own entertainment center, and to the left was a vanity table with a counter that ran at least ten feet to the entrance of her walk-in closet. It was twice the size of Sophia's, with another vanity table and mirrors on the walls.

"I sleep very easily," Fani said. "Everything in here was custom-made for my comfort, even this mattress," she said, pressing down on her bed. "Go on, sit on it."

I did. I really didn't think it was that much more comfortable than my own, but I smiled and said it was amazing.

"Come in here," she said, leading me into her sitting area. "Go on, sit," she commanded, pointing to an oversize ruby-cushioned chair with gold tassels. "I have a bottle of white wine." She went into her closet and returned with the bottle and two glasses.

I watched her remove the cork and pour the wine.

"Daddy put a little refrigerator in there for me," she explained, "so I wouldn't have to bother the servants or go down for something all the time. To thoughtful Daddy," she said, and tapped my glass with hers.

We sipped the wine.

"So, did you enjoy the dinner?"

"Yes, very much. Thank you."

"Personally, I couldn't wait to leave. I thought it was a bit stuffy, everyone watching his or her table manners. I hate having to be so perfect all the time, but my mother keeps one eye on me and the other on everyone else. God forbid I have a strand of hair out of place."

"My aunt was the same before I left tonight. She had to approve my clothes and my shoes, too."

"Exactly. Everyone is so busy impressing everyone else that they forget who they really are. It's like we're all in a play and can't miss a line."

I nodded, even though I really didn't expect to hear such a thing from Fani. In school, she looked as if she thought that was the most important thing, impressing everyone else, parading about as if she were truly on a stage.

"If you are true to yourself, you will probably impress anyone you care to impress," I said.

She smiled and then narrowed her eyes and leaned toward me.

"I like you because you're still innocent, natural, and honest," she said. She sat back and waved the air beside her as if she were chasing a fly. "You probably won't be for long, though."

"Why not?"

"You'll be like everyone else, worried about having friends, being popular. Don't tell me you weren't bothered by the cold shoulder you were being given at the beginning of the week," she said.

"That was because of Sophia, because . . ."

"Doesn't matter whose fault it was. You didn't like it. You were very happy to be rescued. Lucky for you, I could do that."

I felt myself stiffen, a cold chill actually crawling up my spine but turning into a hot flash when it reached my neck and face. I didn't like being thought of as someone who needed to be rescued, and Fani sounded too arrogant about it.

"I don't want to be friends with anyone who doesn't really want to be friends with me, who will only be my friend because I suddenly seem important."

"Then you'll have no friends at all," Fani said. "Don't get too high on a horse. You'll only fall farther down. Relax. Enjoy the moment. We had some fun, and maybe we'll have some more. I don't like your cousin and her friends, but I don't particularly like anyone very much in that school."

"Why not?"

"I told you. They're all too worried about being popular, accepted, important."

"Aren't you?"

"I don't have to worry about it. I know I am," she said without hesitation. "Now I'd like you to tell me about what happened, the incident with Bradley Whitfield."

"Incident? He died," I said. "That's more

than an incident."

"You know what I mean," she snapped, and then smiled. "How did he rape you? And don't try denying it. I have my sources of information, or I should say Daddy does. Well?"

"It is not easy for me to talk about all that," I said. "Please."

"Oh, stop it. It's over and done with. The Mexican boys are in jail, and one is dead, right? There's no one's feelings left to hurt."

"Except mine," I said.

"I did you a favor. You can repay it by telling me everything. I want to know every detail. When something like that happens to you, even the smallest things are significant. Well?"

I felt tears coming to my eyes. To talk about it was to relive it, and I was always afraid that I would say something to lead people to believe Ignacio was not dead.

"It is very painful to remember."

She thought a moment. "Okay, I know what you can do. Pretend it happened to someone else. Pretend you are a reporter writing the story. First, how did he get you to go with him?"

I looked away. Why did she want to know all this? I took a deep breath. She wasn't going to stop until I did tell her.

"He spoke Spanish well and acted as if he wanted to be my friend and help me find my way here in America. I thought he was very nice. One day, he picked me up when I was walking home from where the bus stopped, and he asked me to accompany him to check on a house he and his father were redoing to sell. I didn't want to go, but he made it sound as if it would be very quick. He was Sophia's boyfriend, so I didn't think I should be afraid. I thought he simply wanted to impress me with his accomplishments, but when we got there . . ."

"Yes? What?" she said, leaning forward.

"He forced himself on me, held me down. It was horrible."

"Where exactly did he do that?"

"Where? In the house . . . on the floor."

"So . . . you didn't enjoy any of it?"

"No," I said, amazed at the question. "It made me feel dirty inside and out."

She sat back, looking a little disappointed.

"He tried to get me not to tell, and then he tried to get me to go with other boys."

"What a creep. I remember him well. He was a good-looking boy, and of course he wanted me to go out with him, but there was something about him that turned me off."

"You were lucky."

"He wouldn't have dared try to do that to me," she said. She stared at me a moment and then smiled. "What do you think of Adan?"

"He's very nice and very good-looking."

"He's a man, not a schoolboy," she said. "I'm sure he's been with many women. I imagine that you are quite frightened about being with a boy since the rape, right? You probably have nightmares all the time."

"No. I am sure not all boys are as cruel."

She studied me again. "There isn't anything really going on between you and your cousin Edward, is there? You can tell me. I don't gossip. A secret is as good as locked in a vault when it is told to me."

"Nothing like what Sophia is telling people. Edward is my best friend, and so is Jesse."

"I didn't think so. He doesn't look AC/DC to me."

"What is this AC/DC?"

"Someone who goes both ways. You know, a boy who likes boys and girls, too."

I shook my head. "There are so many confusing things to know about boys and romance, I understand why some women want to become nuns."

She thought that was very funny.

"I am not joking."

"I don't imagine you are. Come to me if

you have any doubts or questions."

"How did you learn so much? Have you had many boyfriends?"

"No, I haven't had that many boyfriends, but I have a built-in sex-trap detector," she replied.

"What is this thing, this detector?"

"It's like an alarm that goes off here," she said, pointing to her temple, "and tells me to back off, stay away from this one or that."

"You were born with this?"

"Yes, it's instinctive. When you are more experienced, you will be able to read boys better and know whom to trust and whom not to trust."

"You are truly a very lucky girl to know so much," I said.

We heard a knock on the door and turned to see Adan.

"May I come in, or is this one of those girls-only discussions?"

"If you mean are we talking about you, the answer is no," Fani told him, and he laughed. "Is the party winding down?"

"Yes," he said, entering. "My father did very well. You can't run a real campaign without lots of moolah, especially if you are running for the United States Senate in California," he added, directing himself more to me.

"This moolah is money?"

"Dinero, mucho dinero," he said. He looked at Fani. "You're wearing that all-too-familiar smirk, Fani."

"You see what you want to see," she told him.

"Yeah, well, I just came up to see if Delia needed a ride home. My father and I came in separate cars."

"She doesn't need a ride home, but she can let you take her home if that is what she wants. What do you want, Delia?" she asked, smiling.

"Oh . . ." I looked at Adan. "I don't want to be trouble."

"I doubt that he sees it as any trouble," Fani said.

"No, of course not," Adan added. "It's not that far out of my way."

"Depends what is your way," Fani told him, and he laughed.

"C'mon, Delia. I had better get you out of here before she convinces you I'm a very dangerous Casanova."

"You mean you're not?" Fani said, and they laughed. I did, too, but mainly because they were laughing.

"Is this all right?" I asked her. "His taking me home? Your parents won't be upset?"

"Hardly," she said. "They are quite unaware of anything but what they are doing at the moment. Go on. We'll talk tomorrow and prepare for the Johnson party. I understand your cousin was invited. She is going?"

"She says yes."

"If Adan offers to take you to the party," she whispered, "go with him. You won't have to be with her that way."

I said nothing, wondering what my aunt would think now.

We walked out and down the stairway so I could say good night to Fani's parents and thank them. They acted as if they didn't know I had been there and barely looked at me. Fani gave me a "See what I mean?" look.

Adan had a beautiful teak-colored Jaguar convertible. Fani walked out with us, and I thanked her again for the invitation.

"You make sure she gets directly home safely, Adan," she warned him.

"Yes, ma'am," he said, saluting, and opened the door for me.

"I mean it. She was my guest tonight, not yours."

"Understood, commander."

"Keep thinking about the sex detector," Fani whispered when I sat in the car.

"Thank you. *Buenas noches,*" I told her.

She smiled and stood there to watch us

drive off.

"How long have you been friends with Fani?" Adan asked as we turned out of the driveway and onto the street.

"Not long," I said.

"I don't think Fani has all that many friends," he said. He looked at me. "Does she?"

"Most of the girls in the school want to be her friend."

"Yes, but she knows it and plays hard to get. There must be something she likes about you for her to invite you to her home." He smiled. "If Fani likes you, you have to be special."

When I didn't answer, he added, "I'll have to find out what that is."

It made me nervous to hear him say such things, so I asked him questions about himself and got him to tell me more about his youth, his education, and his work with his father. He told me he had a business degree from the University of Southern California, and I told him that was where my cousin Edward now was, but I said little more about Edward. Even though I didn't like to think about it, Sophia and her friends spreading nasty rumors made me more aware of mentioning Edward to anyone, especially if I spoke with pride and admiration about him. It made me angry that I had to be so frightened, but I was afraid someone might just think she was right and all the terrible things she was making up about us were true.

Adan wasn't interested in hearing about any other man, anyway. He was just interested in me.

"I really would like to hear more about your life in Mexico and your impressions about people here. I think I'll take up Fani's invitation to that party. How about I pick you up?" he asked as we turned up the street that would take us to my aunt's *hacienda*.

"I must see what my aunt says first. My cousin Sophia has been invited, too."

"Well, if we have to bring her with us, we can. I have three cars, and the two others are sedans."

"Three cars? Why do you need so many?"

He laughed. "It's not because I need them, Delia. I like cars. I'll have more than three soon. I'm going to build up my personal car collection."

I shook my head in amazement. Back in my Mexican village, it would be wonderful to have a bottle-cap collection.

"So, tell me, are there many boys asking you out?" he asked.

"Not many."

"What, are boys shyer these days? I can't imagine you being in my school and not asking you out. No grass grows on this rolling stone," he said, pointing his thumb at himself. He smiled at me, but I couldn't relax. "You look worried," he said, reading the expression on my face.

"I have not been here that long, Adan. I don't always know how to respond or what to say."

"Sure," he said. "That makes sense. I think it would be great fun to show you things, teach you things. You're not one of these twisted sisters most girls your age are. You're a fresh drink of water."

I laughed at that and then looked pensive quickly.

"What?" he asked seeing my expression change.

"I have been compared to water once before, a river."

"You can flow in my backyard any day you like," he said, and laughed.

I started to relax. Now he was the one who suddenly looked very serious.

"I'm glad you were there tonight, Delia. You saw the beginning of something historic. My father is going to be a great man, not that he isn't already; he's just going to be appreciated finally. My family will be an important family in this state. We'll be good people to know."

"Yes, your father is an impressive man, Adan. I understand why you are so proud."

"Thanks," he said. "This is it, right?" He nodded at the entrance to Tía Isabela's property.

"Sí."

"Sí? I love it. Keep throwing in Spanish words whenever you can," he said, and drove up to the front of the house. I was positive I saw Sophia's curtain part so she could gaze out.

Adan jumped out of the car and came around to open my door.

"Gracias, señor," I said, and he beamed.

"Su casa es grande," he said, nodding at the *hacienda.*

"No es mi casa."

"Hey, you live here, it's yours," he said. He took my hand to lead me up the stairs to the front door. "I am delivering you safely," he said, and made a grand bow. "Please tell my cousin I was a real gentleman."

He made me laugh.

"Now, that's better. You have a smile that would tame a wild tiger."

"Buenas noches," I said, and reached for the doorknob. He caught my hand and

turned me to him.

"*Buenas noches, Señorita México*," he said, and kissed me quickly on my lips and bowed again. "I'll call you in the morning to make arrangements for the party, *sí?*"

He was moving so quickly that I felt as if I had been running and had to catch my breath.

"*Sí?*" he asked again.

"*Sí,*" I said, and opened the door. He watched me enter the house. "Good night, and thank you," I said softly, and closed the door. I had the feeling that if I opened it quickly, he would still be standing there.

"Who brought you home?" I heard Sophia ask from the top of the stairway. "I saw you weren't brought back in their Rolls-Royce."

At first, I thought I wasn't going to answer, but I knew that would not put a stop to her questions. I started up the stairway.

"He is a friend of Fani's," I said.

"Who? I know all her friends."

"How could you know all her friends? You have never been to her home, have you?"

"Big deal. I still know who she hangs with. Who was that?"

I paused just a few steps beneath her. "Sophia, it is none of your business who I am with," I said slowly and firmly.

She glared down at me. I lowered my head

and continued up the stairway. Just as I passed her, she reached out and seized my hair. With a short scream of frustration, she tugged so hard on me that I lost my balance and fell backward, slamming down on the corner of a step and turning over and over as I desperately reached out for the braces of the banister to stop my descent. I screamed in pain when my right foot got wedged in one of these braces and abruptly jerked me to a stop. I was nearly to the bottom of the stairway.

Señora Rosario came running down the corridor first, followed by Señor Garman and then *mi tía* Isabela. I was groaning and trying to catch my breath while the pain shot up my leg and into my hip.

"What on earth is going on here?" Tía Isabela asked.

Before I could utter a response, Sophia took a step down and said, "She might be drunk or something. She tripped on a step and lost her balance."

"Drunk?" Tía Isabela said, looking at me.

I shook my head. "No, it is not true, Tía Isabela."

Señora Rosario was at my side, trying to help me get up. In an instant, Señor Garman moved around her and literally lifted me to my feet, but I screamed with pain when I placed weight on my right ankle.

"Maybe it's broken," he told Tía Isabela.

"I'll get some ice," Señora Rosario said, rushing out.

"What a mess, and this time of the night, too. I swear, you girls will be the death of me," Tía Isabela said.

Tears were now streaming down my cheeks.

"I tried to stop her fall, but it happened so quickly," Sophia said. "One minute she was walking up the stairs, and the next she was rolling down. I thought I was dreaming."

"You are dreaming," I managed. "To lie so."

She dropped her hands to her hips and shook her head. "I'm not lying! Don't you dare call me a liar! She's drunk, Mother. Smell her breath."

I looked at Tía Isabela. I had drunk that glass of wine with Fani and imagined the scent of it might still be on my lips.

She stepped toward me and stopped when Señora Rosario returned with the ice and placed it on my ankle, which already was looking swollen and red.

"I don't need to smell anyone's breath. This is a ridiculous scene. Mr. Garman, take her to emergency care, and tell them to bill me," she ordered. "You go up to

157

bed, Sophia."

Sophia smiled contentedly at me. "Yes, Mother. That was what I was going to do before all this stupid commotion." She turned and went up.

"Lean on me, Delia," Señor Garman said.

"Keep the ice on it!" Señora Rosario called to us.

I didn't have to lean on Señor Garman. He practically carried me out of the house and down to the limousine. I sprawled out on the rear seat and closed my eyes. The pain in my ankle was now a dull throbbing rather than a stinging, but it was making me feel nauseous.

"Just relax, Delia," Señor Garman said, his voice more colored by sympathy than ever. "I'll get you there quickly."

He did drive fast, and before I knew it, we were pulling into the parking lot. He came around and this time actually picked me up and carried me into the lobby. There were three other people sitting and waiting: a man with his head in his hands and an ice pack on the back of his neck and a woman with a young child who had been crying.

The receptionist's eyes widened when Señor Garman carried me up to the counter.

"She has had an accident on a staircase

and cannot put any weight on her foot," he explained.

"Take her in that door," she said, getting up.

A nurse came around to show him the way. I was placed on a thick cushioned bed.

"Just keep that ice on your ankle," the nurse said, looking at it, "until the doctor can get to you."

She asked Señor Garman to go out front and give the receptionist the information.

I couldn't believe I was there, that everything had happened so quickly. Just a little while ago, I was at the most expensive home and the most wonderful dinner party I could ever imagine. I was happy, excited, and floating on a magic carpet, and then, in an instant, it had all changed.

Of course, my rage was directed at Sophia. Her temper had seized her, and she had been blinded with rage. Then, as always, she dipped into her bank of lies to come up with another excuse and escape from blame.

It took so long for the doctor to come into the examination room I nearly fell asleep. The pain was duller but still quite loud, I thought.

"Well, well," the doctor said. "What do we have here?"

I started to sit up, and he said just to relax.

He looked at the ankle and turned it slightly. I howled with the new, sharper pain.

"How did you do this?" he asked.

I didn't know whether it would cause even more trouble to tell the truth, so I simply said I had fallen on a stairway and caught my foot.

"You'll need an X-ray," he said. "Just relax."

He went out, and a little while later, the nurse returned with a wheelchair and helped me into it.

She took me to the X-ray room and helped me lie down. The technician set up my foot and took the pictures. I was then wheeled back to the room to wait. It seemed like another hour before the doctor returned.

"You don't have a broken bone," he said. "It's only a very bad sprain. You're lucky."

Lucky? I thought, and nearly laughed.

"I'll wrap it for you. You'll have to stay off it for a few days and keep it elevated for now. Just put some pillows under it when you go to sleep. When the swelling subsides, I'd like you to apply moist heat. You'll be fine," he said.

"How do I stay off it?"

"You can use crutches," he told me. "We can provide you with them. Just have them brought back in a few days. I'm sure you'll be fine by then."

He had the nurse bring me crutches.

"Just try to keep your weight off it for a while," she explained.

I hobbled out to the lobby, where Señor Garman was waiting. The nurse told him what the doctor had determined and the doctor's instructions. He helped me into the rear seat again and fit the crutches beside me.

"Good that it's not broken," he muttered, and we drove off.

Suddenly, all of the pain and fatigue settled in me, and I actually fell asleep before we arrived at the *hacienda*. Rather than have me hobble up the stairway to the front door, Señor Garman scooped me up again and carried me like a baby. I was terribly embarrassed, but to him, I don't think I weighed more than a baby.

My aunt did not come out to see what had been done for me, but Señora Rosario appeared and listened as Señor Garman explained, still holding me in his arms. He carried me up the stairs to my bedroom and set me down just inside the door.

"Remember the pillows under your ankle," he said.

I thanked him. I saw Sophia's door opened just a crack and thought I caught her peering out at us. When Señor Garman turned to leave, she closed her door. I wished I had the strength to go at her, but all I could think of was getting into bed. It was now close to two-thirty in the morning. I fixed the pillows under my ankle and went to sleep so quickly I thought it was more like passing out.

If anyone had come to see how I was, he or she did not wake me. It was my phone that finally woke me, and when I looked at the clock, I saw it was close to noon. It shocked me to see how late I had slept. When I turned to lift the receiver, my ankle reminded me that what had happened was not simply a nightmare.

I croaked a hello.

I heard male laughter. "Don't tell me you're still sleeping, Delia," Adan said.

"Unfortunately, yes," I said, "but not because I am lazy. I fell down the stairway last night and had to be taken to the emergency care. I have a badly sprained ankle."

"You're kidding. How did you fall down a stairway?"

"I was helped," I said cryptically.

He was silent a moment. "You mean, you were pushed?"

"Pulled was more like it."

"Who did this? Sophia?"

"I don't want to talk about it, Adan."

"How horrible. I heard she was pretty bad, but this . . . can you still go to the Johnson party?"

"I don't know. I'm on crutches for a day or so."

"You just won't do any dancing," he said. "I've already spoken with Fani. I can come by at seven to pick you up. Do we know if Sophia is going to go with you?"

"Yes," I said, "we know. She is not. How do you say it? If I do not see her or speak to her again, it would be too soon."

He laughed. "I'll call you later to see how you're doing. Don't let it get you down," he said. "Just think how curious everyone will be to see you on crutches. You'll be the center of attention."

"I'd rather be invisible," I said.

"I like your sense of humor, Delia. Talk to you later," he said, and hung up.

I moaned when I sat up and looked at my poor, bandaged ankle. After I had some breakfast, I would apply the moist heat, I thought.

There was a knock on my door, and Edward and Jesse came in quickly. I had forgotten that they were coming today. They had obviously gotten an earful from Señora Rosario or Señor Garman, perhaps even *mi tía* Isabela.

"Tell me what the hell happened," Edward said angrily. "And don't make any excuses for her or diminish what she has done."

I looked at Jesse's expression, a duplicate of Edward's rage, which now reflected my own.

"Don't worry," I said. "I won't."

7
A GIFT

I am sure *mi abuela* Anabela would not approve of my turning a brother so against his own sister, but with every throb of pain in my ankle, my reluctance to do so was diminished. Edward and Jesse sat on the edge of my bed attentively as I described the evening's events. The moment I finished, Edward exploded in rage and leaped to his feet.

"That little mean bitch! I'm going to rearrange the features on her face."

"Hold it," Jesse told him, reaching out to seize his arm as Edward charged toward the bedroom door. "You're not going to do Delia any good by beating up on Sophia. She'll only go crying to your mother, and your mother will take it out on Delia."

"She needs a good whipping. If there was ever a case of spare the rod and spoil the child, there she is."

"Maybe so, but not now and not this way."

A part of me was disappointed. I would have liked to see Sophia beaten, but the more sensible part of me told me Jesse was right. In the end, Sophia would be the one considered the victim, and somehow I would be the cause of it all, poison making a sick family even sicker. Edward relaxed and returned to the bed. He realized that as well.

"So, what do you suggest, Jesse? We just let her get away with this?"

"No. I'm sure you and I can come up with something that makes more sense."

"Whatever it is, it won't be severe enough," Edward muttered. He looked at me. "Who did bring you home last night, Delia?"

"Adan Bovio."

"Adan Bovio?"

"Maybe the future senator's son," Jesse said.

Edward nodded, but he didn't look happy about it. "What is he, about twenty-six?"

"Yes, I think so," Jesse said. "Maybe even twenty-seven or twenty-eight."

"Fani invited him to the Johnson party tonight."

"Fani invited him?" Edward asked. "It's not her party. How can she invite someone?"

"Don't forget, Edward, she's like a real princess around here," Jesse told him.

"Yeah, right."

"Adan is going to pick me up, if I'm able to attend," I said.

"Well, you won't be doing the rumba, but I don't see why you can't go," Jesse said.

"Pick you up, huh? You'll have to stay on the ball, Delia. He has a reputation."

"What does that mean, Edward, this reputation?"

"He's a well-known lady's man."

"She can take care of herself," Jesse said, smiling. "C'mon. Don't get her nervous. She's been through enough for now."

"That's for sure," Edward said, nodding and still muttering to himself.

Everyone was warning me about Adan, Fani and her sex detector, and now Edward with this lady's man title. I couldn't help it. I was getting nervous.

"Let's go, Delia," Jesse said. "We'll help you down to breakfast."

"I must put some moist heat on my ankle first," I said. "The doctor prescribed it."

"I'll get a washcloth under the hot water for you," Jesse said.

"Yeah, good idea," Edward told him. "She should be resting more, anyway. Delia, why don't you just lie back? I'll bring up some breakfast for you, or is it lunch?" he said, smiling and looking at his watch.

"Brunch," Jesse called back from the bathroom.

"Thank you, Edward. I know Tía Isabela is angry at me. She thinks it's all my fault."

"Don't you worry. I'll straighten that out," he said, walking to the door. "Just relax, and let us baby you."

I smiled, and he walked out, closing the door behind him. Jesse returned from the bathroom with a towel to put under my ankle and a steaming washcloth to put around it. He sat at my feet and carefully removed the bandage before applying the moist heat.

"Is it too hot?"

"No. Thank you, Jesse."

He smiled and looked at my ankle as if he could see it improving every second and then carefully stroked it. While he was leaning over me, Sophia burst into my bedroom.

"Well, look at who's getting tender loving care!" she cried. Her girlfriend Alisha was right behind her, grinning so hard it looked as if the corners of her mouth would touch her ears. "Or is it a little more than that? What do you think, Alisha?"

"More."

"Get the hell out of here," Jesse said.

"Don't tell me where to go in my house, Jesse Butler," Sophia said, clamping her hands on her hips. "Did you know she came home drunk last night?" she asked, wagging her head. "And made a big scene, waking everyone, even my mother? All she can do is cause trouble for us."

"Save your breath and your act. We know exactly what happened last night, Sophia."

"Yes, so do I," she said, and stepped to the side to look at me. "You came home with Adan Bovio. You can't keep a secret from me. I bet you think you're just so wonderful now, but believe me, you'll just become another one of his whores. You'll see, and then —"

Edward had come up behind her with a tray carrying my cup of coffee, eggs and bacon, and rolls and butter with a dish of fruit. He deliberately held it high and bumped into Sophia, causing the cup of coffee to spill out all over the back of her neck. She screamed and nearly leaped out of her skin.

"Oh, sorry. I didn't see you standing there," Edward said. "This damn one-eye problem."

Sophia, now in tears, burst past him and out of the room. Edward reached back with his foot and kicked the door closed in Alisha's face.

"I'll go get some more coffee," Jesse said. "What a waste of good coffee."

Edward laughed and brought the tray to

my lap. "Sorry about the little mess," he said, sopping up the coffee that had spilled in the tray.

"You're just as bad as she is," I said, playfully chastising him but secretly pleased.

"Apples don't fall far from the mother tree," he replied.

"I know she is just being mean and jealous, but she is not all wrong, Edward. I seem to be a sister to disaster."

"Don't you believe it, Delia. She'd love hearing you say that."

"Were you never close as brother and sister?" I asked as I drank my juice and ate.

"Back when my father was alive, maybe. We used to do a lot together, go with him on trips and to events. He did lavish gifts on us both, but more on her. There's no doubt he doted on her, which annoyed my mother more than it annoyed me."

I recalled Casto telling me something like that. For a moment, Edward just sat there, remembering. I ate and thought about it, too.

"Perhaps his death did more to her than it did to you, Edward. Maybe that is why she is this way. She is still suffering inside."

"I don't believe you, Delia," he said, shaking his head at me. "After all this, after what she's done to you, not only now but before, you still find a way to feel sorry for her."

"If you harden your heart too much, it will turn to stone," I said.

"Another saying of your grandmother's?"

I smiled and kept eating, surprised at how hungry I was.

"Can you say that *en español?*" he asked.

"Si usted endurece el corazón demasiado, se convierte en una piedra para apedrear."

"Wow. Don't expect me to memorize that one," he said.

"What one?" Jesse asked, returning with a new cup of hot coffee for me.

"One of her grandmother's sayings."

"Oh." Jesse handed me the new cup of coffee. "I'll put another hot cloth on that ankle," he said, and went to do so. "We'll get you back on your feet before you know it," he called from the bathroom.

Edward watched me finishing my breakfast and then Jesse reapplying the moist heat. "I think I have an idea," he said.

"About what?" Jesse asked.

"About how to take this moment of what she thinks is a victory away from Miss Horror."

"Oh?"

Edward stood up.

"What are you going to do, Edward?" I asked nervously.

"Don't worry about it. You get some more rest, Delia. Jesse and I have an errand to perform. We'll be back in a few hours."

He lifted the tray from my lap.

"I need to get up, shower, and dress," I said.

"No need to do that until you get ready for the party," Jesse said.

"I really don't know if I should go with an injury like this."

"Of course, you should go. You're doing fine. You need to distract yourself and forget the pain. You listen to Dr. Edward and his assistant, Dr. Jesse," he added. "We are the experts when it comes to forgetting unpleasantness, and we prescribe fun and pleasure, food and music . . . well, just listening to music for now, but still music."

"C'mon, you idiot," Edward told him.

"Stay off that ankle," Jesse called back to warn me as Edward pulled him toward the door.

What were they going to do? I laughed to myself. They had come in like a fresh rain shower and cleared my mind of all self-pity and sadness. Once again, I thought how lucky I was to have them.

I let my head fall back to the pillow and closed my eyes. The food did make me feel better, and the pain in my ankle was just a dull ache now. I was able to doze off and on and had no idea how much time had passed. Suddenly, Edward and Jesse came bursting back into my room.

"And how's our patient doing?" Jesse asked.

"I do feel better," I said, bracing myself on my elbows. I looked at the clock. It had been hours since they left. "Where have you been? What have you two done?" I asked, seeing that cat-that-ate-the-mouse look on both of their faces.

"Never mind. We'd like you to get up now. Go shower and put on something."

"Why? Where am I going?"

"You're going to your revenge," Edward said, laughing.

They both wore grins stolen off the face of the Cheshire cat. Suspicious, I started to get out of my bed. Jesse rushed forward to hand me my crutches.

"I'll pick out your clothes for you," Edward said. "Don't worry. Just take your shower, get yourself up."

I hobbled to the bathroom and looked back to see him and Jesse debating what I should wear. It was not easy taking a shower and staying off my injured ankle, but I did so and tried to be extra careful as I moved about and dried myself. I heard a knock on the bathroom door and opened it a little so Edward could hand me my things. They had even picked out panties and a bra and a pair of soft slippers.

"*Gracias,*" I said, more than a little embarrassed.

After I dressed, I stepped out. They were both standing like two palace guards waiting, their arms folded across their chests.

"Just take your time," Jesse said.

Now very curious, I moved quickly to the doorway when they opened it and stood back.

"Careful on the stairway," Edward advised me.

I looked for Sophia when we were out in the hallway, but I neither saw her nor heard her playing her music loudly in her room. I wondered where Tía Isabela was this whole day. I had half expected her to come charging into my room to chastise me and threaten, but she, too, was nowhere in sight.

As we made our way carefully down the stairway, I saw Señora Rosario look up at us with sympathy.

"*Cómo está?*"

"She's fine, Mrs. Rosario," Jesse assured her.

"*Bien,*" I said.

She nodded, smiled at the two of them,

and walked off.

Something was going on, I thought. I looked at the living room and down the hallway but saw nothing. They turned me toward the front door.

"Where are we going?"

"Just outside," Edward said. "Just a little farther."

They smiled like two conspirators at each other. Jesse lunged forward to open the door, and I stepped out to see a bright red sports car with a large yellow ribbon tied around it.

"*Qué es esto?* What is this?" I asked, my breath stolen at the sight.

"This," Edward said, "is your revenge." He did an exaggerated stage bow.

"I do not . . . understand."

"Edward has purchased a BMW sports car for you," Jesse said. "We bought the car, got the insurance, and had it gift-wrapped."

I stared at the two of them as if they had both gone mad, and they laughed.

"C'mon, we'll get you closer," Edward said, taking my arm.

They guided me down the steps to the car. It had beautiful cream leather seats.

"There's a great sound system in there. You'll be singing along," Jesse said.

"And a navigator," Edward added. "We'll

show you how to use everything, so don't worry."

"What is this navigator?"

"It tells you how to get where you're going if you are not sure of the route," Jesse said.

"So, you can never get lost."

"You have bought this for me?"

"It's in your name. Not my mother, nor my sister, no one, has anything to do with it but you."

"Stop looking so worried," Jesse said, laughing. "We'll take turns driving with you until you're perfectly comfortable with it."

"You did pass your driving test and the school driver's course with flying colors," Edward reminded me.

"*Sí*, but I have not driven much since."

"So, now you will, and you won't have to depend on anyone. This, by the way," Edward said, handing me a credit card, "is your gas card. You know how to put gas in a car, right?"

I looked at him.

"Take it."

"But you are giving me so much."

"It pleases me," he said. "Don't you know that it's better to give than to receive? Didn't your grandmother teach you that?"

I shook my head. "*Demasiado*. This is too much, Edward. Your mother will be very angry."

"Won't be the first time," he said, looking at Jesse. They both smiled. "Look, it's my money, Delia. She has nothing to say about it."

"However," Jesse sang, "there will be someone who will have much to say about it."

"Your keys, *señorita*," Edward said, handing me two sets of keys. "You just push this here, and it unlocks the doors and puts on the lights, and here to lock it."

"I'd advise you to keep it locked, even here, especially here," Jesse said.

"By next weekend, you will not be using crutches, and we'll be able to start the driving lessons so you're comfortable with your car," Edward promised.

We all heard the front door open and looked up to see Sophia and Alisha gaping at the three of us.

"Here it goes," Jesse whispered.

"Whose car is that?" Sophia demanded, coming down the steps.

"This car," Edward said, putting his hand on the car's roof and leaning over to look at her, "is registered in the name of Delia Yebarra. Do you know such a person?"

Sophia's eyes widened with such surprise I thought she would tear away her eyelids.

Her mouth opened and closed. "You bought her a car?"

"Not just any car. This is *Motor Scope*'s sports car of the year," he replied. As he came around the vehicle, he casually added, "I kept thinking of all those birthdays Delia had that we missed and thought this might make up for it. What do you think, Sophia? Is it enough or should I . . ."

"You're lying," Sophia said. "You didn't buy her a car."

Edward looked back at the car.

"It looks like a car, doesn't it, Jess?"

"Smells like a car."

"Moves like a car."

Together they cried, "It must be a car!"

Sophia just turned and charged back up the stairs. She rushed past Alisha and into the house. Alisha continued to gape at us for a moment and then followed her in. The moment the door closed, Jesse and Edward burst out laughing.

"Revenge?" Edward asked me.

"I don't know what to call it, Edward. I am in more shock than she is," I said, looking back at the car and down at the keys in my hands. I couldn't even imagine what the look on my father's face would be. Such things were even beyond our dreams.

"C'mon. Let's get you started on preparations for your party," Jesse said.

We were only halfway up the stairs when the front door opened again, and Tía Isabela appeared. She looked at us and then down at the car. We saw Sophia standing behind her with Alisha.

"Is this true, Edward? You bought her that car?"

"Mother, I cannot tell a lie. It is true," Edward said.

"Are you clear out of your mind?"

"I don't think so, Mother. Why do you ask?"

Tía Isabela stared at him a moment and then turned and went back inside.

"The only reason my mother is upset," Edward told Jesse, "is that now she'll really be pressured to buy my sister her car."

"She'll hate me for it," I said.

"She'll get over it," Edward assured me. "She's hated me before, too. Don't worry."

"Just concentrate on your wonderful evening," Jesse said.

When we entered the house, we saw Sophia stumping up the stairway with Alisha. Tía Isabela had returned to her office or bedroom.

"Jesse's right, Delia. You should start thinking about dressing for your party," Edward said. He looked in the direction his mother had gone. "Jesse will help you up the stairs. I'm going to speak with the queen."

"Make sure she knows I did not ask for such a gift," I called to him.

He laughed and walked off. We started up the stairway. When we got to my room, my phone was ringing. Jesse hurried ahead of me to answer it.

"And who's this?" he responded to obviously the same question. He listened. "Well, I'm Miss Yebarra's valet. I'll call her to the phone," he said in an exaggerated correct voice.

It was Adan. "Do you really have a valet?"

"No, it's just my cousin Edward's friend, Jesse. They have helped me today."

"You will go to the party, then?"

"I think I'll feel foolish, but yes," I said. "I will go."

"Great. I'll be by at seven. It's still just you in my car, right?"

"More than right," I said, laughing to myself. I couldn't imagine Sophia sitting next to me. "Oh, wait. How will I get my crutches into such a small car?"

He thought a moment. "Good point. I'll be there in one of my sedans," he said. "Don't worry about it."

"*Gracias.*"

"*Es nada, señorita. Hasta luego.*"

"Yes, see you soon."

When I hung up, I thought about Edward's warning.

"This lady's man," I asked Jesse. "How does such a man behave?"

"You'll see," he said. "Trust in yourself, Delia. Is there anything else you need right now?"

"No, thank you, Jesse."

"We'll be up to help you down and see you off," he said, and left.

For a long moment, I just stood there, reeling from the shock of it all. I went to the window and looked down to be sure the car was really there and it hadn't all just been a dream. The sun glittered off its hood. It was truly wonderful, but then I thought, how would I explain such a gift, and what would people, especially my fellow students, think when Sophia told them it was Edward who had bought the car for me? Wouldn't this just make matters worse?

Should I care?

Having my own car meant I could drive out to see the Davilas anytime I wanted. It would give me great freedom. I might even . . . think of driving to Mexico. Would I dare? What if I were followed or caught? I must get hold of myself and not be too ambitious. I could be like the mythical Icarus, who was given the power and wonder of flight with feathers stuck to him with wax. He was warned not to fly too high, but he did. The sun melted his wax wings, and he fell into the sea.

Would I now fly too high?

My heart raced with fear as much as with joy. *Just get dressed, Delia,* I told myself. *Prepare for your party, and, like an acrobat walking a tightrope, don't think about it, and don't look down. Go forward.*

By the time Edward and Jesse returned to see how I was doing, I was dressed and ready but sitting before my vanity mirror and staring through the image I saw of myself, staring at the face of my mother. With my thoughts so devoted to my own appearance and happiness, I suddenly had the terrifying feeling that I was letting my mother die the third death. All of these events, my life here, the images of new people coming into my life, pushed my past down deeper and deeper into that abyss of forgetfulness, the land of lost memories where loved ones cry out to have their names on your lips.

I am in danger of becoming someone else, I thought. Was this natural? Did everyone undergo such severe changes? Just when I had turned into a butterfly, my mother, whose loving smile and embrace carefully had guided me, was taken from me. I needed her then, and I needed her desperately now. My grandmother, as loving and concerned about me as she was, could not help me understand all of the emotions that swirled under my breast in an electric circle. My own face and body had begun to dazzle me. I had to touch my cheek to confirm that it was truly Delia in the mirror. Something very strong and dramatic had changed inside me. It was as if I were watching the evaporation of my childhood take place right before my own eyes and, with it, the thinning and diminishing of my past, including those I had loved.

"No," I cried as I saw my face returning and my mother's disappearing. "Don't leave me now."

Then came the knock on my door. I sucked back my tears and took a deep breath.

"Yes?"

"Hey," Edward said, opening the door and peering into my room. "How are you doing?"

"I'm still nervous about going to this party," I confessed.

They both entered.

"I love the way you did your hair," Jesse said.

Edward put *mi tía* Isabela's chapeau on me

and stepped back.

"Perfect. You really look beautiful, Delia," he said. "There's no reason for you to be nervous. It will be a fun party, I'm sure. And we'll be here for you. You just call us if you need us."

"I don't know, Edward. I feel . . ."

"It's too late. Someone's downstairs waiting for you," Jesse sang.

"He's already here?"

"And down there talking with my mother, so don't let him wait too long," Edward said. "She could turn Casanova into a monk."

Jesse laughed and went for my crutches. "C'mon. Don't let Sophia get the better of you," he said. "If you don't go to the party, you'll only give her a victory."

"I don't care about her victories," I said, even though I knew deep inside I did. I took the crutches and stood.

Edward opened the door, and Jesse stood beside me.

"We could carry you down, if you like," Jesse said when I didn't move. He made as if to lift me.

"No! I'm going. I'm going."

They both laughed.

We started out and down the stairs. I looked back at Sophia's room.

"I have a suspicion she might not go,"

Edward said, seeing where I was looking. "Drop her from your thoughts."

Adan rose immediately from the sofa and looked at us as we descended. *Mi tía* Isabela was sitting across from him and looked up as well.

"Ridiculous," I heard her say. "Going to a party like this on crutches."

"You once went to a formal dinner with your arm in a sling," Edward reminded her.

"That was different. I was recuperating from a rotor-cuff operation, not from falling down a stairway."

No one spoke for a moment. Then Adan stepped closer to take my hand. "You look fantastic," he said, "and I love that hat. Very French." He kissed my hand. *"Enchanté,"* he said.

I glanced at Tía Isabela. Her eyes widened so that I nearly laughed.

"Oh," Adan continued, "and congratulations on your car. It's beautiful. I was thinking of buying the exact one this week, but apparently, according to your aunt, someone beat me to it." He smiled at Edward.

I thought he looked even more handsome than he had at Fani's. He was dressed in a tailored tuxedo that gave him a breathtaking elegance. He wore a very expensive-looking gold watch and a diamond pinky ring.

"The car is as much of a surprise to me as to anyone," I said, looking toward my aunt. She sneered at Edward, looked away a moment, then stood up and came closer to inspect me.

"Where did you get that dress?" she asked, and before I could respond, she turned to Edward and said, "As if I had to ask."

"The hat really makes the look, don't you think, Mother?" he asked her.

I saw her reluctant approval. "Yes, but the dress doesn't hurt. I know the designer. Well, have a good time, but I would hope," she said, "not to have any repetition of what occurred last night."

"Put a chain on Miss Horror, and you won't," Edward said.

Adan's eyes widened. He looked afraid to utter a word. The silence was too heavy, however.

"Let's be on our way, then," he said, taking one crutch and offering his arm to replace it. I took it, and we headed for the door.

When I looked back after Adan opened his black sedan's door for me, I saw Edward and Jesse standing in the entrance looking at me proudly.

"They do look like two mother hens," Adan muttered, taking my crutches and putting them across the rear seat. "Don't they have anything better to do?"

"What could be better than looking after me?" I asked him, and he laughed.

"I told you. I love your sense of humor," he said, and closed the door. He waved to Edward and Jesse and got in. "We're off," he said, starting the car and driving away.

As we approached the gate, a sports car came rushing in, nearly driving us off the driveway. I had enough time to see who it was, however.

"Who the hell was that?" Adan asked slowing.

"A boy from school, Christian Taylor," I said, looking back. Sophia was coming out of the entrance now.

"Your cousin's date?"

"It looks like it," I said. I couldn't imagine Christian being interested in her. They were both up to no good, I was sure.

Only time would tell me what new dagger she had prepared to stick into my heart.

8
THE PARTY

Danielle Johnson's family estate was as beautiful and as plush as Fani's but smaller and with no heliport. The pool and the tennis court were visible from the driveway. Adan said the Johnsons had only a nine-hole private golf course. Poor Johnsons, I thought. I could see how going from one wealthy person's *hacienda* to another, how living and playing in this world of overabundance, with its servants and gourmet foods, its fountains of wines and glittering gold and diamond accoutrements, could make anyone indifferent to the other world, the world where people struggled to feed themselves, to keep warm and safe. It was truly as if these rich people lived on another planet, and I was like some space traveler who had crossed into another solar system.

As we continued up Danielle's driveway, I saw valets in black pants and white shirts rushing to park everyone's cars. French music was piped out of speakers lining the driveway so people who arrived were immediately bathed in the ethnic nature of the party. Like Fani's home and so many homes of the wealthy here, the front entrance opened to a large courtyard. Tonight, set up inside Danielle's was a replica of the Eiffel Tower in Paris, with all the lights. Later, I learned the replica was done in exact detail and stood twenty feet tall. It even had a small elevator that actually worked.

"So, what do you really think of all this, Delia?" Adan asked me, waving his hand over the sights unfolding before us.

"If you wanted to drown yourself in wealth, this would be the place to die happy," I said, and he laughed.

"I'm really impressed with your wit, Delia. I'm losing all of my stereotype assumptions about rural Mexicans. I guess I have been underestimating my own people."

"And therefore yourself," I said. "Don't forget, your father told me where his family originated and where you still have relatives."

This time, he looked at me less with an expression of amusement and more with an expression of appreciation. The look was so strong it made my heart flutter. A part of me had been afraid of my wanting him to like me this much, and a part of me that I began to sense might be stronger wanted nothing less. At the moment, thoughts of Ignacio were as far away as the moon. Was I slipping off the mountain of faithfulness and love? How far would I fall?

The valet who seized the door handle and opened my door shook me out of my deep thoughts.

"Welcome to the party," he chimed.

"Got to get something out of the rear," Adan told him, and hurried around the car to get my crutches. Then he guided me out, and I put them under my arms. "Okay?" he asked.

I nodded and looked at everything going on around us. It was very exciting. Waiters and waitresses dressed in the costumes of French street vendors were not waiting for people to get into the party. They were coming out to greet guests with the hors d'oeuvres and drinks. No alcohol was being served from trays. Adults had to go inside the courtyard and into the house to the bars that had been set up. I did not know what would keep the underage students from our school from getting the alcoholic drinks, but I did see men who looked like security personnel standing off to the sides watching people, especially young people, carefully.

The entryway and the living room of the huge home had been turned into a ballroom in Paris, even with a small stage on the right. Danielle's father had hired dancers to perform the cancan. They wore costumes as skimpy as possible, and the crowd watching them consisted mostly of the fathers and Danielle's father's male friends. Some were smoking cigars, the thin streams of smoke rising in the air and perfuming it with the heavy, rich tobacco aromas. Deeper inside the house were a half-dozen men and women playing small accordions, juggling, and performing magic tricks for the amusement of the guests. There were kiosks of food almost everywhere I looked, ranging from shrimp, chicken, and meat on sticks to lobster and fish displayed on large colorful plates, breads and vegetables, and in one section a variety of French pastries that surely rivaled anything found in Paris itself. The servers wore chefs' hats.

My first thoughts as I gazed around, drinking in as much of it as I could, was how different from this was a birthday party for a girl Danielle's age back in my Mexican village. I even recalled the fateful night when I had attended Ignacio's sister's birthday party. All of the food was homemade, with friends and family all bringing something.

Here, except for the banner over the front of the main house's entrance that read, "Happy Birthday, Danielle," nothing else suggested that it was a party in her honor. The invitation had forbidden gifts, with the simple statement that your attendance was gift enough. It could be a New Year's Eve party if the banner was taken down. Did such a party make her happy or sad? If this was her birthday party, what would her wedding be like?

"There you are!" Danielle cried, clapping her hands and hurrying over to us. Three of her closer friends at school who were also friends of mine trailed along behind her like the tail of a kite. "I'm so happy you could still attend the party despite your accident. Are you in pain?"

"No," I said, wondering how much she knew about my so-called accident.

"What a beautiful dress, Delia," Colleen said. The other two agreed, their eyes washed in surprise and envy.

"Thank you."

Danielle hugged me but saved her best smile for Adan, whom she kissed on both cheeks as a French girl would.

"I'm so happy you could come to my party," she told him, turning completely away from me, as did the other three. It was as if I had been suddenly changed into a marble statue and no longer commanded even their slightest attention.

"No, it is I who am happy. What a party!"

"Yes, isn't it wonderful?" Danielle leaned toward him so much I thought he would have to catch her in his arms to keep her from falling. "My father looks for any reason to throw a gala."

"He did that," Adan said, shifting so he could be closer to me, and took my hand.

She glanced at me and pulled back. "Fani is talking to my mother," she said. "In French! She speaks three languages."

"Four, really," Adan said. "She can get by with German because of the time her family spent in Berlin."

"German, too! Don't you just hate her for being so perfect?"

"If we hated people for being perfect, we'd have to hate you, too, Danielle," Adan told her, and she beamed again.

"I want to be sure you ask me to dance later." She nodded at me and looked down at my ankle. "It looks like your date can't dance tonight. I'm so sorry, Delia."

Her girlfriends drew closer.

"We all heard about your accident, Delia," Katelynn said. "How did it really happen?"

she asked, with the tone of someone who already knew the answer.

"Oh, not now, girls," Adan said, stepping between us. "We don't want to dwell on sad things tonight. It's Danielle's birthday party." He winked at her. "I'll dance with you later. That's a promise," he said. "Right now, I'm dying of thirst."

She looked at her disappointed girlfriends, who had all been hoping for news bulletins for their gossip. She smiled and stepped aside.

"Of course, you can have something hard to drink, Adan. Just don't you feed anything alcoholic to the underage girls," she added, smiling at me. She was clearly implying that he might just get me something.

Adam laughed. "Looking at you girls, it's getting harder and harder to tell who's underage," he said, and her friends practically exploded with glee. "Later," he added, and pulled me away gently. "Save me," he whispered. "Get rid of the crutches."

"I'm not sure that would be enough. They were like hens clucking at a rooster."

He laughed and plucked a soft drink off one of the trays for me. At one of the bars, he ordered himself a vodka martini. We ate some of the hors d'oeuvres before making our way across the room to join Fani, who immediately introduced us to Danielle's mother.

"Welcome, Delia. I'm so happy to finally meet Isabela's niece. I've heard so much about you from Danielle and now Fani that I feel I've met you already."

"Merci, Madame Johnson. Je suis honore etre ici."

Her eyes widened, and she laughed. "Are all you girls so bright and worldly?"

I shook my head, leaned toward her, and confessed that I had memorized the line. She roared with laughter, her face brightening with delight. I thought she was far more beautiful than Danielle. Fani looked at me with the approval of a mother or guardian.

"What happened to your ankle?" Mrs. Johnson asked.

"A little accident. *Ce n'est rien.*"

"It's nothing? *Bon.* Well, you kids have a great time. I'm happy Danielle has made such nice friends."

She patted my hand and joined some of the other adults nearby.

"That's a pretty expensive dress," Fani said immediately. "Your aunt bought it for you?"

"No. It's a present from my cousin Edward."

"Really? How generous."

Generous? If she thought this was generous, what would she say when she heard about my car?

"Where's your darling other cousin?" Fani asked, looking toward the entrance. "I thought she was definitely coming." I was surprised at how disappointed she sounded.

"She'll be here any moment, I'm sure. Christian Taylor was picking her up."

"Christian Taylor? She got him to do that? Well, this gets more and more interesting. I wonder what outrage the two of them are planning. Don't worry. I've planted the seeds so everyone knows she's responsible for your little accident."

So, Danielle and her friends did know, I thought, and looked at Adan. He surely had told Fani what I had told him on the phone. I was afraid they were all now determined to dig out the nitty-gritty details.

"It is better forgotten," I said, "especially at such a party."

"Didn't you tell me your father told you that if you act like sheep, they'll act like wolves?"

"Yes, but . . ."

"Don't be a hypocrite, Delia. Either be brave and proud, or pick up your cousin's toilet paper," she snapped, her eyes blazing.

"Ugh," Adan said. "You're such an instigator, Fani."

"What of it?" She looked at the grand festivities around us, the food and the music. "These parties can be so boring. All these men trying to pretend they're boys; all these boys pretending they're men."

"Boring? How can you say that? I have never seen such a birthday party," I said.

She grimaced. "Well, don't expect to see a piñata. Get me a glass of champagne, Adan."

"Champagne? Do you want me to be arrested for contributing to the delinquency of a minor?"

"Spare me. It won't be the first time you did so," she said, and he laughed.

"Wait here. I'll have to get it and pour it into a soda glass."

The dancers broke into the cancan again, and men and boys were cheering.

"Adan really likes you," Fani said. "I never heard him speak about a girl as much. I couldn't get him off the phone this afternoon. He thinks you're head and shoulders above other girls your age. What did you do to him on the way home from my house last night?"

"I did nothing."

"Did you go straight home?" she asked, swinging her eyes toward him.

"Yes. Straight home."

"Yeah, well, whatever you did or didn't do was enough to capture his imagination, and Adan has a wild imagination."

She stopped talking when he returned with the champagne in a soda glass. *"Gracias, señor."* She clinked his glass and sipped her champagne.

"Let's get something substantial to eat," she suggested.

As we crossed the room toward the displays of food, Fani paused and nudged me to turn around. Sophia and Christian were just coming into the party.

"This is going to be good," she whispered, and nodded toward Danielle and her girlfriends, who had spotted Sophia as well. Their chatter became more animated. They reminded me of angry bees.

"Oh, I hope they don't make trouble," I said. It sounded like a prayer.

"She'll only get what she deserves," Fani declared. "Besides, it's Danielle's party. She can do what she wants."

"With your little help, I'm sure," Adan muttered. "You so enjoy running everyone's life."

"It's a dirty job, but someone's got to do it," Fani said, and they both laughed.

Adan fixed me a plate of food and guided

me to one of the tables that had been set up like in a French café, with candlelight and baskets of croissants. Looking across the room, I saw Danielle and her friends descend on Sophia, who, although she was dressed more elegantly than I had ever seen her dressed and walked with Christian Taylor holding her arm, still looked like a fish out of water.

Adan fixed Fani's plate of food as well, and she sat beside me. It occurred to me that none of the boys from our school was trying to get her attention. Were they all so afraid of her, of being rejected? She didn't seem to care.

Just before Adan joined us with his food, Fani leaned toward me, both of us still watching Danielle and her friends talking to Sophia and Christian, and whispered, "Adan knows what happened to you. He knows all about the famous Bradley Whitfield affair. He knew more about it than I did."

I nearly choked on the lobster I had started to chew. I turned to her, but before I could respond, he sat next to me.

"What's happening in the soap opera?" he asked, biting into a hamburger and nodding toward Sophia and Christian.

"I'm sure they're cross-examining her," Fani said. "She looks as if she's defending herself. And Christian Taylor looks as if he's here to be her attorney."

They did appear to be in a serious argument now.

"This is not nice for Danielle's party," I said. "She will be upset."

"Are you kidding? Danielle is just like the others. She enjoys tormenting someone. I just provided her with some new ammunition."

"You're such a bitch, Fani," Adan said, smiling.

"I learned from the best," she replied.

Sophia tore herself away from Danielle and her friends and started across the grand room toward us, Christian trailing behind.

"Uh-oh," Adan said. "Here comes trouble."

"You think you're so smart, don't you?" Sophia said when she drew close enough. "Making up that story about me and spreading it so quickly so you could ruin my evening here."

I shook my head. "I said nothing to anyone about you."

"Yeah, right." She looked at Fani. "You'd better pull them off me if you know what's good for you."

"Me? I don't control them," Fani said. "And I don't like being threatened."

"Girls, c'mon," Adan said. "Let's just have a good time tonight."

"Yeah, well, we know what that means for you, Adan Bovio. You probably will have a good time. You have the right girl for it." She nodded at me, turned, and walked away.

Christian shrugged as if there was nothing he could do about her, but we could see he enjoyed it all, perhaps as much as Fani did.

I was sure my face was red. It felt burning hot.

Adan laughed.

"Now, see," Fani said. "Doesn't all this make the party more interesting? I can't wait for the second round."

Like the child's game where a secret is whispered into the ear of everyone in a circle until it comes back to the originator dramatically changed, the gossip began to flow from Sophia and Christian through the ears and lips of the other students at the party. The girls who were my friends in school were again jealous of me because I was with Adan Bovio. They were eager to listen and to unravel the whispers. I had no idea what slurs and rumors were being generated during the evening, but Fani was plugged into the talk and reported to us that Sophia and Christian were claiming Sophia had seen me in bed with Edward and Jesse. She told them my aunt was very upset and had told them to stay away from me. Sophia claimed that was why I had made up this story about her throwing me down a stairway.

I couldn't breathe for a moment. It seemed that everyone at the party was looking my way and shaking his or her head with disapproval. It amazed me that anyone, especially the girls I thought were friends of mine, could believe such a tale, but there was Katelynn describing how I had been so close to my cousin and Jesse at the restaurant, and, of course, there was Christian Taylor claiming I would rather be with them than with him.

Like any terrible rumor, its roots were based on some facts. In this case, it was the fact that Edward had bought me a car and that the two of them had actually picked out and bought the dress I was wearing tonight. Christian confirmed everything. He had seen the car tonight. When I couldn't deny these things, everything else gained validity, and before the night had ended, the target of the ugly gossip had become me and not Sophia.

"Your cousin bought you a sports car?" Fani asked when she had heard that part.

"Sí. It was a surprise."

"I bet it was. No wonder Sophia is wagging her tongue so much. She's probably dying with envy."

To my surprise and disappointment, Fani didn't see this as unpleasant for me. On the contrary, she saw the verbal battle as even more fun. Adan had to dance with Danielle after all, and then another of her friends begged him to take her to the dance floor. Boys even grew courageous enough to ask Fani to dance, but no one else spoke to me. I sat mired in my misfortune, watching them all. The party's strobe lights were turned on and flashed over their smiling faces, making them all look devilish. My ankle even began to hurt again.

How had this wonderful night turned so sour? I couldn't wait to leave, but no one could leave until the huge birthday cake had been wheeled out. Danielle blew out the candles, and there was an explosion of balloons rising into the night. Then, to everyone's amazement, we were paraded out to witness a fireworks display that ended with the words "Happy Birthday Danielle" written in bright lights against the inky night. It was all so overwhelming that for those moments, all thoughts about Sophia and the slanders were forgotten.

Adan held me close. "Your face is lit with the fireworks," he said, and kissed me. It was a warm, soft kiss but passionate enough to send a chill of excitement to my breasts. I felt myself lose all resistance, and he sensed it as well. "Let's get out of here," he whispered.

I looked to the right and saw Fani watching us, a sly smile on her face. She had seen us kiss.

"C'mon," Adan urged. He paused by Fani on our way in to say good night to Danielle and her parents.

"Leaving already?" Fani asked.

"Delia's foot's acting up," he said, and she widened her smile.

"I imagine more than her foot is acting up."

"You're such a bitch," he told her.

"*Bonne nuit, mon amie,*" she told me. "I'll speak to you tomorrow."

"*Buenas noches,*" I replied. She laughed, and we went first to Danielle's parents.

"I'm so happy you could come," her mother said. Her father shook Adan's hand and wished his father luck in running for the Senate. He also said he was sending him a contribution.

All of the students from our school whom she had invited surrounded Danielle, but when she saw us preparing to leave, she broke away.

"Why are you going so early?" she whined. "We're just getting started. The band is going to play until two in the morning."

Adan explained that my ankle was hurting, and we had to get me home to rest.

"Of course," Danielle said. "Feel free to come back after you take her home," she added coquettishly. He didn't respond. "I hope you feel better soon, Delia. See you in school."

"Thank you, and happy birthday."

She smiled and returned quickly to her entourage. I looked about for Sophia and Christian. Adan sensed it.

"I saw your cousin leave a good half hour ago," he whispered. "I'm sure it wasn't to go home."

The valet brought us Adan's car and he put my crutches into the rear again.

"Well, that's one kind of a birthday party," he muttered as we drove down the driveway and out the gate. He looked at me when I didn't respond. "I'm sorry Fani stirred up that hornet's nest. She has lived such a privileged, rich life, traveling to every glamorous and expensive place, and living in that palace that I think she's simply bored all the time and does things like this to amuse herself. I worry about her."

"You worry about Fani? With all she has,

beauty, brains, wealth?"

"Something important is still missing, Delia. She envies you."

"Me? I have nothing compared to her."

"You have a helluva nice new car," he said, laughing.

"You know what I mean, Adan. I have lost my family. My cousin Edward is generous and sweet to me, but I will have to make my own way in this world. I have many burdens, burdens Fani can't even begin to imagine."

"I know, but it's all made you stronger, Delia. I can tell, and so can Fani, and she is jealous of your inner strength, your pride. Believe me."

I said nothing. It was comforting to hear these things, but I wasn't sure whether it was simply flattery.

"I want to show you something, if that's all right," he said. "You don't want to go right home, anyway."

"Show me something?"

Those words, that idea, triggered my painful Bradley Whitfield memories.

"It's just a piece of land," he said. "I know what happened to you. Don't worry. I have never forced a girl to do anything she didn't want to do with me. Men like that are pathetic and insecure."

"Where is this land? Why show it to me?"

I asked, unable to hide my nervousness. Was this the lady's man finally emerging?

"Just be a little patient. And a little more trusting," he said, laughing.

We drove for a while, and then he made a turn that took us away from the lights and houses. The road he chose took us up a small rise. When he stopped, I saw we were looking back at the lights of Palm Springs. It was a breathtaking view.

"This is where I'm going to build my own house," he said. "I own this land myself. My father has nothing to do with it."

"The view is beautiful."

"Yes, and I bought up the land around it for a good four acres of privacy on both sides."

"When will you build this house?"

"I'll start the day I get engaged to the woman of my dreams," he said. "I want it to be the first and maybe only home we have. As you see," he said, smiling, "I do have a very serious side and know when it's time to put my sowing of wild oats aside. You know," he added, looking at his land, "if my father gets elected and serves successfully, it's not unusual for his son to follow in his political footsteps. I may be a future U.S. senator myself. It's very important to be a family man if you want to be in politics."

"Where is this woman of your dreams?"

"In here," he said, pointing to his temple, "and in here," he added, pointing to his heart. "I'll know her when I'm sure."

"I wish you good fortune, Adan."

He sat back, smiling at me. "I'm not going to be one of those guys who fills your head with romantic lies to get you to go to bed with him, Delia, but I will tell you that I've been with enough young women to know when someone is real, authentic, and you are. I want to know more about you, about the family you had in Mexico, about your childhood, everything, because when I learn about you, I think I'll learn something about myself as well."

He put up his hands.

"No more, *no más*. Don't make any judgments about me yet. Be suspicious and skeptical. I want to earn your trust," he said. He put the car into drive again and started back.

I felt myself relax. My mind was reeling with all sorts of thoughts. I was somewhat exhausted from the roller-coaster ride of emotions I had traveled this night. My feelings about Adan were guarded. I liked him, but I was afraid that I would like him too much and in a real sense put Ignacio into the third death even before he had really died.

Every warm feeling I had toward Adan felt like a cold betrayal of Ignacio. He had sacrificed so much for me, for us.

"You're very quiet, Delia," Adan said. "I hope I haven't said anything to offend you."

"Oh, no. I am sorry. I am just very tired."

"Sure. That's understandable. How is your ankle?"

"It feels numb now," I said. "I think it's getting better quickly."

"You'd better get off those crutches soon," he said as we turned into *mi tía* Isabela's driveway. "You have a car sitting and waiting," he said, nodding at my car, glittering in the moonlight in front of *mi tía* Isabela's *hacienda*.

"Yes," I said, still shocked at the realization.

We pulled up behind the car, and he hopped out quickly to get my crutches. He helped me out and then up the stairway to the front entrance.

"Well," he said, "I hope despite some of it that you had a good time with me."

"Oh, yes."

"Great. Then you'll go to dinner with me tomorrow night? I promise to get you home early."

"I'd rather not go out on a night before school. I'm afraid I haven't done any of my homework yet," I said.

"I understand. How about next Friday night, then? A friend of mine opened a great new Italian restaurant in Indian Wells, and I'd like to take you there."

His smile started to fade with my hesitation. My heart jumped a beat when I saw it. It was like watching a kite with a broken string drift off in the wind.

"Yes," I said quickly. "That would be fine. Thank you."

"Thank you, Delia. I had a great evening," he said, and kissed me softly again, but this time more quickly. Then he started down the stairway. "Hey," he said when I opened the door. "Maybe I'll get you to give me a ride in your car. I can help you break it in."

"Soon," I said.

He waited until I entered the house. I closed the door behind me and stood in the entryway a moment to catch my breath. The stairway loomed ahead and above me suddenly looking more like a mountain to climb. I started toward it, holding both crutches in my left hand and then holding on to the banister to keep from putting too much pressure on my swollen ankle. I felt like an old lady, moving as slowly as Señora Baca. I was halfway up when the front door opened and closed. Sophia stood there looking up at me.

"Home before me? That must have been a quickie," she said, starting up. "Maybe Adan's not as good as his reputation."

I didn't respond, but I didn't turn my back on her, either. The way I glared down at her made her hesitate. Her eyes went from me to the stairway and then to her imagination.

"You'd better not try anything," she said.

I enjoyed seeing the fear in her face. She climbed the stairs slowly, staying as far to my left as she could, and when I brought a crutch down a little, she charged up the steps ahead of me. I couldn't help but smile.

"You should go back to Mexico," she cried when she reached the top. "Back where you belong!"

"I should," I muttered after her, but she was already down the hallway to her room.

The commotion was enough to alert Edward and Jesse, who came out of Edward's bedroom and rushed to help me finish going up the stairway.

"I'm fine," I said, but they practically carried me up.

"We want to hear all about the party," Edward said. "You want to come into my room for a while?"

"I'm tired, Edward. Can we talk in the morning before you return to Los Angeles?"

"Sure. You just stay in bed," Jesse said. "We'll bring you your breakfast."

"No. I'll get up," I said quickly, maybe too quickly. I couldn't help but be sensitive to everything they said or did for me. I knew Sophia would make something of it and give the ugly stories more credibility.

Edward narrowed his eyes. "What's wrong, Delia?"

"Was there a problem with Adan Bovio?" Jesse asked quickly.

"No, he was very nice, Jesse. I am going to dinner with him next Friday, to his friend's new restaurant."

"Oh," Edward said, nodding.

"It's fine," I said, smiling. "I am just very tired."

"Sure. Sleep well," he said.

They watched me go to my bedroom. I smiled back at them and went in, closing the door softly behind me.

Now I was keeping another secret from them, I thought sadly, from the two people who had been the most kind and loving toward me. Would they hate me more after hearing the truth or for not hearing it? And how would they behave toward me once they knew of the nasty rumors Sophia and Christian were spreading?

It seemed that no matter what direction I

took or what decisions I made, I was always to be caught in this maze of confusion and danger. My people from Mexico were coming here for protection, security, education, and health, but all I could see was a storm of trouble brewing.

Even in my dreams, the dark clouds were sliding in my direction. The winds blew harder, stronger, and the grasp I had on my grandmother's hand weakened.

I fell through a nightmare into the morning sunlight, terrified at where the hands of the clock were taking me.

9
AN UNEASY DEAL

Despite my telling Edward and Jesse not to pamper me with breakfast in bed, there was a knock at my door in the morning. I had not realized how late I had slept. For a moment, the bright sunlight streaming through my windows confused me, but I called out, "Yes?"

They entered pretending to be waiters, with small towels over their arms, one carrying the tray of food, the other carrying coffee and a local newspaper.

"What are you doing?" I asked, sitting up. "I told you not to bring me breakfast."

Jesse put the tray down, fixed the bed table for me over my lap, and put the tray on it. Edward held up the local paper and smiled.

"That was before we realized how important you have become."

"What?"

"You made the social pages," he said. "And

in a big way, too."

"Me?"

He unfolded the paper to show me a picture of Fani, Adan, and myself at Danielle Johnson's party. Fani was looking at me, but Adan and I were looking toward the camera. Someone had given the photographer my name. Next to it was written, "escorted by Adan Bovio, son of U.S. senatorial candidate Ray Bovio." Fani wasn't even mentioned.

"You didn't know that picture was taken?" Jesse asked.

"There were so many lights going off . . . Danielle's personal photographer, but no," I said, amazed. "I did not know someone was working for the newspaper."

"Delia Yebarra storms into the Palm Springs social scene," Edward said, drawing a headline in the air and laughing. He leaned over to whisper because the door was open. "Seen at the party with the son of the U.S. Senate candidate. This will surely impress my mother. The social pages are the pages of her Bible."

"Sophia will be pouting," Jesse said. "She didn't make the social pages."

They both laughed.

I looked at the breakfast, at them, and at the newspaper.

"It's okay to be a little famous," Edward

said, reading the worried expression on my face.

He didn't understand, but the first thought that had come to my mind after seeing my picture in the paper was that Ignacio's father and mother might see it as well. What would they think of me and my devotion to Ignacio? Could such a picture find its way to Ignacio?

"From what's written there, it sounds like an amazing birthday party," Jesse said. "Magicians, cancan girls, fireworks! What didn't they have?"

"Homemade food," I said, "and family."

They both stared at me with nearly identical smiles.

"You still miss Mexico quite a bit, don't you?" Edward asked.

"Sí. Tanto."

"What exactly do you miss so much, Delia?" Jesse asked.

I smiled, remembering. "I miss the music in the square, the comfort I could find in the church, my grandmother's friends talking softly in the evening, the sight of my father sitting quietly with my mother and talking softly about their day or their own dreams. I miss walking in the streets and smelling the aromas of homemade chile, rice and beans, burritos, fajitas, tortillas, the laughter of the little children, running through our poor streets but none of them thinking about their poverty. I miss the honesty."

I stopped, realizing how I had gone on and that they were both staring at me in amazement.

Edward smiled. "You know, I think we should make a definite decision right now," he said, nodding. "We're going to go to Mexico during the school break, drive to your village, which was where my grandmother and grandfather lived, too. We'll start planning seriously."

"Good idea," Jesse said. "I'll work out the arrangements and the route."

The idea was still as exciting as ever, but I couldn't help but think what such a trip taken by the three of us would do for the nasty rumors once word of it got out. It would be like fertilizing an ugly weed.

"Doesn't that sound good to you anymore, Delia?" Edward asked when I didn't respond.

"Of course, sí."

"Then why this look on your face, the expression of someone who just lost her best friend or something?"

I took a deep breath and shifted myself in the bed so I could move the breakfast aside for a few moments. "Will you promise not to go wild and angry and do something terrible if I tell you something?"

"No," Edward said.

"Then I won't tell you."

"Whatever it is, we're going to find out eventually, anyway, Delia. If something is so bad that you need me to make such a promise, it must be that everyone around here knows about it except Jesse and myself. Okay," he said when I didn't speak. "We'll take deep breaths and not go flying off the handle. You know what that means?"

I nodded. He was probably right. These stories would eventually find their way to his and Jesse's ears.

"Well?"

"Your sister is spreading stories about us. She and Christian tossed them about like grass seed last night at the party, and before we left, everyone was whispering, and the three of us were covered in their slander."

"What kind of stories?" Jesse asked.

"You don't have to answer," Edward told me. He turned to Jesse. "Sophia's made innuendos before, Jess. It's not hard to imagine how she embellished them." He turned back to me. "And people believe her? How can anyone take what Sophia says seriously?"

I shrugged. "People now know what you have bought me and how much you have done for me. She and Christian made sure of that. Tongues were wagging."

"That doesn't automatically mean we're sleeping with you."

"No, but my grandmother used to say, *'La envidia es la madre del chisme.'* Envy is the mother of gossip."

"And we know if Sophia is anything, she is envious," Jesse said.

"Many of the girls were envious," I told them. "As hard as it might be to believe, I think even Fani envied me."

They were both quiet a moment. I was sure their imaginations were flooded with distasteful images. Despite what Edward predicted, I hated being the bearer of such news.

"I am sorry, Edward."

"You're sorry? You have no reason to be sorry. Damn. I'll fix her good for this," Edward swore. "Don't you worry about us, Delia. This won't change a thing."

"What are you going to do, Edward? You said you wouldn't fly off the handle."

"I won't, but I think it's time my mother and I had a real heart-to-heart about Sophia and all this," he said. "We must bring it to a head and end it one way or the other. Obviously, this can't go on. Jesse and I have another life elsewhere and will survive, but you have to remain here and wallow in this muck."

Jesse nodded and then smiled at me. "You know, Delia, ironically, your dating Adan Bovio will be the fastest way to put out this fire."

"That's no reason for her to date someone," Edward snapped at him. "Especially Adan Bovio."

Jesse shrugged. "If she likes him and wants to date him, it won't do any harm. That's all I meant. Of course, you should do only what you want to do, Delia, but it can't hurt if you like him."

Suddenly, I felt even more trapped. It was on the tip of my tongue to tell them the final secret, and maybe I would have done so if it were not for Sophia's standing in the doorway and gleefully smiling in at us.

"I wonder why you don't bring up my breakfast, Edward," she said, "and talk to me while I'm still in my flimsy nightgown."

The moment she said it, I brought the blanket up over my breasts. I could feel Edward's rage. The air in the room seemed to cook in the fire from his eyes.

Jesse stepped in front of him as he started toward her. "Your mother," Jesse reminded him. "Go speak to your mother. That's the sensible solution, Edward. Nothing else."

"Enjoy your breakfast and whatever else you do," Sophia said, and walked away.

I looked at the food. Just the thought of it made my throat tighten along with my stomach.

"C'mon," Jesse urged. "Go do what you have to do. We have to get back to L.A., too. You know what work we have yet."

Edward took a deep breath to put out the fire in his heart. "All right. Get our stuff together. I'll go pay my mother a visit. She doesn't come out of her bedroom on Sundays until midday. You don't have to wonder where Sophia gets her habits." He squeezed my hand gently to reassure me and started out.

"Wait," Jesse called after him. He handed him the paper. "Make sure she sees the newspaper first. It's good psychology."

Edward took it and smiled. "Right. When she hears how darling Sophia is dirtying our reputations in light of this, she'll be even angrier. Maybe she'll take away her breathing privileges," he said, and left.

"Breathing privileges? What does that mean?"

Jesse laughed. "He's exaggerating . . . but not by much," he said. "Eat something, Delia. It's going to be all right. Think about our trip to Mexico, and forget Sophia for a while."

He left to get ready for their trip back to Los Angeles, and I did begin to eat some toast and jam. I thought about our trip to Mexico, too, and how wonderful it could be, especially for Ignacio and me. I would need to get the details to Ignacio as soon as Edward and Jesse planned them. Of course, I had to do all of that without his father knowing. He'd be worried that I would expose Ignacio to the police.

When I got out of bed, I realized my ankle was much improved. I did not need to use the crutches, but I was careful not to put too much pressure on that foot. After I was dressed, I picked up the tray to take downstairs but paused when I heard someone running in the hallway and then Sophia's bedroom door slam shut. I held my breath in anticipation of more trouble.

Almost immediately, there were footsteps. I was expecting Edward, but when the door opened, it was *mi tía* Isabela standing there in her scarlet bathrobe, her hair down around her shoulders. I had rarely seen her without any makeup at all. She looked as if she had aged overnight. There were dark rings around her eyes, and her face was pale, almost sickly.

"With all the spotlights apparently being

turned on this family, I've decided it's time you and I have a real talk, Delia. I have put up with a great deal for Edward's sake as much as for yours, but these petty jealousies and stupid blunders are beginning to take a toll on my health and happiness, and I won't stand for it."

"I have done nothing to bring shame to this house, Tía Isabela."

"Sometimes," she said, moving to a chair by the dresser, "you don't have to invite trouble. It invites itself." She sat. "I didn't think Sophia was this self-destructive, but obviously she is socially suicidal. She certainly isn't worried about my reputation and happiness. I have forbidden her to go anywhere on weekends for the next month, but punishing her for fanning the flames of these disgusting rumors is not going to be enough. Sit," she ordered.

I backed up and sat on the bed.

For a moment, she stared at me and then looked away. "You're much prettier than your mother and I were at your age," she said.

Any compliment from her was unexpected and left me speechless.

"It's proper to thank someone when he or she gives you a compliment, Delia."

"Thank you," I said.

She nodded to herself, confirming a thought. "We have some work yet to be done to build your social graces, but I'm not surprised to see that the social-pages photographer took your picture at the party."

"It was probably because of Adan or Fani," I said quickly.

"You're more prominent in the picture, and they don't even mention Fani. Believe me, that's not an accident. Escort of Adan Bovio, son of a U.S. senatorial candidate," she recited. "So, do you like Adan Bovio?"

"He was very pleasant to be with," I said. "Courteous. He's asked me to go to dinner with him next Friday. To a friend's new restaurant," I added, "so I agreed."

"Good," she said quickly. "Nothing . . . nothing," she repeated with more emphasis and authority and leaning toward me, "will end these stupid stories faster than you having a relationship with someone like Adan Bovio."

Jesse had just suggested the same thing, I thought, but it did not seem to me to be the honest thing to do, and besides, there was Ignacio wearing that face of heartfelt sadness back in the Mexican bus station. Time had not made it any less vivid or painful to recall.

"I do not say it is a relationship, Tía Isabela."

"Don't act the innocent again with me, Delia. If you like him and you see him often, it will be a relationship. Let's just say I'd be very pleased if it is."

"Yes, but —"

"I have asked Edward and his sidekick to give you the breathing space you need to have normal relationships with members of the opposite sex. In light of his buying you this expensive automobile and that dress, among other things, he finally understands how he is not helping to correct the situation. I think this has been a wake-up call for us all. He has promised not to come home for at least a month, if not more.

"In exchange," she added before I could protest, "I have agreed to be more of an aunt, to provide you with whatever wardrobe you require, to introduce you to more well-to-do people and" — she paused and looked back at the door — "to protect you from anything more Sophia might do or attempt to do to harm you in any way. If I should just hear that she said anything more on this subject . . ." She pulled herself up. "I promised Edward I would seriously consider sending her away to another private school, far enough away so she couldn't hurt anyone

225

but herself. Edward was satisfied."

"I do not want to chase Edward away, Tía Isabela."

"You're not chasing him away. He's simply giving you the breathing room you need to develop normal relationships with young men, especially young men of the caliber of an Adan Bovio, Delia. As I said, I would be pleased to see that relationship blossom."

"But —"

"I can't imagine my daughter mature enough to develop such a relationship," she said sadly.

"I have no such relationship," I protested. "I have only attended a party with Adan and agreed to go to a dinner. That might be all we do together," I added, again thinking of Ignacio.

"I hope you're not so cavalier as to toss away someone like Adan Bovio before anything could blossom, Delia." She smiled. "I didn't when I was your age, and I am beginning to think you are more like me than you are like your mother, whether you want to admit it to yourself or not."

I started to shake my head. "I am not cavalier, but —"

Her smile flew off her face so quickly I stopped.

"Edward has asked permission to take

you on some stupid Mexican vacation during your holiday. It appears to be something you all want very much. I told him I would agree only if my terms are followed. I am still your legal guardian and would forbid it otherwise, understood?"

What was she saying? What were her terms? That I develop a romance with Adan Bovio?

"Do you want such a trip, or don't you?"

"*Sí,*" I said. It was my best hope to see Ignacio this year.

She smiled. "A mention of Mexico, and you revert to Spanish. How appropriate. Well, then," she said, rising. "It's all settled. You'll make me proud. Edward will stop hovering over you. The rumors will go away. Sophia will behave, and we'll turn this into a happy, productive family after all."

She started out and turned back to me at the door.

"You and I will spend more time together now, Delia. There are things I can teach you about high society that you might not learn yourself. I didn't anticipate all of this happening so quickly. I'll admit that I underestimated you, but I'm going to correct all that. Someday you'll thank me. Someday," she added, "you will even respect me."

I said nothing.

She nodded and left. I sat there looking at the floor.

Why did I feel as if I had just been forced into a bargain with the devil?

There was another knock at the door. Edward entered.

"We're on our way back to L.A., Delia. I think you're going to be all right now."

"You should not have made such an agreement with your mother, Edward."

"It's all right for now. Let's see if she lives up to her part of the bargain. She knows if she doesn't, you'll be on the phone to me immediately, and she knows I'll be doing my own checking up periodically. I'll say this for the queen, Delia, when she promises to do something, she does it. In that sense, she is most trustworthy. Often my mother is the harshest critic of herself.

"She's right about much of this, anyway. I suppose Jesse and I in our own way have been holding you back. You should have had some boyfriends by now, been dating more."

"No," I said. "It has nothing to do with you."

Ignacio's name and all that had been kept secret were once again about to spill from my lips.

"It certainly has nothing to do with you,"

he replied. "My mother admits that you are an outstanding Latin beauty. I even heard some faint notes of family pride in her voice. Maybe this is what she needs, what will bring her back. I do not hate my mother, Delia. I hate what she has made of herself, but I understand some of it, too. Let's just give it all a chance. I think Miss Horror Face is steaming in regret right now and realizing she has only hurt herself. Who knows, maybe this will help her, too, although it's hard to believe anything will."

"Edward —"

He put his finger on my lips.

"Shh . . . don't worry. Maybe Adan Bovio will help you get used to your new car. Anyway, he's had more experience with cars than I have. Enjoy, Delia. Have some fun. Don't live every day so seriously, intently. You'll miss some of the best times of your life. Listen to me. I'm talking as if I were already on social security. I'd better get out of here."

He kissed me on the cheek and left before I could say another word. I wanted to run after him, but instead I went to the window and watched him and Jesse get into his car right after Jesse looked up at me and waved. I waved back. Despite all Edward had said and hoped, I felt as if a lifeboat were sailing off in the distance when they drove off the grounds and disappeared behind a turn.

Almost as if he were watching from somewhere very close by, Adan Bovio called me moments later. "How's your ankle?" he asked first.

"It's much improved."

"Good. Maybe you'll be dancing sooner than you think. I suppose you've seen or been told about your picture in the newspaper today?"

"Yes, my cousin Edward brought it to me," I said, and Adan was quiet a moment. "He and his friend Jesse have started back to Los Angeles."

"Right. Well, if I can, I'd like to swing by in an hour or so just to give you something."

"Give me something? What?"

"It's a surprise. Nothing big. Not like a car," he added, and laughed. "I won't stay long. I know you have work for school."

"Yes, I do," I said.

"I'll be in and out. See you soon," he said, and hung up before I could think of any other reason to keep him from coming. Maybe . . . maybe I didn't want to think of one, I thought.

I brought my tray down and spoke to Señora Rosario and Inez for a few minutes. They were both concerned about my ankle, but I reassured them that I was doing well. They had both seen my picture in the newspaper, too, and they were impressed.

"I remember the first day you arrived from Mexico," Señora Rosario said. "You looked so frightened."

"You know that I soon had reason to be."

"*Sí,*" she said. "But those days are gone. You are no longer a little girl, Delia. You are a young woman, and remember, *vale más una madura que cien verdes*. One ripe fruit is worth a hundred green ones."

Inez nodded in agreement. I thanked them both and returned to my room to start on my homework. Soon after, Inez came up to tell me Adan Bovio had arrived and was waiting for me in the living room. I looked at Sophia's closed door as I followed Inez out and downstairs. Unlike Tía Isabela's confidence in her own power, I had no faith in her threats and punishments. Sophia was a wild thing and would surely wait. Her silence now was deceptive. *"Guardate del agua mansa,"* I could hear *mi abuela* Anabela warn. Beware of still waters.

I had faith only in my own eyes and ears.

Adan stood as I entered the living room. He wore a beautiful red shirt and white pants with a pair of white boat shoes. He looked even more handsome than he had the night before.

"Walking without your crutches?"

"I'm limping, but it's okay," I said.

He handed me a single yellow rose.

"Gracias." I smiled at the simplicity of his gift.

"I was worried about you, about all that had happened at the party. I thought you were somewhat saddened by all of it and did not have much of a good time despite the festivities."

"I was fine, Adan. Do not worry."

"The picture in the paper was quite exciting. The moment I saw it, I knew I had the perfect gift."

"It's a beautiful rose."

"No," he said, laughing. "That's just a small token. Here." He reached down to pick up a small wrapped package I hadn't seen on the marble coffee table. "For your desk, perhaps."

"Qué es?"

"Open it to see," he said.

I tore away the paper and looked at the picture that was in the newspaper. It was cropped so it was only of Adan and me, and it was in a beautiful gold frame. It wasn't a reproduction made from the paper, either. It was the actual photograph of us.

"How did you get it?"

"We know the publisher. I called first thing this morning and then hurried over to a gift shop. I hope I picked out a nice enough frame."

"Yes, it's beautiful."

"I think," he said, "that this will be the first of many pictures of you in newspapers."

It frightened me to hear that. "Why?"

"It just will be," he said. "Okay, I'm off. I promised not to take up much of your time."

He leaned over to kiss me on my cheek just as *mi tía* Isabela stepped into the living room.

"Oh, Mrs. Dallas. How are you?"

She looked from him to me and smiled. "Very well, thank you, Adan. I gather you two had a nice time last night."

"It was quite a bash."

"Yes, well, I would have gone myself, but I had a commitment I couldn't change. What do you have in your hands, Delia?"

"Oh, that's just a little something I thought she might enjoy having," Adan said quickly.

I showed it to her, and she nodded and smiled. "Very thoughtful, Adan. It's a particularly good picture of you both as well." She handed it back to me. "And I see you've brought her a beautiful rose as well."

"Yes. My father always brought my mother

233

glasses. She also put placemats on the patio table. I caught her looking at Adan and then smiling at me as she raised her eyebrows. Everyone was imagining too much, letting their fantasies run away with them, I thought, but I had no idea how to change their thinking, not with Tía Isabela behaving like a matchmaker.

She joined us, and soon after, Inez brought out the shrimp salad and bread. Tía Isabela got into a conversation with Adan about his father, the campaign, their home, or I should say homes. I learned Señor Bovio owned a condo in Los Angeles and a house in Big Bear, the mountains not far away. I sat and listened to them reminiscing about the grand social events they had both attended in the past and for the first time wondered how Tía Isabela had dealt with all of this the first time she had been shown the great wealth and glamour. She came from the same poor world from which I had come. There were things yet to learn from her, things she would rather teach me now than teach her own daughter.

I was afraid to ask about Sophia. Was she still up in her room pouting? Had she been invited to join us for the lunch? Did she even know Adan was here?

Adan and Tía Isabela had coffee after our

lunch, and then I walked him out to his car. We stopped to look at my yet-to-drive new sports car.

"It's a beauty," Adan said. "Since your foot isn't as bad as feared, do you think you would have time one day this week for me to help you get used to your car? I could come by after work. Since I'm the boss these days, I can make my own hours and come whenever you have the free time."

He walked around the car and looked at it with more desire than he was looking at me, I thought, and laughed.

"What?"

"You do love cars, Adan."

"I admit, they are my weakness." He smiled. "Some weaknesses aren't terrible to have. What do you say? We can't leave this beauty languishing."

"Call me tomorrow."

"I will. I hope you're not angry at my taking more of your time today."

"No. As *mi tía* Isabela said, I had to have lunch, too. Perhaps not as elaborate. I usually make my own lunch."

"I bet."

He kissed me on the cheek, then paused and kissed me on the lips. "I'll call you tomorrow evening," he whispered.

"Thank you for the gift," I told him. He

got into his car and looked out at me through the open window.

"That picture was a gift for both of us. I had two copies made, and mine is on my night table next to my bed. I'll be looking at you when I wake up every morning."

That idea sent a chill down my spine. Everything between us was moving too quickly. It was like trying to hold back a flood of emotions with a dam made of paper. I said nothing. He smiled and drove off. When I turned to go back into the house, I saw Sophia. She was in my room, looking down at me from my window. The moment I looked up at her, the curtain closed, and she was gone as quickly as a streak of lightning.

Despite Tía Isabela's assurances, I had no doubt that Sophia was also as dangerous even now. I hurried inside and up to my room, expecting to see some damage. I even pulled back the blanket on my bed to see if she had put something terrible in it, such as tacks or even a snake. When it came to Sophia, there were no limits on what terrible thing to imagine.

I found nothing, but it was obvious she must have seen the photograph in the gold frame. She kept track of everything I had and was given.

Tía Isabela had told Inez exactly where

to put it.

Mine, too, was on the night table next to the bed.

Adan would be the first face I would see when I woke up.

I dared not put a picture of Ignacio anywhere except in the front window of my memory.

And for the moment, Adan's handsome face was pushing Ignacio's into the shadows claimed by the third death.

10
BEWARE OF THORNS

At dinner that evening, I decided Sophia had lost a battle but not the war. When she finally came out of her room, she was neatly dressed, with no rings in her nose or anything else that usually annoyed and disturbed Tía Isabela. Her hair was brushed and pinned very neatly, and she wore one of her prettier blouse-and-skirt combinations. She wasn't overly made up. In fact, she wore no lipstick, black, which Tía Isabela especially hated, overly bright red or otherwise.

At the table, she was Little Miss Politeness, performing perfect dinner etiquette and saying nothing that could disturb her mother. She was even polite to me, passing dishes and thanking me for whatever I passed to her, but I didn't for one moment believe in her performance. It would take more than being grounded on the weekends for a month and threats of greater punishments to rehabilitate Sophia Dallas. If she really did turn over a new leaf, it would be a leaf with new thorns as well, the only change being that they might be more difficult to see.

Nevertheless, she began the dinner by reciting a speech she had surely read in a book or gotten over the phone from a friend.

"I'm sorry about my behavior. I know I have no justification for it. My excuse is only that I have been miserable myself. I'm disappointed in my failure to lose weight, and I've been a little bitch, especially to you, Delia. I admit that I have been jealous and done things I shouldn't have done. Some of my so-called good friends have instigated a lot, too. I'll try to be a better cousin."

I looked at Tía Isabela, expecting her usual skeptical expression. Surely, I thought, she knew Sophia was not sincere, but to my surprise, she pretended to believe and accept her apology.

"I'm happy to hear you say those things, Sophia. I hope that's all true."

"It is."

"Good. Let's see how it goes," she added, holding up the promise of a reprieve.

"Do you think I can get some help with that math tonight?" Sophia asked me, with one eye on her mother. "I didn't really pay enough attention in class, and as usual, it all looks like gibberish to me."

"Yes, I'll help you with it," I said.

"Thank you," she said. She flashed another smile at her mother.

Am I in the middle of some play? I wondered. Do they lie so much to each other that they have learned to accept and to live on them?

"Mother," Sophia sang, "can Delia and I go to school in her car tomorrow?"

"Oh, I need to practice with it first," I said quickly. "And I should give my ankle another day or so."

"Yes, you should," Sophia agreed. "You know, Mother, it is a very complex automobile. You should hire someone to teach her about the car."

"I think she has a very good teacher already," Tía Isabela said. That surprised me as much as it did Sophia. How did she know what Adan had offered to do?

"Who?" Sophia asked.

Tía Isabela smiled at me and nodded to urge me to tell her.

"Adan asked to do it," I admitted. "He'll come by one day this week."

For a moment, Sophia lost her deceptive sweet face but quickly brought it back.

"That's a good idea. He owns a lot of sports cars, I hear. Doesn't he?" she asked me.

"I do not know how many cars he owns or what kind of cars they are."

"I'm sure you will soon," she muttered. It fell out of her mouth the way water or something she had gulped too much might dribble. She dropped her gaze quickly to her food and began eating again. I looked at Tía Isabela.

She wore an odd expression. She looked troubled more than angry. Was she worried that somehow, some way, Sophia would turn Adan against me?

The remainder of our dinner was passed in the all-too-familiar silence. Afterward, Sophia came to my room with her math book and tried to be attentive as I explained the homework. I could see talking about the homework and making her do the problems herself was like forcing her to take some bitter herb to cure a headache or a stomachache. She listened and successfully completed the problems, but she hated every moment of it.

"How can you care about any of this?" she asked, gazing at the textbook pages with disgust.

"I would never have had such opportunity back in Mexico," I told her. "Thinking about going to college was like thinking about going to the moon. When I was a little girl, my father always told me never to turn away any knowledge or information, for it has a way of finding a place sometime in your life, often when you least expect it."

She flashed a smirk and then became a little thoughtful. "How come if your family was so poor and everyone worked so hard, you had so much time to spend with your parents?"

I smiled.

"What's so funny?" she asked angrily.

"I am not laughing at you. I am laughing at what you would think if you saw a party in my village or parents out on what we call here an evening out. The family is always together. There is no such thing as a babysitter. Most of the homes in the village have only one bedroom. Parents and their children are together much, much more. Some children even go with their parents to work. I worked on the soy farm at a very young age, actually as soon as I could become a pair of fruitful hands, as my grandmother would say."

As if she realized she was getting interested, she shook her head emphatically and scooped up her books. "Sounds like a terrible life. I would have run away."

"You're running away from your life here, aren't you?" I shot back, perhaps a little too sharply.

She did pause as if she had been slapped. "Huh?"

"You mock your school even though it's an expensive school with more opportunities for students than the public schools provide. You don't want even to know about your mother's businesses. You say you don't want to go to college. You dislike so many of the other students. You seem bored all the time."

Her eyes actually became glossy with tears, and I felt guilty. "Well, maybe you'll rub off on me, and I'll go pick soybeans and be happy," she said. "Thanks for helping me with this stupid math."

She turned and rushed out, closing the door sharply behind her. I couldn't become close to her even if we were stuck together in the same dress, I thought.

The next morning, she came down to breakfast rather than demand that it be brought up to her. I found out later, however, that Tía Isabela had instructed Inez not to bring Sophia her breakfast. It was part of her punishment. She was told to return directly home from school, too, and Señor Garman would be there at the end of the day to get her. Violate one of the new rules, and she would extend her punishment.

The sword of threats over Sophia's head

worked like a steel cage and at least kept her contained at school. I could see her friends were disappointed in her. They had so wanted to continue the onslaught on my reputation and have fun, or what they considered fun, tormenting me. My picture in the paper with Adan and Fani's continued friendship with me depressed them as well. It was as if I had been installed in the house of royalty. The girls, including Katelynn, who had helped flame the flames of the nasty stories by reporting me at the restaurant with Edward and Jesse, were now attending to me as if I were the princess and not Fani, or at least as important. Everyone wanted to know about Adan and what it was like going out with an "older man."

I was flattered but simultaneously depressed about it. Apparently, what Jesse and *mi tía* Isabela had suggested was true. Having a relationship with Adan, or at least having it appear so, was the best antidote for the poison Sophia, Christian, and their clique of friends had tried pouring into everyone else's ears. I had the distinct feeling that if I didn't get along with Adan and continue dating him, the rumors, like some aggressive cancer, would come charging back to destroy me and infuriate Tía Isabela. The trip to Mexico would be forbidden. I would soon be the one in a cage and not Sophia. I felt like a prostitute who couldn't deny that her client was desirable, for I had yet to discover something distasteful or unpleasant about Adan Bovio. A part of me hoped I would, and a part of me feared I would.

He called that night, and we made plans to meet at my aunt's house the next day to practice with my car as soon as I returned from school. My ankle had improved enough so that I had barely a limp now. Señor Garman returned the crutches to the emergency care. Sophia continually asked me when Adan would be coming around to help me learn how to drive my new car. I knew that she was hoping Tía Isabela would then give permission for me to drive her to school. Perhaps she harbored the belief that she could talk me into taking her other places as well.

I discovered that Fani knew what was happening between Adan and me almost as soon as I did or perhaps a little beforehand. I had the sense that they spoke often and that I was the chief topic of their conversation. I began to believe Fani was acting as a matchmaker almost as enthusiastically as *mi tía* Isabela.

"You two really looked good together at Danielle's party," Fani told me.

"With my crutches? We couldn't even

247

dance."

"You still made a good impression, and that photographer managed to keep the crutches out of the picture, didn't he? All I've heard are good things about the two of you. My parents said it, too, and they spoke to other adults at the party. You're the talk of the town, Delia, our own Latina Cinderella."

All of this talk made me very nervous when Adan arrived on Wednesday. He brought me another gift, a pair of designer sunglasses that I later found out cost hundreds of dollars. Even my aunt would be jealous of them.

"You can't keep giving me presents," I told him when I unwrapped the box.

"You can't drive a car like that wearing an ordinary pair of sunglasses, Delia. It's practically a sin."

I laughed and put on the glasses. When I looked in the mirror in the entryway, I was impressed with myself. Immediately, I studied the shadows behind me, too, searching for some sign of the *ojo malvado*. Adan was watching me, a slight smile of amusement on his lips.

"What?" he asked, seeing the expression on my face.

With Ignacio, I would not have hesitated

to explain my belief in the evil eye, but I was afraid Adan would laugh at me and perhaps not want to have anything to do with a girl who was so superstitious.

"Nothing. They are beautiful. *Gracias,* Adan. But you spend too much money on me."

"Nothing compared with what your cousin Edward spends," he said. It was like a sharp cut. He saw the pained expression on my face and quickly added, "Besides, I like buying you things. You really appreciate it. Most of the girls I know and have known are so damn spoiled I'd have to buy them a jumbo jet to get a sincere thank-you."

I continued to look at him in the mirror. It seemed safer to talk to him this way. It was more like a dream, a fantasy, an imaginary relationship that didn't compare to the reality of Ignacio and me. It was as if Adan and I were characters in a movie we were both watching. To the other girls at school, it truly seemed that way. We had quickly become what our English teacher would say, quoting from Shakespeare, the stuff that dreams were made of. Maybe if I, too, believed this and conducted myself this way, I would not put Ignacio and myself into any real danger. Could I treat it all as lightly as air, slip in and out of my own body, and speak like a puppet? Would Adan notice, and would that make him angry?

"Thank you, Adan," I said, and he smiled and reached for my hand when I turned to him.

"C'mon. Let's get to that car. You have the key, right?"

"Right," I said, laughing at his enthusiasm.

We went out quickly. I opened the locked doors as Jesse had shown me, and Adan got into the driver's seat. First, he went through every button, every control. He had me get into the driver's seat so we could put the seat's position and height into memory. All I would have to do was touch a number, and the seat would move to fit me. Even the side mirrors moved to fit the way I would look out at them.

We went through the climate-control system and the audio, and then he started to explain the navigator. We put in the address of *mi tía* Isabela's *hacienda* first.

"All you'll have to do," he explained, "is push this location icon that says 'home,' and the car will tell you what turns to make until you are here."

I could see he enjoyed my astonishment. "Most of the roads outside our village have no signs," I told him. "However, there is always someone who can tell you where to go or how to get there."

"There's not always someone here," he said. "And you can't depend on their directions, anyway. Besides, you have to be careful about whom you talk to when you're driving this car. A beautiful young woman who looks well-to-do is a moving target."

I nodded, impressed with his concern.

"Do you want the top up or down?"

"Maybe down," I said.

"It's a hardtop convertible. Watch this," he said, pressing the button. The top lifted up and back. "Neat, huh?"

"Yes, it does so much."

"Only what you tell it to do," he said, smiling.

We started away, and he explained more about the engine, the gears, and the driving. Finally, he pulled to the side of the road, and we changed seats. I pressed the memory button for my seat, and it moved closer and higher. I screamed with delight, and he laughed. It took awhile for me to get used to the accelerator. The car was so powerful that if I pressed too hard, too quickly, we both were snapped backward, screaming. Eventually, it all became much easier, and I became comfortable.

"It's a beautiful piece of machinery," he

said, stroking the dashboard as if to him the automobile was really alive. "You're going to enjoy it."

"Thank you for helping me," I said when we pulled up to the *hacienda*.

We put the top back up.

"You did great. I imagine you are quite a good student, Delia. Your teachers must enjoy having you."

"Thank you, Adan."

"Can I dominate your weekend this weekend?" he asked before opening the car door.

"Dominate? What does this mean?"

"Well, we're going to dinner Friday night, right?"

"Yes."

"I'd like to take you to Newport Beach on Saturday and give you a ride on my boat."

"You have a boat, too?"

"Yes," he said, laughing. "It's not a big yacht, but the weather is supposed to be perfect, and we can go to Catalina Island for a nice lunch. We'll have dinner on the way home from Newport."

"This is so much," I said. "I cannot imagine it all."

"Don't. No need to imagine it. We'll do it," he said. "Okay?"

I hesitated.

"Do you think I should go in and ask your aunt's permission?" he asked, thinking that was the reason I had not yet replied.

"No," I said. It almost made me laugh. She would probably leap at saying yes.

"Then I can make plans for Saturday?"

"I have not gone in anything but a rowboat," I said.

"You're in for a great time, Delia. You know," he said, reaching over to take my hand, "when you can enjoy the things you have with someone who really appreciates them, you really appreciate them, too. You become grateful, and that's a good thing, no?"

"Sí."

"Then you'll be doing me a big favor by coming with me," he said.

He was either very sincere or very clever, I thought, but at the moment, I didn't want to work too hard at figuring it out. He leaned closer to kiss me, and then we got out of my car. We walked hand in hand to his.

"It was a great afternoon," he said. "Thank you, Delia."

"No, thank you for helping me."

"Don't go rushing off to pick up some new guy in this car," he warned playfully. "I don't want to be responsible for driving you off, too."

"I wouldn't do such a thing," I said.

"I'm just kidding, Delia. You're fantastic," he said, and kissed me again.

Then he got into his car, smiled at me, and drove away. I stood watching him disappear around the gate before turning to go inside. When I closed the door behind me, Tía Isabela appeared so quickly I had the sense she had been watching us from some window.

"What a beautiful pair of sunglasses," she said, walking over to me. She plucked them off my head and looked at them. "I imagine Adan gave them to you."

"Yes."

"Do you have any idea how much these cost?"

"No."

"I have a similar pair but not as nice as these. Just take good care of them," she said, putting them on me again. "They look very good on you."

"Thank you, Tía Isabela."

"Well, how was your driving lesson?" she asked.

"It was good. He says I'm competent enough to drive the car myself."

"That's nice. Anything else?" she asked. The way she asked with such expectation made me wonder if she didn't have secret microphones planted in the bushes to overhear our conversation.

"He asked me to go with him on Saturday to Newport Beach to go on his boat."

"That's wonderful, Delia. I'm happy for you."

We both suddenly realized Sophia was standing at the top of the stairway.

"Where did you get those sunglasses?" she asked, taking a step down.

"Where do you think she got them, Sophia? It's too early for Santa Claus."

"Not for her," she said. "They look beautiful on you," she added, quickly realizing she had reverted to her normal nasty, jealous self.

"Thank you," I said.

"So, you had a good lesson?"

"Yes, I did."

"Good. Can she drive us to school tomorrow and always, Mother?" she asked.

"It's up to her. It's her car," Tía Isabela said.

Sophia looked at me hopefully.

"We're just going to go to school and back," I said firmly.

"Fine. Where else can I go, anyway?" she said petulantly.

"Exactly," Tía Isabela said. "And don't let me hear that you tried to talk Delia into going anywhere else."

She glared threateningly at Sophia, then turned and walked away.

Sophia stood gazing down at me. If her eyes were daggers, I'd be bleeding to death, I thought. But she smiled quickly and returned to her bedroom, confident, I was sure, that she could manipulate me soon and get what she wanted.

I went up to my room to write a letter for Ignacio. My conscience was dictating the words in my head so quickly I had to get to pen and paper.

Dear Ignacio,

I continue to miss and pray for you daily. My cousin Edward has given me a very generous gift. When I see you, I will explain some of the reason for it. It has to do with his relationship with his sister and how difficult she has made life for me here, as you know.

The gift is a car. I imagine you are shocked to hear it, but not as shocked as I was to see it. I have learned how to drive it and will drive it to and from school, as well as to your family's home now. In fact, I hope to do that very soon, although it will be hard during the week, because my cousin Sophia will be riding home with me. Maybe I will drive there this coming Sunday after your family has returned from church.

I paused and held my pen in the air. I did not want to lie to Ignacio, but I didn't want to tell him very much about Adan. Still, I was afraid the newspaper picture would somehow find its way to him and if I mentioned nothing, he would surely be suspicious and hurt.

Because I am now attending the private school where only the most wealthy people here send their children, I have been invited to some gala parties. I have tried not to become too friendly with too many other students. I don't think they will be good friends, but I am also afraid that if I behave strangely, it might create some suspicions.

A picture of me attending one of these parties was in the newspaper.

Attending these parties is not going to cause me to forget you. I promise that, and now I have a wonderful surprise to tell you.

My cousin Edward and his friend Jesse want to take me to Mexico during the next school holiday. They want to go to my village. As soon as I know the details, I'll get them to you. Perhaps somehow, some way, you can meet me there.

I have not told them about you, of course, so we'll have to figure out a way, but isn't it wonderful?

I will count the days until it happens.

Love,

Delia

There, I said to myself, *I have told him the truth, without revealing anything that would make him sad, and I have even given him hope.* However, if and when I sent this letter, I had better be sure the Mexican trip with Edward and Jesse would happen, I thought. Of course, this meant I would have to keep Tía Isabela pleased.

I gazed at myself in the mirror. I was still wearing my new designer sunglasses and hadn't even realized it.

I wondered if I was really concerned with only pleasing Tía Isabela.

Snapping out of my musings, I folded the letter and put it into an envelope, hoping to deliver it to the Davilas on Sunday. Somehow, I would sneak off, and now that I did not have to depend on Casto for a ride, I should have an easier time of doing it.

Right after dinner, Adan called me. I had just begun my homework.

"I know you're doing your schoolwork,"

he said, "but I just wanted to see if you had mentioned Saturday to your aunt."

"Yes."

"No problem, I hope."

"No," I said. If he only knew how hard she was pushing me in his direction, I thought.

"Good. Then I'll make the calls I have to make to set things up for us. Enjoy your new car," he added.

"I'll try," I said.

"Uh-oh," he said. "I think I hear something unpleasant in your voice. That means you have a rider along, doesn't it?"

"*Sí, señor,*" I said and he laughed.

"They should make these cars with an eject button, so you can send your passenger out through the roof like a jet pilot."

I laughed at the image of Sophia flying up and out.

"It's good to hear your laugh, Delia. It's like music," he said.

I went to sleep thinking of those sentences. "It's good to hear your laugh, Delia. It's like music."

I used to go to sleep thinking of Ignacio.

When I went down to breakfast in the morning, I was surprised to find Sophia already dressed and waiting. Tía Isabela had yet to come out of her bedroom. She would be pleased, I thought. Sophia was dressed quite differently from the way she usually dressed for school. She wore a very nice light yellow skirt and matching blouse, had her hair brushed and pinned, and again wore hardly any makeup. She wore a pair of earrings that actually were coordinated with her outfit, too. Instead of her usual dreary, half-sleepy self, she was bright and cheery.

"Good morning, Delia. I told Mrs. Rosario to make you her scrambled eggs. I know how much you like them. You need a good breakfast today. It's a big day for you," Sophia said. "Driving your own car to school. How lucky you are. But I'm not jealous," she added quickly. "I know my mother will be buying me my own car soon. With your help, I'll get my school grades up. You'll want that to happen. That way, you won't have to drive me everywhere, and you can take someone else in your two-seater." She winked.

"I'll help you in any way I can with your work, Sophia, but I can't take the tests for you. You have to spend more time studying."

"Oh, I will. I will," she promised.

Señora Rosario brought out my scrambled eggs.

"Gracias, señora."

She glanced at Sophia and gave me a subtle

look of warning. I nodded.

"No se preocupe," I told her. I wanted to assure her that she did not need to worry about me. *"Antes se atrapa al mentiroso que al cojo."*

She laughed.

"What did you say?" Sophia demanded.

"I thanked her for the eggs and told her she made them just like my grandmother used to make them," I said, which was, of course, ironic because it was a lie. What I really had said was "It's easier to catch a liar than a cripple."

For Sophia, who was so accustomed to lies and lying, it was also ironic that she could be fooled so easily. Perhaps she had left the truth so far behind that she could never find it again.

"Good," she said. "Very good, Mrs. Rosario. Thank you."

Señora Rosario couldn't hide her smile, so she quickly left.

"You know," Sophia said, leaning toward me to whisper, "I really do have to pay more attention in Spanish class as well. I should learn how to speak it so I know when the employees are saying things behind our backs."

"There are better reasons for you to learn how to speak Spanish, Sophia," I said, laughing.

Tía Isabela was also surprised to see Sophia up and ready for school so early and so well dressed. She looked at me as if I had been somehow a good influence. I felt guilty about taking any credit for any change in Sophia that was good.

"What are you doing today, Mother?" Sophia asked, which was something I had never heard her ask. She usually had no interest in her mother's business affairs or even her social life. Tía Isabela's eyebrows lifted.

"We're closing on a strip mall, Sophia. Do you know what that means?"

"No."

"We're going to own it, and everyone, all the stores in it, will be paying us rent. It's a steady stream of income."

"Damn, there is so much I have to learn," Sophia said, shaking her head and finishing her coffee. "I'll just be a minute, Delia."

She hurried out to the stairs.

Señora Rosario brought Tía Isabela her juice and coffee and her newspaper.

"I think I'll have your famous scrambled eggs, too, this morning, Mrs. Rosario."

"Very good, Mrs. Dallas."

She hurried back to the kitchen. Tía Isabela and I looked at each other. She smiled.

"I know what you're thinking, Delia, but

take my advice, accepting even the illusion of happiness and hope is better than the alternative. It enables you to go on. *Comprende, señorita?*"

"*Sí*, Tía Isabela."

Why shouldn't I understand? I thought.

That was exactly what I was doing now and had been since the day I had arrived.

11
DRIVING SOPHIA

One of my Mexican classmates in the ESL class at the public school I attended when I first arrived here had told me the easiest way to make new friends in America was to have a car. I quickly discovered she had not been exaggerating. With the speed of a lightning bolt, Sophia spread the news about my driving her to school in the sports car her brother, Edward, had bought for me. I could practically feel the way the other students were now looking at me. Many who usually hardly said a word to me smiled and tried to start conversations. It was as though I had been accepted into a private club.

It amused me to hear the way Sophia described the car to her friends, emphasizing "we" with everything. She also made it clear that now that I had a car, her mother was soon going to buy her one. In fact, Tía Isabela, according to Sophia, was already researching models and prices.

"You know my mother," she told Alisha and the girls who had gathered outside the Spanish classroom. "She has to be sure she's not being ripped off and that she makes the best possible deal. She has friends in the automobile business. In fact, she bawled out Edward for not coming to her first before he spent the money on Delia's car. She could have saved him thousands, not that he cares."

She also let some of her friends believe that I would soon be willing to let her use my car.

"Until I get my own," she emphasized.

Overhearing Sophia's conversations amused me, but they also confirmed that she was not going through any real personality changes. Her sweet talk and her smiles for me were like flies hitting a closed window. I doubted there would ever be a time when I would open it and let her inside, a time when I would trust her with anything more than hello.

Christian Taylor was quite impressed with my car. During the lunch hour, he went outside with some of his amigos and looked it over. Sophia tried to get me to give her the key so she could show the car to Christian and his friends, but I politely told her I would rather not.

"Then you come out and show it to them," she urged.

"I want to do some reading for social studies," I told her. "Maybe later."

"You've got to learn how to relax, Delia. You're too intense. Social studies class won't go away."

"Maybe later," I repeated, and she pouted.

"You know," she said, "you could meet me halfway. I'm trying to be a better cousin."

Halfway, I thought, recalling something Edward had once told me. "You give my sister an inch," he had said, "and she won't just take a foot. She'll take all of you."

"I'm sorry," I told her. "I do not like Christian Taylor. I'd rather ignore him."

"He's just another boy. Don't get so uptight about him," Sophia advised. "I can handle Christian Taylor."

"I can handle a rattlesnake," I said. "In fact, I have, but I'd rather not."

"You have?"

"Where I lived, you learn to get along with everything in nature. If you leave them alone, they will leave you alone, unlike Christian Taylor. Snakes may be smarter than us. They'd rather ignore us."

She shook her head. "I don't know if I'll ever understand you."

"Work harder in Spanish class," I said. I knew it wasn't what she meant, but I was feeling more confident and wanted to tease and frustrate her.

She made a face and walked off, but at the end of the day, she was waiting at my car with her girlfriends.

"It's a beautiful car, Delia," Trudy said. "I bet it can go very fast."

"Too fast," I said, "if you're not careful."

"Who wants to be careful?" Alisha said, and they all laughed.

I unlocked the doors, and Sophia opened hers and stood there smiling at her friends.

"Just feel the leather," she told them, and stepped back so each could touch the seat.

I got in quickly and started the engine. "We must go home now," I said.

"Right. Talk to you all later," Sophia told them. "Do you want to stop for a frozen mocha or something, Delia?" she asked, loudly enough for them all to hear, before she closed the door. "I'll buy them for us."

"No, thank you, Sophia. Your mother might be waiting for us."

"She's probably at some meeting."

"Maybe," I said. "It's better we just go straight home as we promised."

"Can you put the top down, at least?"

I thought about it and nodded.

The girls squealed with delight when they saw the roof lift up and go back. Sophia sat back, gloating.

I drove us out slowly, and it was lucky I did so, too, because before we reached the entrance to the parking lot, Christian Taylor stepped in our way, smiling. I had to hit the brakes fast.

"Estupido!" I screamed at him.

He laughed and leaned over the car. "Wow. Isn't this too much car for a girl like you? I know I'm too much man."

"You're the only one who knows it," I told him, and accelerated.

He leaped back, and Sophia roared with laughter.

"Now you're turning into my kind of girl," she said. "Cousin."

I looked at her and back through the rearview mirror at Christian, who was complaining to his friends. Sophia turned on the radio loudly and lit a cigarette.

"You want one?"

"No," I said. "I am not that kind of girl," I said. "I am sorry for my behavior, but he makes me . . ."

"I know what you mean," Sophia said. "You don't have to explain when it comes to Christian Taylor or any other boy, for that matter."

It seemed no matter what I said, she would find a way to become my new pal, and all because of the car.

I drove on, fuming inside.

Adan called that night to see how I did, and we talked for almost a half hour. He was very excited about an important political endorsement his father had received. He said it was looking good for him to receive some labor and police endorsements as well.

"I'm beginning to think my father could really win," he said, which surprised me.

"Didn't you think so before?"

"I hoped, but now it's more than hope. There's a big Latino vote in this state, and we're going to get a sizable portion of it," he added. "But that's all boring stuff. I'd rather talk about you."

If he could see through the phone, he would see a very thoughtful face and not a face full of delight. Every warm feeling I had for him and every moment of pleasure we had together were truly like pins in my heart because of my feelings for Ignacio. Later, when I went to sleep, I dreamed he had heard about Adan and me and it had driven him to become a criminal in Mexico. His family, especially his father, cursed me. I woke gasping and nearly cried because of how vivid the nightmare had been.

My letter to Ignacio still lay under my panties in my dresser drawer. I struggled to come up with a way to drive to the Davilas' home, but with Sophia clinging so closely to me now, it was difficult. I had been hoping that my company, even in my sports car, would bore her eventually, but she was still basking in the glow and enjoying the way her girlfriends envied her. Finally, on Thursday, she asked me for a favor I was perhaps too eager to grant.

"My mother is at a meeting in Los Angeles today and won't be home until evening. She told me last night after dinner," she said as we drove to school. "We can go meet my girlfriends at Alisha's house for a while. It will be fun. We can talk and have something to drink and listen to music and —"

"No, I cannot go there," I said. "I have too much to do."

She was quiet until we were nearly to the school.

"Okay, but will you at least do me a favor and not tell on me? I'll go home after school with Alisha, and she'll bring me home at dinnertime."

"What you do and where you go are not my business," I replied, instead of saying I would lie for her. It was enough to please her.

"You're making a mistake not coming with

us after school," she said when we parked. "But," she added quickly when I started to look angry, "that's fine as long as you don't go blabbing to my mother. We have to trust and help each other if we're to be real cousins, Delia."

"Tía Isabela did not ask me to spy on you," I said. "What I don't know I don't know."

She smiled. "Good. Have a nice day," she said, getting out.

If you only knew how much nicer it will be now, I thought, and followed. Knowing that I was free to drive to the Davilas' home later made me fidgety and impatient in my classes and even at lunch. Fani noticed and remarked about it.

"Something bothering you?" she asked. "Adan, maybe?"

"No, nothing."

"Let me know the moment he does something that displeases you, Delia. Although he is older than I am, I am more like a big sister to him."

"Has he not had any serious love affairs?" I asked her.

"Adan?" She laughed. "To him, every love affair is serious, but serious is not a long-term condition. Perhaps he's changing," she added quickly when she saw my reaction and thought I was terribly disappointed. Part of me was relieved. I was still walking a tight-rope of emotions. "After all," she continued, "he's getting older, and now with his father a serious contender for a U.S. Senate seat, he's got to at least appear more stable. His playboy days are numbered. Maybe you're numbering them even less and less."

I said nothing. My mind was on Ignacio and the Davilas now. As soon as the final bell of the day rang, I was out the door. I drove off before Sophia and her friends could corner me and try to talk me into going to their after-school party. I drove a little too fast to get home and to the letter I had written, but this was my opportunity.

I scooped it up and was out the door again before anyone even realized I had come home. On my way down the driveway, I did wave to Señor Casto, who was doing some work with a gardener down near the east wall of the property. Then I shot out of the gate and was on my way. Ignacio's father and brother weren't home when I arrived, but his mother and his youngest sister were there, preparing the evening meal. When his sister let me in and I entered the kitchen, I saw the look of happiness and relief on his mother's face.

"Delia, it has been so long since we last saw you," she said, wiping her hands on a dish towel and then hugging me. "How are you?"

"I am fine. It has been difficult for me to get away," I said.

She nodded, but I saw her eyes shift toward the newspaper on the small table by the pantry door. It was open to the picture of me and Adan and Fani. I went to it.

"This was a birthday party I had to attend," I began.

"Ignacio's father wanted to send it to him, but I begged him not to do that. He says Ignacio should get used to the idea that you are off to a new life, and he must be off to his new life."

"No!" I said. "This is nothing. I am planning on returning to Mexico during the school holiday, in fact, and I will see him if he can meet me in my village."

"Oh," she said, impressed. She thought a moment, glanced at the article, and shook her head. "For now," she said, "it would be better not to mention the trip to my husband. He will find something wrong with it."

"Sí. This is my letter to Ignacio. I will get the information on the trip for you to get to him as soon as I know the details."

She took the letter.

"It will get to him?" I asked, worried that Ignacio's father had forbidden new letters.

"Sí," she said. *"I will make sure."*
"Gracias, señora."

She insisted that I sit and have a glass of Jarritos lime soda with one of her just-baked Mexican chocolate meringue cookies. I told her they were as delicious as I remembered my grandmother's cookies. I was there more than an hour, telling her about my school, my new car, and life at my aunt's *hacienda*. Every once in a while, I looked toward the door, anticipating Ignacio's father's arrival, but he did not come while I was there. She could see the anticipation was making me nervous and reassured me that she would make things okay.

We hugged, both near tears thinking about Ignacio, and then I left. When I made the turn onto the main highway, I passed Ignacio's father and Ignacio's brother coming home in their truck. I had the top down, and they both turned in surprise at the sight of me driving such a car. I barely had time to nod.

My stomach was a hive of mad bees all the way home. I was afraid for Ignacio's mother when she defended me. Now I was the source of arguments in their *casa*, I thought. I was still bringing unhappiness to the people who should love me and whom I loved. When would that end?

Driving up to *mi tía* Isabela's *hacienda,* I was surprised to see Alisha's automobile. Why had she brought Sophia home so early? I was anticipating her not returning until just before dinner. She would surely be afraid that Señora Rosario would mention her not being at dinner. I parked and went into the house. It was quiet downstairs, but as I ascended, I could hear the music pouring out of Sophia's bedroom. The door was partially opened. I quickly discovered that was so one of them could spot me entering my bedroom. Instantly, Sophia, Alisha, Trudy, and Delores marched in behind me.

From the expressions they all wore and the glassy look in their eyes, I could see they had all been drinking, probably vodka, because they were able to disguise it in fruit juices. Trudy carried a paper cup and sipped it, smiling.

"So, where were you?" Sophia asked. "I thought you had too much work to do and couldn't go to Alisha's house after school."

"Why are you here?" I asked, instead of answering.

"Alisha's mother didn't go where she was supposed to go. It wasn't . . . what's the word, Trudy?"

"Conducive."

"Yeah, conducive. You know that word? It

275

means favorable for what we wanted. Right, Trudy?" she asked before I could respond.

"That's it. It was not exactly the right situation for our festivities," she said, giggling.

"So? Where were you?" Sophia asked. "Huh?"

"I had some chores," I said.

"Chores?" She looked at her girlfriends, who were all smiling. "It couldn't have been the chore of being with Adan Bovio, could it?"

I had no hesitation about lying to Sophia, and she had, after all, given me a good excuse.

"Yes, it could."

"That's bull crap!" she screamed, her hands on her hips now. "Adan Bovio called here for you just a half hour ago. I heard your phone ringing and answered it."

I just stared at her. Even lying to her caused more problems. Lies never work for long. Some die the instant they're born.

"You didn't just happen to go and meet another boy, did you? One of your Mexican boyfriends, maybe?" She glanced impishly at her girlfriends, who drew closer to her as if to add their support. They all wore the same look of self-satisfaction.

"What I do and where I go are not your business," I said.

"Ha!" She swayed. The vodka was settling into her brain. "What did I tell you, girls? The Latina Cinderella has found another Latino prince. Who is he? How's Adan going to feel about it? Where did you meet him? It's no one from our school, is it? Well?"

"Your mother will not be happy to hear about this after-school party," I replied, focusing sharply on her. I took a step toward her. "She might very well add on to your punishment."

"She won't be happy about you going off to be with other boys, your whoring around."

"Get out of my room! All of you!" I said, pointing at the door.

"I guess I touched a sensitive spot." She nodded and held her cold smile on her lips.

"Yeah, her G-spot," Trudy said, and they all laughed.

"You know what that is, Delia?" Alisha asked.

"She knows," Sophia said. "Bradley Whitfield showed her."

Something broke inside me. It was as if a dam holding back the heat in my blood burst and all of it rushed into my head. I spun around, seized the footstool at the base of my bed, and turned on them with the stool's legs forward. They screamed when I charged at them. Trudy dropped her cup, and they all ran out of my room. I slammed the door closed.

I would ask Tía Isabela to install a lock on the door, I thought, gasping and fuming. I heard them close Sophia's door, too, after Sophia screamed about me being dangerously crazy.

It took me awhile to calm down, but after I did, I actually laughed at how I had frightened them. They were nothing to fear after all.

Adan called again about a half hour later. I expected that he would ask where I had been, but he didn't. Instead, we talked about the weekend, Friday night's dinner, and the schedule we would follow on Saturday. I actually listened much more than I spoke. He realized that I was unusually quiet and he asked if everything was all right.

"It's my cousin Sophia," I said.

"What is she doing now?"

"It's better just to ignore her. *Ella cocinará en su propio jugo.*"

"What's that mean?"

"She'll cook in her own juice," I said.

"I'm going to need your help with some of those great Spanish sayings. I'm helping my father with his speeches."

"It's not a great saying. I make up my own sometimes. I'm like my grandmother in that way."

"It's great to me. What works works. I'll see you tomorrow night," he said. "I have the number for animal control if you need it for your cousin."

"Maybe I will," I said, laughing.

I heard Sophia's friends leave, and then I showered and changed to go down to dinner. Sophia came to the table timidly but gathered her courage after Señora Rosario and Inez had brought in the food and left.

"If you don't say anything about me, I won't say anything about you," she offered.

"I don't have to make any bargains. I have nothing about which I am ashamed."

"Still, it's better we don't go ratting on each other to my mother. Deal?"

"Stay out of my room, and never answer my phone again," I said firmly. "If you don't —"

"Okay, okay. Who cares what you do in your room or who you see, anyway?"

She pouted and picked at her food, leaving most of it on the plate.

"My mother better get me my own car soon," she muttered. "Or she's going to be sorry when my trust kicks in. If I have anything to do with any of these properties and businesses . . . I'm going to hire my own attorney to look at all the documents my father left."

I said nothing to encourage her or discourage her.

"I don't want any dessert," she told Inez, and rose from her seat. She walked to the doorway and turned. "I'm not going to school with you tomorrow. Christian Taylor is picking me up and will bring me home."

"You keep saying you don't think much of him, but you do things with him," I reminded her.

"We have things to discuss. You can dislike someone and still have things in common, you know."

"No, I don't know," I said, shaking my head and smiling at her.

"That's right," she said, her eyes small and cold. "You don't. You don't know everything, Delia."

She stomped out and up the stairs.

Later, Edward called me. "I waited as long as I could," he said. "How's the new world going?"

"Sophia is not really changing," I told him. "But I can handle her. Don't worry, Edward."

"No one can handle her, Delia. I do worry. And Adan Bovio? How are things with the possible new senator's son?"

I told him of Adan's invitations and the

things we were planning to do.

"I'm happy for you if you're happy, Delia. I saw my mother today, by the way. She actually stopped by while she was in Los Angeles and took Jesse and me for coffee. She's really buying into your relationship with Adan, so if you end it, let her down slowly. That's the only advice I'll give you about it. I'm no expert when it comes to these sort of things."

"Thank you. Have you thought more about Mexico?"

"You still want to go with us?" he asked with surprise.

"Oh, yes, very much, Edward. Yes!" I said. My enthusiasm made him laugh.

"I just thought you might be spending that time with Adan Bovio, but if you're sure . . ."

"Yes, yes."

"Okay, then. We'll leave the day after you get out. Jesse says it would take too long to drive our own car, so he suggested we fly to Mexico City and rent a car. We can get to your village that night or the next day or so, depending on what we do along the way."

"I'd rather we get there quickly and stop to see other things on the way home," I said.

"Yes, that sounds like a plan."

"I have some people I'd like to tell we are coming, some of my grandmother's friends."

He turned to Jesse to explain, and then Jesse got on the phone.

"You can tell them we'll be there by the Sunday following your last day of class," he said. "I've plotted it out with the computer. What is this hotel like, this Hotel Los Jardines Hermosos?"

I laughed. "That is the hotel in the village. It has maybe six rooms and a patch of land with some cactus flowers, but the owners are nice people, and the rooms will be clean. It's just a place to sleep," I said. "Don't expect any more."

"Six rooms? I had better make reservations, then," he said.

"They will be shocked to hear the request."

"I'll use your name."

"Yes, use my name," I said, smiling to myself at how they would react. "Thank you, Jesse."

Edward came back on the phone to tell me he would book our tickets and advised me again to watch out for Sophia and be careful. He wished me a good time on the weekend, too.

It was hard to get to sleep afterward. My anticipation of this trip to my village was overwhelming. I couldn't wait to write down the details and get them to Ignacio. For me to send them so soon after I had told him of the possibility would be wonderful for him.

And for me, I thought.

For a while, I completely forgot about Adan and our upcoming weekend. The only name on my lips and the only face in my dreams and thoughts were Ignacio's. It helped me to have a good, restful sleep.

Tía Isabela was at the breakfast table before either Sophia or I was the following morning. If Señora Rosario had told her anything about our dinner the night before, she did not reveal it when Sophia greeted her. I was already at the table, and we were talking about my upcoming trip to Newport Beach with Adan. She was telling me about the time she and her husband had owned a boat she described as a small yacht. They had kept it at Newport Beach and had even traveled to some ports in Mexico. She said it slept eight people, and they often had guests, business associates and their wives, with them on their trips. It sounded as if they rarely had taken Edward and Sophia, and she did reveal that most of the time on the boat was before the two of them were old enough to enjoy it.

"After my husband got sick, we sold the boat," she explained.

"What about the boat?" Sophia asked as

she entered.

"Well, I'm glad you got up, dressed, and down to breakfast before it was time to leave," Tía Isabela said.

Sophia plopped into her seat. "It would be great if we still had that boat, not that I remember it much," she said. "Why are you talking about it now?"

I realized she didn't know about my plans for Saturday with Adan.

"We were talking about Delia's excursion with Adan on Saturday," Tía Isabela said.

"Excursion?"

"They're going on the Bovio yacht."

"You are?" she asked me. "How come you didn't tell me?"

"Why does she have to tell you?" Tía Isabela asked.

Sophia looked at her mother with such hate I felt my heart stop and start.

"You're treating her more like she's your daughter and not just your niece."

"When you show me you respect your family, respect me, I'll have an easier time thinking of you as my daughter," Tía Isabela replied.

"I'm doing what you want," Sophia whined. "I got an eighty-five on the math quiz and an eighty on the social studies quiz, didn't I, Delia?"

I nodded.

"Good. Keep it up," Tía Isabela said.

"We've come right home every day and started our homework, too," Sophia added, glancing at me.

"That's perfect."

"I told Christian he could pick me up for school today," Sophia inserted. "I'm just going to school and back."

"You should have asked permission first," Tía Isabela said.

"Why? I would go with Delia otherwise. It's just a ride to school, Mother."

"Be careful, Sophia. I know when I'm being deceived."

"I'm not deceiving you! Damn."

"Watch your language at the table."

Sophia looked down at her plate.

"You can go with Christian, but I don't want to hear anything about speeding or side trips or anything else, understand?"

"Yes, Mother," she said.

Sophia looked satisfied, which only made me worry more.

Tía Isabela returned to her reminiscing about happier days with her husband, but some warning was buzzing in the back of my mind. It would be with me all day. I tried to think about anything but my schoolwork, and when I had the opportunity, I wrote the additional letter to be given to Ignacio.

When the school day ended, I hurried out to my car. Fani, who had her own car, too, was already in the parking lot.

"You want to come over to my house for a while?" she asked. "We can discuss you-know-who a little more."

"Thank you, Fani, but I have an important chore I must do."

She bristled. No one turned down an invitation from Estefani Cordova.

"Can I come over right after I do the chore?" I quickly added.

"Well, how long will you be?"

"Not more than an hour," I said. She wasn't happy, but my quick thinking saved me.

"If you're much longer, just don't come," she told me, and got into her own car.

I hurried to mine. All of the students were leaving the school now, and I caught sight of Sophia and Christian walking quickly to his car. I sped up and nearly got a speeding ticket, because a policeman who was following me pulled up alongside and wagged a warning finger at me. I smiled, nodded, and slowed down. He drove on.

Ignacio's brother, Santos, was out front when I arrived. I was surprised to see him. If he was finished with school, he would usually go to work with his father's crew. I noticed he was carrying some tools. He paused when I drove into the driveway.

"Where did you get that car?" he asked immediately.

"My cousin."

"You're really rich now, aren't you?"

"I'm not. *Mi tía* is. What are you doing?"

"I'm repairing these steps," he said, nodding at the front steps.

"Your mother is inside?"

He nodded. "Can I look at your car?"

"*Sí*," I said. I handed him the keys, and his eyes filled with excitement.

Then I went in and found Señora Davila folding towels she had just washed.

"Back again so soon? Is something wrong?"

"No, something is right, Señora Davila. Did you get the letter off to Ignacio?"

"This morning," she said, nodding.

"I need now to get this to him," I said, handing her the additional letter and information. "It will tell him about my trip."

"So, you are really going?"

"*Sí*."

"You will come back before?"

"If you like."

"I have some things I would like you to bring him," she said.

"Then I will be back. I have to rush off now," I said. "I'm sorry."

She took the letter, and we hugged. I hurried out. Santos was sitting in the car, dreaming of driving it. He got out quickly, surprised at how short my visit was.

"It is a beautiful car," he said. He handed the keys back to me.

"Maybe next time I come, I will have time to take you for a little ride in it."

"Maybe," he said.

I got in and started the engine

"The top goes down?"

"Yes," I said. "I'll show you."

I lowered the top, and his eyes widened with appreciation.

"When you take me for a ride, I'd like the top down, too."

"Okay. I will see you soon," I said, and backed out. I was very excited about everything and had to remind myself to keep my attention on my driving.

When I turned and started away, I checked my rearview mirror.

My heart sank.

There, parked on the street, watching me, were Christian and Sophia in Christian's car.

They had followed me.

That was why she had asked him to pick

her up and why the alarm was going off inside me. Instinctively, like a wild animal in the desert, I sensed the danger. I should have listened to the alarm and anticipated something like this.

I slowed down to see if they would follow me again. When I reached the corner, I stopped and watched them. Christian started his car and drove up to the Davilas' house. I saw Santos turn with surprise when Sophia got out of the car. She walked toward him.

A car had come up behind me, and the driver leaned on his horn, making me jump in my seat. I accelerated quickly and drove on, my heart pounding harder than the engine, all the way to Fani's house.

12
Blackmail

I knew Santos would not intentionally reveal his family's great secret, but I was afraid of what Sophia would say or ask. She was the most conniving, sly person I had ever met, and there was no doubt in my mind that she hungered with all her being for some way to ruin me. At a minimum, she could go to her mother now and tell her I was continuing my relationship with the Davila family. She knew her mother had forbidden me to have anything to do with them.

But I feared more. I feared that somehow she would figure out what was going on with Ignacio.

"Nadie reconoce el engaño asi como alguien que engaña" my grandmother would say. No one recognizes deception as well as one who deceives.

"It takes one to know one," I had heard other students at the school say. It was never truer for anyone than it was for Sophia. I was playing on her playground, and she was far better at the game of lying than I was, for she had been doing it all her life.

My nerves were on fire. I was shaking so much I thought I might make a mistake driving. Every few minutes, I checked my rearview mirror to see if they were still following me, but I did not see them. Where were they? Why were they remaining so long at the Davilas' home? What trouble would Sophia cause for them? Had Ignacio's father returned to find them there? Did Sophia have the nerve to knock on the door and question Señora Davila? What would Ignacio's mother think? She would surely wonder why had I brought these people to their house. What new danger had I created for the family?

My own imagined questions and concerns brought tears to my eyes. I was actually sobbing by the time I reached Fani's front entrance. I stopped to wipe the tears from my face and catch my breath. If Fani saw me like this, she would want to know why, too. For a moment, I wondered if I could trust her with the truth. She would surely tell it to Adan, though, I thought. The secret must remain tightly locked in my heart.

I had to buzz in through the intercom at the gate. The house manager opened it, and

I drove up to the house. Fani's parents had more full-time servants than Tía Isabela. A woman younger than Señora Rosario was in charge inside and greeted me at the door. Fani came out quickly to meet me.

"You're here in less than an hour," she said, leading me back to her room.

"I nearly got a speeding ticket," I told her, and described the policeman wagging his finger.

"You're lucky. He was in a charitable mood. My father probably could have fixed the ticket for you, anyway," she said smugly. "He has fixed a few for me."

"A few?"

"Policemen love giving tickets to beautiful women in fancy, expensive cars, Delia. Expect it," she said. "So, what was this important chore?"

It seemed impossible to avoid lies in this world, I thought. If you were always honest, you were often in great danger, or someone you loved was. However, whether the lie was to protect someone else or to avoid hurting someone you loved, it was still a deception, and it still required you to be accomplished enough to convince the listener.

And then, of course, there were those who were experts at lying to themselves. *Mi tía* Isabela was the best one at doing this, I thought.

I had learned well from Sophia. The best liar was one who used part of the truth and first won the listener's faith in what was being said, and the best way to do that was to pretend to be giving the listener some secret.

We went into Fani's bedroom and to her sitting area. She sat first and waited for my response.

"It is something that would not please *mi tía* Isabela," I said. "In fact, she has forbidden it, but I can't help but do what I think is right."

"What is it?"

I sat across from her. "Visiting the Davila family," I said.

"The family of the boy who died?"

"Yes. I am very fond of Ignacio's mother, and I was always saddened and troubled by what had happened."

"So?"

"Today is Ignacio's birthday, or what would have been," I said.

Her eyes widened as she sat back. "Really? So you went to see her?"

"Yes, I have just come from there. They live up in Indio." This was another part of the truth I could reveal.

"Well, it's a very nice thing to do. I'm sorry

293

I put so much pressure on you and rushed your visit, but if you would have told me right away . . ."

"I am so afraid, and now I have more reason to be," I added.

"Why now?"

"I was followed to the Davila home."

She stared and then brightened. "Your bitch cousin?"

"And Christian Taylor."

"What did they say?"

"I didn't speak with them. When I came out of the house, I saw they were there and they had followed. When I started away, I saw Sophia get out to talk to Ignacio's brother, Santos. I'm sure she'll run home to tell *mi tía.*"

"You did well to confide in me, Delia," Fani said after a moment. "I can help you."

"You can? How?"

She smiled, stood up, and went to a closet. I waited as she opened a box on the floor and sifted through some files. She pulled out something and returned to hand me a picture.

"This should help," she said.

I looked at the picture. It was Sophia, maybe a year or so younger, naked on someone's sofa with a boy named Gregory Potter. He was in our class, but I didn't see him spend any time with Sophia or give any attention to her.

"How did you get such a picture?"

"It was about a year and a half ago, a wild party. Another boy in our class, Danny Rosen, has all this equipment. He took secret pictures. I found out and bought some from him."

"Why?"

"First for my own amusement and then to have something on Sophia as well as some other girls."

"Do they know?"

"Some suspect, but Sophia doesn't. I haven't had any reason to tell her yet, but now there's a reason. She tells on you, you'll tell on her, and what's worse for her is that you can prove it. If Isabela Dallas thinks people can get pictures of her daughter in such a compromising way, she'll not only be furious, she'll have a nervous breakdown and probably ship Sophia off to some behavioral modification camp, maybe as far away as Europe or South America."

"What is this camp?"

"A behavioral modification camp is one of these places they send very, very bad children, children whose parents can't control them, and the children are basically imprisoned with no way out and no way to contact anyone. There was a boy in our school, Philip Deutch. He ended up in one of those places."

"What happened to him?"

"I don't know. I never heard, and he's never been back. His family acts as if he never existed. I'm sure that would be the way Isabela would feel or want to feel. You have a lot of power there, Delia," Fani said, nodding at the photograph in my hand. "Sophia doesn't know if there are other pictures or where the negative is for that picture. It was actually taken with a digital camera, and it's on a computer file. I don't have the file, but I could get it for a price, I'm sure."

"Is this why so many of the girls in our class are afraid of you, Fani?"

"Some. Others are just . . . frightened rabbits. Go 'boo,' and they'll jump out of their shoes." She sat.

I looked at the picture again and shook my head. "How terrible."

"Disgusting, isn't it? She's a good fifteen pounds overweight, and the boy she's with is a zero. Put it in your purse, Delia. As soon as you get home, you confront her. She might try to confront you first with a threat or some blackmail, I'm sure. Then you whip that out and tell her to fade into the woodwork, or else you'll show the picture immediately to your aunt. If she wants to know where you got it, you can tell her it was from me. That will be more convincing and make her even more afraid, because she knows I don't like her. It might be the end of all your troubles with her."

I shook my head sadly and looked again at the picture. Tía Isabela would definitely have this nervous breakdown Fani described.

"It's sad to have to live with your own cousin like this," I said.

"How about living like this with your own daughter? If Sophia could blackmail her mother, do you think she would hesitate?"

I looked again at the picture. How could Sophia be caught this way? She was surely *borracha,* probably from vodka.

"I don't know if I can do this."

"You'll know you can do it the minute she threatens you. You want to protect the Davila family, too, don't you? Stop being so weak. Put it away. Forget it for now. Let's talk about Adan," she said, pulling her legs up and under her. "He is a handsome man and quite a catch. I've played with the idea myself from time to time. We're only third cousins or something, but he's not for me."

"Why not? Who is for you?" I asked, putting the picture into my purse.

"I'll know when the time comes, when I'm

297

ready. Let's talk about you, not me. Do you like him a lot?"

"He's very nice, yes. We're going to dinner tonight," I said, glancing at the clock.

"I know, and on his yacht tomorrow. He's taking you to Catalina. You're getting the full treatment. Adan doesn't spend his full treatments on just anyone. I told you he liked you very much. This is becoming a real romance."

She thought a moment. I thought she was studying me too closely, and it made me look away.

"Aside from this terrible experience you had, have you ever been intimate with a boy or a man, Delia? What about the Davila boy, the one who died?"

"I am embarrassed by such a discussion, Fani."

"Get over it. You're here now. You see the way the other girls are. No one has any bashfulness anymore."

"What about you, Fani? Do you talk about your romances?"

She smiled. "I see. We're going to play that 'I'll tell you if you'll tell me' game, huh?"

"No, I don't want to do that. I don't want to play such games, but can't we be friends and still keep some things private, Fani?"

She stared at me very intensely again and

then nodded to herself. "You know something, Delia Yebarra," she said, "you might just be different and authentic enough to win the heart of Adan Bovio. Okay." She stood. "Go on home and get ready for your hot date. If you want to confide any more in me, I'm here for you. And use that picture. If you're too nice to do it, she'll grind you into sawdust right at your aunt's feet, and Adan Bovio or anyone like him will be a distant dream."

"Thank you, Fani," I said, rising. "I am indebted to you."

"I know," she said. "One day, I'll ask you for a favor, I'm sure, and you can repay me."

I couldn't imagine having or doing anything Fani Cordova might need.

She walked me out to my car.

"Call me on Sunday," she said, "unless you have the confrontation before you go to dinner tonight. I want to hear about it in detail."

"I will."

I got into my car and drove off, looking at her in my rearview mirror. She stood there watching me, and I wondered what her life was really like, this girl who had everything but seemed disinterested in her own life and more interested in manipulating the lives of other people, as if we were all pieces on a chess board. She was the one stuck in a castle living through fantasies, not me. I turned out of her gate to head home.

What would face me there?

The house was deceptively quiet when I entered. My heart was still thumping in expectation. I had half expected and feared that Sophia had gotten home already and gone right to *mi tía* Isabela. Both of them would confront me the moment I stepped into the entryway, but there were no signs of anyone, not even Señora Rosario or Inez. I moved quietly to and up the stairway. Walking down the hallway, I saw that Sophia's door was shut. I hadn't seen Christian Taylor's car, so there was the possibility he had dropped her off and gone or that they were still not back.

I had my head down and was in deep thought about it all when I entered my bedroom, so I didn't see Sophia there at first. I put my purse down and started to think about what I would wear to dinner. That was when she spoke up.

"Who else did you visit today?" she asked. I turned sharply and saw her lying on my bed, my pillows up behind her head. She wore a deep, self-satisfied smirk.

"What do you want?"

"You didn't come right home, so who else did you visit? What, were you making the rounds, seeing all the families of your Mexican boyfriends?"

I didn't answer.

"What I'd like to know," she continued, "is how you got up there to visit the Davila family so often before you had the car. That bus ride has got to be close to an hour and a half with all the stops it makes. Don't try to deny you've been visiting them, either. Ignacio's simple-minded brother revealed it. I had the feeling he's not all that crazy about you. Well? I want some answers, and fast. My mother is not going to be very pleased when she finds out you're still so friendly with those Mexicans."

Fani was right, I thought. Sophia was capable of driving me down to places so dark inside myself that I did not realize or believe they were there. I wanted to do more than show her the picture and counter her threats with threats of my own. I wanted to wring her neck, to toss her out of the window and out of my life. She put a hot poker into my heart and set me afire. Seizing my purse, I stepped toward her. The look on my face actually frightened her.

"You'd better not swing any footstools or anything at me, Delia, and you'd better not put any of your Mexican curses on me, either. I mean it," she said, but pulled herself back into a defensive posture.

"I won't throw any stools, and you put curses on yourself. You don't need me to do it. I need not tell you anything, and you will do nothing to hurt or displease me," I said.

That sent a smile rippling through her face, curling the corners of her mouth. "Or else what, Delia?"

"Or else your mother will see more of this, as well as other students at school and who knows who else," I said, plucking the picture out of my purse and tossing it onto the bed. It fell facedown at her knees.

She studied me a moment and then slowly picked it up and looked at it, her face collapsing in defeat and fear.

"How did you . . . where do you get this?"

"Fani Cordova," I said. "She has them all, many copies to hand out whenever I tell her to do so."

She glanced again at the picture. "Who took this?"

"What difference does it make? You think your mother would go rushing out to buy you your car or end your punishment if she saw that and more pictures of you like it? And if the boys at school saw such pictures, would you want to stay there?"

I could see the defiance and strength drain from her face the way I might see water disappear from a glass with a crack at the bottom.

"You're disgusting," she said.

"I am only what you make me be," I said. "You can have that picture. As I said, there are many others. Take it, and get out of my room, and never, ever follow me with Christian Taylor or anyone. I don't want to hear the Davila name come from your lips in this house or anywhere. They have suffered enough, thanks to what you and your girlfriends did that terrible night, stirring up Ignacio and his friends."

She slipped off the bed but kept her distance from me. "I tried to be your friend and get my friends to like you," she moaned.

"The way a spider befriends a fly. No, *gracias*."

"You'll be sorry. You'll see," she said. "Fani will betray you, too. When she gets bored with you, she'll toss you off like some empty bag."

"Don't worry about me. I don't depend on anyone here," I said. "Friends here sway too easily in the wind. You know that, too, and you will see it all your life."

"Right. You know everything, as usual,"

she said. "You can tell Fani Cordova that if she shows any pictures like this, I'll get her good."

She tore the picture into pieces and threw it at me before running out of my room. The pieces floated down to my feet. I heard her door slam, and then I picked up the pieces and put the pile into a corner of a dresser drawer. Someday I might put them together again like a puzzle, I thought. She was mean-hearted but cowardly and stupid.

To calm myself as much as anything, I took a hot shower and washed my hair. It was getting later, and I had to prepare myself for my dinner date. Despite my liking Adan, my heart was heavy, and I was afraid I would be terrible company both tonight and tomorrow. I considered getting myself out of going sailing with him, but then I realized that would disturb Tía Isabela and might stir up some suspicions.

Sophia was defeated tonight, but she was not simply going to retreat. She would hover in the corner and in the shadows, waiting for some opportunity to strike back at me. I must do nothing to give her that opportunity, I thought. If anything, I had to be even more careful.

I fixed my hair and chose my dress and shoes and a pair of earrings. The makeup I wore was still quite understated compared with what Sophia and the other girls at school wore. I was still at my vanity table when Tía Isabela knocked and entered my room. I turned in fearful anticipation, worried that despite it all, Sophia had decided to tell her mother where I had been.

"Very good, Delia," Tía Isabela said, inspecting me. "You chose the right dress to wear, and I like what you've done with your hair and makeup."

"Thank you."

"I had occasion to meet Adan's father today," she continued, coming farther in and sitting. "Apparently, Adan has told him a great deal about you. His father is impressed and happy about it. These days, the families of candidates for high office are scrutinized almost as much as the candidate. I'm here to tell you that you should expect people, photographers and reporters, will pay more attention to you. You must think carefully before you speak, especially if you are asked any questions about your family or about the terrible thing that happened to you here."

So, that was the reason she was being so friendly. She wasn't pleased so much with me as she was worried about herself and her reputation. How fortunate I was to have Fani give me that picture and stop Sophia before she planted the story in *mi tía* Isabela's mind. She would certainly see it as a threat to her image and reputation, and the explosion would have been so great all of us would have suffered.

"I will," I promised.

"No. I mean you must be careful," she emphasized. "They are bound to ask you questions about the death of Bradley Whitfield. You simply say you've been told by our attorney not to discuss it.

"And if they ask you about your life in Mexico, our family," she added, surprising me with the word *our*, "don't make them sound so poor and uneducated. You can say your father was a foreman in charge of many men.

"Of course, you can tell them about our home here, our grounds, the nice things you have, and how wonderful it has been to be here and have these opportunities. *Comprende?*"

"*Sí.*"

She rose. "I wouldn't be surprised if some reporter from a Spanish newspaper approaches you. It would be fine to speak to him in Spanish."

"Where will all these reporters and questions happen?"

"Anywhere! That's the point I've come up

here to make. Because Adan's father is now such an important figure, they'll be looking for material, for things to write. You look very nice. You've been taught how to behave in society. You will continue to make me proud," she said, making it sound more like an order than a conclusion.

She paused at the doorway.

"Did my daughter behave today, or did she and Christian do something I should know about?"

"I will not spy on Sophia, Tía Isabela," I said firmly. I would never forget how she used me to spy on Edward, and she knew it, too.

"I'm not asking you to spy. You have to help me with her, help us both now. Never mind. Just continue to get yourself ready for your date," she said, and left.

If I had ever felt as if I were moving through a minefield, I felt it now. Suddenly, every word I said, every little thing I did, would be magnified and have some importance or possibly a disastrous result. Worrying about it all, I remembered I had promised to call Fani with the results of my confrontation with Sophia.

She listened and said something that frightened me. "She gave up too easily." She actually sounded disappointed. "At least, I expected she would challenge you to show the picture to your aunt. You'd better keep your eyes and ears open and watch for some trap she'll set. I'll talk to you on Sunday, and we'll think and plan some more. Besides, I want to hear how your weekend with Adan went. Have a good time."

Why wasn't she going out on date tonight, too? I wondered. Wasn't there anyone she had interest in? It was on the tip of my tongue to ask, but I was afraid to do it. I thanked her, hung up, and went down to wait for Adan.

Sophia's door was still shut, and I heard no music or anything coming from her room. She was probably in a deep pout. Maybe Fani was wrong. Maybe all of this would finally drive her to be decent.

Adan was right on time and as handsome as ever, in an emerald-green sports jacket that highlighted his eyes. He brought me another single rose. I half expected to see Tía Isabela there to greet him and fawn over him as well, but she didn't appear. We went out to get into another one of his sports cars. He said it was an Aston Martin, and when he told me what it costs, I lost my breath for a moment. He laughed at my reaction.

"I didn't pay that much," he said. "We have some influential friends in the car business. I'm sure you know the irony, Delia. People with the money to pay for things also have the connections to get them for a much lower price. It's the same everywhere."

"Yes," I said. "I am sure."

We drove off. I looked back once and thought about Sophia stewing in her pot of anger back in her room. Fani's warning was like a persistent chant. Sophia wouldn't simply fade into the woodwork. Every day, I would have to be alert and expect some new trap set for me.

"You're in very deep thought tonight," Adan said. "Everything all right?"

"*Sí*," I said.

He didn't believe me, of course. He told me that when I had a delicious dinner and met his friend, I would cheer up.

"Charles Daniels is a world-class chef," he said. "His close friends call him Chuck. He's been to what is known as a *cordon bleu* cooking school in France, but he's better when he cooks Italian. We went to undergraduate school together, and then he veered off and followed what he always wanted to do, be a chef. His father, who owns public storage facilities and a good-size trucking business in Los Angeles, wasn't too happy about him not joining their business. He didn't see his son becoming a chef as anything to brag about, either. He does have an older brother, however, who is working with his father."

"Like you."

"Yes, like me, which isn't lost on Chuck's father. He's always pointing me out to him, but Chuck's happy about owning his own place and doing what he loves. He's a jolly guy, lots of fun. He treats the dishes he creates as works of art. Wait until you see how he presents everything.

"I'll tell you a secret," he added, whispering as if there really was someone else in the car who could overhear. "Someday, I'm going to build a bigger restaurant for him, and we'll go into business together."

He looked at me to see my reaction.

"I'm serious," he emphasized.

"Oh, yes."

He shook his head. "I see you're not easily impressed," he said. What kind of reactions did he expect from me? "Actually, I like that about you, Delia. I don't think there's an artificial bone in your body."

"Artificial bone?"

"You know, phoniness. You're authentic from your head to your feet," he explained. It reminded me of when Fani had first begun speaking to me and telling me I was an authentic Mexican who could work in an authentic Mexican restaurant.

"I am only who I am," I said.

The restaurant was somewhat smaller than I had expected, but I was not disappointed in the food or Adan's friend Chuck. When he was able to do it, he joined us at our table, and he and Adan told one funny story after another about their college experiences.

The contrast between them physically couldn't be any greater. Chuck Daniels looked like an authentic chef, rotund, with premature jowls and roller-pin forearms. When Fani first showed me any attention at the private school, Sophia, jealous, of course, tried to turn me against her quickly by telling me that beautiful girls and handsome men like to be friends with people who are less attractive. It makes them stand out more. It was another way for her to insult me. I thought about it and asked her, "So, then, why are you not her best friend?"

I didn't ask it with any nasty tone, but it was enough to send her flying off to complain to her girlfriends about me and how I was impossible to help. Nevertheless, I couldn't help but wonder if what she had said could be true. I wondered about it now. What did Adan and Chuck have in common that would make them so close? Perhaps I was hoping to find something that would turn me away from Adan, but it didn't take long to see that he and Chuck had a defi-nitely warm and sincere friendship. Later, Adan would tell me Chuck was the brother he had never had.

"I'd do anything to help that guy," he said. "And I will. His father gets me that angry."

He slipped out of his unpleasant mood quickly, however, and talked excitedly about our boat trip to Catalina.

"I'd take you someplace else," he said after we had left the restaurant, "maybe dancing, but I want to get you home early. I want you to be fresh and awake tomorrow so you don't miss a thing."

When we drove up to *mi tía* Isabela's *hacienda,* he didn't get out immediately, how-ever. He shut off the engine and sat there. I didn't know what to make of his silence. I was getting nervous.

"I'm glad I met you at this particular time in my life, Delia. I feel my father and I are starting the final liftoff of a rocket ship. I imagine you've been told some pretty racy stories about me. I know I have something of a reputation. I'm sure your cousin Edward has warned you about me."

I started to protest, but he put his hand up.

"It's all right. I'm not saying I don't de-serve the notoriety. I just want you to know you're the kind of girl who can make a guy like me grow up."

He smiled and leaned in to kiss me softly. Then he pulled his head back a little and looked at my eyes. If I ever sensed I was losing my grip on any restraint, I sensed it at that moment. It would make me feel so guilty later, but I brought my lips to his waiting lips and kissed him. He held on to me firmly. Then he lowered his head to my shoulder and whispered, "I'd better get you out of this car now, or I won't let you out at all."

He sat back, opened his door like someone truly trying to oppose the demands made by his own body, and got out to come around and open my door. In silence, he walked me to the front door of the *hacienda,* where he pretended to be a gallant Zorro and kissed my hand.

"Buenas noches, señorita," he said. *"Sueños dulce."*

"Pleasant dreams to you, too, Adan," I said in a voice that seemed to rise out of my heart.

He smiled and hurried down to his car. I waited until he got in and started away, and then I entered the house in a daze. I felt as if I were floating up the stairway. Sophia opened her door as I approached my bedroom. I imagined she had been sitting at a window and watching for us. She was in her nightgown and barefoot.

"I do not want to fight with you anymore, Sophia," I said.

She folded her lips into a wry smile. "That's okay. I'm not going to start an argument or anything. In fact, I'm going to be your friend. I just thought you'd like to know where my mother was tonight, or rather, who she was with."

"I do not —"

"She went out with Adan Bovio's father," she said quickly. Then her smile widened. "She's just using you, just like she uses everyone else."

She stepped back into her room and closed her door.

I stood there listening to her words echo in my ears.

Maybe I should be grateful she was so spiteful. Adan's words and good looks, the whole warm evening, and his kisses had lifted me into a place so high I could no longer see Ignacio's face. It was truly like personally delivering him to the third death.

Now, thanks to Sophia, like a balloon losing air, I sank back to the earth, where promises like beautiful bubbles floated by and then burst.

I hurried to bed and the sanctity of sleep, where I could escape from Fani, from Sophia, from Tía Isabela, and from Adan Bovio and see only my grandmother and hear only her voice.

But just before I got into bed, I saw the headlights of an approaching vehicle wash over my windows. I looked down and watched as Adan's father got out and opened the door for Tía Isabela. He kissed her when she stepped out, and they held each other very closely. They looked like serious lovers already. A terrifying thought sizzled in my mind.

If I did something to ruin her pursuit of Adan's father, she would see me as she saw my mother, once again ruining her plans for a loving relationship.

It was the emotional world in which she lived and from which she could never escape.

We were all in little traps, perhaps of our own making.

13
OPEN WATER

I almost overslept and probably would have if it weren't for Tía Isabela. She came bursting into my room, carrying a large shopping bag.

"Why are you still sleeping? You didn't come home very late," she cried angrily. "Get up, get up, get up!"

I ground the sleep out of my eyes and sat up.

"I know they didn't serve you anything alcoholic at the restaurant. You're underage, and if there's one thing Adan Bovio has to avoid, it's corrupting the morals of a minor, or at least being caught doing so. Well?"

"No, I was just —"

"Just get out of bed," she said. "I want you to put this on today."

I watched her dig into the bag and pull out what she called a sailing outfit. First, there was a beaded screen-print tank top. The print was of a small island with palm trees.

Then she pulled out a hooded light green jacket and a pair of light green elastic-waist pants with front pockets.

"I'm sure you've noticed that green is Adan's favorite color," she remarked, and set the clothing on my bed. She pulled out a matching green sailing cap from the bag and reached in again to produce a pair of what she called women's navigator shoes. "They're made to walk on slippery decks. Well," she said, "why are you still sitting there gaping at me?"

I got up quickly and headed for the bathroom.

"Get into these clothes, and come down for a light breakfast. We don't want you getting seasick," she called after me.

If I ever felt I had pressure on me to perform and make her happy before, I had twice as much now. I was surprised at how well the outfit she had bought fit me, including the shoes. When I went down to breakfast, I discovered she had already dictated to Señora Rosario what I would eat. It was to be merely one poached egg on a single slice of toast.

"No, no, no," she said, coming into the dining room while I was eating. "Don't pin your hair up like that. It makes you look too severe. I want it loose. Let it blow in the wind. Men like to see that."

She didn't wait for me to take out the pins. She went ahead and did it herself, fluffing my hair the way she wanted it to set.

"Has Sophia risen and eaten her breakfast already?" I asked. I didn't think Tía Isabela had relented to let her be served in bed again.

"Sophia? She's probably competing with you. I relented a little on her punishment and said she could go out if she kept decent hours and behaved. We're better off keeping her from being too idle around here. She'll only get into more mischief by pouting. I know her too well."

"What do you mean, she's competing with me?"

"She went with Christian Taylor an hour or so ago, supposedly to a picnic up in the mountains in Idyllwild. I can't imagine her settling for a picnic. Frankly, I'm disappointed in Christian. I thought he had better taste."

How could a mother speak so about her own daughter?

"I'm going to lend you this bag," she continued, and showed me a green bag that looked as if it had been purchased to match my outfit. "You can carry your change of clothes in it. I just decided you should put on your new bathing suit now and wear it under your outfit."

"Bathing suit?"

"I expect you'll do some swimming, but even if you don't, you'll probably do some sunbathing with Adan."

She took the bathing suit out of the bag to show me. It looked like something a stripper would wear. She glanced at her watch. "Hurry and finish. I'd like to see how you look in this."

She stood over me to encourage me to gobble down my last two bites.

"Come into my room," she ordered. "You don't have to go back upstairs."

I followed her out and down the corridor. She tossed the bathing suit at me and stood back.

"Well, put it on," she ordered.

"It looks too tiny."

"Nonsense. It's very becoming. You have a great body, perfect for such a suit. There are literally thousands of girls your age who would kill to have your figure and be able to wear a suit like that. Put it on. We don't have time for false modesty."

"It is not false, Tía Isabela."

"Whatever. Just put it on."

I took off my new clothes and my bra and panties while she stood by waiting. Then I slipped into the abbreviated bottom and the small top. There was little left to imagine about my body, I thought.

"I had a figure just like yours once," she said, admiring me. "I remember when my husband first saw me in a bathing suit like that. I knew from the look on his face that I had hooked him like a fish and would reel him in."

She stuffed my bra and panties into the bag.

"I've put in a small makeup kit for you, tissues, and a new hairbrush. You have everything you need now. The restaurants you're going to for lunch and dinner are not formal. They're both beach restaurants. Because you've been so good these past few days and listened to what I tell you, I've bought you this," she added, and handed me a small case. "Go on, open it. I want you to wear it today."

I opened it and saw a beautiful watch with an emerald-green leather band.

"It's beautiful," I said.

"Of course, it is. Now, have a good time, and don't say or do anything to embarrass me."

Señora Rosario came to the doorway. "Señor Bovio has called from the gate," she said.

"Which Señor Bovio? Adan?"

"Yes, Mrs. Dallas."

"Okay, Delia. Go on. Get dressed."

I hurriedly did so.

"I won't be home when you get back," she told me as I put on my new outfit, "but we'll have time to talk about your day tomorrow at breakfast. Late breakfast," she added.

She handed me the bag and nodded. Adan was waiting in the entryway. He wore his own sailor outfit and cap and looked as if he belonged in a movie.

"Wow," he said when he saw me. "Perfect. That's a perfect outfit, and we have terrific weather today. The sea isn't too bad at all."

He opened the door quickly. I supposed I looked so nervous he was afraid I might change my mind. Instead, I smiled at him and hurried out. I couldn't help feeling I was being swept along in a wind I couldn't possibly resist. We were on our way.

"Did you enjoy last night?" he asked.

"Yes, very much. I like your friend."

"Yeah, he's great. Fani is fond of him as well."

Since he had brought up her name, I thought I could speak about her. "Why does she not go out more?"

"You mean on dates?"

"Yes, *sí.*"

"Fani is a little too particular about the men she sees. Sometimes I think she's asexual, not interested in men or in women."

He laughed at the expression on my face.

"I'm just kidding, but she is too into herself to be in a relationship. She puts herself too high up. No one can reach her. Don't worry," he added quickly. "I'm not speaking out of school. I have this same argument with her all the time."

As we drove to the sea, he talked more about his youth, the times he and Fani had been together, once when their families even met in France.

"She's probably the closest friend I ever had who happens to be a girl," he said. Then he turned to me and smiled to add, "Until I met you."

In my mind, I was imagining a boat perhaps a little bigger than a fishing boat, but when we parked and Adan nodded at his boat, I was amazed.

"That's it."

"Where are the sails?" I asked.

"There are no sails. It's a powerboat. My father bought it last year from a friend of his, and we actually have used it only a half-dozen times since."

He grabbed his small bag, and we stepped out of the car.

A tall, thin man in a T-shirt and jeans stepped out onto the deck as we walked to the boat's slip.

"Everything's set for you, Mr. Bovio," he said. "The kitchen's stocked just as you requested. She's gassed up and ready."

"Thank you, Bill," Adan said, and turned to me. "I was thinking last night and decided it would be stupid to get off the boat for lunch. We'll dock and have our own lunch on the boat, okay?"

"Yes," I said, still wide-eyed.

"Let's tour the boat first," he said, and the man he called Bill extended his hand to help me board. Then he nodded at Adan and got off.

"Thanks, Bill. See you later," Adan told him.

He brought me first to the bridge to show me the boat's sophisticated electronics. We had to climb a short ladder. There were two brand-new-looking comfortable chairs in front of the panel in the up position. He explained it all, the radar, the sonar, all of it, but I heard very little. It wasn't that it was too complicated for me as much as that I was still in awe.

Through a portal under the bridge, we entered a small living room with a television set, leather sofa and salon chairs, a small kitchen with modern appliances and a small dining table. There was a short stairway from the salon to the staterooms, where there were two queen-size berths and room for two more in bunks, bathrooms, a sitting area with a desk and two full bathrooms with showers. There was even a clothes washer and dryer.

"You could live on this boat," I said, and he laughed.

"Don't think I haven't thought about it from time to time. C'mon, let's get started."

We went back upstairs, and he got the engines going. He was very proud of the boat and couldn't stop explaining and describing everything about it. Soon he realized he was going too quickly and too far over my head.

"Don't worry about any of it," he said, laughing again. "You're here to enjoy the day, not buy the boat."

"Buy the boat?" I couldn't imagine anyone having enough money to do so.

He smiled and began to take us out to sea, moving slowly at first. I could see from the concentration in his eyes that when it came time to do what had to be done, he was very serious and precise. Then he smiled a little impishly and sped up. We bounced over the waves so hard I screamed. But it was very exciting. After a while, he let me steer the boat and taught me some of the most basic things. I had no idea how much time had gone by, but when we were far enough out, he cut off the engines and said it was time for a cool drink. He lowered the anchor and we returned to the galley, where I saw the refrigerator had been stocked with far more food than we could eat.

"There's cold lobster salad, shrimp salad, cold cuts, a Greek salad, breads, delicious desserts, and champagne if you want any. You ever had a mimosa?"

"Yes. I know what it is," I said.

"Good. I'll make you one. For today, I'll be the waiter. You go up to the deck and make yourself comfortable. You have your bathing suit?"

"*Sí,*" I said, already blushing at the thought of stripping down to it.

"Perfect. It's going to get hot. Even just dipping into the sea will be delightful."

I went up to the deck. The boat bobbed in the ocean but not badly. He was right about how hot it felt with no clouds and the sunlight reflected off the surface of the ocean. Very self-consciously, I took off my outfit and spread one of the large terry towels on a chaise. There was even sunscreen set out for us. I rubbed it into my much-exposed body and lay back on the chaise. Except for the occasional sound of a tern or another motorized boat in the distance, it was peaceful. The movement of the boat quickly lulled me into a comfortable daze, bordering on sleep. I didn't even realize Adan had come up with a tray carrying two mimosas in champagne-style glasses and a platter of cheese, fruit, and crackers. When I opened my eyes, I saw him standing there gazing at me.

"Oh," I said, sitting up.

"You are truly a beautiful girl, Delia. Woman, I should say."

"*Gracias,* Adan."

"Here, try one of these."

He set the tray on a small table and organized a chaise for himself. I sipped the drink. It was refreshing and didn't taste at all like anything alcoholic, but I knew it was, of course.

"It's good?"

"Yes."

"Nice drink for this time of the day."

He took off his shirt and pants. His body was lean and tan.

"I was on the swimming team in college," he explained before I could even think of complimenting him. "I'm still always training."

"I'm not much of a swimmer. We swam in a small lake near the village sometimes, but not much more than that."

"So, your village was inland?"

"*Sí*. The biggest industry is the soybean farms. My father was a manager on the biggest one."

"And he and your mother were killed in an accident caused by a drunken driver."

"Yes," I said.

"I know you don't like to talk about it. I don't like to talk about my mother's death, either. I'm sure they wouldn't want us to dwell on it. They'd want us to be happy," he said. *"No más,"* he added. He reached for the sunscreen and began rubbing it into his body. "You put some of this on?"

"Yes."

"Turn over, and I'll put it on your back and the backs of your legs. It doesn't take long to wish you had," he added.

"Gracias," I said. He rubbed in the lotion, taking his time. I felt his fingers over my upper thighs, moving all around my legs.

"We don't want anything bad to happen to this skin," he said. He even did my ankles.

I turned around, and he smiled and drank some of his mimosa.

"We need music," he cried, and turned on the boat's stereo system.

The radio went on immediately to a Mexican station, and he came out dancing. He beckoned for me to join him, and I did. In minutes, we were both laughing, drinking more mimosas, and eating some of the fruit and cheese. Every once in a while, another boat would draw near, and the driver would play his horn. Most of them had tunes instead of just a blaring noise. The people aboard would wave and scream. It seemed as if everyone on the ocean had been invited to the same party.

I didn't know how much time went by. I didn't think about it, but at one point, Adan decided it was too hot, and he dove into the sea. He beckoned for me to join him, to climb down the ladder and dip myself at least. I was afraid, but he called and called until I inched myself down the ladder and, still holding on to it, lowered myself into the ocean. He swam over to me, and we bobbed about. I was screaming half in delight and half in fear when he kissed me and kept his arms around my waist.

"I've got you," he said. "You can let go of the ladder. Go on. Swim a little, so you can say you've swum in the Pacific. Go on," he urged, until I did let go, swam a few feet, swallowed some salt water, and gagged. He immediately wrapped his arm around my waist and brought me back to the ladder.

"You have to keep your mouth shut, silly,"

he said. "Are you all right?"

I nodded, but I had been shocked enough to want to go back up the ladder. He helped me, and I flopped onto the chaise. I quickly discovered that the bathing suit *mi tía* Isabela had bought me wasn't really made for swimming. It was translucent. My breasts, my nipples, were as exposed as if they were uncovered. I seized another towel as he climbed up the ladder and threw it over me quickly.

"Wasn't it great?" he asked, grabbing a towel for himself.

I nodded.

"You did okay for the first time. Cold?" he asked.

"A little," I said.

"You'll warm up in minutes," he promised. "I'll get us moving again. I want you to see Catalina. Rest," he told me, and went to bring up the anchor and restart the engines.

I did dry quickly and was soon warm again. As my bathing suit dried in the sun, it became less translucent. I was soon comfortable enough with myself to join him at the helm. I took the other seat and enjoyed the ride, once again steering the boat, too. He pointed to Catalina when it came into view. He explained that he was going to rent a slip, and then we could get off the boat and walk in the village, visit the shops, and when we were ready, return to the boat for our lunch.

The fun and excitement, the new things I learned and discovered, all conspired to drive back any thoughts of Ignacio or my life in Mexico. This is how *el diablo* wins our souls, I thought, but it was only a fleeting thought. When we docked the boat, I put my clothes on over my suit, and we got off to walk through the village. Adan bought me souvenirs, a funny sun hat and two T-shirts from Catalina.

Afterward, when we returned to the boat, I insisted that I be the one to prepare the lunch. He set the table, and we had more mimosas and a wonderful lunch, talking and watching the tourists and the other boats and listening to our music. Afterward, while I cleaned up, he sprawled on a chaise, and when I returned, I found he had fallen asleep. I sat in a shady area and dozed a little myself. Time didn't seem to matter anymore. I worried about nothing, thought about nothing serious, and had never felt as relaxed.

He woke and told me we would start back to Newport. We were both more subdued during the return trip. He talked again about his future, his father's ambitions, and all of the possibilities that seemed to lie out there on the distant horizon. When we reached the dock in Newport, the day had cooled but was still very pleasant. He told me about the reservation he had made at a great steakhouse on the beach.

I went down to take a shower and wash the salt off my body and out of my hair while he spoke with the man who was caretaker for the boat. Wrapped in a large towel, I came out and sat at the vanity table in the master bedroom, where I brushed out my hair. I saw him come down the stairs and stand for a moment watching me. He approached slowly, took the brush from me, and started to brush my hair. Neither of us spoke.

Then he stopped and leaned to bring his lips to my neck. The tingle that went down my spine seemed to form into fingers that sent a warmth over me. He held my shoulders and then slowly lifted me until I turned to accept his kiss. I felt the towel slip away from my body. Like someone trying to resist, he kept his eyes on mine, and then his hands moved over my breasts and down around my waist as he drew me into another kiss. My resistance softened. He whispered my name and told me how beautiful I was. I thought I had said, "No, please stop," but perhaps it was only in my imagination. He didn't appear to hear or sense any restraint. He scooped me up in his arms and carried me to the bed, covering my body quickly in kisses, his lips moving lower and lower.

I mustn't let this happen, I thought. I even pictured myself standing at the side of the bed and shaking my head, but I only weakened more and closed my eyes. His lips were on mine again, his body naked and firm against me.

And then, like a streak of lightning across my eyes, I saw Ignacio's face.

Back in Mexico, he had stood with me at the bus door until the driver said it was absolutely time to go.

"Don't go rushing into another marriage before I get back," he had said.

"I won't," I had promised.

"I will cross again, Delia, even if I have to battle the desert to get to you."

"I'll be waiting," I had said, and we had kissed.

"Wait!" I cried suddenly. "Please." Adan paused and lifted his head to look down at me.

"I really like you, Delia. You can trust me," he said. "I know you have not had good experiences with men, but I am different. I promise."

I took a deep breath, gathering my wits. I should have told him about Ignacio then and there, but instead, like some frightened young girl, I said, "Please, wait."

He smiled. "Sure," he said. "I understand. I can be patient, because I know how wonderful you are and what lies at the end of the rainbow."

Recoiling himself like the anchor he had pulled up from the sea, he sat back, took a deep breath, smiled, and said, "I'm taking a cold shower."

He went into the stall, and I quickly hurried to put on my clothes. Since he didn't force himself on me and try to persuade me to end any resistance, he was surely a good man, I told myself. I felt bad, and when he came out of the shower, I tried to be as pleasant and affectionate as I could. He dressed for our dinner, and we walked off the boat to the restaurant, where he had reserved a table that looked out on the ocean. We had a wonderful dinner, neither of us talking about what had just almost happened.

Later, the full day in the sun, the champagne, the food, all of it, finally caught up with me. I fell asleep during our ride back to Palm Springs and woke with a start when we were on the main street. He laughed, and I apologized.

"It's okay. I liked watching you sleep, Delia. You look like an angel."

From where did he get all these wonderful lines? I hoped they were sincere and from his heart and not some book instructing him how to win the love of a young woman.

It was late when we arrived. *Mi tía* Isabela's *hacienda* was very quiet. I remembered that she had told me she would not see me until late breakfast in the morning. Adan walked me to the door, where we kissed good night, and I thanked him for a most wonderful day.

"No," he said. "It is I who thank you for the day. Nothing I have brings as much pleasure without you. You make it all complete, Delia. I'll call you tomorrow."

His words took the breath from me, and I could only nod, kiss him again, and go inside. When I closed the door behind me, I juggled mixed feelings in my heart and mind. In one sense, I felt as if I had escaped making a commitment I would regret, and in another sense, I felt guilty for letting Adan believe I was just asking him to move slower.

Was I becoming more like *mi tía* Isabela than I would like? Was I lying to myself, using people, being unfaithful to the things that were true and important? Was it because I lived in this house and had this new life? Had the old Delia slipped away? Did I really leave her behind at that bus station? Was I fooling myself in thinking otherwise?

A day like this should fill a heart with only joy, not more turmoil and trouble, I thought. I should not be feeling so sad. I plodded up the stairway with my back bent and my head lowered, as if I were carrying a weight on my shoulders. I thought I would fall asleep before I could brush my teeth. I had just prepared my bed and was about to get into it when Sophia opened my door. She had obviously just come home herself.

"Well, I'm sure I don't have to ask you if you had a good time," she said when I turned.

"I did," I said. I wasn't in any mood to argue with her or trade insults, so I continued to slip into my bed and pull my light blanket up as I adjusted my pillow. "I'm very tired, Sophia. Let's talk in the morning."

"Oh, I'm not here for a long conversation, Delia. Don't worry. Christian and I had an interesting day, too, and I thought you'd like to hear about it. Just close your eyes and listen, if you like."

"Please, in the morning," I said.

She came farther into the room. "So, we went to that park where all the Mexican kids go to play ball, you know, and watched some baseball game. That Davila boy is a good baseball player."

I opened my eyes.

"Got your attention? Good. Yes, he hit a home run, and he was the pitcher on the team, too. Afterward, they have a picnic. The young boys sneak some, what do you call it, *cerveza?* Boy, what's his name, Santos? He can put it away. He outdrank Christian the big shot. Not me, of course. I don't drink *cerveza.*"

I just stared at her.

She smiled. "We took him home. He wanted a ride in Christian's new BMW. You still want me to wait until the morning?"

"What is it you want, Sophia?" I asked, holding my breath.

"Why would you be bringing his mother a letter?" she asked. Something in her tone of voice told me she didn't know. "Well? Were you giving her money in an envelope? Money you took from us? Were you?"

"Didn't I specifically tell you not to mention the Davila family or have anything more to do with them?" I asked. "Did I not tell you that?"

"If you or Fani show any of those pictures to anyone, my mother will go to the police for sure. Fani will be in big trouble, despite her father's money, and you, you will be deported or something. Christian told me to call your bluff."

I shrugged. "I'll let Fani know tomorrow. She doesn't do anything she doesn't want to do herself, and she doesn't frighten too easily. We'll see."

She stared at me. "I bet that's what you were doing, right? You were giving them money. How much have you given them?"

I just stared at her.

"I'll find out eventually, you know, so you might as well tell me now. Maybe I won't tell my mother."

"You're like Fani, Sophia. You will do what you want to do, no matter what I tell you, and if you think going to the police afterward is enough, then that's it."

Now she was the one staring. "I'm not saying I'm going to my mother for sure. Look, I'm just trying to be friendlier."

I started to laugh.

"I am! I came here to give you advice, not to threaten you."

"Oh?"

"Yes. You should stop giving them money. Eventually, it will get out, and not because of me. Someone else will talk, maybe Santos when he gets drunker or something, and my mother will find out that way, so for your own good, stop going there. That's my advice."

"*Gracias,* Sophia."

She pressed her lips together and shook her head. "You're an idiot, Delia. I don't have to do anything to you. You'll do it to yourself. I'm sure of it. All I have to do is be patient and wait," she said gleefully. She turned and walked out of my room.

I felt my body slip out of the grip of terror that had seized it despite the act I had put on for her. I was safe for now.

But Santos had slipped dangerously near the edge of the cliff over which he would go and pull his family and me and Ignacio down into the depths of more pain and agony than he could ever imagine.

I closed my eyes and said a prayer before I rushed into sleep like someone who had stepped onto a train that would take her to freedom.

14
CHANGE IN PLAN

Tía Isabela predicted well when she predicted we would meet at a late breakfast the following morning. I slept so deeply and was so tired, but I was still shocked at how late it was when my eyes finally were nudged open by the bright sunshine that had been pouring vainly through my windows until that moment. I glanced at the clock and saw it was already after ten. By the time I drifted down to breakfast, it was nearly eleven, and she appeared only moments after I did.

"Well, I can tell from the way you look this morning that you had a full day. Tell me about it," she said, sitting. She didn't ask about Sophia, where she was, whether she had eaten breakfast, anything.

"His boat is beautiful, and I had a wonderful time in Catalina. We had lunch on the boat."

"Yes, that's smart. And you went swimming?"

"A little."

"What did he think of your bathing suit?"

It brought a blush to my face to answer, but her eyes were like doctor's eyes, searching for signs that would reveal what was going on inside me.

"He liked everything I wore," I said.

She smiled. "I'll bet he did. And afterward, you had dinner in Newport Beach?"

"At a steak restaurant on the beach, yes."

"Good. Since you and Adan are doing so well, I think I will take you with me to the fund-raiser for his father next weekend. It is a dinner at one of the bigger hotels here. There will be more than a thousand people. We'll sit at the Bovio table, of course. I'm going to take you for a new dress, something more appropriate, and shoes to match. We'll do it on Wednesday."

Finally, she glanced at Sophia's empty chair.

"And where is our own little princess this morning?"

"I have not seen her, Tía Isabela."

"She did come home last night, didn't she?"

"Yes."

Inez began to serve breakfast. Señora Rosario brought in the newspaper.

"Will Sophia be going to the fund-raiser,

too?" I asked.

Tía Isabela lowered her paper to look at me.

"Whatever for?" she replied, and returned to her newspaper. "Besides, it's a thousand dollars a plate."

"A thousand dollars! For a plate?"

She lowered the paper again and smiled. "Yes, Delia, you're in a different world now, a world you could never imagine. In time, like me, you'll forget you were ever in that dirty little Mexican village. It will seem like someone else's bad dream." She snapped the paper.

"That will never be, Tía Isabela," I said defiantly. She heard me but chose to pretend she hadn't.

After a while, Sophia entered the dining room, wearing a long shirt and slippers, her hair disheveled. Tía Isabela looked at her askance.

"That's not a proper way to dress for breakfast, Sophia."

"I just got up!" she cried. "And I'm hungry." She turned to me, smiling. "You had a phone call. I heard your phone ringing and ringing. That's what woke me up, actually, so I answered it for you."

I grimaced. I had asked her never to answer my phone again.

"Who was it?" Tía Isabela asked first.

"Adan Bovio. I told him you were down at breakfast and would call him when you were finished," she told me.

"You didn't say anything nasty to him, did you, Sophia?"

"Oh, no, Mother. Heaven forbid I ever do anything like that to Adan Bovio."

"It would make me very unhappy to hear you had done anything to interfere. I am quite fond of the Bovio family."

"Oh, we all know that now, Mother." She picked at some toast.

"Where did you go last night, Sophia?" Tía Isabela asked her.

She looked at me. "We ended up at a movie and had some Chinese food," she told Tía Isabela, and then she smiled at me. "Goodness knows, I wouldn't want to get in anyone else's way."

Tía Isabela glared at her and then turned her suspicious eyes toward me for a moment. I looked down, and she returned to her paper, mumbling to herself.

Sophia's smile brightened and widened. She so enjoyed frustrating and annoying her mother. As soon as I finished, I excused myself and hurried back up to my room, first to call Fani and then to call Adan back.

"You were right about her," I told Fani

immediately. "She isn't that frightened of us. She thinks I go to see the Davilas to give them money."

"Do you?"

"No, never. Señor Davila is far too proud a man to take money from me, even if I had it to give him."

"I'd advise you to stay away from the Davilas for a while, then. Don't give Sophia any more opportunities. Now, forget about her. Tell me about your day."

"Adan hasn't called you yet?" I asked, and she laughed.

"I'd rather hear it from you, Delia. Was it wonderful?"

"Yes, it was," I said. I could not say otherwise.

"You know, he never took me to lunch on his boat."

"He is very fond of you, Fani. He speaks of you often."

"He should. I've done many good things for him, including you."

"Me?"

"Why do you think I invited you to my parents' dinner party, just to annoy those idiot girls at school? No, I knew you and Adan would hit it off."

Why wasn't she concerned about her own romances and not the romances of others? I wondered again.

I told her about Tía Isabela taking me to the fund-raiser for Adan's father.

"Good. I'll be there as well. Now, tell me a little more, Delia."

"More. *Por qué?*"

"Just give me the juicy details. Did you or did you not make love with Adan on his boat?"

"He was a gentleman," I replied.

"I take that to mean no, which I don't believe. If there is anyone you can confide in, Delia, it's me. I would think you would know that by now."

Why was she so determined to hear such news?

"It's nothing to be ashamed about," she continued. "Well?"

"We did not, as you say, make love on his boat, but we were romantic."

"Romantic?" She laughed. "I know Adan Bovio. He invented seduction. Okay, my bashful one, keep your secrets."

She sounded so confident. Had Adan told her some other story?

"I'll see you in school," she said.

Before I called Adan, Edward phoned also to hear about my weekend. He listened to my descriptions of everything, and then, after a moment of silence, he said, "You sound ambivalent. You know what that means?"

"I think so. Not sure?"

"Yes, as if you are both happy and sad. Maybe things are happening too fast for you, Delia. My mother sounds like a mad-woman matchmaker."

I didn't like to gossip, but I mentioned that Tía Isabela was seeing Adan's father.

"Oh. The plot thickens," he said. "Anyway, to change the subject, Jesse has made all the arrangements for our Mexican trip. We'll be down for lunch on Saturday to review everything. It's not that far off now."

"I look forward to seeing you both," I said.

"As for everything else, Delia, take it slowly. The right way will show itself to you in time," he said, "and I'm confident you will make the right choices."

"*Gracias,* Edward."

"*Hasta luego.*"

"*Sí,* see you soon," I said.

I sat thinking for a while after I hung up. I had promised Ignacio's mother I would stop by one more time to bring him things she wanted him to have. I would just be more careful about it, I thought. I wondered if I should speak with Santos, too. He had to be warned about Sophia.

Adan didn't wait for me to return the call.

He called again, sounding a little worried because I hadn't rushed to call him back.

"I was just about to call you," I said. I made my conversation with Tía Isabela sound longer, but he knew I had already spoken with Fani. He said a strange thing.

"Be careful about how much trust you put in her, Delia. I love Fani, but she is almost her own species."

"What does this mean, this species?"

"She can change moods, allegiances, very quickly and without any apparent warning or reason. She's been good to me and sometimes bitterly cruel to me. Of course, she immediately regrets it, but she's a complicated person, and you're a sweet and innocent young woman who may be a little too trusting still."

I'm not as innocent as he thinks, I thought. He would come to that conclusion quickly if he knew the truth about Ignacio. Thinking about it, I told him of Edward, Jesse, and our plan to take a trip to my Mexican village.

"If those two weren't gay and he wasn't your cousin, I'd be very, very jealous," he said. "I'll miss you, even for that short a period."

I quickly told him about Tía Isabela taking me to his father's fund-raiser, and that returned a cheerful tone to his voice. He went on and on about it, the food, the entertainment, the people we would meet.

"There's a good chance the governor might stop by. He has a vacation home in Rancho Mirage, you know."

I agreed to try to see him during the week, but I soon discovered Tía Isabela had seen to that. She had him meet us at the dress shop the following Wednesday so he could take us to dinner. I was surprised that Sophia showed no signs of envy when she heard about her mother taking me to the fundraiser. She told me she hated those sorts of things.

"You've got to watch everything you do and everything you say. And the people there are mostly old and stuffy. You'll see," she said. "I'll have my girlfriends and some boys over for a party around the pool," she told me. "Just don't dare say anything to my mother about it. I don't care if she finds out as long as it's afterward."

Maybe because she knew Adan was going to meet us at the dress shop, Tía Isabela spent nearly two thousand dollars on a gown for me. The shoes were seven hundred. She promised to lend me some more of her jewelry as well. Even though I knew in my heart that she had other motives for doing what she was doing, I let myself be treated like her daughter. The salesgirl, excited about the purchases Tía Isabela was making, had to comment and tell me, "Your aunt must be terribly fond of you. You're lucky."

I welcomed her envy. Perhaps I shouldn't have, but at least for a short while, I could feel loved and imagine what it would have been like if my mother had been blessed with Tía Isabela's wealth and opportunities, and we could have gone off together, perhaps to Mexico City to shop and eat at fine restaurants, laugh and take delight in each other's company. Maybe, just maybe, I hoped, Tía Isabela had longed for such a relationship with her own daughter and was at least enjoying these moments the way I was.

But as soon as Adan arrived, she transformed from a loving aunt and surrogate mother into a socialite. Her voice took on a more correct and formal tone. Even her laugh was different. It was more of a forgery, dishonest, affected. She treated Adan as if he were a little prince and we had to pay royal homage. She laughed hard at all of his jokes, widened her eyes at his comments as if every one of them were brilliant enough to be written into books.

What threw me the most, perhaps, was how much and how enthusiastically she built me up, boasting and bragging about my achievements at school, my grasp of English, even my cooking abilities, even though she had never tasted anything I had made. After a while, I was so embarrassed I could barely glance at Adan.

Adan was polite and went along with everything she did and said, but once in a while, he winked at me to let me know he wasn't as gullible as he pretended. I was relieved when the dinner was finally over and we could go home. My body had been frozen in such a tense state the whole time I was actually exhausted. Señor Garman had already loaded the car with my things. We said good night outside the restaurant with Tía Isabela standing off to the side to watch Adan kiss me. As if it were a stamp of approval, she kissed him on the cheek, and we got into the limousine.

"What a wonderful young man," she said as we were driven away. "It's nice when a father can be proud of his son and a son can be proud of his father. Do you realize what it would mean for you if Señor Bovio was elected, Delia? You would be in Washington society, mingle with the powers that be. It's incredible to think that a girl who lived in a house that was more like a barn would exchange greetings with a president or ambassadors. Aren't you excited?"

"I am not married to Adan Bovio, Tía Isabela. I have only gone on some dates with him."

She laughed. "You can't be that dense. I saw it in his eyes when he looks at you, Delia. You've hooked him. He's head over heels in love with you."

I turned away so she couldn't read the expression on my face. She was already imagining Adan's and my wedding, calling it the biggest social event of the decade. More to put an end to all of this fantastic talk than anything, I mentioned that Edward and Jesse were coming on Saturday to review our trip plans.

"What? You can't tell me you're still considering doing something as stupid as that. You can't!"

"Why not? I have promised them, and they are very excited about it."

"This is ridiculous. And it's dangerous," she added, nodding. "I won't permit it."

"But you said —"

"I don't care what I said. I never believed you would go through with such an idea. It's absolutely the wrong time for you to do such a thing. Don't worry. I'll take care of Edward," she said, as if my only problem was disappointing my cousin.

"No, I must go," I said, a little more firmly

than I had intended.

"What do you mean, you must? Why must you go?"

"I need to visit my grandmother's and my parents' graves."

"Why? It is not the *Día de los Muertos.* That was last November."

"I don't wait for the Day of the Dead to pay my respects," I said. "I need to thank them for all the good things that have happened for me and will happen."

"Oh, please. Thank them. What did they do to bring any of this about? You must lose these foolish, ignorant superstitions. You're about to become a modern woman, an American woman with prestige. You can't go babbling about evil eyes and blessings from the beyond. And I want you to stay away from these ignorant Mexicans who hold on to these ideas," she added. She fluffed her dress and pouted. "Now you've gone and upset me, and we were having such a wonderful day and evening."

"I am sorry," I said.

She grunted but said nothing more until we arrived at the *hacienda* and entered.

"I'll speak with Edward tomorrow first thing," she told me. "Just do your schoolwork and prepare for the wonderful weekend."

Before I could respond, she turned and

marched off. I carried the boxes containing my gown and shoes up to my room. Sophia had her door shut. I could hear the music. I was sure she was on the phone with one of her girlfriends plotting and planning their own festivities for the weekend. I was so conflicted I didn't know if I could ever get to sleep. I had already had Ignacio's mother and father send him the letter that told him of my trip. I would have the specific details for them to get to him this weekend. What if Tía Isabela was able to get Edward to change his mind about going?

And what about all these things she described? Could I deny that they sounded wonderful? I felt as if I had been tied to two donkeys that wanted to go in opposite directions. The beautiful new gown hung in my closet. My memories of the day on Adan's boat were still vivid. Poor Ignacio's face was fading. Was it dreadful to wish that *mi tía* Isabela would make the decision for me? What was happening to the Delia who had struggled and suffered to cross the desert with Ignacio? Where was the Delia who worked happily beside her grandmother preparing tortillas and singing old songs? Had my parents' tragic deaths and my grandmother's passing taken that Delia's soul along with them? When I looked into my mirror in my beautiful new home, did I see only the shell of the girl I had been, and were *mi tía* Isabela and everyone else I now knew filling me with a new identity?

Maybe in so many small ways that we don't even realize and rarely understand, we confront our own Day of the Dead. We visit our own graves and finally see that the memory of who we were and where we had been was dwindling like some distant star that had died light-years before and was now only the empty illuminated echo of itself. If you could reach out to touch it, your fingers would pass through to nothing, and you would be left concluding that it was gone. Rather than be alone, you would turn to another star.

And you would be happy and sad at the same time, just as I was this night when I lowered my head to the pillow and fought back the darkness like one terrified of her own dreams. The weight of night was too great to resist, however, and I was soon overwhelmed with sleep.

Tía Isabela said nothing about my Mexican trip in the morning. Apparently, she had forgotten about it for the moment. She was too involved thinking about her own preparations for the weekend, her nail and hair appointments. Someone was coming to

the *hacienda* to do her makeup profession-
ally. She explained that television and other
media people would be at the fund-raiser, so
she had to be "up to snuff."

When she spoke about it, I watched Sophia
to see her reactions. It was as if she didn't
hear her. She ate or did whatever she was
doing and never asked a question or made a
comment.

Before Friday, however, Tía Isabela had
called Edward about our Mexican trip. They
apparently had an argument on the phone,
and then Edward called me and told me to
disregard whatever his mother had said. He
and Jesse were coming down on Saturday,
and that was that.

Adan was busy on Friday with his work,
and then he was going to some campaign
events with his father. He wanted to see me
and asked if I wanted to go along as well, but
I told him I was tired and would rather rest
for the bigger night on Saturday. He said
he understood and admitted he probably
wouldn't have had that much time for me
anyway, and I might have been uncomfortable.

Neither Sophia nor I knew where Tía Isabela was Friday night. She left no instructions. Sophia went out with her girlfriends,
and I had dinner alone, watched some televi-

sion, and tried to distract myself from thinking about the tension now between Edward and Tía Isabela.

It wasn't until Saturday morning at breakfast that she brought it up.

"Your cousin and his companion are coming here today. I want you to tell them in no uncertain terms that you will not go to Mexico. Is that clear?" she asked me at the table moments after she entered. Sophia strutted in, half-asleep as usual, but she perked up at the tone in her mother's voice.

I didn't respond.

"You'll ruin everything by doing something that stupid," Tía Isabela continued.

"I told Adan about my trip already," I said, keeping my gaze on the plate. "He wasn't upset."

"Of course, he wasn't upset with you on the phone, but he thinks you're doing it for your cousin, and he wouldn't want to get into any argument with you about it. He's too much of a gentleman."

"Oh, please, spare us," Sophia said. "Adan Bovio is too much of a gentleman?"

"Don't you dare contradict me, Sophia."

"Yes, your highness."

I was happy they were at each other, and Tía Isabela was not concentrating on me.

"Don't take that tone with me. Did you go

out of this house last night?"

"You said I could if I came home early."

"Did you come home early? I can ask Mrs. Rosario."

"It was early to me. It was before midnight. Wasn't it, Delia?" she asked, turning to me.

I looked at Tía Isabela. "I was asleep early myself," I said.

"You'd never stand up for me, would you?" Sophia complained. "But you expect me to come to your defense all the time."

"I didn't say you were lying. I just said —"

"Yeah, yeah. I came home early, Mother, earlier than you."

"That's enough. You've spoiled my appetite. I will not allow myself to get stressed out today. It does terrible damage to your face, deepens lines, not that I have that many."

She suddenly remembered what she had said to me.

"Just be sure to make it clear to Edward, Delia. I expect nothing less from you."

Again, I said nothing. After breakfast, I went up to my bedroom anticipating Edward and Jesse's impending arrival. I tried doing some reading for school and some math homework just to keep myself from thinking about it all. I think I dozed off for a while, because suddenly, Sophia was at my door, a gleeful smile on her face. I could hear shouting below.

"Hear that?" she said. "They're fighting about you."

I stepped out into the hallway. Edward and Jesse had arrived, and Tía Isabela had intercepted them before they started up the stairway.

Sophia held her smile and followed me to the top of the stairway.

"Do you fools realize how dangerous it is nowadays to travel those back roads in Mexico to that decrepit village? Why would you want to go there and see that poverty? And what about the health issues?"

"You hid our heritage from us all our lives," Edward responded. "We have a right to know and understand from where we have come."

"Understand?" She laughed. "Now, you listen to me, Edward Dallas, you can threaten to do whatever you want with your money. I no longer care. I have through my own business associates created a strong financial foundation. What we lose because of you, we lose and you lose, but I am that girl's legal guardian, not you. She is still in my care and control, and I absolutely forbid your taking her on this idiotic Mexican trip. That's final."

I took a few steps down.

"If you defy me, I swear, I'll go to the police and have them pick you up for kidnapping."

I saw her pointing to Edward and then to Jesse.

"Don't either of you test me on this," she said, turned, and walked to her side of the *hacienda*. Edward and Jesse stood there looking after her. Then Jesse saw me on the stairway and nodded.

Edward turned to me. "C'mon," he said. "We're taking you to lunch. That we can do without the police coming after us."

I hesitated and looked up at Sophia. She was as pleased as a hog wallowing in cool mud. I hurried down the stairway.

"Hasta la vista," Sophia cried, laughing.

We hurried out to Edward's car.

"Just get in," he said. His face was red with rage. Jesse said he would drive.

"What turned her off on all this?" Edward asked as we pulled away from the *hacienda*. "She wasn't so against it when we first told her."

"It doesn't sit well with her matchmaker plans, is that it?" Jesse asked.

"Sí. She is afraid it will upset Adan and Señor Bovio."

"That's a twist," Jesse said. "Ray Bovio

is running as a Latino candidate, and she's saying he'd be upset if you took a trip to Mexico."

"She wants me to forget my past and think only of the future."

"Think only of *her* future," Edward said. "That's what she really means. Well, we're not going to do it," he said.

"Not go to Mexico?" Jesse asked, surprised.

"No, not listen to her. Don't worry about it, Delia. Her threats are empty threats. She'd never put the police on us. It would bring too much shame to the Dallas name.

"But for now," he continued, thinking aloud, "we'll let her believe she's frightened us off. Don't mention the trip anymore to anyone, Delia. If anyone asks, it's off, especially Sophia. Put on an act for her or something. Act very sad about it. She'll enjoy seeing you sad and believe you."

"And then?" Jesse asked.

"And then we'll go as planned," Edward said, smiling. "You'll sneak out of the house that day, and we'll pick you up. Before she knows anything, we'll have flown to Mexico City," he said. "She'll get over it just the way she gets over everything. One thing about my mother, she never lets anything annoy her too much. She's afraid it would age her.

This is one time I'm grateful for her vanity."

Jesse smiled.

"Okay, Delia?" Edward asked.

I had my chance. I could have stopped it all then.

But I didn't.

I nodded and added one more secret to my backpack, another burden to weigh on my soul.

We drove on now talking about Mexico.

All I could think about was how I had to sneak up to the Davilas' and give Ignacio's mother the details.

And then, after that, there was just the waiting and constantly looking for the evil eye.

15
GIVE THE DEVIL HER DUE

It was hard for me to concentrate on preparing for the fund-raiser dinner. After lunch, Edward and Jesse spent another hour or so with me. They complimented me on the dress and shoes Tía Isabela had bought me. Edward said he had to give the devil her due. His mother had impeccable taste. They left to return to Los Angeles. Moments after they had, Sophia came to spy. Of course, she pretended only to be interested in my new dress at first, and then, in a by-the-way tone of voice, asked, "Well, what are you going to do about the trip to Mexico?"

"We can do nothing," I said, and as Edward advised, I pretended I was about to break into tears. "I had so wanted to show them where I had lived, where your mother had once lived, but Edward says it is true. Your mother is my legal guardian, and it would cause much trouble if we defied her wishes."

"Really?" she asked, sounding disappointed. "I would never have thought Edward was such a coward."

"Jesse is worried, too," I said.

"Yes, I can understand that. He should be worried. He's not related. He probably could get into serious trouble, and his parents would be quite upset. My mother would have him charged with kidnapping. Maybe," she added, still looking for a way to tease and disturb me, "Edward isn't trying to make you happy anymore because he's simply too upset about your budding romance with Adan."

"He is not!"

She laughed. Then she grew serious. "Or maybe you're just pretending to be upset about not going yourself, huh? Maybe you've finally learned how to kiss up to my mother and get things out of her, like that expensive dress and those shoes. Maybe you just love being wined and dined and being with the wealthy like Adan and Fani."

"Think what you like," I said. "You will, anyway."

She nodded, happy about her conclusions. "You're not so innocent anymore, Delia Yebarra. In fact, you're more like me than you'd care to admit. That's all right," she said. "Eventually, we'll help each other get what we want."

She laughed and left.

Rather than be like her, I thought, I'd trade places with my poorest girlfriend back in my Mexican village.

Once again, Tía Isabela was up in my room to supervise my makeup and hair. She brought the jewelry she had promised. My eyes widened so dramatically at the size of the diamonds on the bracelet and necklace that she laughed.

"Before you ask, Delia, yes, they are real. My husband would never buy me fake jewelry, and I certainly would never buy any for myself. Wear that watch I gave you. I want you to try on some of these rings as well," she suggested, opening a small box to show them to me. "You and I have the same ring size, I'm sure."

The rings did fit. She chose the one I should wear.

While she hovered around me, fixing strands of my hair, making me do some of my makeup over, trying different shades of lipstick, Sophia came to the doorway and watched. Despite the way she had belittled going to the fund-raiser, I saw the look of envy in her face, and I couldn't help but feel sorry for her. Her mother was treating me just the way she wished she would treat her, despite the act she put on, pretending not to care about such things.

Tía Isabela glanced at her from time to time but said nothing. Couldn't she see how much pain Sophia was feeling? I did not understand how a mother could be so indifferent to her own daughter's feelings. Perhaps more puzzling to me was how *mi tía* Isabela could be so different from her sister, my mother. Some selfish coyote surely had peered into our house the night Tía Isabela was made. Despite all I had learned, I couldn't help but believe in such superstitions. *Mi tía* was living proof.

Finally, she spoke to Sophia.

"If you would take some interest in your own appearance and stop hanging around with losers and riffraff, Sophia, you could enjoy social events, too."

"I'd rather hang around with riffraff," Sophia said, grimacing.

"I know you would," Tía Isabela said, pausing to look at her. "That's the pity of it all. We can thank your father for it."

"Right. Blame everything on a dead man," Sophia fired back, her eyes actually filling with tears. She stormed away and slammed her bedroom door.

"I was hoping something good from your new life would rub off on her," Tía Isabela said, "but I'm afraid she is doomed to suffer great unhappiness."

She stood back to look at me.

"Perfect. You'll sparkle beside Adan Bovio, especially in the photographs. Come down in twenty minutes," she said, and left.

I gazed at myself in the full-length mirror. In the new dress and shoes, with my hair styled, the makeup highlighting my features, and the jewelry dazzling, I dared to think I was a good candidate for princess. Why shouldn't I be, couldn't I be, just as pretty and impressive as Fani or any other girl at the event? Was it really so sinful to take pride in your appearance? Was I guilty of too much vanity? Would I open the door for the devil and the evil eye? How does anyone ever enjoy good fortune and pleasure if she is always worried about being too lucky? Why couldn't I have the same thick skin as Tía Isabela and think of myself as someone special, no matter what anyone else thought or said? Hadn't I already paid the high price for any happiness I would enjoy? Did even thinking of such questions mean I had gone too far and crossed over into the world of the damned? I'll never enjoy anything in my life as long as I feel this way, I thought. In that sense, Tía Isabela was right and someone to admire.

Hoping that I wasn't turning my back completely on the honest and pure things my family in Mexico had given me, I set out for the fund-raiser, feeling proud and confident in my looks and appearance.

"Have fun with the snobs," Sophia called to me as I passed her door.

I didn't respond.

Tía Isabela joined me in the foyer, and we walked out, both elegantly dressed, both bedecked in jewels, looking like birds of a feather. Even though I knew in my heart that she was using me in her pursuit of Señor Bovio, I permitted her to take me under her wing and turn me into the Latina Cinderella Sophia mocked. Señor Garman looked at me with some astonishment and hurried to open the limousine doors for us.

"*Usted es muy hermosa, Delia,*" he whispered as I slipped into the limousine. Hearing him say I looked beautiful brought a blush to my cheeks.

"*Gracias,* Señor Garman," I whispered back. Even so, I saw Tía Isabela had heard and smiled to herself as if I were entirely her creation.

When we arrived at the hotel, I realized all the plans and preparations were justified. It was like the movie premieres I had seen on television. There were spotlights in front of the entrance, and when we drove up, men in tuxedos were there to greet us immediately with glasses of champagne. Tía Isabela permitted me to have one.

"Tonight," she whispered, "you cannot be a girl. You are a woman."

Still, it made me nervous to walk into the ballroom with a glass of champagne. The guests who were arriving and had arrived were just as dressed up as we were, some even more so. Women were wearing tiaras that looked as if they cost thousands of dollars, and every gown I saw was surely as expensive as, if not more expensive than, the ones we were wearing.

There was music, and waiters and waitresses went about with more glasses of champagne and hors d'ouevres. Almost as soon as we entered the ballroom, an assistant for Señor Bovio rushed over to lead us through the aisle of tables dressed in beautiful centerpieces to the front tables, where Adan and his father were waiting and being greeted by one guest after another. Fani and her parents were there as well.

"That," Tía Isabela said, nodding to my right, "is the current U.S. senator, not running this time, and over there is the attorney general of California."

She identified all of the major local officials, mayors of cities and towns, state assemblymen, and state senators. She even pointed out old movie stars and singers and especially directed my attention to the billionaires and millionaires. It was all so overwhelming and dazzling I didn't know where to look first. Fortunately, Adan pulled himself away from the guests and greeted me with a kiss on the cheek.

"You look fantastic," he said. "I had to look twice to be sure I wasn't dreaming."

He took my hand and brought me to his father, who looked at me with more interest than I had expected. He gave Adan a look, too, and nodded his approval. After that, Adan began introducing me to other guests while *mi tía* Isabela stood off to the side near Adan's father and met people as well, pausing every once in a while to give me a nod of approval.

Fani, who was with people I did not know, smiled and waved and nodded her approval. She finally excused herself to join me for a few moments.

"You look like you have arrived, Delia. I have to hand it to your aunt. She's remade you, turned you into one of us. How's sweet Sophia taking all this?"

"Badly," I said and she laughed.

"Remember my warnings. Sophia doesn't

give up easily."

When Adan returned this time, he looked at Fani and asked, "Well?"

"I love you, cousin," she told him, and then, looking at me, she added, "but when it comes to men, Delia and I would rather put our faith in scorpions."

He laughed, and Fani returned to her parents' table.

"What was that about?" I asked.

"Fani refuses to be convinced about how much I like you, but she'll come around and become a believer," he said, kissing me softly on the cheek.

By the time we sat to start the dinner, my stomach was tied in such knots I didn't think I could eat a morsel. I soon discovered that two of the empty chairs at the Bovio table were being held for the governor and his wife. When he entered the room, the band stopped, and the master of ceremonies introduced him. Everyone stood to applaud. He was just as he appeared on television. He spoke fluent Spanish, so when he finally reached our table and everyone was introduced, he turned to Adan and smiled at me when he said, *"Menos mi esposa, ella es la mujer más bonita aquí."*

I didn't think it was possible to blush any redder than I had already, but I felt the heat in my cheeks.

Adan leaned over to whisper, "He had to say except for his wife, but I could see it in his face. He thinks you're the prettiest woman here."

Mi tía Isabela was beaming. I had come to California hoping that somehow she would accept me as her flesh and blood and together we would find ways to get beyond the ugliness of the past. Until this moment, nothing had ever given me hope of doing so, but I sensed that if she could exchange Sophia for me, she wouldn't hesitate.

There were famous singers at the dinner to entertain. There was dancing to the twenty-six-piece orchestra and afterward some short speeches by other politicians praising Adan's father. Before the evening was over, Adan told me his father's campaign had raised nearly two and a half million dollars, with other pledges coming.

Sometime during the evening, while Adan was talking to other people and Tía Isabela was with Señor Bovio, I had time to think about something Tía Isabela had said. I had been defiant when she told me I would forget my life in Mexico, but sitting here among all these wealthy people, these glamorous celebrities and powerful politicians, it was nearly impossible to remember the dirt streets of my village, the tiny homes and poor laboring families. I had the strange feeling the old Delia was drowning in a sea of opulence and riches once beyond her imagination. The *hacienda,* my car, my new clothes, the jewelry I wore, all of it was far too bewitching. I even questioned the wisdom of sneaking off with Edward and Jesse to make the trip to my village.

Perhaps, I thought sadly, I was weaker than I had thought. Perhaps there truly was more of *mi tía* Isabela in me than I had believed.

"Why so long a face, Delia?" Adan asked, surprising me.

I quickly smiled. "Long face?"

"You look like you're unhappy. Aren't you having a good time?"

"Oh, yes."

"I wish we could do something more tonight, but —"

"Oh, this is enough," I said, perhaps too quickly. He laughed.

"I guess it is," he said. He kissed me on the cheek and then got pulled away to meet another politician's son. Fani joined me again to tell me how good an impression I had made on everyone I had spoken to.

"You're a quick learner, Delia. You're going to be a big success."

"At what?"

"At getting what you want," she said, smiling coyly. "Just like the rest of us."

She left me with that remark. I wasn't happy about it, though. It made it sound as if Sophia was right. We were like each other, all of us, using each other for selfish goals.

I was happy when Tía Isabela told me we would be leaving. Adan promised to call me the next day with plans for another dinner or maybe just to have something simple and go to a movie.

"Whatever you want," he said, walking us out to our limousine.

"Delia wants whatever you want, I'm sure, Adan," Tía Isabela said, overhearing.

Adan smiled. "Thank you for your generous donation to my father's campaign," he told her.

"There are few causes as worthwhile," she replied.

He kissed me softly on the lips, and then we got into the limousine. He remained there until we pulled away. Looking back at him resurrected my memory of Ignacio when I went off in the bus back in Mexico City and he waved his good-bye.

Only he now seemed much farther and smaller in my mind.

It brought tears to my eyes.

"You did well, Delia. I hear only good

things about you. You're on your way to becoming a real lady. I only wish I could say the same about Sophia," Tía Isabela muttered, turning away.

Her wish would be reinforced moments after we arrived at the *hacienda*. The number of cars parked in front was the first warning. When we pulled up, Tía Isabela didn't wait for Señor Garman to open her door. She lunged out. Even though the pool was a good distance behind the house, we could hear the loud music, laughter, and shouting going on. Sophia had either neglected to watch the clock or had decided to do something else to infuriate her mother.

"What the hell is going on?" Tía Isabela cried, and charged into the house, through the living room to the French doors and out the back, almost before I had entered the house. Señora Rosario was standing off to the side, shaking her head.

"I kept them from taking any of Señora Dallas's whiskey," she told me, "but they brought their own and other things as well, I'm sure."

"What's going on?"

I went through the French doors to see.

Many of the boys and some of the girls had either been thrown into the pool with their clothes on or had jumped in themselves. Tía

Isabela's looming appearance silenced them. Someone turned off the music. Sophia, who was sprawled on the diving board, sat up in surprise and saw her mother. Everyone scurried to climb out of the pool. I saw Christian Taylor take off his shoes to empty the water out of them before putting them on again.

"I want every one of you off my property in five minutes or less," Tía Isabela said, "or I will call the police. I know who you all are, and I will make sure that every parent is informed."

They all stood staring.

"Get out!" she screamed, and they hurried to gather their things. "Don't dare walk through my house. Go around to your cars."

Sophia simply dropped herself from the diving board into the pool and swam to the other side. Christian Taylor helped her out and then moved quickly to follow the others, some of whom were still laughing.

"Thanks a lot for making me look like an idiot, Mother!" Sophia cried.

"You *are* an idiot, Sophia," Tía Isabela said. "You are not to go anywhere but to school and back until further notice, maybe until you're eighteen and out of my house. If you disobey me this time, I will ship you off in a straitjacket," she added, glanced at me, and marched back into the house.

"You can have her for a mother if that's what you want," Sophia said, wobbling toward me.

"She is not my mother. She can never be my mother. She is your mother," I said.

"Yeah, well, I'm giving her to you, whether you like it or not," she said, slurring her words.

I watched her head toward the house, stumble, and then continue.

She'd be sorry in the morning, I thought, and followed her in. She didn't get far. Tía Isabela was right at the French doors.

"Take off those wet clothes now. You don't track in that water and ruin my rugs. Do it!"

Sophia wobbled and then began stripping off her clothes, smiling as she did so. She dropped everything at her feet. Totally naked, she walked to the stairway without any embarrassment, paused to smile back at us, and then went up.

"She has no shame," Tía Isabela said sadly. She told Señora Rosario to get rid of Sophia's clothing, and then she went to her own bedroom.

When I looked in on Sophia, she was still naked and lying on her stomach on her bed. I closed her door and went to my own room.

It was difficult to fall asleep. I truly felt as if I had been on a merry-go-round. Ending the night with this terrible scene at the *hacienda* only added to the confusion and excitement. My nerves buzzed like neon lights. Visions of my parents, *mi abuela* Anabela, Ignacio, my classmates in Mexico, all commingled with visions of the people I knew now. By the time I fell asleep, the morning sunlight was peeping over the horizon. I didn't rise until the phone rang at midday. It was Adan. I told him to give me a chance to wake up. He laughed and said he understood. I said nothing about Sophia's wild pool party.

Sophia, probably suffering a hangover, never came out of her room all day. I saw Tía Isabela briefly after what was my breakfast. She told me she wouldn't be home for dinner, but if Sophia ever came out, I was to tell her she would be home early enough to check up on her. I was supposed to warn her again that her mother's patience had run out and she was prepared to send her to a special camp for impossible children. Fortunately, I didn't see Sophia all day. If I was the one to give her such a message, I knew she would hate me more, if that was possible.

Since Sophia was so under the weather, I thought I had my best opportunity to visit Señora Davila. Adan called again and suggested we go for an early bite and a movie, but I thought that would put too much pressure on me to get back in time from the Davilas' home. I told him what Tía Isabela and I had found going on at the *hacienda* when we had returned from the fund-raiser and how terrible the atmosphere was at the house.

"It feels as if a bomb is set to go off. I'm tiptoeing around," I told him. "Because of the commotion, I didn't get to bed until late and had trouble falling asleep."

"I can imagine. She's headed for big trouble," he said, and then suggested we go to dinner. "You need to get out of there for a while, Delia."

He promised it would be a quieter evening. I agreed to end the conversation and started out before Sophia came down. I had been hoping to find Santos at home and the opportunity to speak with him, but he was somewhere with his father.

Señora Davila was happy to see me and ecstatic that I was really going to Mexico and would see Ignacio.

"He has sent back this note, telling you where to meet him in your village. I would appreciate your giving him this," she said, handing me a cross on a chain. In the center of the cross was a tiny diamond. "It was my grandmother's, my mother's, and mine. I want Ignacio to have it. I want him to have hope again," she said.

I promised I would give it to him. She also gave me a letter she had written.

"Rather than send it the usual way, I'd like you to hand it to him personally. My husband is already nervous about sending your letters to him."

"I understand."

"I am not one for writing letters. My writing skills are poor, but there are things sometimes better said like this. Also, he can hold on to the letter, hold on to the words, and read them whenever he wants."

"*Sí, señora.* I will hand it to him myself."

"*Gracias.* Be careful yourself, Delia."

She hugged me, and I left, wondering if I should say anything to her about Santos talking to Sophia. I thought it might add to her heavy worries, however, and decided not to speak of it. I couldn't imagine Sophia coming here anymore, anyway, now that she was literally under house arrest.

She had still not emerged from her room when I returned. The door remained shut, and I didn't bother to check on her. Instead, I hurried to shower, do my hair, and dress for my dinner with Adan. Tía Isabela called from wherever she was to ask me what Adan and I were doing. She sounded worried that I would have somehow not agreed to go out with him.

"It's an exciting time for both of us," she told me. The way she had included me in her happiness surprised me but also disturbed me. It was almost as if Sophia had died and I had truly taken her place.

Despite my fear that I would be terrible company and ruin the evening for Adan as well, I soon found myself relaxing. He was very upbeat, perhaps to overcome my dark mood. He talked optimistically about the future, his business, his father's election, parties we would attend, more trips with his boat, describing days and weeks of future activities as if we were already engaged or even married.

"Soon you'll graduate from high school and be out of that house and away from all the tension and trouble," he said.

We had gone to a fancy French restaurant, and I had permitted him to order for both of us. He surprised me with his command of French and his knowledge of the menu, the sauces, and even the preparation of the dishes. Once again, he reminded me of his travels in Europe, and I realized how wide the gap between us really was. Despite all that Tía Isabela had done to prepare me for this high social life and despite the progress I had made with my education, I was still a stranger in a strange land. Adan didn't seem to care about it, however. In fact, he enjoyed being my teacher, telling me about things I had never seen.

"I want to do all these things over, go to all these places again with you," he told me.

"How can you be so certain about us, about me, Adan?" I asked him before we had finished our dinner. I had waited as long as I could to ask. "After all, we have not known each other that long."

He smiled, thought a moment, and said, "Because of the way you make me feel, the way I feel when I'm with you, and I don't mean just having a beautiful young woman on my arm. Some men wear their women like another piece of jewelry, but for me, being with you . . . is different."

"How is it different?" I pursued. I wanted to know what it was he felt so strongly.

He smiled again. "I like that," he said. "I like that you're making me dig deeply into myself to answer."

"And what is the answer, Adan?"

He thought before speaking, just as before. "You make me aware of what it means to have family," he said. "I haven't felt this way since my mother died, even though my father tries the best he can."

He couldn't have said anything that would have endeared me to him more, but he couldn't have said anything that would have given me more pause, either.

Family was what Ignacio had lost and what I had hoped to bring back to him.

Family was what I had lost and what I had hoped to regain myself when I was with Ignacio.

In the end, the rich and the poor want the same things after all, I thought. We are all desperate for the same real love, the same sense of belonging, the same comfort that came with loyalty and devotion. Money couldn't buy it, and it was not something luck brought. You had to have an honest heart that you were willing to open to someone else, someone you would trust with your very soul.

He reached for my hand.

"Adan," I began.

"No, no, don't apologize. I'm glad you made us have this serious conversation, Delia," he said. "When you return from Mexico, I want to continue it."

My heart began to pound. I had not told him that mi tía Isabela had forbidden the trip. Apparently, she had not told him, either, or even mentioned it to his father.

I smiled. Maybe it was deceitful giving him such hope, giving such hope to myself, in fact, but I was too much of a coward to do or say anything that would change it. I held his hand as tightly as he held mine.

But the back of my neck felt hot. Behind me, in the shadows, the evil eye was surely beginning to open.

16
ESCAPE

Schoolwork, studying for exams before our vacation break, kept me busy during the following ten days. Adan was busier as well, because his father's campaign had picked up its pace. He traveled with his father all over the state and at the same time had to look after their business concerns. Edward and Jesse visited once more and again went into detail about our trip, which was now our secret escape. Sophia hovered about like some buzzard waiting for something, some mistake, some opening that would give her an opportunity to pounce on any of us, but we were all very careful. Tía Isabela's rage the night of Sophia's wild swimming party didn't diminish all that much as time went by. She still refused to permit her any privileges and kept her from seeing her friends after school and on weekends. It made her more sour and bitchy, but Tía Isabela seemed determined this time to break her spirit. She kept reminding her of the alternative.

"Disobey me once more, Sophia, and you're gone. I'm not kidding. Preliminary arrangements are all in place. You know I have friends high up in the judicial system who will take you in hand."

Sophia was quite aware of what had happened to that boy, Philip Deutch. He was something of what they called an urban legend at our school, used by more than one parent from time to time to threaten a child. It was as if they said the wicked witch would get them. He loomed out there, embodying a punishment so severe it actually gave some of the students nightmares, including, I imagine, Sophia. Tía Isabela reminded her that she had already been in juvenile court. She had a record, so to speak, and was a prime candidate for more severe punishments.

She cowered and backed away but, like some rat in the corner, waited patiently for her opportunity. During the ten days, she wasn't nasty to me, but her friendliness and at times overly sweet manner only put me on my guard even more. Fani was always there as well, chanting, reminding, warning.

Because I had said nothing more about Mexico, Tía Isabela dropped the subject, too. Edward and Jesse did a fine job of making it seem we all had moved off the idea. When they were home, they talked about college activities, their classes and plans for other trips. I thought Edward was being more pleasant to his mother than I had ever seen him while he winked at me behind her back. It all made me feel more deceitful, but I saw no other choice. Señora Davila's cross and letter remained close to my heart. I dreamed of handing them both to Ignacio and finally seeing him again. Every night, I read his note describing the cantina where we would meet. I memorized every letter in every word, even the way he formed them with the curves in his S's and the slightly tilted crosses in the T's.

I was actually trembling the day school broke for the holidays. Everyone was excited about his or her time off. Most were going places with their families. Tía Isabela never once mentioned such an idea. She was even more involved now with Señor Bovio's political campaign and attended a number of functions with him. She planned to attend many more. Adan still believed that I was off to Mexico with my cousins for a trip my aunt had sanctioned. He didn't suggest any dates or dinners during the holidays. It seemed to me that he was so overwhelmed with new responsibilities he was grateful I would be on a holiday anyway.

Fortunately, Tía Isabela was so distracted preparing for a cocktail party that she didn't notice just how nervous I was. Sophia looked at me suspiciously at dinner when I had trouble eating. I told her I was just not feeling well because I had gotten my period. She accepted that excuse readily. Whenever Sophia had hers, she acted as if the world were coming to an end. She moaned and groaned about her cramps and made all the servants miserable. Tía Isabela hated hearing about it.

After dinner, I packed a small satchel with what I considered essential. The plan was for me to sneak out at three A.M. and walk down to the road, where Edward and Jesse would be waiting. We would then drive off to the airport in San Diego, where they had booked a nonstop flight to Mexico City. They had reserved a rental car, and Jesse had the route all worked out. We would be in my village well before nightfall and check into the small hotel.

As if she could sense that something was happening, Sophia barged in on me twice. Fortunately, both times I was lying on my bed. I didn't have the headache and cramps I had described to her, but I was so tense I felt better just lying still until the hour to leave had come. My appearance bored and disappointed her.

"Are Edward and Jesse coming down to spend time at home, at least?" she asked me.

"I don't think so," I said. "I think they're going away with friends on a trip."

She smirked skeptically. "My mother doesn't know anything about any trip."

"Maybe she does and just hasn't said so," I remarked as casually as I could. "Maybe she doesn't think it's any of your business or mine."

"I don't believe you," she finally concluded. "You've become too good at lying."

I looked at her and shook my head. She left, and when she returned a second time, I pretended I was fast asleep, but she kept her bedroom door wide open, and I had no doubt she was waiting and watching my door all night. My hope was that she would get bored and distracted and fall asleep herself. At ten to three in the morning, I opened my door just enough to slip through. Crawling, I moved as softly and silently as I could. Sophia still had a light on, but I could also see the blinking images from her television set bouncing off the walls. I was grateful for the soft carpeting on the stairway. Barefoot, my feet whispered me down and to the front door. I didn't open it until I was certain there was no one nearby. Then I opened it as slightly as I had my bedroom door and seemingly glided on a shelf of air into the night.

My heart was pounding so hard I thought I would faint and be discovered at the entrance in the morning. Keeping myself as much as possible in the shadows, I made my way down the driveway. When I reached the gate, Edward triggered it with the clicker in his automobile, and it swung open. Jesse held the rear door open for me, and without a word, I got in. In fact, none of us spoke until we were well away from Tía Isabela's property.

"Anyone suspicious?" Edward asked.

"Sophia was. She kept asking questions. She asked about you two, as well."

"Figures. Being a sneaky person herself, she has a nose for anything sneaky," Edward said. "But you feel sure no one saw you leave?"

"Yes, I feel sure."

"Good. We're on our way, then," he said. "We've got the first flight out. By the time they realize you're gone, we'll be halfway to Mexico City."

"Tía Isabela will hate me," I said.

"And how," Jesse added.

Edward nodded. "She'll be angry for a while, but, as I told you, my mother doesn't like airing her dirty linen in public, especially now. She'll rant and rave and then just forget it. She'll try to make you feel sorry for her having to put up with two reckless teenage girls. Believe me, she'll be working at being the victim here."

"Nevertheless, don't sugarcoat it, Edward. Isabela Dallas is not exactly going to treat any of us with kid gloves," Jesse said.

"It will all be bluster," Edward insisted, giving Jesse a look of reprimand. "Don't worry about it, Delia. Just enjoy the trip, and start thinking of all the places and things you want to show us. For now, lie back and get some sleep."

"*Sí,*" I said, and sprawled out on the rear seat. I closed my eyes, not realizing just how exhausted I was from the tension. In moments, I was asleep. I woke up when I heard Jesse say we were approaching the airport parking lot.

"From here we'll take the shuttle bus," he told me when I sat up, grinding sleep out of my eyes.

After we parked and while we were waiting for the shuttle bus, I felt as if we had become three shadows. They were tired themselves. None of us said much. Finally, the bus arrived, and we rode to the terminal. Edward gave me my airline ticket, and we went through the process of checking in for our flight. We didn't have to wait too long before boarding, but I almost fell asleep again in the chair by the gate.

When we entered the plane and took our seats, I felt a new cold rush of fear wash over me. We were really going. There was no turning back now. Edward squeezed my hand gently to reassure me. I didn't imagine I was doing a good job of hiding my anxiety. I kept looking at the airplane door, expecting policemen to come charging aboard at any moment to take the three of us off in handcuffs. But the door was closed, and the pilot addressed the passengers. We felt the plane move back out of its docking, and moments later we were rolling along, heading for takeoff. I gripped the armrests and closed my eyes as the plane lifted. I tried to concentrate on images of Ignacio.

"Take another short nap," Edward whispered. He closed his eyes himself. Jesse was already asleep. I nodded and did exactly that.

I slept until the flight attendant announced that we were preparing for our descent to the airport in Mexico City. There was just enough time for me to go to the washroom and soak my face in cold water. I returned to my seat and saw the excitement on both Edward's and Jesse's faces.

"Welcome to Mexico," Edward kidded when the wheels of the plane touched down.

We hurried off the plane when the doors were opened. Like me, they had brought only carry-ons, so we didn't have to go to the baggage carousels. We went directly to the rental-car desk, where Edward and Jesse finished the paperwork. Another shuttle bus took us to the lot, and we found our car. They had rented a nice-size SUV.

It was somewhat hazy when we set out from the airport, but as we went west, the sky cleared. Seeing the *campesinos* walking along to their work on the larger farms, the women and children walking along, some with donkeys, some pulling little wagons filled with vegetables to sell in the markets, passing cantinas, open markets, and villages with squares built in front of their churches, just as in my village, drew me back through time until I felt as if I had never left. It took only minutes to remind me how much I loved my country and, despite its hardships, my life with my family in our poor village. I couldn't look at everything enough, and looking at it all quickly brought tears to my eyes.

Jesse and Edward were full of questions about everything.

"What exactly is a *campesino?*" Jesse asked.

"Rural people who have a little land but not enough to provide for themselves and their families. They have to work on the bigger farms, but they still take pride in what they own," I quickly added, "even though people back in the U.S. would laugh at what they own."

"I guess owning a car is a big thing out here," Edward noted.

"They don't go very far from their work and their *casas*. In the village, they find their entertainment, their religion, their schools."

Little children waved at us as we drove by, and Jesse waved back.

"They act surprised at seeing us. This isn't exactly tourist territory, is it?" Edward asked.

"No. You will not find English spoken at all in some places."

"I never fully appreciated the enormous changes you've had in your life until now," he said.

"*Sí,*" I said, unable not to sound sad.

"You've done very well, Delia," Jesse immediately told me. "You should be proud of yourself."

I smiled at him and said, *"Gracias."*

Everyone was hungry, so we stopped at a roadside cantina and had some soft tacos and beans. They both drank bottles of Mexican beer, and then we continued on. The going became slower as the roads narrowed and turned into broken macadam, gravel, and just dirt in places. Edward was glad they had decided to rent an SUV and not some fancy automobile. The newer road construction was uneven. At times, we would ride for miles on good roads and then turn onto the older, broken ones.

Finally, I began to recognize the area just outside my village. I sat up with renewed energy and excitement. I was truly coming home, and even though neither my parents nor *mi abuela* Anabela were alive, I looked forward to going to our *casa* and walking the same streets. Of course, I would get to the cemetery as soon as possible.

"Is this it?" Edward asked as we approached.

"Sí. Es todo. This is all of it," I said, smiling.

Jesse turned to me. "Funny how you went right to Spanish," he said. "You really have come home."

"Sí, Jesse. *Estoy en casa otra vez.* I am

home again."

I told them where the Hotel Los Jardines Hermosos was located. As we approached it, we passed by Señora Rubio's *menudo* shop, and I smiled at the realization that I had almost ended up there married to her son. Ignacio had saved me, and now I was returning in hopes of saving him.

"This is our town square," I said the moment we reached it. "At night, there is music and food. You'll see tonight. That's our church."

"I think we can see that," Jesse said, laughing.

"Don't tease her," Edward said, then winked and added, "too much."

They both laughed at me.

"I want to see the house in which my mother lived. I brought a camera for that," Edward said. "I plan on blowing the picture up into a poster and putting it on the wall in the living room."

"She'd kill you," Jesse said. Edward gave him an impish smile.

When they saw what was the hotel, they laughed again.

"And you called ahead and made a reservation," Edward reminded him.

"Stop, please, Edward!" I cried.

"What?" he asked, stopping.

"These two women looking at us. They are the Paz sisters, friends of *mi abuela* Anabela."

I lowered the window and waved to them. They stared confused for a moment and then both simultaneously brought their hands to their hearts.

"Delia?" Señora Paz said, walking slowly toward us.

"*Sí, cómo está*, Señora Paz?"

"*Mi dios*," her sister Margarita said. "*Es Delia*."

They looked at me as if I were a ghost.

"You are a grown woman," Señora Paz remarked.

I quickly introduced Edward and Jesse and explained that we were there to visit. I knew they were full of questions, so I promised to stop by to spend time with them.

"You are a grown woman?" Edward quipped.

"They knew me only as a young girl. They helped me when I . . ." I stopped myself.

"Ran away?" Edward asked.

"*Sí*."

"But, like Batman and Robin, we came to your rescue," Edward joked.

"Your mother calls you the Lone Ranger and Tonto."

They laughed, and we pulled up to the

hotel. The owners, Señor Agular and his wife, Teresa, remembered me, of course, and, just like the Paz sisters, remarked about how grown-up I looked. They gave us the two best rooms of the six, both with windows looking out on the main street. None of the rooms had bathrooms, but there were two in the hallways, and at the moment, as was true most of the time, there were no other guests in the hotel. They made their living mostly from the small cantina. The cost of the rooms in American dollars brought smiles to Edward's and Jesse's faces, especially when they heard the price also included breakfast.

"Three lattes at Starbucks would cost more," Jesse said. "Maybe we oughtta look into buying up some real estate."

They were laughing at everything now, and even though I had anticipated it, I couldn't help being a little annoyed.

"This isn't Palm Springs," I told them, "but you will not find the people less friendly."

"She's right," Edward said. "Besides, I come from this place, too. Let's go right to the house, Delia."

It didn't take us long to settle into the rooms, and then we started up the street.

"Where's the school?" Jesse asked.

"Back there," I said, pointing behind us.

"We can see it later, if you like."

When we reached the town square, I told them how, as a child, I believed the prayers said in church went up through the steeple and directly to God's ears.

"Maybe it's true," Edward said.

"You see what that boy is eating?" I asked, nodding at a little boy enjoying a chocolate-dipped *churro*. "It's nothing more than chocolate-dipped fried dough, but it's delicious. You'll have to have one before we leave."

We walked past the *menudo* shop, and I saw Señora Rubio's son, Pascual, serving a customer. He looked even heavier. It was hard now to imagine that I had almost married him. Neither Edward nor Jesse noticed how I looked back and shook my head. They were taking in everything as if they had gone to Disneyland.

We turned down the dirt street to my family's *casa*. There was still no lawn or even any grass in front of it, just some shrubs, stubble of grass, stones, and the remnants of the faded pink and white fountain that no longer had water running through it unless it rained hard. We hadn't sold it or removed it, because it had an angel at the top, and *mi abuela* Anabela believed that if you had a replica of an angel in or around your house,

397

real angels would stop to bless you.

"This is it, Edward," I said.

He and Jesse stopped and just gaped at it for a few moments, before Edward took out his camera.

"I can't imagine Isabela Dallas living in this," Jesse muttered. "In fact, Delia, I can't imagine you living here."

"I did, Jesse, and I didn't think myself so bad off. In fact, this *casa* is one of the nicest in the village. My grandmother and I had slept in our own bedroom."

"You are truly a remarkable girl," he said.

Edward agreed, took more pictures, and then, because of the time and the heat, suggested we return to the hotel and cantina and have some *cerveza*.

"I want to go to the square tonight and hear the music and see the people, the artisans, all of it. We have to do some shopping and bring back some nice gifts for Sophia and my mother."

All the while, I was trying to think of a way to separate from them so I could meet Ignacio at the cantina just a little ways north of the village. I thought I might use the excuse of visiting with some old girlfriends. I would tell them they would be bored, so I would visit and return to be with them in the square.

I waited until darkness began to fall and they had become very relaxed, drinking their beer. Neither objected. In fact, Edward said I should feel free to do whatever I liked.

"I know you want very much to go to the cemetery yourself, Delia. Don't worry about us. We'll amuse ourselves fine."

I went up to my room and changed into the dress I had brought for my meeting with Ignacio. Now that I was literally only an hour or so away from seeing him, I was trembling with excitement and nervousness. Would he think I had changed? Would I bring disappointment instead of great happiness to him? Would our reunion be sad or wonderful? Had I done the right thing by coming here, or should I have waited for him to make his way back?

I knocked on Edward and Jesse's door and told them I would meet them in the square later.

"If you get hungry, don't wait for me," I said.

"We'll wait," Edward insisted. "We've been gorging on the chips and salsa and some *empanadas* in the hotel cantina."

"Okay," I said. "See you later."

I hurried out. It would be a long walk that would take me past the cemetery. I decided I would stop there on my return.

As I walked, I did see some of my girl-friends and some of the boys I knew, but I didn't approach them. I did not want to do anything to delay my reunion with Ignacio. I clung tightly to my purse, which contained the cross his mother had given me for him and her letter.

When the cantina came into view, my heart started to pound again. My legs felt wobbly, and my stomach did flip-flops. I saw some trucks and some cars nearby, but I did not see Ignacio. What if he had been unable to come? How would I know? How would he get a message to me? How long could I wait? Why wasn't he standing outside watching for me?

Drawing closer, I could see men and women and some children eating in the outside patio, but I did not see Ignacio. My heart seemed to drop in my chest. I had come all this way to be disappointed, and I would have to bring back his mother's cross and letter. I looked inside but still did not see him. For a few moments, I just stood in front looking down the street and then up from the way I had come. No one approaching from any direction looked at all like him.

Suddenly, I felt someone touch me at the waist, and I turned around to look into his smiling face.

"Ignacio!" I cried. "Where were you?"

"In the rear watching you."

We stared at each other a moment, and then he embraced me.

"You are more beautiful than I remember," he said. "Life in America has been good for you."

"And you look older, more mature."

"You either grow up quickly or die when you're desperate," he said.

"I brought you this from your mother," I said, before I forgot, and handed him the cross and the letter.

He looked at the cross and shook his head. "She was saving this for my wedding."

"She thinks you need it now," I told him. "It was very important to her that I get it to you, and her letter."

"Sí. So," he began, "how long . . ."

He paused, and the expression on his face changed quickly to a look of shock and fear. I turned to see what had so frightened him and gasped. Seemingly out of thin air, a half-dozen federal police officers appeared. Police cars came flying down the street as well.

Ignacio looked at me with such accusation in his eyes I couldn't speak. All I could do was shake my head.

"What did you trade for this? What will your aunt give you?" he asked.

"No. I did nothing. I did —"

Two of the officers rushed at him to seize his arms.

"Ignacio Davila, we arrest you. You are wanted for murder back in the United States."

"No, he is not! No, it wasn't murder!" I cried.

They pushed me aside and put handcuffs on him. When they did, the cross and the letter his mother had sent with me fell. No one stopped to pick them up, so I did. I started after him.

"Ignacio!" I screamed as they led him toward the police cars that had now appeared.

He turned and looked back at me with such pain I thought my heart would literally tear in two.

"I did not do this! I swear. Ignacio! Your mother's cross, her letter," I said, holding them up.

"Take them back with you!" he cried.

They stuffed him into the back of a police car. I started toward him.

A police officer seized my arm.

"You will have to come with us," he said. I was taken to another car, but I was not put in handcuffs. I put the cross and letter back into my purse quickly. They drove me to the local police station, where I was taken to a small room with two chairs and a table and told to wait. While I did so, I went through my purse to look for some tissues to wipe the tears from my face and suddenly realized I was missing something.

Where was the note Ignacio had sent me through his mother, the note that had described where we would meet, the note that I had read often before we had left for Mexico?

A cold realization made my body shudder.

Sophia, I thought. Sophia had found it but had not said a word. She had let us go, and then she had told. Why hadn't I noticed? Why hadn't I realized it was missing? Why hadn't I torn it up the way Ignacio's father had torn up every correspondence from him? Look what my carelessness had brought down upon us.

I lowered my head to my forearms on the table and sobbed.

Ignacio would never believe me.

And worse, maybe, neither would his parents.

Nearly an hour later, the door opened, and

Edward and Jesse stepped in along with a police officer. They both looked down at me in disbelief.

"He's alive?" Edward began. "All this time, he's been alive, and you knew?"

I took a deep breath and nodded.

"And you got us to make this trip just so you could meet up with him?"

"No, not just —"

"You used us," he said.

"No, Edward. Do not think that."

"What else should we think, Delia? All this deception. This is very, very serious."

I started to cry.

"Why didn't you trust us with the truth, Delia?"

"I . . . was afraid you would get into trouble, too, Edward, both of you."

"What do you think we're in now?" He nodded at the policemen. "They think we knew and that we brought you specifically to meet him."

I didn't know what else to say. I just lowered my gaze to the floor and cried.

"You know what's the worst thing about all this, Delia?" Edward said.

I looked up and shook my head. What was worse than any of this so far?

"The worst thing," he said, "is we're going to have to call on my mother to help us."

It was as if a flag had been lowered to the ground, and there was truly nothing else left to do but surrender.

17
SURRENDER

The journey back resembled a funeral procession. Even when we sat in the airplane, there was a heavy cloak of morbid silence draped over the three of us. Before we boarded the plane, I tried once again to explain to Edward and Jesse why I had kept Ignacio's existence a secret from them, but I could see they were still so hurt that my words were like bubbles bursting in their ears.

"Let's just not talk about it, Delia," Edward said, sounding totally emotionally exhausted. He sighed deeply. "Let's just not talk at all."

I closed my eyes, swallowed back my tears, and waited for the horrible journey to end.

I did learn some things from them. Tía Isabela had to get Señor Bovio to contact the Mexican ambassador to intercede on our behalf. I couldn't imagine how Adan might be reacting to all the news. We had been told that the Mexican legal authorities were being cooperative and sending Ignacio back to be tried in the United States. Bradley Whitfield's father still had a great deal of influence. The fact that Ignacio's death was faked and the secret kept not only by his family but by friends in Mexico and the United States proved to be too great an embarrassment. No one could defend such a thing. We heard the local newspapers and television and radio stations, as well as some of the state and national newspapers, were reporting it all in great detail.

I felt like running away again and might have, but the police and government people were all around us, making sure we were quickly sent off. No one wanted me here, and certainly no one wanted me now in America, either. I hadn't even had the chance to visit my parents' and my grandmother's graves. I wished I could disappear, form a shell around myself, and crawl into it. I had even disappointed the dead.

Despite the newspaper accounts and television stories directing the spotlights toward us, however, Tía Isabela and her influential friends were able to keep the cameras away when we arrived at the airport. Señor Garman greeted us and led us to a different automobile in order to keep us incognito. In minutes, Edward and I were on our way to the *hacienda*. Jesse's parents had made separate arrangements for him. They scooped him up so quickly we didn't even say goodbye.

If I had ever felt I was entering a courtroom to face an unmerciful, cruel judge, I felt it again when Edward and I, both entering the *hacienda* with our heads lowered like flags of surrender, confronted Tía Isabela. She sat in the heavy cushioned chair facing the entryway and waited for us to walk into the living room. Sophia was nowhere in sight, which I thought was a little blessing.

"Now, before you start, Mother," Edward began, holding his hand up like a traffic cop, "I think you should know —"

"Just sit on the settee, Edward. I know all that I need to know," she interrupted. She turned to me. "Sit," she ordered, pointing down at the floor as if I were a dog.

Edward and I looked at each other and then sat across from each other. Tía Isabela pressed the tips of her fingers together and brought her thumbs to her chest as if she were going to begin a prayer.

"The damage you two have done to this family is irreparable. If it had been created and caused only by Delia, I could have faced the community and even been the object of sympathy. After all, I have tried to civilize this third-world wretch, given her the finest education, provided far more than her necessities of life, housed her in luxury, and introduced her to the highest levels of our society. I taught her etiquette and thought I had begun to turn her into a classy young lady.

"Instead," she continued, her eyes now narrowing into hateful, angry slits, "you took everything I offered, and you crushed it, spit on it, destroyed it, and delivered a serious blow to my reputation, a reputation I've taken years to build. Whatever motivated me to bring you here and get you out of poverty and ignorance was surely my undoing. Yes, I blame myself, too, blame myself for believing I could turn a pig into a princess."

"Stop it, Mother," Edward said. "Enough."

She turned so slowly to him I held my breath.

"You're a bigger fool than your sister and even a bigger disappointment to me and to your father's memory. Supposedly, you have brains, an honor student, and you go along with this deception?"

"He did not know, Tía Isabela. I swear," I said.

"Then he's a bigger fool for not knowing, for being sucked in by your sweet, false act.

I guess you're more of a man than I thought, Edward, just as blind when it comes to a female's guile."

"I'm not going to sit here and listen to much more of this, Mother. What's done is done."

"It's only done because I've been able to put an end to it, you fool."

She sat back and pulled up her shoulders, as if her spine had suddenly hardened into a steel rod.

"You're right. You're not going to sit here and listen to much more of this. You're going to leave this house, get into your car, and go back to your campus. You are not to return until the end of the school year or unless I call for you to return. You are not to have anything more to do with your . . ." She turned to me and nodded. "Your cousin. I want the registration to the car you foolishly gave her, and I want that car sold immediately. I can't imagine why you would ever do it now, but should I hear that you've bought or done anything for her, I'll see to it that the authorities reconsider your actions in Mexico. That goes for you both and for Jesse, especially Jesse. Am I clear?"

Edward glanced at me and then looked down.

"Am I clear?" she repeated.

"You're clear," he muttered.

"I think your, what should I call him, friend? Your friend Jesse might not even return to college."

Edward looked up quickly.

"His family might not be as capable of rebounding. His father and mother are both in a deep depression. We met to discuss you both, and we all agree that neither of you is good for the other."

"None of you has a right —"

"We'll see about rights," she said confidently. "Pack whatever you want, and go. The sooner you are out of the house, the better it will be for all of us at the moment."

"Gladly," he said, rising.

"Where's the registration to her car?"

"It's in the car with the title and insurance cards."

"You'll bring me the keys," she told me. "As soon as we're finished here. Get your tail between your legs and go, Edward."

He looked at me again and walked away.

"Do you have any real idea what your conspiring with this Mexican family has done to them and to their son? He will spend more time in prison than he would have had to spend, and unless there is some arrangement made, his parents could be tried for obstruction of justice. They could both go to prison, too."

"Mi dios," I said.

"Yes, you're right to call to the Almighty for help. He's the only one who might provide it."

She pulled herself up again in the chair.

"I will keep you here until you're old enough to be on your own, and then I'll send you back into the world to fend for yourself. You'll have what you need to survive but nothing more. I'm having you transferred back to the public school. The other students at the private school would ostracize you, anyway. Their parents wouldn't permit any of them to have anything to do with you, and by now, all of the teachers at the private school know about you and would certainly look at you differently. Every one of them would feel he or she had been duped to believe you were a sweet, innocent, bright star and would be embarrassed.

"And don't expect Fani Cordova to help you in any way," she quickly added. "Her parents are quite upset about her friendship with you as it is. So I'm doing you a big favor by taking you out of the private school.

"You'll go on the bus and be with your own common stock, where you belong. I'm reestablishing your chores here at the house. You'll earn your keep again. Mrs. Rosario has already been instructed to give you a list of your duties. You'll begin immediately. I'll permit you to remain in the room. I can keep a closer eye on you that way. The phone has been removed, however, and I've taken back some of the clothing, jewelry, and cosmetics I gave you. You won't be needing any of it, since I forbid you to do anything off these grounds but attend school. The less you are seen in public, the better it will be for Sophia and me and even my idiot son.

"Do you have anything to say?" she asked. I felt like someone about to be executed asked to utter her final words.

I took a deep breath. I wanted to say much. I wanted to tell her again that Edward and Jesse were innocent. I wanted to explain why I had helped Ignacio, how he had been trapped, and how his family had suffered, but I could see no warmth in her eyes. The revenge she had sought and perhaps been prevented from achieving before was now hers, and she was basking in the pleasure. Surely, in her mind, she had reached beyond the grave and given my mother great pain.

I shook my head.

"Good. Go up to your room, get the car keys, and bring them to me immediately. Then stay out of my sight. You're to take your meals with the help from now on, by the way. *Comprende?*"

I looked up sharply. From her lips, Spanish had become profanity.

"*Sí,*" I said.

"I hope you realize how lucky you are to be my niece. Any other girl who had done what you did would be looking at jail time. I think I deserve to hear a thank you. Well?"

"Thank you, Tía Isabela," I said, without a speck of emotion.

"Go on and do what I told you to do," she said, and turned away.

I rose and went quickly up the stairway. Edward was in his room, getting things together. I paused at his open doorway, and he looked out at me with an expression of helplessness that made me press my lips together to stop myself from bursting into tears.

Before I reached my room, Sophia stepped out of hers. The moment that I had so dreaded was here. She gloated and smiled and then threw her head back and laughed.

"I know you did this," I said. "I know you stole the note that was in my purse."

"Of course I did, you *stupido*. You thought you were so superior. You were in control of everyone, my brother, my mother, even me. Now you're no better than you were the day you arrived. You're just a poor slob of a Mexican. I really have to thank you for giv-

414

ing me the opportunity to show my mother who her real daughter is and who isn't."

"Oh, you're your mother's daughter," I said. "I never doubted it."

"You did this?" we both heard. I turned. Edward had come to his doorway and had listened to our conversation. "You caused all this trouble?" he asked, stepping toward Sophia.

"I saved us," she claimed.

"Saved us? You're lower than I ever imagined."

"You're still taking her side? Even after the way she used you?"

He looked at me. "That's between us," he told her. "What she did she did for someone else, to help others, but what you did was purely and simply selfish and cruel. You hurt me and Jesse as much as you hurt anyone. I don't want to think of you as my sister any longer. I can't imagine you married to anyone, but I pity him. I pity all your friends, but I don't pity you, Sophia. You make me sick to my stomach," he concluded, turned, and walked back to his room.

"Go to hell yourself!" she screamed at him. "I don't care what you say or do, either."

She glared at me, went into her room, and slammed the door shut.

I got the keys to my car and hurried downstairs with them. Tía Isabela was talking with Señora Rosario. She turned, took the keys from me, and turned her back to me. Before I reached the stairway, she called to me, however.

"Get changed," she said. "Mrs. Rosario has work for you to do, bathrooms to clean and floors to wash."

I did not look back. I went up the stairs quickly. Edward, carrying his bags, stepped out of his room.

"Please don't hate me, Edward," I said, and rushed past him.

During the remaining days of the spring vacation, I realized Sophia was right to make her hateful prediction. I had returned to the poor Mexican girl I was when I had first arrived. Once again, I worked beside Inez, cleaning toilets and sinks, washing floors, doing laundry, serving food, and polishing furniture. Whenever she could make more work for me, Sophia did it. She left things lying about, deliberately made things dirty, or messed up rooms. I avoided her as much as I could, but she found ways to hover around me or nearby, making her comments, laughing.

I was actually grateful when the vacation ended and I could go to school. I didn't mind returning to the public school. The students and teachers there weren't as into the news about me, Edward, and Jesse as I was sure the students and teachers at the private school were. Sophia would keep the topic alive, anyway. At least, Tía Isabela had been right about sending me back to the public school, I thought. The work was easier for me, but I had lost so much spirit I did little more than was required. I decided not to make any new friends, because I was so restricted that I wouldn't be able to do much with them, anyway.

The news about Ignacio and his family trickled in slowly over the following weeks, but Sophia was happy to bring any of it to my attention. Ignacio had avoided a trial by plea-bargaining. He received the most severe sentence of all the boys involved, however: six years. It was devastating news, and I spent that night crying and choking back tears until I fell asleep. His parents were severely reprimanded but were not charged with any crimes. Fortunately, Señor Davila held on to most of his customers and did not go out of business.

Although Tía Isabela still saw Señor Bovio from time to time, they were not together in the public eye as much. I had yet to hear a single word from Adan. If he had tried to call me, I was never told, and he never came to the *hacienda*. I imagined he and his father had discussed me and had concluded that I would only bring negativity to the campaign. I was sure Adan felt betrayed by my secret rendezvous with a former boyfriend. After all, I had told him nothing as well, and I hadn't told him that Tía Isabela had forbidden the trip.

Jesse did return to college and to Edward. He did whatever he had to do to win the concession from his parents. I felt certain one of the things was to promise never to have anything to do with me again.

These days seemed to take longer. Weeks were more like months. I drudged along, taking little care of my appearance. My hair looked straggly and dirty most of the time. I didn't even wear lipstick. If any boy at school even glanced my way, I turned my back on him quickly. Vaguely, in the back of my mind, I looked forward to the day Tía Isabela described, the day I turned eighteen and she sent me packing. I had no idea whether I would return to Mexico or not, but just the idea of being on my own, being released from this new prison, was enough to keep me going.

Of course, I couldn't stop thinking about Ignacio. It took awhile for me to learn what prison he had been sent to, but when I did, I wrote him a letter and prayed he would write back. He didn't, but I wrote him again and again. I waited for a response in vain. Nothing I told him seemed to please him or get him to forgive me. I decided to stop writing to him. Even if I could show him that none of this was my deliberate doing, I was sure that he saw me as the cause of all the pain and trouble his family was suffering.

I began to believe and accept this way of thinking, too, and therefore quietly accepted all of the abuse, the extra hard work, and the drudgery of my life as proper punishment. I almost welcomed whatever mean thing Sophia could say or do. I saw that this diminished her satisfaction. She was gradually getting bored with me, anyway, and returned to her own pleasures with her friends. She had something to hold over her mother now. She had been the one to expose it all and save her mother from even greater embarrassment. If Tía Isabela tried to discipline or restrict her in any way, she was quick to throw it back in her face, and her mother retreated. Sophia was as wild as ever, and reckless. I knew her schoolwork suffered, but the only thing that mattered was keeping herself from being bored or unhappy.

It had been so long since I had been happy myself that I actually began to envy her. I'd watch her parade by with her friends, laughing and talking excitedly, or see her being picked up to go places on weekends night and day. I was truly once again the Cinderella who had gone too far beyond her midnight curfew and had been returned to her lowly status.

And then, one day, without any warning or preparation, I was summoned by *mi tía* just as I began washing the kitchen floor.

"Leave it. Inez will finish that. Señora Dallas wants you right now," Señora Rosario told me.

When I started out, she stopped me to fix my hair and straighten my clothes. Confused by her attention, I walked into the living room to find Adan Bovio sitting with *mi tía* Isabela. He stood up immediately, looking as handsome as ever in his tight, hip-hugging jeans and silk turquoise short-sleeve shirt. He looked tanned and rested and wore a beautiful thick gold chain around his neck.

"Hello, Delia," he said. *"Cómo estás?"*

I looked at *mi tía* Isabela. She nodded slightly, as if to give me permission to speak.

"I am okay, Adan, and you?"

"As busy as ever. My father let me take a short holiday in Hawaii, however, and I've just recently returned."

Again, I looked to Tía Isabela.

"Unless you have something on your clothes that will stain the furniture, you may sit, Delia."

Surprised at the invitation, I did sit quickly. Adan sat as well.

"Would you like something cold to drink, Adan?" Tía Isabela asked him.

"No, I'm fine, Mrs. Dallas."

"If I've told you once, I've told you at least a dozen times to call me Isabela, Adan. Don't make me sound old."

He laughed.

I looked from one to the other, amazed at how they both were acting as if nothing terrible had occurred. What was going on? Why was Adan here, and why was *mi tía* being so pleasant to me?

"Adan has asked for permission to take you on his boat again, Delia. He would like you to accompany him this coming Saturday. I told him I would give it serious consideration, since you have been behaving and could use the fresh air."

I was speechless.

"You still have the bathing suit and boat clothing I bought for you," she added.

I looked at her. I didn't have them. She had taken it all back, but I could see she didn't want me to say that.

"*Sí,* Tía Isabela."

"Yes?"

"Yes."

"Okay, then, Adan. You're coming by when tomorrow morning?"

"I thought about nine, if that's all right, Delia."

"It's all right," Tía Isabela quickly answered for me. "Is this a party, Adan, some of your friends?"

"No, Isabela. For now, I thought it would be better if there was just the two of us." He looked at me. "We have a lot of catching up to do."

"Yes, I imagine you do," Tía Isabela said.

Adan nodded. "Well, then, I'll see you tomorrow morning," he said, standing. "It's nice seeing you, Isabela."

"And nice seeing you, Adan," she said. She followed him to the doorway and said goodbye. Then she turned quickly and walked back to the living room.

"That's a man for you," she said. "See how stupid they are? After the way you treated him, he's still infatuated with you. If you're smart, have any brains at all, you'll take advantage of it. This is absolutely the very last opportunity I'll provide for you. When you drive him away this time, you drive it all away," she concluded. "Come to my room, and I'll give you the clothing and the bathing suit."

I rose and followed her. When she handed the clothes to me, she looked more closely at my hair and face.

"You can stop your working today. Go do something about your appearance, your hair, your nails, everything. It will probably take you until tomorrow to get yourself presentable again. How he didn't see that just now is beyond me. Well, maybe not so beyond me. Men are blind when it comes to women. Look at your father. Go on, get to it," she ordered, and waved at the door.

I hurried out, feeling very confused. What had brought Adan Bovio back? Was I happy about it or not? What definitely did make me happy was the reaction Sophia had when she heard. She came running up the stairs to my room. I had just washed my hair, using the hair softeners and treatment Tía Isabela had given me and not taken back. I was sitting at my table brushing out my hair and drying it when Sophia burst in.

"Is it true?"

I shut off the dryer and turned to her. "What?" I asked, pretending ignorance.

"You know what. Don't play dumb with me, Delia. Did Adan Bovio come here and ask you on his boat again? Well?"

"I think it's true," I said.

She stared, fuming. I saw her mind spinning. "My lying mother had something to do with this. She's still after his father. I can't believe it," she said, and then smiled. "You'll do something to mess it up, I'm sure. On the other hand, maybe he's taking you out to sea to drown you. Or maybe my mother asked him to do her a favor." She left with a smile on her face.

As foolish as that sounded, the image frightened me. Was Adan angry enough to do something that drastic and horrible? Certainly, I could believe *mi tía* Isabela would. Then I shook my head at myself in the mirror, laughing at how paranoid I had become.

That evening, Tía Isabela did another surprising thing. She had Inez set out a place setting for me to have dinner with her and Sophia. I could see how displeased Sophia was, but Tía Isabela was acting as if nothing much had happened since I had sat with them at this table before I went to Mexico. In fact, her topics of conversation were centered all around social events and the upcoming political events that were being held for Señor Bovio. When she talked about my boat trip, Sophia was so infuriated she interrupted her mother to say she was finished eating and wanted to go up to prepare for going out. She jumped out of her seat before Tía Isabela could respond, but at the doorway, she turned, her eyes blazing with rage, and said, "You're still the laughingstock of Palm Springs, Mother, because of what you did for her, and this isn't going to change it."

She ran to the stairway before Tía Isabela replied. She didn't seem to want to reply, anyway. She simply smiled, shook her head, and continued talking about people and events that were filling the social calendar. I listened, nodded, and smiled whenever I thought I should, but to me, it was as if I were humoring someone who had gone mad.

By the time I went up to my room, Sophia was already gone. She came home very late and made enough noise to be sure she would waken me. I heard her open my door, but I kept my eyes closed to pretend I was asleep. She laughed and came to my bed.

"I know you're awake," she said. "You're probably having a hard time staying asleep because you're so excited about tomorrow on the boat with Adan."

I groaned and turned over to look at her. "What do you want, Sophia?"

"Nothing."

She wobbled a bit, and I could smell the alcohol on her breath. There was a rum drink they were all into now.

"Then go to sleep," I said, turning back, "and give the rest of the world a rest."

"Very funny. Ha-ha. For your information, I have some information for you."

She waited, but I didn't ask what, and I kept my back to her, hoping to discourage her.

"It's about Adan Bovio."

"Right."

"It just so happens he's been seeing someone else very seriously all this time. In fact, he took her to Hawaii with him. Her name is Dana Del Ray, and her father is the CEO of Atlantic Air. They live in Beverly Hills, and everyone says they're minutes away from becoming engaged."

I didn't reply or look at her.

"So, I wouldn't put too much hope in this date tomorrow. It sounds like he's toying with you."

I pressed my lips together to smother a cry. She's lying, I thought. She's simply trying to do anything she can to hurt me. I heard her giggle and then turn and start away, but at the door to my bedroom, she turned back.

"If you want, I'll lend you my spermicidal foam. I'll even show you how to use it. Just knock on my door in the morning. I don't mind."

She laughed again and left.

For a long time, I lay there, unable to move. Her words circled my head like wasps.

I finally fell asleep but nearly overslept. I rose, showered, and dressed quickly. When I opened my door to go downstairs, a box of Sophia's birth-control foam was there on the floor.

I scooped it up, and then, as if it was a hot potato, I quickly dropped it in front of her door before I hurried downstairs to have some coffee and a piece of toast and wait for Adan. My stomach was in too much turmoil for me to be very hungry. I couldn't even eat the toast.

Maybe because of the little sleep I had gotten or the confusion and excitement I was feeling, I felt dizzy. I sat at the table with my eyes closed most of the time. Tía Isabela did not come out to join me, which surprised me. By the time I heard the door buzzer, I was ready to go back upstairs to bed. I started toward the entrance, but Tía Isabela was there before me and before Señora Rosario.

"Why, Adan," she declared, "you're right on time."

He stepped in, and she turned toward me.

"And so is our dear Delia. The two of you,

so anxious to be together. How nice."

Her smile put ice in my veins.

It was as if the devil had crawled into her and was urging me on through the gates of hell.

18
ROUGH SEAS

"Are you all right with this?" Adan asked as soon as we closed the door behind us. "You're not upset about my coming to ask you on the boat?"

"I'm not upset, but I am surprised."

He nodded and opened the car door for me. I glanced at him and slipped into the seat. After he closed the door, he stood there for a moment, looking back at the house as if he were deciding whether or not to go through with this date. Then he hurried around and got into the car.

I waited for him to say more, but he drove away with just a smile flashed in my direction. Finally, after we had driven off *mi tía* Isabela's property, he turned to me and asked, "How are things going for you, Delia?"

I remembered an expression my father would use whenever someone asked him that, especially after a hard day's work in the fields.

"I'm doing well, if I count tips," I said, and he laughed.

"I missed your sense of humor."

I could see that he was thinking carefully before he spoke, combing through the words he was going to use. It made me uncomfortable. It was as if we were both in court, taking great care not to say anything offensive or anything that would bring up unpleasant things. How could we spend hours with each other this way, not to mention being alone so much on a boat?

"I'm sorry I haven't come around sooner," he began, "but I'm sure you can understand that it's taken me time to work through everything."

He paused so long I thought that was all he was going to say, but then he asked, "Have you been in touch with your friend Ignacio Davila?"

"I tried writing him, but he does not reply."

"If you feel like it, you can tell me what happened. It's all right if you don't want to talk about it," he quickly added.

At first, I thought I wouldn't, but so many times I had gone over it all myself to try to understand what had brought us all to this place, this situation. One more time didn't seem to matter and might get me to see something I had missed. Perhaps he would say something wise as well.

I began by going as far back as the first day I had come to America to live with my aunt and described what it was like then and going to the ESL class and being so alone in a foreign country. I explained how Ignacio and I had become friends and how I had enjoyed being with his family, how it had helped me get over my homesickness.

Adan listened attentively, obviously afraid to utter a sound that might stop me from continuing. When I described crossing the desert in flight, he did shake his head and said, "It's impossible to appreciate how desperate people can get."

"I am sorry for how I have hurt my cousin Edward and his friend Jesse," I added.

Adan nodded. "I'm sure you are, but I'm also sure they'll be all right," he said, smiling. "And so will you."

When we reached the dock, I thought about all the mean things Sophia had said to me and the warnings she had delighted in giving me. I hesitated in the car. Adan, who had gotten out, leaned in to ask if I was all right. I gazed at the boat.

"I have been honest and open with you, Adan. Please be the same with me."

"What?" he asked, surprised, sitting back

in the car.

"Tell me why after so long you decided to call on me."

He stared a moment and then shrugged. "I wanted to come to see you earlier, but . . ."

"Yes?"

"My father was very upset with it all. He told me your aunt was near a nervous breakdown."

"I don't think so," I said, smiling. "She could win what is called the Academy Award."

"Whatever, it made it very difficult for me."

"And this other girl you have been seeing? She, too, made it difficult?"

"What other girl?"

"Dana Del Ray."

He turned so quickly toward me that I thought he had snapped his neck. "Who told you about her?"

"Who tells me anything she can to make me unhappy?"

"Oh. I thought it might have been Fani."

"No, I haven't spoken to Fani since I left with my cousin to go to Mexico."

"She has never called you?"

"Never. You told her you were coming to see me?"

"No," he said.

"And you haven't told your father, either, have you?"

He played with the steering wheel a moment and then shook his head.

"Why did you come? Why did you ask me out on your boat, Adan?"

"It's true I've been seeing other girls, and even one in particular, all this time, Dana Del Ray," he began. "Her father's very wealthy and powerful. My father is very good friends with him." He laughed. "It's almost like one of those arranged marriages in Mexico you once described. She's nice, attractive, but an airhead. You know what this is?"

"I've heard about it."

"After what happened with you, I felt I had to do things to please my father, but I came to the conclusion recently that if I'm not happy, in the end, I won't be pleasing him. I didn't know if you would want to see me again. I wasn't sure what your relationship was with this Mexican boy, whether it was some family thing or what. You know, one of those arranged relationships.

"When I phoned your aunt, she was very encouraging, enthusiastic. She told me you weren't seeing anyone. I thought, maybe if she approves again, my father would come around, but none of it would matter if you didn't want to be with me.

"So," he continued, "this was a way to find out. That's it, as honestly as I can tell it."

"Gracias," I said.

"Let's just go for a nice boat ride, have a wonderful lunch, swim, and enjoy the day. If it makes you happy, good. If not, I'll bring you home and wish you good luck. Okay?"

"Okay," I said.

The man who looked after the boat appeared on the dock, looking our way and wondering, I felt sure, why we were taking so long. When he saw us get out of the car, he headed our way.

"Might be a little rough out there today, Adan," he said. "Winds are up. The front is very unpredictable."

"Maybe we'll just go south, then, to Coronado. It's not far," he told me. "Good places for lunch."

"Everything's set."

"Thank you, Bill," Adan told him. He nodded at me and walked off.

Adan helped me onto the boat. Nothing much had changed on it. I went up onto the bridge with him and sat while he got us under way. As soon as we left the dock, we felt the swell and the wind. The boat bounced. Adan kept the speed down to keep us from bouncing too hard, but it was obviously not going to be as soft and gentle a trip as it had been the first time.

"I'm sorry," Adan said, as if the changes in weather were his fault. "Are you all right with this? We could go back."

"I don't mind, as long as it's safe," I said.

He nodded, but I could see he was unhappy about having to pay so much more attention to navigating. At one point, there was a small inlet, and he headed us into it just to get some rest. It wasn't as bad, and he was able to shut the engine and drop anchor. We had some cold plain soda and then sprawled out on the cushioned matting on the deck. I stripped down to my bathing suit, and he did the same.

"My father's campaign got off to a great start," he said after we had both put on some sunscreen. "But the polling statewide is not promising. We've actually lost some ground. It's made him more irritable."

"I'm sorry."

"Which is another reason I didn't bring you up in a conversation," he admitted. "Everything in this world is timing. Something good today will sound bad tomorrow or did earlier. I'll tell you what I have learned these months without seeing you, Delia. I've learned to go slower, think longer before acting. Maybe I'm getting older," he concluded, and turned on his back again. "I sound like a man who wants to be settled down."

"Is that bad?"

"Part of me says no, but sometimes I think I'm not willing to give up being young and foolish just yet. Like most people my age, I'm more afraid of missing something than I am about anything else. Stupid, I know."

We were both quiet. The boat bobbed and swung, and the sun found cover behind a stream of clouds that looked like spilled milk. Birds circling seemed curious enough about us to draw closer and a seagull did land on the railing and strut for a few seconds before lifting back into the wind, perhaps to report to his brothers and sisters that we were boring. There was no food set out. The clouds looked as if they were racing across the sky, some appearing like soft but smeared marshmallow.

"What are you looking for now, Delia? Surely, all that's happened has had an effect on you."

"I want to graduate from high school, of course."

"And then?"

"I've decided I might go to nursing school," I said.

"Really? Nursing?"

"Yes. I'm doing well in science classes, and medicine has always been intriguing to me. I think I'd like to care for other people and help them get well. Back in my village, there were no sophisticated medical facilities. Every family used old remedies for minor ailments, and they often worked. I know real doctors here would laugh, but sometimes the cure is right in front of us. I suppose you have to have some faith. Or maybe, as you said, it's all just the right timing."

Adan turned on his side and looked at me with a deeply quiet, studious expression.

"I know I've said this before, Delia, but I like being with you because you're so much older than the girls your age here. That is why I have no difficulty thinking of you in more serious terms."

"Serious terms? What does that mean, Adan?" I asked, turning toward him.

"I'd like to give you a special gift on your graduation day."

"What is this special gift?"

"An engagement ring," he said. "Don't look so shocked and frightened," he added, laughing.

"But I am," I confessed.

"What would you do if I gave you such a gift that day? Would you accept it?"

"I don't know," I said. "I know I want to do what I said. I want to become a nurse."

"There's no problem with that."

437

"I don't know."

"You still have strong feelings for Ignacio?"

"I'm going to sound like — what you call it — a broken record."

"You mean you don't know?"

I nodded. "I am very confused," I said.

He smiled and reached for my hand. "You have every right to be, but maybe I can help you get rid of the confusion."

"How?"

"Like this," he said.

He leaned in to kiss me and then kept his face close to mine so we could do nothing more than look into each other's eyes.

"I can't get your eyes out of mine," he whispered. "Even when I look into the eyes of other girls, I see your eyes, Delia. Whether you realize it or not, you've set your anchor in me."

He kissed me again, longer this time. The taste of his lips made my head spin.

"Delia," he said, his lips grazing my cheek and my earlobe, "I need you and want you to need me. Nothing that's happened has changed that or ever will."

All my days of pain and turmoil had cut the legs out from beneath my sense of caution. I brought my lips back to his, I felt his level of excitement. His hands moved up and around to slip under the top of my bathing suit and easily lift it away from my breasts. The cool air felt good on my hardened nipples, which eagerly accepted his lips and the tip of his tongue. I moaned as he kissed his way down to my belly button and below, gracefully undoing the bottom of my suit. In the distance, I heard the birds cawing as if they were trying to warn me against myself, as if the voices of my ancestors were being transmitted from beyond.

But I was unable to deny that I had fantasized about this moment many times, that I had struggled, mostly in vain, to put it out of my mind. He was mounting me and chanting my name as if not saying it would shut some door and destroy the magic bubble around us. I didn't surrender to him as much as I drew him into me, demanding that he surrender all of his essence, uncover his soul, be completely naked and honest. When I realized there was no turning back, I surged forward. The ocean lifted and dropped us gently, as if it were trying to mimic our love rhythms. The wind eagerly scooped up my cries and carried them over the water. We held each other so tightly it was as if we were literally trying to absorb each other.

I heard my cries of pleasure as they echoed down the corridors of ecstasy leading to my very soul. "Delia," he whispered. "Delia, I love you."

We did not let go of each other when it ended, either. We lay there entwined until both of us began to breathe normally and both our hearts stopped thrashing inside our chests. Then he turned over, quickly put his bathing suit on, and tossed a towel over me. I closed my eyes and turned on my side.

"Just relax," he said. "I'll get us under way. I know this great restaurant that has its own dock. It's not far."

I didn't reply, and I didn't open my eyes until I felt the boat moving quickly and bouncing harder on the water. I had been lying there anticipating my inner voice start to reprimand me, stir regrets, bring me to tears, but I heard nothing but the echo of my own pleasure. I'm still smiling, I thought. This must be right.

I dressed and took a cold drink. Adan beckoned for me to climb up to the bridge. He held out his hand, and I stood beside him looking out at the water while he put his arm around my shoulders to draw me closer to him.

"You okay?" he asked, and kissed my cheek.

I nodded, but I wondered if he could feel me trembling inside.

"I'm really hungry," he said. "You?"

"Yes."

"I really do love you, Delia."

"Sí, yo lo creo."

I did believe him, and I didn't think I was gullible or just vulnerable because of all that had happened. I had confidence in my own feelings and what I could see in his eyes.

I knew that he was waiting for me to say I loved him as well, but those words were still forming. He would have to be patient.

I went down to put on the rest of my clothing as we drew closer to the restaurant he had described. Then I helped him get the boat tied to the dock, and we went off to eat. Adan was even more animated, excited, and happy at the restaurant. I regained an appetite as I calmed down and really enjoyed the lunch. Afterward, the winds seemed to calm as well, and the ocean was not as rough. He felt it was safe enough for him to show me how to navigate to keep the course steady. When he was confident that I knew what to do, he had me drive the boat while he took a nap.

It was exhilarating, and I began to wonder if I was made for this life after all. The contrast between it and how I had been living was even greater. I tried to envision what it would be like to be Adan Bovio's young wife.

What would our children be like? Would I become very much like *mi tía* Isabela, concerned about social position, clothes, and jewelry? My life in Mexico would drift farther and farther away, disappear in the distance as the shore disappeared. Everyone I had loved and lost would move closer and closer to the third death.

But I would be building a new family and a new life, and I would carry as much of what I loved and cherished into this new life. That can't be terrible, I thought. Abuela Anabela used to say, *"En la casa de la rica, ella manda y ella grita."* In a rich woman's house, her hollers and orders ring out. That was certainly true for *mi tía* Isabela. Would it be true for me? Was it important to be important, respected, obeyed? She certainly didn't have love. Could I have both?

I looked back at Adan. Even asleep, he looked as handsome as Adonis. I would certainly be the envy of every woman. Sophia would come close to committing suicide. It was all so complicated. Did I love him at all? Were those words finally coming to my lips, words I would say before this day ended? And if I did, did I love him for who he was or what he was? Was his love for me so strong that it would answer all questions and wipe away any troubles and pain? Should I consider myself lucky and be done with it?

When he gave me that ring on graduation day, would I take it and put it on or shake my head and softly say, "I can't. Not yet." In his eyes, postponement meant never. He would take it back, but he might never again offer it to me. I knew what *mi tía* Isabela would say. "Seize it."

"How are you doing?" I heard him say.

I had been in such deep thought that for a moment I panicked when I saw I had gone off course.

"Sorry. I wasn't paying good attention," I confessed.

He rose, stretched, and came back to the controls.

"I'll say," he said, laughing. "You must have been sleeping or daydreaming. It's all right," he added quickly. "I'll get us back on course."

He took over, but the wind stirred up again, and our ride became quite rough. He kept apologizing for it.

"You don't control the weather, Adan," I told him.

"Yeah, but I shouldn't have let us get out this far. It's going to take longer to get back. Sorry. You'd better sit," he added when I wobbled from side to side.

While he stood spread-eagle at the wheel,

I could sit right behind him and hold on to the armrests. We were rocking that much now. The sky had clouded up quickly, too. I actually felt a little cold.

"Damn," he muttered. "I didn't want to take you out on such a rough ride. I should have listened to Bill back there."

"But it became so nice."

He looked back at me, and I blushed. I wasn't referring to our lovemaking, but I could see he thought I was.

"I'm not saying it wasn't worth it," he told me, and then turned back to the wheel. He looked at his gauges and shook his head.

"What?" I asked. The brisk wind and the higher waves were beginning to frighten me.

"We're not moving as fast as the RPMs indicate we should. Sometimes you pick up something and drag it, like seaweed, even an old fisherman's net. I'm going to go back and check it out, Delia. I'd like you to take the wheel and just hold it steady like I showed you before, okay?"

I nodded. When I stood up, the rocking threw me back to the seat. He held my arm when I stood again and planted me at the wheel.

"Hold on tightly," he said. "We'll be all right. Don't be afraid."

"*Sí*," I said.

He braced himself and carefully went down the short ladder to move toward the rear of the boat. The wind ripped at his blazer and combed up the strands of his hair. I was worried about him, so I kept turning to look back to check on him. At one point, he lost his balance but caught himself quickly on the side of the boat.

"Adan!"

He waved back at me.

"I'm all right," he called, and leaned over the boat to look at the rudder and propellers.

I was half turned, watching him, and I let go of the wheel with my right hand just as a rather strong, high wave crashed against the side of the boat. I was the one who lost balance this time and felt myself falling to my right. I reached out frantically for the wheel, and when I seized it, I turned it sharply. The boat turned sharply too.

Adan looked as if he was lifting off the floor of the deck the way the gull had lifted earlier off the side of the boat. In an effort to prevent himself from going overboard, he reached for the side of the boat, what I would later learn was called the gunnel, and he struck his head hard and sharply. He fell back to the deck instantly.

"Adan!"

I straightened myself, and, clinging to anything and everything I could, I hurried down the ladder. I made my way back to him. He hadn't stirred since hitting his head. I fell to the deck beside him and shook him. Without anyone steering it, the boat wobbled and bounced dramatically.

"Adan! Adan!"

His eyes were shut, his face in a grimace of pain, but he did not regain consciousness. When I saw a trickle of blood begin to flow from his scalp, I went into an even greater panic. I knew I had to get back to steering the boat. The ocean was tossing us about as if we were in a toy. Practically crawling on all fours now, I scurried back to the ladder and up to the bridge. When I seized the wheel, I spread my legs apart as I had seen him do and steadied the boat. I had no idea which way to turn to reach shore, but I turned all the way to my right. I looked for a way to keep the wheel from turning while I returned to Adan, but I couldn't find one.

Tears were streaming down my face now, tears of panic, not tears of sadness. I moaned and prayed. Suddenly, I saw another boat in the distance and turned to head in its direction. I knew the people on it were too far away to hear my cries, and the wind would carry them off, anyway. Fortunately, they were heading in our direction, so the time it took to draw closer was reduced. It seemed to take forever to me, however.

Adan had still not moved. I could see the trickle of blood was now a clear red line down the side of his temple and over his cheek. How could all this have happened so quickly? I complained aloud, as if some god of the sea would hear me and fix everything. It wasn't fair.

When I could clearly see the people on the other boat, I waved and screamed. Someone pointed at me, and they all looked my way.

"Adan is seriously hurt!" I shouted, as if I believed everyone in the world knew who he was. I pointed to him, but there was no way they could see him yet.

I listened to the tall man in a dark blue shirt and pants and followed his directions to slow our boat. He told me to hold it steady, and soon they were close enough to lower their dinghy. The man got into it and started for our boat. The moment he was able to board, I felt myself spin around. The excitement and panic were too much. He seized my arm, but I sank to the floor.

When I woke, I saw there was now another man, shorter and stocky, and a woman beside him on our boat. They had managed to get Adan onto the cushion on the deck. The woman came to me immediately. She had long red hair and freckles peppered over her cheeks, even at the sides of her chin.

"What happened?" she asked when I sat up.

"He hit his head on the side," was all I managed to say before my throat choked up.

"You take it easy," she said. "We'll get you both back. Felix, my husband," she said, nodding at the man standing at our steering wheel, "will handle your boat. My son is on ours. C'mon," she said. "I'll help you lie down on the cushion beside your . . . husband?"

I shook my head. "No, he's only a friend."

"All right, honey. Lean on me," she said. Somehow, she guided me back to Adan, and I was able to sprawl out beside him. His eyes were still shut, but they had bandaged his head enough to stop the bleeding. I reached for his hand, and then I lay back and closed my eyes.

Soon, I thought, I'll wake from this nightmare. *Please, mi dios,* I prayed, *make it only a nightmare.*

Maybe I fell asleep again. I can't remember now, but when I opened my eyes again, we were closing on the dock. They had put a blanket over Adan. He didn't look as if he was cold, but I thought the way he was right now, he wouldn't know if he was or not. They had radioed ahead, so when we reached the dock, I could see the paramedics waiting. There was an ambulance parked nearby.

"It'll be all right," the woman told me. "We're almost there, dear."

She squeezed my hand. I looked at Adan and prayed she was right.

Once we docked, the paramedics quickly boarded. They asked me what had happened, and I described Adan's accident quickly while they prepared to take him off the boat. I was crying so hard that I wasn't sure they understood my explanation. I know I was blaming it all on myself. If I hadn't lost my balance . . . if I hadn't pulled the steering wheel too hard . . .

"Did you hurt yourself in any way?" the paramedic asked me.

I showed him my hands. They were burning because of how I had skinned my palms in my desperation to get up the ladder to the bridge.

"We'll take care of that. Don't worry. Take it easy," the paramedics told me. "Just stay calm."

"Gracias," I said.

I watched as they strapped Adan into a

gurney, securing his head and neck, and lifted him gently. On the dock, they had another gurney with wheels. I was wobbly when I stood. The woman with red hair held my arm and helped me get off the boat.

"How are you doing?" one of the paramedics asked me.

I just shook my head. I felt nauseous now and very dizzy. I took deep breaths to keep myself from passing out.

"C'mon," he said, taking my arm. "We'll bring you along and get you checked out."

He led me to the ambulance. I watched them load Adan in, and then they helped me in and had me sit while one of the paramedics began to take a reading of Adan's vitals. Moments later, the ambulance started away.

Before I closed my eyes and sat back, I glanced through the rear window and saw that a small crowd had gathered on the dock, and the red-haired woman and her husband were telling everyone what had happened.

Mi dios, I thought, I hadn't even thanked them.

19
Loss

When we reached the emergency room at the hospital, they took me to a room next to the one Adan was in, so I was able to hear them working frantically on him. Before anyone came in to examine me, I heard them wheel Adan off to radiology. The nurse at the desk came in to see me and ask questions about our identities and the accident. Finally, the emergency-room doctor came in to see me to treat the palms of my hands.

"Did you injure yourself in any other way?" he asked.

I shook my head. I think I was on the borderline of being hysterical, and he could see that in my face.

"Just relax," he said, getting me to lie back. "Everything's going to be all right."

"Can you give us a phone number of someone to call for you?" the nurse asked me.

Can you call the beyond? I wanted to ask.

Can you reach my parents or my grand-mother?

There was no point in delaying it, I thought, and gave her *mi tía* Isabela's home number.

"Will Adan be all right?" I asked quickly.

"We'll know everything soon. Just try to rest. We'd rather not give you any medications right now, Delia. Will you be all right?"

I nodded.

"We'll look in on you frequently. Just close your eyes and rest," she said.

I did, and I was blessed with sleep and grateful for it, even though it was obviously a result of mental and physical exhaustion.

When I woke, I clearly heard Señor Bovio's voice in the hallway. I trembled at the thought of seeing him. Moments later, he looked in on me. The nurse came in before him and checked my blood pressure. He stood staring at me until she nodded and left the room.

His face was grim, dark, his lips trembling. Then he held out his arms and looked as if he would break into tears.

"How did this happen to my son?" he asked.

I began to explain, taking deep breaths between sentences. My chest ached with my own sadness and agony. I know I was practically blubbering, rattling off insignificant details, mixing English and Spanish, but he picked up on my mention of the RPMs as Adan had described them.

"So he went to check the propellers?"

"*Sí*. And the boat was rocking so much and so hard, I was worried for him."

He nodded. "And then?"

"Then I lost my balance," I said, and he looked up quickly.

"What happened?"

"I was falling over, so I grabbed the wheel, and it turned, and that's when Adan went flying into the side of the boat."

"Into the gunnel? When you lost control?"

"*Sí*. I hurried down to him, but he was unconscious, and the boat was tossing so hard —"

"You let go of the wheel?"

"Just for a little while to see how he was."

"No, I mean before, when you lost your balance."

"*Sí, señor.*"

He stared at me.

"How is he now?" I asked.

"They are looking at the results of his CT and his MRI," he said abruptly. "Your aunt is on the way," he added, turned, and left me.

It was almost another hour before Tía Isabela arrived with Sophia. Amazingly, she looked bored, even angry, about being dragged along. She was behaving as if I had arranged all of this in order to be the center of attention and take the spotlight off her. From the look on Tía Isabela's face, I knew that things were very serious. I almost burst into tears. She looked at the bandages on my hands and then asked me to tell her exactly what had happened, too. Sophia stood off to the side, staring down at the floor, her arms folded across her breasts.

"I just don't understand how things always turn out bad for you, Delia," Tía Isabela said. That was to be the softest, most considerate thing she would say to me about all this. "I'm going up to the OR waiting room. They took Adan in for an emergency operation."

"On his brain," Sophia added. "Ugh."

"Maybe you should stay down here with Delia, Sophia," Tía Isabela told her.

"I'll go into the lobby and read whatever magazines they have or watch television. I don't know why you made me come," she said.

Tía Isabela shook her head and left.

"I heard my mother talking with Mr. Bovio," Sophia said as she turned to leave the room. She paused at the door. "I could tell he blames you. He didn't want his son to be with you in the first place."

Her words were as painful as a dagger driven into my heart. She left, and I fell back against the pillow and stared up at the ceiling. He doesn't have to blame me, I thought. I blame myself, my clumsy, stupid self.

As I lay there, I could think of few things worse than being trapped in this limbo of tension. I was afraid to move a muscle or call to a nurse to ask a question. I couldn't even cry. My well of tears was long dry. Sophia came back once to complain about how long it was all taking. I turned away from her rather than respond, and she left quickly, mumbling to herself. Minutes moved like snails on a bed of dry earth.

Finally, Tía Isabela returned. It had been nearly four hours. She stood there just inside the doorway and looked at me when I sat up.

"Get yourself together," she said. "We're leaving."

"How is Adan?"

"Adan died twenty minutes ago," she said. "I've been holding Señor Bovio, keeping him from tearing himself to pieces."

"Why?" I said, now replenished with tears

streaming down my face. I thought my own heart had stopped. "Why did he die?"

She shook her head.

Sophia came up beside her, now looking shocked herself, looking more like a helpless little girl than ever.

"I listened to the doctor explaining it to Señor Bovio," she said in a tired and defeated tone of voice. "There is no room in the brain for extra blood. The skull does not expand, so the blood presses on brain tissue, which is delicate, and with large amounts of bleeding, the pressure can make critical areas of the brain stop working. He had what they called a contracoup injury. His brain had microscopic tears. They went in to see if they could stop the bleeding, but . . . it was too late. Let's go," she concluded. "I'll wait in the lobby."

Sophia looked at me with less accusation than pity. Apparently, finally, there was some part of her that had reached the bottom of the pit, the end of the envy and belligerence. I was too pathetic to be worthy of any more of her anger. In her eyes, and truthfully, in my own as well, I was gone, diminished to the point of bare existence, as empty as a shadow, dark and enslaved to follow my skeleton about like a chained prisoner who lived only to die.

It was reflected in the way I moved —
stunned, my legs following some reflexive
orders because my brain had shut down.
The nurses and the ER doctor looked my
way with funeral faces, their eyes shrouded
with sympathy. Did everyone blame me?
Was I wearing some mark of Cain on my
forehead? Señor Garman was waiting for
us with the limousine doors open. To me,
he now looked like an undertaker, and the
limousine looked like a hearse. I was already
buried in my own body, not quite awake
but not quite asleep, trapped like a hopeless
vampire eagerly waiting for a wooden stake
to put me out of my misery.

Sophia snapped out of her moments of
shock, moments when, for a little while at
least, she had connected with someone else
and had empathized, felt sorrow and pain,
and was somewhat sympathetic. But as if
that realization hit her, she slapped on her
earphones and listened to her own rock
music, trying to drown out the shreds of hu-
manity that had bubbled to the surface. Tía
Isabela was silent, staring out the window at
the hospital. When we pulled away, however,
she sighed and said, "That poor man."

I shrank into myself, embraced myself, and
hovered as close to the corner of the seat as I
could. Tía Isabela did not look at me or talk

to me until we were nearly home. Then she spoke in a voice that sounded like the voice of some judge sitting above the clouds and looking down at me.

"I want you out of that room now," she began. "Take your things, and move into the old help's quarters, to the room you had when you first arrived, the room I should have kept you in and not been persuaded otherwise by my gullible son. Perhaps none of this would have happened. Do your chores, and finish your school year. Then go back to Mexico, or do whatever you want, only leave.

"You make me believe in the *ojo malvado*, the evil eye," she said, and I turned sharply toward her. "Yes, those stupid, old, backward ideas I have ridiculed all my life seem to have validity when it comes to you. I don't want you bringing any more bad luck to my home, to my family, to my world."

I had no fight left in me and no words to contradict her. I had come to believe these things about myself. I turned away again, and when we arrived, I got out, went up to my room, and gathered my things together as she had commanded. Even though it was late, Sophia charged up ahead of me to get on her phone and report everything as if she were some foreign correspondent with breaking world news. In a matter of hours, if not minutes, everyone who knew of Adan and of me would know what had happened. And she would feel important.

Tía Isabela told Señora Rosario and Inez what had occurred and what she wanted done with me. They were waiting to help move my things when I came down. They looked sorry for me, but I could see they were also afraid to say anything that might be critical of *mi tía* Isabela. I imagined how angry and terrifying she had looked to them when she described the events and what were her new orders. I moved silently, truly believing I had become that shadow of myself. I didn't mind the cold, dark, dusty room and the uncomfortable bed. I didn't mind the insects and the poor lighting. Señora Rosario left me cleaning liquids, a mop, and washcloths. The palms of my hands still burned with pain, but I worked anyway, welcomed the pain, welcomed anything that resembled punishment I thought I deserved. When I was finally too exhausted even to cry, I went to bed. At the moment, I felt even too unworthy to say a prayer. I battled back sleep, because I was afraid of the nightmares that would surely come thundering through my mind, but eventually, I could not stay awake.

I didn't dream. Maybe I was too tired even for that, but when the morning light streamed into the little room and nudged my eyes, I was happy to see I had slept. I rose, washed and dressed, and, moving like a robot, went to the main house to begin my morning chores and help with the breakfast. Both Tía Isabela and Sophia slept late. Señora Rosario risked some expressions of sympathy and comfort, and Inez even cried a little for me. I smiled and thanked them and went about my work.

I wasn't sure Tía Isabela would want me to serve the late breakfast, but I accompanied Inez as usual, and *mi tía* said nothing. Sophia came bouncing down the stairway, declaring she was starving, and immediately demanded more of this and more of that. Then, while I was still in the dining room, she turned to Tía Isabela and said, "Everyone thinks this is going to be one of the biggest funerals here ever."

"I imagine it will be," Tía Isabela said. She sipped her coffee and stared at the empty chair her husband had once filled.

Sophia, not satisfied with that, turned her attention to me. "Guess who wishes she had never met you and never made you her friend. Just guess," she pursued.

I didn't respond, but I glanced at Tía Isabela. She looked pleased at how Sophia was trying to torment me.

"Fani," she volunteered. "Fani Cordova, who was once your savior. So I wouldn't bother calling her for help. Ever."

I cleared the dirty dishes and went into the kitchen. I tried to block out their words, but I could feel myself cringing and finally doubled up at the sink. Señora Rosario saw me and quickly came to my side.

"Go. Take a rest, Delia. Go," she told me. I started to shake my head, but she literally pushed me toward the rear door. "Rest," she ordered, and I left.

Inez and Señora Rosario covered for me, and I spent the rest of the day in my room. Inez brought me something to eat, but I barely touched it. I returned to help with dinner, but Tía Isabela had gone to Señor Bovio's home, and Sophia had gone with some of her friends to gossip, especially now that she was seen as someone with privileged information about it all. I ate a little and returned to my dark, lonely room to pray.

I returned to school the next day. Many had heard about Adan, but not that many knew I had anything to do with him. For most, he was like some celebrity. It held their interest for only a little while. The newspapers I saw showed Señor Bovio in postures of mourning. There was great sympathy for him, but from what I heard and read, few thought it would have any positive effect on his campaign. In fact, they talked about his simply clinging on to save face, but they described his effort as empty and futile.

What amazed me, but for which I was grateful, was the fact that my name had somehow been kept out of the news stories. It was almost as if he had been alone on the boat. There were no follow-up stories, either. However, there was no doubt that the students at the private school and the families knew all of the details, including my involvement.

In fact, Tía Isabela called me into her office to tell me she had decided that under the circumstances, I should not attend Adan's funeral.

"It would be too painful for his father," she said. "And it would only attract more unnecessary mean gossip, something neither he nor I need at the moment."

I didn't have much choice about it. Sophia and her friends went. Edward came back from college with Jesse, and they attended as well. I kept anticipating them coming to see me, but Tía Isabela must have issued some new threat. They went directly to the church and cemetery and then returned to college.

Sophia was so excited about everything that she had to come to my room in the old help's quarters to tell me about the funeral. I was sitting on my bed trying to read one of my English assignments when she appeared in the doorway.

"It stinks in here," she complained. I just looked at her. "The church was so packed that people were standing outside. There were lots of politicians, too. Mr. Bovio was practically being held up and carried by two of his close friends. He looked like he was the one who died.

"And there were just as many people at the cemetery. Of course, everyone was asking about you. My mother should have let you come. It looks worse because you didn't come.

"What a waste. He was like a movie star. Are you going back to Mexico right after your graduation?" she followed almost in the same breath.

"I don't know."

"You should. That's where you belong. You're never going to meet or find someone like Adan again. What can you do but become someone's maid or watch someone else's kids? You'll get fat and ugly like most of them and marry some toothless gardener.

"God," she said, shaking her head as she

looked at me. "Remember when you were so damn high and mighty, threatening me with Fani's pictures and everything?"

I looked at my book.

"You can pretend you don't care, Delia, but you don't fool me." She laughed. "Forget about that idea of becoming a nurse, too."

I looked up sharply. How did she know that? She saw the surprise in my face and laughed.

"You told the guidance counselor at the public school, and he mentioned it to my mother. You know what she said? She said with your luck, every patient you touch will drop dead. This room really smells," she concluded. "I think the sewer is backing up or something. Ugh."

She turned and left.

I waited until I heard the outside door close behind her, and then I stood up and screamed in silence, the sound echoing inside me and traveling down into the very bottom of my soul.

And then everything went black, and I seemed to take hours crumbling and sinking, my body folding cell by cell, until I poured onto the cold cement floor and drifted through a dark tunnel in which memories flashed on walls, faces, places, laughter, and screams.

I had no idea how long I was unconscious, but that was the way Inez found me. Señora Rosario came quickly, and the two of them got me into my bed. Señora Rosario hurried back to tell *mi tía* Isabela. She came to see me, but I remember when I opened my eyes, she looked as if she was standing very far away, and everything and everyone else was quite out of focus. I could barely hear them speaking, too. Their muffled voices ran into each other.

I closed my eyes again and turned away.

Apparently, *mi tía* Isabela's first reaction was to leave me alone.

"It's just a hysterical, self-serving cry for pity. Let her sleep it off. She'll get up and come out when she's hungry enough, believe me," she told them.

Everyone was ordered to leave me alone.

Later, I was told that for nearly twelve hours, I didn't move, didn't turn, didn't open my eyes. Tía Isabela was brought back to look at me. What convinced her to do something else was the sight of my having messed myself.

"Ridiculous!" she cried, and left.

She called her personal physician, Dr. Bayer, who, after examining me, told her I was in what he believed was a hysterical coma, especially after he reviewed the past events.

"Well, can't you give her a shot or something?"

"We'll give her a mild tranquilizer," he told her, "but this is more of a psychological problem."

"It's just an attempt to get people to feel sorry for her," *mi tía* Isabela insisted, but her doctor shook his head.

"No, Isabela, she's not faking it."

Apparently disgusted, but unable to ignore me now, she agreed to have me taken to the psychological ward at the hospital. She even agreed to an ambulance. I was unaware of any of it, but later, I learned it all from Inez, who found time to visit me and describe the scene.

Actually, *mi tía* Isabela found this all to be quite convenient. With her money and power, she had me transferred to a nearby clinic for continued treatment and psychological counseling. I became responsive a day after I was placed in the clinic, and out of shame, she came to see me. She acted concerned, especially when she spoke with the doctors and nurses.

When we were finally alone, the motherly demeanor left her, and the Tía Isabela I knew so well instantly returned.

"Well," she said, "you outdid us all when

it comes to drama. Even Sophia couldn't achieve such a performance."

I said nothing. She looked around my room.

"You have a nice private room here, Delia. I'll see to it that you are kept comfortable. It's the ideal place for you right now. No one can get to you, and you can think about your future in Mexico, because that's where you should go now. Go back to the pathetic village. I'll stake you to some money, and you'll return like a heroine."

I didn't reply, but I could see that for her, her so-called guardianship would be ended, and her conscience, if she had any left, would be soothed.

"Sometimes solutions find themselves," she continued. "You obviously have no future here. If anything, you should be grateful and thank me for all this." She lifted her arms to indicate the clinic. "All I ask is that you keep up your performance so no one badgers me about taking you home. *Comprende*, Delia Yebarra?"

I looked away.

I heard her laugh before she rose. She stood there for a few moments to see if I would respond, and then I heard the whispering sound of her skirt as she left my room. For a long moment, I just stared at the wall. When

467

I saw that she was truly gone, I closed my eyes again and fell asleep.

Days went by very slowly. I did have a very nice psychiatrist, Dr. Jensen, who happened to be fluent in Spanish. He was in his mid-fifties and very kind and caring. He kept me on some mild medications. He told me it wasn't a bad thing for my aunt to be able to afford to keep me in his care.

"We have to address this deep-seated guilt you feel, Delia," he said. "You have taken on far too much blame and responsibility for people and events you really could not control. You did not hurt anyone deliberately. In time, I hope you will realize this.

"As for this evil eye you speak of," he added, smiling, "it's really more like an excuse, a way to blame something else for your misfortune, rather than coincidence or events caused by someone else." He laughed. "Don't worry. I'm not going to attempt to wash away centuries of superstitions. I'm not that arrogant."

I really did like him, and he helped me to feel better about myself much faster than I thought possible.

I did some reading and some arts and crafts, watched a little television, gradually developed more and more of an appetite, and started to do exercise.

It was well into my third week before Inez came to visit me and describe what had occurred. She told me things were quite back to normal, which meant Sophia was her usual obnoxious self and Tía Isabela was once again absorbed with her social life.

"No one is permitted to speak about you," she said. "Señora Dallas didn't come right out and say it, but it's very clear."

"And Edward?"

"He hasn't been home. I don't know, but I don't think he calls much."

"Maybe you shouldn't have come here, Inez," I said. "It's liable to get back to my aunt."

"I'm not afraid." She leaned closer. "I have another employment opportunity which will pay as much. I just have to wait another two weeks." She sat back, smiling.

"That's good. Señora Rosario will be upset, I'm sure."

"She's talking more and more about retirement. It won't be much longer for her, either."

"Who would think looking at *la hacienda de mi tía* that it was a place where people would not want to work?"

Inez laughed. "We would!" she cried.

We hugged before she left, and we promised not to forget each other.

Two more weeks flew by, because I was doing more and keeping myself quite busy. I really did think I was recuperating and getting stronger, until I woke up one morning sick to my stomach. At first, I, and my nurse, thought the medication might be responsible. Then she looked at me askance and asked me about my period. I wasn't that overdue, but her next question and my answer raised her eyebrows.

"Are your breasts tender?"

I had felt that and nodded.

"Do you notice yourself urinating more, Delia?"

Again, I nodded.

She stepped back, as if I had slapped her across her face. "I'll be right back," she said.

When she returned, she had Dr. Jensen with her. He looked at her, and she left us alone.

"Delia," he asked me directly, "could you be pregnant?"

For a long moment, I wondered why such a realization would come as a complete surprise to me as well as to him.

And then I thought about how all of the events of the immediate past were like some chain of dreams, distant, vague, and deliberately repressed. There was so much I didn't want to remember. It was more comfortable to think of it as all in my imagination, part of some childlike pretending. I was more comfortable now living only in the present. I didn't want to think of the past or the future, only the very moment I was in.

But Dr. Jensen's question revived my wonderful lovemaking with Adan on the boat. The images came up like bubbles in water, bursting around me.

My answer came in the tears streaming down my cheeks.

He put his hand on my shoulder. "It's all right," he said. "Don't worry. I'll speak with your aunt, and —"

"No!" I screamed.

He lifted his hand away as if my shoulder had turned into the top of a hot stove.

"Please!" I moaned.

"Okay, Delia. Calm down. What is it you want?" he asked.

I shook my head.

I only knew that I didn't want *mi tía* Isabela involved with any other decision or event in my life.

"She will make me have an abortion," I told him.

"You want to have a baby?"

I didn't answer, but I could see the same future he saw — another young, unmarried woman, a Mexican woman, returning to a life inches above poverty, to a world where she would not have respect or any man eager to take her as his wife and be a father to her child.

But I would do it, I thought, perhaps with foolish determination. I would cross that border again.

Dr. Jensen shook his head. "Okay, let's just stay calm," he repeated. "Everything will be fine."

He left me sitting there, stunned.

The tears that had started and stopped started again.

I felt them moving down my cheeks, but I didn't wipe them away.

They dropped onto the backs of my hands like drops of salty rain, like drops of the sea upon which Adan and I had conceived the child forming inside me.

What was the greater sin?

Letting a baby come into this world under these circumstances?

Or sending the baby back to the peacefulness of the third death, forgotten before he or she could be remembered?

I sat there waiting for the answer.

20
ADAN'S GIFT

"Now you've gone and done it, you absolute fool!" *mi tía* Isabela practically spat at me the moment she entered my room. She hadn't been back since that first day. "Why did you have unprotected sex? Sophia told me she gave you protection the night before you went on the boat. Have you no brains at all? Are all you Mexican girls just stupid?"

"You're a Mexican girl," I said defiantly.

Ironically, one of the consequences of her putting me here was to give me a sense of security. She couldn't reach me, torment me. She had given up her control.

"That is an honor I'm glad to refuse," she said, and flopped into the chair. For a long moment, we simply stared at each other. Then she smiled. "I am not going to arrange for an abortion for you, Delia. As they say, you've made your bed. Now you sleep in it. The harder your life becomes, the more you'll appreciate what I offered you. You could have had a life like mine."

"No, *gracias,* Tía Isabela. Your life is an empty promise. If you didn't love yourself, you'd have no one to love you."

Her eyes nearly exploded. "You insolent . . . this is too much. You don't need any more psychiatric treatment. Stupidity is not a mental illness. I'm going to end your stay here. You can go right back to Mexico now instead of later. Arrangements will be made immediately. And you'll leave with exactly what you came with and no more."

"No," I said.

"No?"

"I can't leave with what I came with, Tía Isabela. I came with hope and love, with prayer that somehow we would be a family."

She nodded. "I wouldn't expect you to accept any blame for any of this. Not that I care, but I'm sure you'll go back telling anyone who will listen that it was all my fault."

"No. I don't think I'll mention your name," I said.

Again, her face tightened, and her lips stretched so that two pale white spots of rage formed in the corners. "I can tell you now, don't bother ever to write to me to ask for any help."

"And you, *mi tía,* don't write to me to ask

for any help, either."

This brought a smile and a laugh to her face. "You are a little crazy after all," she said. "Now I don't feel so bad about sending you here."

She stood up and pulled up her shoulders to give herself even more stature.

She really does think she is a queen, I thought.

"I'll make arrangements immediately. Get yourself prepared. Go back to speaking Spanish."

She turned to leave.

"The truth in any language is still the truth, and the truth is that you are the one who suffers, Tía Isabela. You have no family. You will suffer all three deaths the same day your body dies, but don't worry, I'll light a candle for you."

She glared back at me and walked out.

It didn't make me feel any better to say these things to Tía Isabela. Whether I was able to pierce her armor and reach into her heart or not no longer mattered. I certainly didn't feel as though I had accomplished anything or got the better of her. Events in our lives had seriously wounded us both, perhaps fatally. The truth was, she and I had more in common than she would ever admit or realize.

I was anticipating someone coming for me as quickly as she had promised, but no one came to tell me to get ready to leave all afternoon. Finally, right before dinner, Dr. Jensen stopped in to see how I was and told me that *mi tía* Isabela had seen the chief administrator, and I would be leaving the clinic sometime late in the morning.

"You're off all of the medication, Delia. There's no need for any drugs. You'll be fine, I'm sure," he said. "Are there any questions I can answer, anything else I can do for you?"

"No, Dr. Jensen. I am grateful for what you have done already. *Gracias.*"

"You can still make a very good life for yourself, Delia," he said, and patted me on the back of my hand.

"Not only for myself now," I reminded him.

He smiled and then thought about another patient and left. I sat staring out the window until I was told to go to the cafeteria for some dinner. I went and ate, thinking that now I should try to take better care of myself. I could see from the way the staff looked at me that news of my pregnancy had spread quickly.

After dinner, I tried to distract myself by watching some television, but I found I was too jittery. I had so much to think and to worry about very soon. Exactly what arrangements would Tía Isabela be making for me? Would she give me any money when she sent me packing off to Mexico? Would I be simply dropped over the border? I had to think about who might take me in and what I might do to keep myself from starving.

I wondered if Tía Isabela would tell Edward about my pregnancy. If Sophia knew, which I suspected, she would surely enjoy calling him to tell him. Would it make him angry, or would he feel sorry for me?

Every time I heard footsteps in the hallway outside my room, I anticipated seeing Edward in the doorway, but he did not appear. It grew later and later, and finally, I was too tired to stay awake and went to bed.

I dressed quickly in the morning, anticipating a long day of travel. It was overcast outside and quite a gray morning. Lights were still on in the hallway. No one came before breakfast, but just afterward, I heard male voices in the corridor and thought about Edward again. I smiled in anticipation of seeing him, but the figure who appeared in the doorway, shrouded for a moment in shadows, was older and broader in his shoulders. The shape of his head was familiar. For a moment, I thought I was about to confront a ghost, and then he stepped into the light, and I gasped.

It was Señor Bovio.

He stood there looking in at me and then took off his hat.

"Do you mind if I come in?"

"No, *señor.*"

"*Gracias,*" he said, and sat across from me. He gazed around the room and nodded. "Your aunt put you in a very fine clinic, and a very expensive one, I might add."

I didn't want to say anything bad about Tía Isabela, so I just nodded.

"I know your doctor. I saw him before I came to your room. He says you're doing well."

"He's been very kind," I said.

He nodded and tapped his hat on his knee. "You know I stopped campaigning after Adan's death."

"I am sorry, *señor.* Maybe you would still win."

He shook his head. "I wasn't doing that well before Adan's death. As hard as it might be for you to believe, I've been outspent. Television advertisements, campaign committees, all of it goes into the millions and millions. My opponent is up to thirty-two million."

My jaw dropped, and he laughed.

"The best government money can buy." He stopped smiling and stared at me for a long moment, a moment so long, in fact, that I became a little uncomfortable and fidgeted. I had to look down.

"You are pregnant with my son's child," he finally said. It wasn't a question, but I nodded anyway. Of course, I wondered if Dr. Jensen or *mi tía* had told him.

He saw the look of surprise on my face.

"I've been interested in your treatment and progress ever since you were brought here. I couldn't help but keep track of how you were doing. I was sure it was something Adan would have wanted me to do."

"Gracias, señor."

"I understand that you are leaving the clinic today?"

"Sí."

"And you are intending to return to Mexico?"

"I am going home, yes," I said.

"To what?" he asked, sounding angry. "Do you have family back in this village?"

"No, not in the village."

"And your family *casa?*"

"It was sold soon after my grandmother's death."

"What will you do, sleep in the street?"

I didn't want to cry, but I couldn't stop the

tears from filling my eyes. "There are friends of my grandmother . . . I'm sure . . ."

"This is foolish," he snapped. "And I won't permit it!"

I looked up at him. "But *señor* . . ."

"Why your aunt is turning you out is not my business, but my grandchild will not end up in some hovel in some Mexican village lucky to have running water. You are going to leave here today, but you are going to come live in my home. When my grandchild is born, if you want to leave, you can leave, but not with my grandchild. *Comprende?*"

I looked at him firmly. "I will not go from one prison to another, *señor.*"

His face softened, but his eyes seemed to get sharper, cooler. "You still have your Latin pride. That's very good," he said, nodding, and then changed his expression to a softer one. "No one says you'll be living in a prison, Delia."

"And my child is my child first and your grandchild second. I would never leave my child."

He smiled skeptically. "I should only have a dollar for every woman who has left her own child to go chase some thrill."

"I am not every woman, *señor.*"

"We'll see."

"Why should I do this, go live in

your home?"

"It was Adan's home, too," he countered.

I looked away, the tears now defiant enough to leave my eyes. "I meant only to help him."

"I know. I know," he said. "I was over-wrought with grief. I don't blame you."

I looked at him sharply. "You don't know yourself if you do or you don't. Besides, you would say that now to get me to go to your home."

He sighed deeply. "I can see why he defied me and returned to you. Look, you will have your own wing of the house, servants at your beck and call, your own car, an expense budget for any clothing, anything you want or need. You can see whomever you want whenever you want. I ask only that you do healthy and prudent things until you give birth, and I will make sure you have the best possible medical attention."

"*Sí, señor,* I'll have everything I want and need except the most important thing."

"And what is that, Delia?"

"Family," I said.

"You want me to get your aunt to take you back?"

"No. There is no family there for me. My cousin Edward is the only kind one and he is out of the house. That's not the family I mean."

He shook his head. "I can't promise you I will be the father-in-law I would have been or could have been. I'll do my best. You don't have family back in Mexico!" he added, frustrated at my silence. "You have only graves to visit."

"And I want and need to visit them."

"And I will personally take you to them."

"When?"

"Soon. We'll fly to Mexico City, and I'll hire a helicopter to take us to your village and land right in the cemetery."

I had to laugh at the image of that. "You'd scare the whole village."

"I'll make it look like a piñata."

I laughed again.

Then I thought about *mi tía* Isabela.

"This will not please *mi tía* Isabela," I warned him.

"At the moment, you are the only woman I care to please," he replied.

He could have said nothing better.

"Today?"

"The car is waiting for us. Your aunt's already signed you out."

"Will you first tell her you intend to do this?"

"She'll hear about it soon enough,"

he said.

I couldn't help but smile at the image of her hearing about it this morning.

"I know you will want to get your high school diploma. I will arrange for a tutor to help you finish up and take the exams. I can do all of these things for you," he continued. "You have only one thing to do for me."

"Which is?"

"Give me a healthy grandchild."

He stood up.

"I am afraid, *señor*," I said.

"If you're afraid about going home to live in my house, imagine what you would fear being tossed over a border."

"All of our lives we cross borders, Señor Bovio. Going to your home is just another crossing."

"*Sí,* Delia, but I'm reaching out for you," he said, extending his hand, "to make it easier and safer."

I stared at his hand a moment and then reached for it. I truly felt like someone drowning who had been rescued. He pulled me gently toward him.

This is Adan's gift, I thought. It was he who was reaching for me, reaching from beyond the grave.

His father tightened his grip on my hand to lead me out.

What was I really giving him in return for this rescue?

A grandchild.

And what did a grandchild really mean to a man who had lost his son?

For the answer, I was thrown back in time to the day *mi abuela* Anabela and I buried my parents. When we walked away, she was holding my hand as tightly as Señor Bovio was holding it now.

And she was smiling through her grief and her tears.

"Why are you smiling, Abuela?" I asked. *How can she smile?* I wondered.

"Because I have you," she said, "and because of you, they will never die."

Señor Bovio wore *mi abuela* Anabela's smile all the way home.

ABOUT THE AUTHOR

One of the most popular authors of all time, **V.C. Andrews** has been a bestselling phenomenon since the publication of her spellbinding classic *Flowers in the Attic.* That blockbuster novel began her renowned Dollanganger family saga, which includes *Petals on the Wind, If There Be Thorns, Seeds of Yesterday,* and *Garden of Shadows.* Since then, readers have been captivated by more than fifty novels in V.C. Andrews' bestselling series. The thrilling new series featuring the March family continues with *Scattered Leaves,* forthcoming from Pocket Books. V.C. Andrews' novels have sold more than one hundred million copies and have been translated into sixteen foreign languages.

The employees of Thorndike Press hope you have enjoyed this Large Print book. All our Thorndike and Wheeler Large Print titles are designed for easy reading, and all our books are made to last. Other Thorndike Press Large Print books are available at your library, through selected bookstores, or directly from us.

For information about titles, please call:
(800) 223-1244

or visit our Web site at:
http://gale.cengage.com/thorndike

To share your comments, please write:
Publisher
Thorndike Press
295 Kennedy Memorial Drive
Waterville, ME 04901